IMITATION OF LIFE

T0364864

IMITATION OF LIFE

FANNIE HURST

Edited and with an Introduction by

Daniel Itzkovitz

Duke University Press

Durham and London

2004

CONTENTS

INTRODUCTION

Daniel Itzkovitz

It happens every two years . . . the new novel by Fannie Hurst. . . . Book critics moan. The public buys it like mad. — "Books," *Newsweek*, January 17, 1944

"A hundred years from now," journalist Kathleen Norris mused in 1918, "when the children of a democratic world are patiently memorizing the dates of the Great War, it might be interesting to see what place Fannie Hurst will hold in American literature."[1] She leaves the matter unsettled, of course, but it's doubtful that Norris, in her *Cosmopolitan* profile proclaiming Hurst "A Genius of the Short Story," would have predicted the near-complete obscurity into which her subject has fallen by the twenty-first century. Brilliant, charismatic, and remarkably prolific, Hurst was a major celebrity in the first half of the twentieth century. By the time she published *Imitation of Life* in 1933 she had written numerous best-selling melodramatic novels and stories so popular they earned her the rumored place as the "world's highest paid short story writer" (she denied it).[2] And Hurst's celebrity reached far beyond the literary: she was regularly interviewed, profiled, and exposed in newspapers and magazines, and she periodically starred in her own very public real-life melodramas, most explosively in 1920, when front-page headlines across the United States revealed the scandalously unconventional nature of her secret marriage. The critics who embraced heroic male modernists like Ernest Hemingway and Sherwood Anderson for their distinctly unsentimental literary experiments were uniformly horrified by Hurst's unapologetic and sentimental appeal to women readers — and by her popularity.[3] But her masterful storytelling and unrelenting attention to the underdog helped win her multitudes of adoring readers.

Accustomed to extreme responses, she nevertheless was stunned when she found her best-selling novel *Imitation of Life* the subject of fierce debate and parody. Little prepared Hurst for the response to her tale of Bea Pullman and Delilah Johnston, white and black single mothers who together raise their daughters and build an international restaurant empire using Bea's business savvy and the Aunt Jemima–like Delilah's servile demeanor and irresistible southern recipes. Her massive audience was familiar with her extraliterary, outspoken commitment to progressive political causes, especially women's and antiracist issues. With *Imitation of Life*, however, Hurst's investment in the politics of race suddenly became a rather unsettling matter of public interest. The nurturing and self-effacing mammy Delilah and her tempestuous light-skinned daughter, Peola, added a new dimension to the sentimental formula Hurst had perfected, but they also became the subjects of vigorous debate across the United States. Hurst had created black characters with depth and humanity, many argued, something to celebrate in the era of Amos 'n' Andy and Stepin Fetchit. But *Imitation of Life* soon came under attack by those who understood it to be perpetuating the kind of literary stereotypes that, ever since Harriet Beecher Stowe's *Uncle Tom's Cabin* (1852), had seemed to justify a condescending kindness toward the black community that was worse (as Langston Hughes pointed out in his 1934 story collection *The Ways of White Folks*) than outright hatred. In the immediate aftermath of the novel's publication, a wildly popular movie version was released featuring Hollywood starlet Claudette Colbert and Louise Beavers, the most celebrated black actress of her day, and *Limitations of Life*, a one-act parody by Hurst's friend Hughes, played to a raucous Harlem audience appreciative of the simple but deadly switch that left a white woman in the role of the obsequious, dialect-speaking domestic servant who, "like a faithful dog," yearns to rub the feet of her wealthy black mistress, a woman who speaks "perfect English with Oxford accent."[4] Each retelling helped to fuel the ongoing debate and solidified the significance of *Imitation of Life* in the complex cultural scene of the 1930s.

The seventy years that followed have done little to blunt the force of Hurst's tale. Her novel's concerns, in particular the confusions of racial identity and the tensions between sacred ideals of motherhood and the culture of success and consumption, remain recurring tropes of Hollywood and mass-market publishing alike. The two Hollywood adaptations that followed the novel, in 1934 and in 1959, each of which utilizes the connections among gender, race, and consumption that characterize Hurst's unique vision, have both met with great success. The second film, directed by Douglas Sirk, quickly became the most profitable in the history of Universal Studios, a distinction it held for decades; in 1995 it still numbered, according to a *New York Daily News* poll, among America's ten favorite films.[5] And there have been other successful retellings as well, including a classic Mexican version, *Angelitos Negros* (1948), and more recently, a stage parody, *Imitation of Imitation of Life*, featuring drag divas Lypsinka and Flotilla DeBarge, which performed to sold-out crowds in Manhattan in 2000. An unnamed Hurst even shows up simply as "a poet" in the 2001 REM song "Imitation of Life," which muses, like the novel, on the emptiness of fame and success. Hurst's anonymity here is telling: despite *Imitation of Life*'s hold on American audiences, the novel and its author have for decades virtually disappeared.[6] Long out of print, *Imitation of Life* and Fannie Hurst are both ready for a reexamination.

. . .

Hurst's audience was not always so sharply divided between the adoring American masses and the critics who despised her; the story of her critical reception reveals a great deal about not only the complicated cultural politics behind *Imitation of Life*, but also the shifting face of the twentieth-century American literary tradition. Hurst was still a young woman in the early 1910s when her popularity began to soar, thanks to her intuitive brilliance and the growing influence of commercial magazine culture. She was initially hailed by critics who saw — in her passion for the unseemly realities of city life and her attention to the world of newly arrived immigrants — a writer whose interests and style matched the increasingly urban sensibilities of the literary marketplace. The influential editor Edward O'Brien suggested in 1917 that Hurst's stories "may prove to be the most essential literary documents of our city life to the inquiring literary historian of another century."[7]

Born in St. Louis, Hurst moved to New York after graduating from Washington University in 1909, and after a brief period of searching for success, she found it. Her early fiction chronicled the trials of lowly, and mostly Jewish, city dwellers. It followed shopgirls, immigrants, mistresses, and romantic and aspiring dreamers, living lives in New York City boardinghouses and the ghettos of the Lower East Side of Manhattan. Though

The young Fannie Hurst in New York. Fannie Hurst Collection, Robert D. Farber University Archives and Special Collections Department, Brandeis University Libraries.

Hurst herself was a product of assimilated and rather antisemitic German Jews of middle America, her early reputation developed, in the words of the great novelist and editor William Dean Howells, as both a potential New York "genius" and one of the foremost writers of "the Hebraic school."[8] Howells was impressed with the way Hurst gave her Jewish stories broad American appeal, her ability to find in her "Hebraic comedy . . . the depths of true and beautiful feeling."[9]

By the time she composed *Imitation of Life* her attention had shifted from Jewish immigrants to race relations, but readers of her early stories will recognize in *Imitation of Life*'s mammy Delilah Hurst's numerous portrayals of all-loving Yiddishe Mamas. These stories — she published well over a hundred — were sentimental tales marked by Hurst's desire to capture, with photographic accuracy and a hint of romance, the everyday reality of ordinary women. Her frequent research excursions to the sweatshops and dark tenements of the Lower East Side were widely known and admired and lent an authentic stamp to her work. Informed by these trips, and more generally by the vast changes taking place on the American cultural landscape, her catchy, emotionally devastating plots found their profundity in the everyday disparities of modern city life. A typical Hurst story might detail the fraught romance between a wealthy American man and a poor immigrant woman, or the spurning of a supportive mother, not long removed from the old country, by the new wife of her Americanized son. She seemed to speak directly and intimately to her vast audience, imagining characters who struggled to live the American dream and who often failed to find happiness even when they succeeded in finding "success." A Hurst story meant massive sales. Only a few years after she arrived from St. Louis, still in her twenties, such magazines as *Cosmopolitan*, the *Saturday Evening Post*, and *Harper's Bazar* were competing fiercely to publish them.

Hurst's most discussed story of this period, "Sob Sister" (1916), follows the downward-spiraling life of Mae Monroe, a "kept woman" who dwells "outside the barbed-wire fence of respectability," along with "a great army of street-walking women."[10] She gains weight and grows increasingly isolated until Max, her boyfriend of six years, finally abandons her. Their final exchange comes in an explosion of sadistic cruelty and raw emotion, his freedom to walk away revealing a painful double standard between the sexes. Readers were stunned by her frank attention to a subject usually ignored by polite society (a *New York Times* review specifically describes the story in terms of its unblinking realism: "brutal, but . . . also strong, a bit of realism that grips in every line of its tense dialogue, in its impassive objectivity")[11] and by her sympathies for Mae. Despite these sympathies, however, the story also ultimately punishes its suffering female protagonist, who has pushed the boundaries of societal norms, a pattern in Hurst's work that emerges even in *Imitation of Life*.

With her flamboyant style and her natural inclination for the spotlight, Hurst's celebrity quickly moved beyond her many stories, novels, and films, and her name, like those of her *Imitation of Life* heroines Bea and Delilah, became "a national commodity."[12] While other writers of her era cultivated the ideal of the lone suffering artist, Hurst developed into a glamorous and sometimes scandalous personality so generally recognized that the magazine *Metropolitan* put her portrait on every streetcar in Manhattan after closing a multistory deal with her in 1916.[13] Even when not writing, Hurst was in the papers, often for her unconventional acts and opinions. Her pronouncements were regularly sought on matters ranging from communism to America's racial situation to the state of fiction writing. The revelation in 1920 of her secret marriage and unusual matrimonial living arrangements (she and her husband, pianist Jacques Danielson, shared neither a home nor a name) made the front page of newspapers across the nation, including the *New York Times*, where it appeared above the fold:

FANNIE HURST WED;

HID SECRET 5 YEARS

Sailed Into Matrimony with
Pianist "in a Bark of Their
Own Designing."

LIVE APART, THEIR OWN WAY

Meet By Appointment — It's a
New Method Which Rejects
"Antediluvian Custom."[14]

But because of the peculiar politics of early-twentieth-century literary culture, her great success inevitably led to questions about the "greatness" of her work. If in the 1910s she was widely accepted as a brilliant up-and-coming ethnic writer by such significant luminaries as Howells and

O'Brien, by the 1920s the elite literary world was coming increasingly under the sway of the modernist movement, which defined itself specifically against the sentimental style in which Hurst felt at home. Writers who wanted to be taken seriously rejected sentimentalism as crude and tawdry, overly popular and overly feminine. By the mid-1920s, her prolific outpouring of stories and her massive celebrity led to the dismissive notion shared by many highbrow critics that Hurst pandered to the buying public at the expense of "beauty and truth."[15] Such was the accusation of critic and novelist Waldo Frank, who, in a 1925 *New Republic* manifesto against "Pseudo-Literature," used her as a central example of how not to write, cautioning would-be writers not to push for mass-market Hurstian rewards over artistic integrity. In the evolving intellectual world of the 1920s and 1930s, to be a commercial success came increasingly to mean one's work was both apolitical and without artistic merit — and despite her feminist and antiracist politics and her professed desire to be thought a true artist, Hurst's work was generally felt by the new generation of critics influenced by the modernist movement to be lacking on both the political and the aesthetic fronts. Though she continued to publish for a popular audience and found some recognition among middlebrow critics who cared less about the purity of modernist aesthetics, she was terrorized by the implications: "Fears and doubts smote me," she writes in her memoirs. "Did my mass appeal prove lack of stature? Why the implication that one could not simultaneously be a popular and an important author?"[16] Insisting that she "had not the skill to tailor [her writing] to fashion," she later seemed more reconciled to her situation. "Please make no mistake," she announced in a 1942 *New York Times* interview, "I am very clearly aware that I am not a darling of the critics. I have a vast popular audience — it warms me; it's a furnace."[17]

She may have longed for highbrow approval, but Hurst's strident and unsubdued work pleased her massive audience by being unapologetically melodramatic and unapologetically plot-driven. *Imitation of Life* is no exception, and though the novel itself stages a struggle between "success" and "meaning," it did not dissuade Hurst's critics from the notion that her main literary interest, and fault, was in writing "sentimental hokum," as one review of *Imitation of Life* put it.[18] "Sentimental" here is a charged term, one that calls on a history of extremely popular, yet degraded and critically dismissed nineteenth-century American women's writing which focused on home, relationships, and the intricacies of human emotion — "women's interests" — at the expense of the "serious" political and aesthetic concerns of the public sphere. This charge was nothing new for Hurst: by the early 1920s reviews of her work regularly pointed out and degraded her sentimentalism. (It was "her worst vice," a *New York Times* reviewer sniffed in 1922, and the *New York Evening Post* sighingly agreed: "Her ever-gushing sentiment" did not "show any signs of drought").[19] Such writing was understood to fail the test of true literature by the consensus of mostly male critics and authors of Hurst's era, whose work came to constitute for decades the heart of the twentieth-century American literary canon. The response of these critics tells us as much about attitudes toward women and the popular as it does about the reception of Hurst's fiction; that her work is for the most part completely out of print is strong testimony to the power of this elite in shaping lasting literary tastes.

Only recently, since the introduction of women's and popular culture studies into English departments, has the academic establishment begun to take more seriously the work of sentimental writers. Feminist critics have argued not simply for the inclusion of these writers, most of whom were women, into the traditional canon, but, more significant, that the evaluative criteria that have largely been in place since the advent of literary modernism need to be rethought. Moving beyond the widely held position that equates popular literature with the mindless regurgitation of empty and repetitive formulae, these critics argue that many of the sentimentalists were able to be politically powerful precisely because they reached vast audiences and because, in taking their female readers seriously, they were able to speak to ordinary women about everyday issues of real concern. Following the success of Stowe's *Uncle Tom's Cabin*, which famously worked to convince northern white women with its fiery righteousness that abolitionism was a women's issue, sentimental fiction became an important forum in which women writers could discuss grander political issues as well, such as women's independence and racial justice — themes that become central to Hurst's work and, soon thereafter, to the tradition of melodramatic film.

But by the time Hurst wrote *Imitation of Life*, the politics of both race and gender had changed tremendously from the days of Stowe. The dominance of the nineteenth century's feminine ideal, the True Woman, who was expected to maintain her exclusive domain over the private world of the home, was challenged by the suddenly more visible New Woman — the working girls, flappers, and suffragettes — who found to a limited but significant degree new jobs in the workplace, new educational and social possibilities, and, by 1920, voting rights. The years leading to the novel's publication also saw radical demographic shifts, due to ethnic whites flooding the United States from Eastern Europe (and who had been the subjects of Hurst's early writing) and due also to the "Great Migration," in which tens of thousands of African Americans abandoned the rural Jim Crow South in search of higher wages, better homes, and political rights in northern urban centers. Hurst and many of her contemporaries — Harlem Renaissance writers Nella Larsen and (Hurst's protégées) Dorothy West and Zora Neale Hurston, and others such as Anita Loos and Anzia Yezierska — grew up in the midst of these historical developments, which inevitably helped to alter the subject of women's writing.

But unlike many of her contemporaries whose work has been revived by the recent interest in women's and African American studies, and unlike her nineteenth-century predecessors, popular women authors such as Stowe, Louisa May Alcott, and Susan Warner, whose writing has recently been recuperated by feminist scholars, Fannie Hurst remains largely forgotten. When she has been noticed in recent years, it is usually either as a footnote to discussions of Zora Neale Hurston, the great folklorist and novelist of the Harlem Renaissance with whom she had an intimate friendship, or, following the lead of critics from Hurst's era, in dismissive nods to her image as a one-note literary hack whose bad work has been converted into a few influential melodramatic films. One more recent critic writes, for instance, that the novel *Imitation of Life* is little more than a "tawdry bestseller . . . celebrating the American success ethic, romantic love, and the nuclear family."[20]

As with all caricature, there is some truth to such readings: the plot does begin something like a classic American success story, in the tradition of Ben Franklin's *Autobiography* and Horatio Alger's archetypal "American dream" novels of the post–Civil War era. In these texts, the young hero journeys to the cold city and, through "pluck and luck," rises from impoverishment to success. But Hurst is not complacent in following this traditional formula. As readers will discover relatively early in the narrative, this is hardly a novel that simply and unambiguously celebrates family, romance, and American success. Indeed, the novel is fueled by its lack of faith in, and its challenges to, these familiar institutions, though it is equally apprehensive about any alternatives. Balanced between its significant stake in the power of traditional sentimental ideals and its very modern aspirations for women's success in the marketplace, the novel might instead be read as a meditation on the emotional and ideological confusions behind the emergence of the New Woman. And crucially, in *Imitation of Life* the New Woman is as much a racial as a gender category. Herein lies its singular, engaging power.

• • •

"What happened to girls thrown on their own resources?" the narrator asks a few pages into *Imitation of Life*. For a 1933 American public still reeling from the stock market crash and trying to understand the massive waves of young women who left home to enter the workforce in the decades that opened the twentieth century, the question had broad resonance. The novel responds with both excitement and trepidation. At a moment when increasing numbers of women were leaving their traditional roles behind, *Imitation of Life* holds tightly to certain sentimental ideals, even as it seems clearly aware that these ideals no longer provide such solid ground for a young woman to stand on.

Bea Pullman's initiation into the repressive and confusing world of middle-class America occurs in the novel's early chapters, before Delilah enters her life, against a background of devastation in her formerly stable home. Here the novel explores classic sentimental distinctions between public and private, men and women. Bea's father and her husband, Mr. Pullman, typically sit and talk politics while she serves them; Bea's husband lectures on U.S. commercial and political history (his specialties: "the life history of the tomato from the vine to the ketchup bottle" and Abraham Lincoln), while Bea develops an anxious secret self and frets about her bland sex life. But there are early intimations that these realms are far from stable. For instance, although Bea's romantic and feminine obliviousness to the public sphere is underscored by the narrator, who juxtaposes her attention to the "frivolous details" of their courtship and marriage with references to the more serious male domain of the presidential election of 1912, one such passage also reveals an early-twentieth-century uncertainty about American masculinity (as embodied by presidential candidate Woodrow Wilson): "Thus in the year when men were debating whether a college professor was of sufficient stamina for Presidency of the United States, Bea lifted her face, which intimated yes, for the betrothal kiss of Mr. Pullman." When Bea finally begins crossing lines after Mr. Pullman's sudden death, posing as her dead husband to earn a living, her mother's ominous warning, that work "made a girl mannish," stands in for a more general anxiety that the clarity of sentimental distinctions has begun to crumble.

The novel was first published in serial form in the women's magazine *Pictorial Review* (1932) under a title, *Sugar House*, that itself captures a sense of fleeting domesticity. But the early advertisement campaign describes the novel's subject in terms seemingly calculated to reaffirm the safe clarity of separate gendered spheres in the face of new possibilities for women. Curiously, there is no mention of race: "Beginning Next Month: SUGAR HOUSE. A novel of human emotions . . . told in the story of Bea Pullman as a girl, a bride, a mother, and, finally, as herself. . . . [A] revealing study of the eternal feminine."[21] Bea does of course finally move beyond the suffocating limitations inherent in all of her specifically feminine roles: as daughter, wife, and mother. She moves so far beyond these traditional roles, in fact, that when her own alienated daughter addresses letters to Bea as "Dear household word," the household word she has in mind is not "mother" but "B. Pullman," the name of her business. But it's less clear that this mobility leads her any closer to her femininity. Rather than highlight her femininity, such moments indicate how Bea's success in the public sphere has ironically and impersonally infiltrated the no longer private world of the "household." Ultimately, Bea is far more comfortable, if sexually repressed, in "the uncharted seas of big business for women." And although she confesses to being a "home wench," the place to find "home" in this novel is in the homey atmosphere of the B. Pullman restaurants. Bea's house, on the other hand, is merely "a halfway house in which to steam up for the new day." Bea spends most of her time at work, and any fleeting yearnings or regrets she has about childrearing are postponed to a later date.

Such a point of view, dismantling conventional notions of instinctive motherhood, is consistent with what we know of Hurst's own beliefs about motherhood, which were hardly cut from sentimental cloth. Rather, her thoughts on the matter seem more suitably expressed in the business jargon of modern efficiency experts: "If a woman can sell insurance or run a paying beauty parlor or write a book," the childless Hurst argued elsewhere, "the chances are ten to one that she can hire vastly more efficient service to train her children than she could give them. . . . Motherhood does not automatically bring with it the knowledge of child training. The maternal instinct is not infallible. It can kill the thing she loves."[22] There will perhaps be little surprise, then, that by novel's end "the eternal feminine" noted by the advertisement remains difficult to locate. Indeed, if "eternal feminine" and the sentimental focus on "human emotions" imply a removal from historical influences, we are instead presented with characters whose lives are profoundly influenced by the ineluctable pressures of history and the sweeping social changes of the early twentieth century.

The advertisement is telling, however. The novel's great power and tension emerge in large part from its troubled relationship with these changes: its insistent awareness, even celebration, of them, and its simultaneous anxiety about what has been lost. Even her career choice reveals Bea's uncertain place in the conflict between New Woman and True Woman. Feeding legions of America's young men in B. Pullman restaurants across the nation, she clearly has not entirely forgone the traditional maternal role. But importantly, her contribution to the burgeoning restaurant industry is fueled primarily by a desire for profit, not the warmth of her heart.

Accordingly, the novel seems to view twentieth-century motherhood specifically through the lens of an alienating and omnipresent consumer society. Setting the novel's early chapters in an emerging consumer Mecca, an Atlantic City populated by the hustling salesmen, concession workers, and storefront dentists working the newly constructed boardwalk, Hurst creates an atmosphere defined by ephemeral consumption. The novel puts great emphasis on the tawdry minutiae and consumer goods of this world: the shoes worn by Mr. Pullman (congress gaiters); the best-selling historical romances Bea borrows from the public library (*When Knighthood Was in Flower*); "the great pickle-and-relish firm" whose interests Bea's father represents in Atlantic City. The characters here are delimited and identified by what they consume, and by the time Bea and Delilah reach Manhattan we see realized the potentially alienating and devastating effects of this consumer-oriented urban world. Bea's restaurants emerge into a world populated by "lonely city souls" who seek "respite from the duress of that strife and stone and steel out there." The solution offered by Bea's restaurants is rather circular: more consumption, with Delilah standing in as a surrogate mother (as one character puts it, a "kind substitution for his old mother") for the masses of lonely urbanites.

Given the mixed messages here, it is hardly a surprise that the novel, which at first cheers Bea on as she struggles to survive, finally sours on her success. Bea is not a perfect mother, but she nevertheless yearns to be, and the novel's grim finale might easily be read as a punishment for Bea's ultimate choice of ambition over motherhood. This punishment — the perverse collapse of her momentarily promising love life — seems to suggest a failure of imagination, but Hurst was not alone during this period in doling out poetic retribution to her successful New Woman. The sentimental logic developed here, by which female protagonists move into traditionally male roles with tragic consequences, has its literary and Hollywood corollaries: disasters such as Bea's quickly became a commonplace in the melodramatic novels and films of the 1920s, 1930s, and beyond.[23] Certainly this logic operates powerfully in Olive Higgins Prouty's enormously popular novel *Stella Dallas* (1923), a clear forerunner to *Imitation of Life*, which was itself made into a play and three films and also depicts a working woman whose economic aspirations and desire to be a good mother ultimately reveal themselves to be disastrously incompatible. A similar sensibility informs James M. Cain's novel *Mildred Pierce* (1941), made into an Academy Award–winning film (1945), whose plot, like that of Hurst's novel, involves a single mother who becomes wealthy in the restaurant business and who is caught in a sexual competition with her daughter.

Unlike *Stella Dallas* or *Mildred Pierce*, however, *Imitation of Life*'s interest in the maternal failures of the New Woman is inextricably linked to U.S. racial politics. Hurst codes her novel's New Woman as necessarily white; as Bea's traditional feminine identity becomes less stable and certain, Delilah fills the void left behind in the home, taking on a powerful symbolic presence. The situation grows even more complex when Delilah acts not only as mammy to Bea's daughter, but as "mammy to the world," her face the very public trademark image of Bea's business. Certainly her dual role as both homely support and commercial spokeswoman signals the novel's awareness of the profound intermingling of racial, gender, and economic meanings in early twentieth-century American culture.[24] In its insistence that these matters are fully bound up with one another, Hurst's tale is thoroughly unique.

Readers of *Imitation of Life* will no doubt see in "Aunt Delilah," whose "chocolate and cream" face first adorns the maple sugar candy boxes and then the B. Pullman restaurant logo, an echo of Aunt Jemima, the instant pancake icon who rose to great prominence in the 1920s. Delilah's uncomfortable similarity to Aunt Jemima, the stereotypical mammy who became a consumer symbol of domestic salvation for middle-class white women, was clearly a self-conscious choice for Hurst. Thanks to Aunt Jemima, as well as other similar mammy figures hawking home economics goods during the early decades of the twentieth century, U.S. advertising had for years been steeped in images of black women that called on precisely the set of responses inspired by Delilah, responses that reveal the thorough interweaving of racial and gender ideologies in an ever-expanding culture of consumption.

The strange career of Aunt Jemima is instructive: the fictional brainchild of two white Reconstruction-era pancake mix manufacturers, Chris L. Rutt and Charles G. Underwood, Aunt Jemima had become omnipresent by the 1920s, when white American nostalgia for an idyllic southern rural past reached its peak. In the face of a cosmopolitan present growing increasingly anxious and alienated, in which the popular understanding of a white woman's role as natural caregiver was less certain than in previous generations, Aunt Jemima's cheerful and nurturing echo of the minstrel show mammy provided welcome guidance and support. Rutt came up with the marketing ploy to jump-start his struggling instant pancake business after hearing a song called "Aunt Jemima" at a blackface performance, and the idea quickly caught on with consumers. Through the years the brand (sold in 1926 to Quaker Oats) hired a succession of black models to pose as the smiling Aunt Jemima, for whom the company had created a fictional biography rooted in a fantasy South of warm kitchens and benevolent whites. The fictional Higbee Plantation was her home, Colonel Higbee and his endless stream of guests Aunt Jemima's hungry and appreciative audience (similarly, in the novel we learn that Delilah formerly worked for "Cunnel Glasgow"). Nancy Green, the first model who posed as Aunt Jemima, from 1893 to her death in 1923, was herself an ex-slave. By the time of Green's death, Aunt Jemima had become one of the most successful and recognizable brands in U.S. history.[25] Aunt Jemima products were advertised regularly in *Pictorial Review*, the women's magazine where *Imitation of Life* first appeared. In advertisements there Aunt Jemima was marketed to northern middle-class white women who, like Bea, increasingly found themselves spending more time in the workplace than in the kitchen.

Acutely aware of the economic and emotional power behind Aunt Je-

Guests as long as they might, guests at Colonel Higbee's plantation never could get from Aunt Jemima the flavor secret of those wonderful pancakes.

What Aunt Jemima would never tell them...she got her matchless flavor with a blend of four flours

Wheat, corn, rye and rice flours were blended in the treasured Aunt Jemima recipe to give the tenderest, best-tasting pancakes anyone ever had.

Today, Aunt Jemima Pancake Mix is faithful to that recipe. It's produced now, of course, with all the advantages of modern milling methods.

Over the years as other pancake mixes have come and gone, none ever made pancakes with such flavor as the Aunt Jemima brand. Reply, it's true: You can't duplicate in a homemade batter or get with any other mix the matchless flavor of Aunt Jemima pancakes. For a special treat team up that flavor with fresh asparagus in the delightful springtime way shown here.

ASPARAGUS ROLL-UPS. Prepare pancakes according to Deluxe recipe on the Aunt Jemima package. Roll each hot pancake around several spears of cooked asparagus. Serve with cheese sauce. Garnish each roll-up with a strip of pimiento or sprinkle with paprika.

Aunt Jemima charming the plantation guests of the fictional
Colonel Higbee with her secret pancake recipe.

mima, Hurst's novel both reflects and satisfies white fantasies and desires for a mammy, with all the maternal and racial connotations of this term fully intact. Accordingly, white reviewers, even those who disliked the novel, reserved their strongest praise for Hurst's Delilah.[26] The "black, bulging Delilah," according to the *New York Herald Tribune*, "abounds in the warm vigor which is Fannie Hurst at her best. I can think of no character of [Hurst's] since *Lummox* who is as actual a creation as the mammy whose face and skill were the foundation of Bea's fortune."[27] Others agreed: Delilah was, according to the *Cincinnati Enquirer*, "one of the most magnificently drawn characters in all the great store of literature depicting Negro life." The *Christian Science Monitor* exclaimed that "it is Delilah's story really," and while admitting that Hurst "overcolored her portrait a little," proclaimed that "most of us have at some time known a servant who partook in some measure of the nature of Delilah."[28] It is an "us" that speaks volumes.

In Bea Pullman, Hurst created a protagonist whose genius in large part lay in her understanding of the power of race in U.S. consumer culture: her knowledge of Delilah's potential as "a walking trademark" and her ability to create an atmosphere of "food that seemed flavored of romance." The food in Bea's restaurants was flavored with the romance of race. Delilah, like Aunt Jemima, develops as a character antithetical to, and supportive of, the New Woman, and Bea's imperfect embodiment of traditional femininity is brought to a finer point with the advent of her housemate and business partner, "the enormously buxom figure of a woman with a round black face that shone above an Alps of bosom." Bea needs to pretend to be a man to commence her economic rise, but her real success, and her distance from her earlier life as a housewife and mother, is solidified by Delilah's inescapably black and maternal body. Delilah's monumental bosom, which requires two mentions in this sentence just to capture "the limitless reaches of its warmth," is immediately set against Bea's work-ravaged and "constantly perspiring" body, certainly not maternal, let alone traditionally feminine.

Together, Bea and Delilah build what is in some ways an extraordinarily unconventional household. The novel even signals Bea's remove from a traditional gender economy when she begins to inspire spontaneous crushes among her female employees. They "adored her . . . with a dangerous kind of intensity" until Frank Flake, Bea's business manager and, eventually, her love interest, "ridiculed . . . out of practice" the anonymous gifts and letters they send to Bea. The "dangerous" desires of Bea's female employees seem a natural extension of Bea and Delilah's Boston marriage; perhaps this is why they need to be so sharply disciplined out of existence. But between Bea and Delilah there are no unruly desires that need ridiculing: the racially determined hierarchy that divides the characters deflects potential readings of these companions as romantically, as well as domestically, connected.

Despite its objectification of Delilah, the novel does briefly foreshadow potential interpretive tensions concerning the character in the voice of Delilah herself, in her protests over her own representation. When Bea first decides to market Delilah's cooking, using Delilah's face as her trademark, the cook grumbles about the photograph of herself that is to adorn the boxes of her maple syrup candies. "This heah ain't no rig for to have your picture taken in," she protests, requesting instead a photograph that demonstrates her true "style," and one "to keep a record for mah chile of how her mammy looked." Instead, Bea succeeds in imposing her vision of Delilah on the box: "the chocolate-and-cream effulgence that was Delilah. The heavy cheeks, shellacked eyes, bright, round and crammed with vitality, huge upholstery of lips that caught you like a pair of divans into the luxury of laughter." Delilah wants her uniqueness, her "style," to come across for future generations to know her; Bea imagines Delilah to be an exemplary mammy, lovable and self-sacrificing, whose very body is converted in Bea's observations here into food and furniture — objects of consumption and comfort. Bea's assumptions about Delilah enable the possibility of hiring many substitute "imitation Delilahs," all with "round black faces . . . shining over the waffle irons of the cities of a nation." The luxury Bea is ostensibly afforded in the *Pictorial Review* advertisement, to move beyond predetermined social identities ultimately to become "herself," is apparently not available to Delilah. Bea laughs off Delilah's protests and ignores her occasional insights about race politics (Delilah is, after all, the only character to describe with sober awareness the prejudices of white people, "broad minded as mah thumbnail"). Bea knows her audience. The candy boxes appear to great financial reward with the photo chosen by "Miss Bea." And Delilah, driven to embody and to teach to her daughter Peola acceptance of a meager lot in life, ultimately voices a politics of complacency to her noncompliant daughter.

Delilah's largely unquestioning acceptance of the traditional racial power dynamic helps undergird changes in the American gender landscape; her light-skinned daughter, on the other hand, continually disrupts the seeming certainties of race. The novel holds tightly to its fantasy of Delilah's authentic blackness, but just as its understanding of the New Woman is steeped in ambivalence, so too is its investment in racial authenticity, as its response to Peola's "cheatin' on color" makes quite clear. Peola is one of many mixed-race characters in literature of this period who, fitting definitively in neither racial camp, attempts to pass for white. Early-twentieth-century novels and stories about passing repeatedly rehearsed American anxieties about the color line, ultimately demonstrating both the incoherence of racial distinction and its steadfastness. The lives of these "tragic mulattos" generally end in sadness or death (*The House Behind the Cedars, Passing, Plum Bun, Flight*), and if a character does successfully pass, it is usually to his or her detriment — and that of the character's abandoned black community.[29] Such is the case with Peola, who hardly deviates from the standard trajectory of these characters. Like Angela Murray, the light-skinned protagonist of Jessie Redmon Fauset's *Plum Bun* (1929), Peola chooses a white husband, frets over the color of her children (she ultimately abandons the possibility of having children to assure that her child's skin color won't give her away), and moves far away (Angela to New York, Peola to Bolivia). And like Clare in Nella Larsen's *Passing* (1929) and the unnamed protagonist of James Weldon Johnson's *Autobiography of an Ex-Colored Man* (1912), she learns that going to such measures is, first and foremost, a form of self-alienation. Nevertheless, Peola's very presence here, and her ultimate escape/banishment, provide a counterpoint to Delilah's solid embodiment of authentic blackness, itself so ideologically powerful in a world marked by familial and political turmoil.[30]

There is a subtext that holds in such passing novels as Johnson's and Larsen's, as it does in Hurst's. Each of these ultimately relates the theme of racial authenticity and alienation to an anxiety about a more pervasive cultural inauthenticity. Written with an eye not only to the tragic mulatto but also to the emerging New Woman, for instance, *Imitation of Life*'s interest in the broad implications of American "self-making," heretofore generally a male domain, is extensive. The novel juxtaposes racial and gender passing, along with a more general social chameleonism rooted in class, with provocative results. Beginning with Bea's assumption of her husband's identity, most of the women here find mobility through self-transformation. Bea's friend Virginia Eden, for instance, has made millions in "beauty culture" and was "born Sadie Kress in Jersey City."[31] Juxtaposed with Bea and Virginia, Peola comes to embody a distinctly American dilemma, in which idealized narratives of self-making bump up against the rigidity of U.S. racial categories. The novel's central figure of rebellion against an oppressive social order, Peola attempts to find a way, like Bea, to transcend the identity into which she is born. But according to her devastated mother, passing is akin to "sinning," and her escape from blackness is ultimately presented as perverse — a fact that hits home when she performs two acts unforgivable in a sentimental economy: she abandons her mother and has herself sterilized.

It should be clear, however, that *Imitation of Life* does not rely on a simple double standard to divide the possibilities presented to Bea and Peola. Indeed, if Peola's woes highlight the real possibilities that exist for white New Women, Hurst also uses the literary stereotype of the mulatto to underscore the New Woman's limitations. The novel's more general uncertainty is implicit in the analogy that connects tragic mulatto and New Woman. Peola finds herself in the irresolvable position of being "neither black nor white yet both," but Bea too lands in an impossible place. Torn between career, romance, and motherhood, Bea finds her success in the marketplace accompanied by devastating and irreparable loss. Hurst's surprising conclusion, that a woman *can't* "have it all," arrives as one of the novel's most unsettling implications. Given her own success as a writer and entrepreneur driven to challenge the status quo and experiment with romantic and domestic arrangements, it is curious that Hurst did not come up with more alternatives for her heroine.

· · ·

The complex personal and historical pressures of race and gender were certainly alive for Hurst, whose Jewish parents felt it to be an utmost goal that their daughter not marry a "kike" (as they called Jewish men).[32] She defied them in her marriage to a Jew, but nevertheless seems to have absorbed their discomfort. She spent much of her life bumping uncomfortably against her Jewish identity, describing in her memoirs an intense childhood shame strikingly similar to Peola's relationship to blackness. "I would have given anything," she says, not to have had her mother tell people they were

Jewish.[33] But her interest in the culture of American race was enlivened in new ways when she became a friend and patron of some of the most prominent Harlem Renaissance writers in the mid-1920s. And if *Imitation of Life* depicts a rather clumsy understanding of cross-racial companionships, the story of Hurst's African American friends' relationship to the novel provides a more nuanced portrait of cross-racial friendship in the 1930s. These were relationships clearly complicated by the difficult interplay between patronage and racial and class power, complications that played a substantial role in the unfolding history of *Imitation of Life*. When *Imitation of Life* came under fire, Hurst turned for support and justification to her black friends, some of whom clearly experienced the novel as troubling. The year before his parody *Limitations of Life* skewered *Imitation of Life* on the Harlem stage, for instance, Langston Hughes, who relied at times on Hurst's benevolence as a literary supporter and political comrade, wrote her a letter thanking her "as a Negro" for being responsible for the 1934 film *Imitation of Life*, Hollywood's "first serious treatment of the Negro problem in America."[34]

Even more suggestive is her relationship with Zora Neale Hurston, the great Harlem Renaissance novelist and folklorist. Their companionship seems to have directly influenced the novel's composition. In 1926 Hurst judged a writing contest in Harlem and was immediately taken with Hurston, the second-prize winner. Hurst hired her as secretary and then driver, and the two became close friends and regular companions in the years prior to the composition of *Imitation of Life*. As Hurst biographer Brooke Kroeger recently discovered, in the months before Hurst began writing her novel, the pair took a road trip together to Canada. It is easy to imagine the basic image of her novel developing in Hurst's mind out of this trip, not least because it mirrors the central image of so many classic American novels, which bring together a white person with a person of color (usually both of whom are men) in an unlikely, spiritually fulfilling, and at times homoerotic companionship (*Huckleberry Finn, Moby-Dick, The Last of the Mohicans,* etc.). By extension, it is tempting to try to read Zora and Fannie into Delilah and Bea, though Delilah is of course no Zora Neale Hurston, and Fannie and Bea share little in common beyond their unusual success. However, even if the parallel can be taken only so far, Hurst was clearly inspired by their companionship, especially Hurston's interest in the everyday lives and folklore of African Americans. When the novel came under attack, Hurston, herself a target for some (most notoriously, novelist Richard Wright) who felt her work was full of racist caricatures and not sufficiently political, became one of its staunchest supporters. Years after the novel's publication, Hurston lived in Durham, North Carolina, the same southern town as Sterling Brown, one of *Imitation of Life*'s fiercest critics. He confronted Hurston about the book, accusing her of being the source of the material Hurst ultimately turned into the novel's troublesome racial imagery. The accusation proved, Hurston noted in a letter to Hurst, "the truth of [*Imitation of Life*]. What he and his kind resent is just that. It is too accurate to be comfortable. . . . You have," Hurston reassured Hurst, "a grand set of admirers in this part of the world because of *Imitation of Life*."[35]

But although Hurston attests to the accuracy of Hurst's racial representations, there are intimations elsewhere that Hurston was not quite comfortable with the racial dimensions of their relationship. Hurston's biographer Robert Hemenway, for instance, reports her observation to a friend that Hurst liked being seen in public with Hurston because her blackness highlighted Hurst's own white complexion.[36] This rings true, especially given Hurst's anxiety about appearing Jewish and her desire to be considered simply a white American. Such objectifying, of course, goes hand in hand with Hurst's investment, shared by many of her era, in a notion of blacks as fundamentally different from whites. As late as 1961, in Hurst's memorial essay on Hurston, she writes with touching intimacy and with a clear condemnation of racism (she even gently chastises Hurston for her lack of sensitivity to racism), but also with a firm hold on what seems a profound fantasy about blackness. "Uninhibited as a child," Hurst writes of her old friend. "She sang with the plangency and tears of her people and then on with equal lustiness to hip-shuddering and finger-snapping jazz."[37] No wonder, then, that blackness, with all of its imagined "plangency and tears," lends such powerful symbolic force to a novel so consumed with its sense of an otherwise impossible authenticity.[38]

. . .

Moviegoers in the 1930s were well familiar with the degrading images of African Americans prevalent in Hollywood films of that era. Black comic actors such as Stepin Fetchit, for example, were rarely at a loss for work in the 1930s: Fetchit appeared in some forty films between 1927 and 1939, delighting whites and outraging many African Americans with his lazy, language-slurring characters. In 1934 alone, Louise Beavers, the most prominent and well-respected African American actress of her day, appeared in eighteen films, nearly always as an inarticulate servant, as comic relief, or simply as part of the scenery. That year, she appeared as a "Reno Hotel Maid," for instance, in *Merry Wives of Reno*, "Suzy the Cook" in *Gambling Lady*, and "Crystal, Mayme's Housekeeper" in *Palooka*; she also played "Mary's Maid," "Hattie's Maid," "Sadie's Maid," "Azais' Maid," and so on, that year, in a frenzy of typecasting. Beavers got only fifth billing as Delilah in John Stahl's Oscar-nominated film version of Hurst's novel, also produced in 1934, but *Imitation of Life* provided her with something different: the chance to play a dignified woman with a degree of depth and with aspirations for her family. Compare this role to, say, the superficially similar character named "Aunt Jemima" in the 1934 Shirley Temple musical *Stand Up and Cheer*, played in blackface as cheerful, plump, and depthless by the white Italian American actress Tess Gardella, and we get a sense of how far Stahl's film reaches for a psychological complexity not available to black characters in other films of the era.

Indeed, film proved to be an especially powerful vehicle for Hurst's tale, particularly insofar as *Imitation of Life*'s concerns are so invested in questions of visibility — from Delilah's physicality, to Peola's desire to hide behind her light skin, to Bea's struggles with her femininity. This breathtaking assortment of concerns electrified audiences, who "seemed to find [the film] gripping and powerful," according to a bemused *New York Times* reviewer. The review archly rehearsed the film's "topics": "the mother love question, the race question, the business woman question, the mother and daughter question and the love renunciation question."[39] The only slightly veiled scorn here is unmistakable, but the film has remained an object of fascination and debate for contemporary scholars precisely because of its unusual appetite for, and nuanced management of, such a broad spectrum of "questions." This is especially the case insofar as it takes on and engages the relationship between the themes of *both* race and gender, which were nearly always "segregated" (to borrow historian Ruth Feldstein's apt term) in Hollywood film.

Although it covered much of the same ground as Hurst's novel, Stahl's film provided significant and meaningful revisions. Responding to the constraints of the newly developed Hollywood production code and the demands of Hollywood storytelling, the film's rather cheerful demeanor stands in stark contrast to Hurst's often dark novel. The film, for instance, has a far smoother understanding of what it means to be a woman in the workforce. As played by actress Claudette Colbert, Bea experiences only sporadic tension between her private life and marketplace success; they are successfully bridged by her persistent and extraordinary feminine allure and a buoyant faith in consumption. So, rather than start her business career by posing as a man (as in the novel), here Bea uses her flirtatious charm to convince a parade of men to invest in her business. The *Hollywood Reporter* is near breathless in its praise of Colbert's look in the film, using language that would never be associated with Hurst's Bea: "Miss Colbert looks like a million, giving the character a superb treatment and wearing gowns that will make the femme fans gurgle and gasp in admiration."[40] With its abiding faith in the marketplace, Bea's uncompromised femininity, and a new ending that provides a version of reconciliation between both sets of mothers and daughters, Stahl's film comes across at once as more optimistic and ultimately much less vexed than Hurst's novel. Bea *is* allotted punishment for attempting to be both a mother and an entrepreneur, but importantly, unlike in the novel, her ultimate punishment is a self-imposed choice.

Peola poses the greatest threat to the film's ultimately more ordered vision and proved a more difficult puzzle than Bea's femininity; if the tragic mulatta had become a stock literary character by the time Hurst wrote her novel, she also remained threatening. As Susan Courtney has demonstrated, this becomes remarkably clear in the debate concerning the film among the Production Code Administration (PCA) members, who felt that the film was "definitely dangerous" because it violated the clause forbidding miscegenation on screen "in spirit, if not in fact!" There is no portrayal of miscegenation in the film, but Peola makes "the suggestion [of miscegenation . . .] omnipresent."[41] The unacceptable suggestion is, of course, that somewhere in the past Peola's black ancestors had sexual relations with what can only be Peola's white ancestors. PCA Director Joseph Breen wrote in a letter about the film, "It is our conviction that any picture which raises and elaborates such an inflammable racial question as that raised by this picture is fraught with grave danger to the industry."[42]

As in the novel, Delilah's authentic blackness stands as a counterpoint to the confusions wrought by Peola. Her iconic blackness becomes par-

Bea (Claudette Colbert) uses her flirtatious charm to convince a parade of
men to invest in her business in John Stahl's 1934 film, *Imitation of Life*.
Fannie Hurst Collection, Robert D. Farber University Archives and
Special Collections Department, Brandeis University Libraries.

ticularly forceful because her role as "walking trademark" for the B. Pullman pancake flour recurs as a powerfully visible trope throughout the film.
And her refusal of payment for the use of her own recipe is baffling, except
insofar as it helps maintain a recognizable economic order that matches the
racial power dynamic. After Bea's offer to Delilah of a 20 percent share for
the sales of her own recipe (!) and the promise that Delilah will soon be able
to purchase a car and house, Delilah's response seems quite a stretch unless
one also imagines that she takes great pleasure in her racially driven subser-
vience: "My own house? You gonna send me away, Miss Bea? I can't live
with you? Oh, honey chile, please don't send me away. . . . How I gonna
take care of you and Miss Jessie if I ain't here? I'se your cook. And I want
to stay your cook. I gives it [the pancake recipe] to you, honey. I makes you
a present of it."[43]

Louise Beavers, as Delilah, in John Stahl's *Imitation of Life*. © Photofest.

Even after her death, the camera continually finds Delilah's neon image flashing above the lives of her survivors, as if to remind everyone of the stabilizing power of her authentic, certain, and fully marketable blackness. It is a vision that gets the final word: in Hurst's novel, the passing Peola marries a white man and is forever exiled to South America; the film's final scenes, by contrast, return a contrite and devastated Peola to her mother's somber funeral march, to a "negro college," and consequently back into the fold of blackness.

The film's depiction of race relations and its representation of relatively respectable and complex black characters did not go unnoticed. In the words of one historian, *Imitation of Life* "was the talk of Harlem. It came back every year and played to full houses. Grown men and women sobbed in the theater."[44] Many African Americans expressed pride in the film's depiction of a dignified and religious black woman who diligently saves for her child's education: "Everyone in America should see the motion picture play *Imitation of Life*," gushed a reviewer in the African American newspaper the *Philadelphia Tribune*, "it is more than a movie, it is a sermon . . . the strongest possible condemnation of racial prejudice."[45] In *The Crisis*, a reviewer suggested that, "as propaganda favoring the American Negro in his struggle for recognition as a human being, no picture has been as effective."[46]

Not everyone agreed. Black audiences became increasingly uncomfortable with the novel's and film's well-intentioned but crude and simplistic depictions of black characters. This discomfort was most clearly formulated in Sterling Brown's searing and influential review of both novel and film in the magazine *Opportunity*, which, to Hurst's great shock, paid less attention to *Imitation of Life*'s honorable antiracism than it did to Delilah and Peola as racist icons. False and degrading, he argued, these characters were little more than remnants of the traditions of racist literature and blackface minstrelsy, nineteenth-century America's most popular form of entertainment. "It requires no searching analysis," Brown observed, "to see in *Imitation of Life* the old stereotype of the contented Mammy, and the tragic mulatto; and the ancient ideas about the mixture of the races. Delilah is straight out of Southern fiction. . . . Her idiom is good only in spots; I have heard dialect all my life, but I have yet to hear such a line as 'She am an angel.' "[47]

Brown's assessment struck a chord, as the sizable response to his article attests: after months of debate, an overwhelmed *Opportunity* editorial staff formally announced that it would no longer publish responses to Brown's piece.[48] Hurst was horrified by the sharp criticism. She called Brown's attitude "ungrateful" and "unintelligent" in her reply to *Opportunity*, her indignation buoyed both by the support of her black friends, such as Hurston and Hughes, who supported her strongly to her face, and by the response of the white reviewers who had especially loved Delilah.[49]

Like Brown's review, Langston Hughes's brief satire *Limitations of Life* (1938), performed in Hughes's Harlem Suitcase Theatre, seems to arrive from a world that Hurst and her white reviewers have no idea exists. In the process, it exposes the earnest blind spots and implausible assumptions about African Americans made by *Imitation of Life*. Setting the action in "Harlem. Right now," even the stage setting reveals what is just barely unspoken in *Imitation of Life*'s racial scenario. Set in a "luxurious living room," the stage comes complete with "electric stove, griddle, pancake turner, [and a] box of pancake flour." However, there is one important change to the box: "Aunt Jemima's picture is white." The largely black audience clearly appreciated the play for undermining the sober absurdity of Bea and Delilah's relationship. Like Hurst's Delilah, Audette, the play's white servant, refuses to accept reasonable compensation. In fact, she refuses anything having to do with her own comfort, suggesting that a nice funeral is all she needs. "I want to do something for you Audette. Something you'll never forget," her wealthy black mistress pleads. She then suggests Audette's gift: a meager day off. Audette refuses: "Ah wouldn't know what to do with it."

The debate about the status of race in what film historian Donald Bogle has called "the first important 'Black film' of the 1930s" continues among contemporary film critics. Many agree with Brown and Hughes that the film is tainted by Delilah's role as an embarrassing and simplistic mammy figure. But others, most notably Lauren Berlant, read Delilah as a far more subversive and challenging figure, claiming that her most demeaning moments in the film are rendered ironically, "ironizing the tradition of grotesque African American representation in American consumer culture, which includes the distortions of the Hurst novel itself."[50] On this reading, Delilah is not simply a racist icon; rather, she voices and embodies the film's subtle critique of the relation of race to national politics. It is clear that many in the film's audience agreed.

. . .

Two decades after Hughes's parody, film producer Ross Hunter gave director Douglas Sirk a copy of Hurst's *Imitation of Life*. He didn't like it and quickly stopped reading. "After a few pages I had the feeling this kind of American novel would definitely disillusion me," Sirk told an interviewer. "The style, the words, the narrative attitude would be in the way of my getting enthusiastic."[51] Sirk's comments may come as a surprise to those familiar with his work, which was itself disdained for its "narrative attitude" by many 1950s critics who loathed the self-conscious melodrama of his three-hankie "women's weepies." Sirk's ironic directorial stance does seem far from the earnest tones of Hurst's novel, but if the novel's sentimental style, language, and attitude rubbed him the wrong way, Sirk's response in his 1959 remake was not to abandon a style built around highly fraught emotional intensity and narrative excess, but to dive in. And though it deviates greatly from Hurst's novel, in some ways Sirk's film is far more faithful than is Stahl's to the novel's uncertainties.

Sirk hired an astonishing cast, including film diva and former sweater girl Lana Turner, who was at the time embroiled in one of the biggest Hollywood scandals of the 1950s. Months before filming commenced, Turner's fourteen-year-old daughter, Cheryl Crane, murdered Turner's boyfriend, gangster Johnny Stompanato, in their Beverly Hills home. The sensational crime was ruled justifiable homicide; a judge nevertheless took Crane from the custody of her often absent celebrity mother, whose teary testimony at the trial was deemed "the performance of her life." The details of Turner's domestic life, revealed at the trial, played out uncannily in Sirk's film, and the film played up its similarities to the real-life scandal (the junior high school Crane attended, for instance, was featured in the film as the school from which Turner's fictional daughter, played by Sandra Dee, graduates).[52] Both film and trial enacted powerful midcentury anxieties, pitting sacred ideals of motherhood against the culture of success and consumption, in the process agitating the uncertain distinctions between Hollywood imitation and "real life."

With a self-conscious sense of drama and high gloss, the film worked as a skewed mirror of very real issues of public concern. Reviewers in the late 1950s read this distortion with virtual uniformity as a problem and deemed the film a failure. Many focused their central critiques on the film's excesses, from the staging, costuming, and acting to its overwrought stories. Compare the *Hollywood Reporter*'s near paroxysms of excitement about Claudette Colbert's gowns in the 1934 film to the review of Sirk's version in *Cue*, which simply misses the film's self-conscious attention to excess and artificiality in blaming Lana Turner for her wardrobe in the film, calling her a "glossily artificial clotheshorse . . . more concerned with clothes, coiffure and profile than with valid performance."[53] By the 1970s, however, many film historians came to a new appreciation of Sirk's work, reexamining its lush excess as an ironic commentary on the excesses of 1950s consumer society. The critical attention intensified as feminist and race studies gained prominence, and critics recognized in the hugely popular and politically complex film an attempt to explore the social disjunctures of postwar America. As such, *Imitation of Life* serves, too, as a fascinating counterexample to the problem films of the 1950s, which took on such social issues as racism with a straightforward, well-intentioned, and often hamfisted earnestness.

If the Depression-era United States provided an important cultural con-

Lana Turner with (from left) Karin Dicker, Juanita Moore, and Terry Burnham in Douglas Sirk's 1959 film *Imitation of Life*. © Photofest.

text for Hurst and Stahl, the 1950s, with the emerging Civil Rights and women's liberation movements and the far-reaching concerns about the stultification of consumer society, rendered the tale of single working mothers, black and white, shockingly current. Dispensing with the Aunt Jemima premise — the film's protagonist, now called Lora Meredith, becomes a famous actress rather than a restaurateur, eliminating the need to market her loyal African American maid Annie's (Juanita Moore) culinary skills — Sirk's version of the tale is recognizable in only skeletal ways. The changes are more than superficial; indeed, they represent a sea change in attitude toward working women and consumer culture. To Stahl's straightforward celebration of the career woman and the salvation of the marketplace, Sirk responds with an ironic critique of the dangers and allures of the postwar boom in consumer spending, staging this critique as a struggle between normative and perverse modes of femininity. In the logic of the film, Lora fails romantically and as a mother and lives a life of "imitation," failing to follow the standard script for women, insofar as she indulges her outsized ambition. Obsessed with her career and celebrity, disinterested as a mother, involved in a loveless long-term career-driven relationship, she is told by her true love, Steve, early in the film, "What you're after isn't real." Throughout the film, Lora responds to Steve's pleas for stability by making dubious-sounding claims about her desire to "settle down." But, as director Rainer Werner Fassbinder commented in an appreciative essay about Sirk, the characters in Sirk's *Imitation of Life* "are always making plans for happiness, for tenderness, and then the phone rings."[54]

The melodramatic tone of Hurst's novel derived from an earnest sense of her characters' impossible dilemmas. Sirk takes a more savage and campy approach: in his take on cold war America, all gestures are theatrical, including those that strive to seem authentic, and the desire for fame and success overrides love and motherhood. So, while maternal self-sacrifice is an idealized act in the first film, in which Bea ultimately sacrifices her love interest to preserve her fragile relationship with her daughter, such behavior is hopelessly suspect in Sirk's film. When Lora dramatically offers to abandon Steve to save her daughter Susie's feelings, she receives a sharp and incisive response: "Oh, Mama, stop *acting*!" Lora gets equally cynical responses from Steve himself, who also urges her to "stop acting" when Lora puts her desires and ambition first in one heated conversation. Of course, it is precisely as an actress that Lora finds her success and public adoration, an indication that the film is challenging audiences to think about their own role in this circuit of desire. The point is made stronger insofar as Lora is not alone in her performances: hers is a world of pervasive inauthenticity. Annie's light-skinned daughter, now called Sarah Jane (played by the Jewish actress Susan Kohner), again plays a crucial role in this conversation. In this retelling, we learn that as she passes for white, Sarah Jane earns her money in a series of demeaning, hypersexualized performance jobs, clear echoes of, and commentary on, Lora's profession.

The film's racial subplot, and its interest in a black identity informed by the burgeoning civil rights movement, underscored its unsettling vision. Annie does ultimately act as Lora's domestic servant, but in this film blacks have traveled a long way from the subservient mammies of Hurst's novel and Stahl's film. The distance is marked in one remarkable scene in which a disgusted Sarah Jane, asked to help serve at a function for Lora, enters performing a parody of a southern servant, carrying a tray on her head, her

Passing for white in Douglas Sirk's *Imitation of Life*, Sarah Jane
(Susan Kohner) works as a dancing girl. © Photofest.

voice a distorted and thick imitation of southern dialect. "Oh, no trick to
totin', Miss Lora," she sarcastically explains. "Ah l'arned it from my
mammy . . . and she l'arned it from old Massa . . . 'fo she belonged to you!"
But if she is allowed to voice a critique of old models of racial hierarchy,
Sarah Jane certainly does not provide a solution sanctioned by the film.[55]
Her passing, modeled, it seems, on what she learned in "Miss Lora's"
house, is presented as yet another false performance of identity. And like
Lora, Sarah Jane's self-creation as an object of consumption in the mar-
ketplace comes to define, and overwhelm, her.

Annie presents a dignified, but still subservient, alternative. She is not
crippled by self-hatred or artifice, but neither can she offer a viable response to the frustrations voiced by Sarah Jane, frustrations that were in
part informed by the civil rights movement. Like the tale's previous manifestations, then, while there is something at stake here in a vision of black

authenticity, there is a pervasive sense of its precariousness. We learn, along with Lora, that Annie has a life separate from the one we witness onscreen ("It never occurred to me that you had many friends," Lora tells her in a particularly thick-headed moment. "Miss Lora, you never asked," is Annie's reply), and it is here, the film implies, that "real life" has taken place. But even in what seems the film's most "authentic moment," the final, somber, African American funeral procession, with gospel star Mahalia Jackson voicing the searing soundtrack, the camera acts as a distanced onlooker, at one point watching the proceedings from inside a store whose window reads "Costume Rental."

It is a telling moment: despite the film's clear condemnation of Lora's chosen path, the sense of being trapped in a world of performance pervades. Steve consistently urges her to abandon her acting career and devote herself to her family, but he keeps returning to her despite her failure to do so. And there he is again, among Lora's rapt audience in the theater scenes, seemingly addicted to the illusions he wants to destroy. A similar point might be made about Annie, despite her being the conduit to "real life." It is she, after all, who introduces Sarah Jane into the world of wealth and performance she comes to covet and emulate, and who voices an outlook focused on creating illusion: "No sin in looking prosperous," she tells "Miss Lora" early on in their relationship when she is mistaken for Lora's maid. When the loose ends are tied at the film's conclusion, both Lora and Sarah Jane become acceptable women, doing race and gender the "right" ways. "I didn't mean it!" Sarah Jane screams to her mother's casket, echoing Peola's final words in the first film. Yet one gets the sense that here, despite the film's tidy end, such problems will never resolve. Soon, as Fassbinder pointed out, the phone will ring again.

. . .

Hurst's novel, like Sirk's film, refuses to resolve its dilemmas — dilemmas that still haunt America in the twenty-first century — with simple and satisfying answers. To the question asked early in her novel, "What happened to girls thrown on their own resources?", Hurst offers myriad responses: women who are "thrown on their own resources" defy expectations: they become independently wealthy despite the sexist assumptions of a business world otherwise closed to women; they become single mothers; they create alternative households; and they break from social conventions. But the new possibilities explored by *Imitation of Life* are far from ideal. Bea Pullman consistently feels the need to choose between financial success and the fulfillments of love and family. And even Delilah, whose role as caregiver seems so obviously prescribed and accepted by her, cannot find contentment insofar as she succeeds as mammy only for her white audiences. Crowds of white consumers clamor for Delilah's waffles and love; her own daughter is less impressed. So, despite their respective relationships to being women in the twentieth century, neither finally translates her "own resources" into a situation in which either motherhood or ambition is enough.

Some readers have understood Bea's and Delilah's unhappy endings as a shortcoming in Hurst's novel. Certainly the implications here, both about race and about the impossible relationship between motherhood and success in the marketplace, are troubling. But if troubling, Hurst's work is also reflective of concerns of the 1930s, concerns still shared by many today about the difficult balance of career and family, the relationship between blacks and whites, and the aggressive lure of consumer society. And the novel is all the more interesting precisely because it does not pretend to provide easy solutions.[56] The novel may punish Bea for her transgressions against traditional feminine roles, but it also takes great pains to showcase her remarkable abilities. She negotiates a perilous world hostile to a woman forced to be both mother and breadwinner, hardly imagining marriage as an idealized alternative, nor men as somehow more naturally suited for the public sphere. Bea's father, emblem of a reduced patriarchy, signals quite the opposite, quickly demoted here to an "impotent" and silent spectator, a nonearning "chair baby," with a wilted arm.

The films' long-term successes serve as an unusual response to Kathleen Norris's 1918 question, with which we opened, about Hurst's longevity. Her writing now largely out of print except for this new edition of her classic novel, it makes sense that the work of this once popular author has thrived longer on film, a medium more forgiving than American Literature to popular texts.[57] Such longevity would no doubt be mystifying to Hurst's critics, but not to her loyal audience. Since its initial publication, *Imitation of Life* in its various manifestations has occupied a singular position in American culture, haunting it more persistently perhaps than any twentieth-century popular text about race other than *Gone With the Wind*. Together, novel and films provide a lens through which readers of the early-twenty-first century can explore the evolution of the most fundamental American cultural issues of the twentieth.

Notes

1 Kathleen Norris, "A Genius of the Short Story," *Cosmopolitan*, September 1918, 134.

2 See Fannie Hurst, *Anatomy of Me: An Autobiography* (New York: Doubleday, 1958), 242.

3 Among critics more generally, for decades Hurst inspired a steady flow of wildly extreme responses. She was immensely popular and deeply scorned, "among the four or five permanent short story writers of our generation," according to one hopeful reader, and according to another — F. Scott Fitzgerald — a "fifty thousand dollars a year" sensation who produced not "one story or novel that will last ten years." She was a "genius" who left readers "breathless with her roaring power and erratic beauty," and her writing was "a serious insult to her readers." Edward O'Brien, letter to Fannie Hurst, October 25, 1916, cited in Brooke Kroeger, *Fannie: The Talent for Success of Writer Fannie Hurst* (New York: Random House, 1999), 47; F. Scott Fitzgerald, *This Side of Paradise* (1920; New York: Cambridge University Press, 1995), 201; Robert Littell, review, *New Republic,* February 3, 1926, 302–303; Harry Longan Stuart, "Matter Wins over Form in *Appassionata*," *New York Times Book Review*, January 24, 1926, 1–5.

4 Langston Hughes, "Limitations of Life," in James Vernon Hatch, ed., *Black Theater, U.S.A.: Forty-five Plays by Black Americans, 1847–1974* (New York: Free Press, 1974), 656. In his biography of Hughes, Arnold Rampersand gives a brief account of the play's performance and reception: *The Life of Langston Hughes,* Vol. 1: *1902–1941* (New York: Oxford University Press, 1986), 364–365. See also *New York Amsterdam News*, November 5, 1938, 20.

5 David Hinckley, "Rites of 'Passing,' " *New York Daily News*, December 5, 1995, 36. Both films have recently enjoyed a renaissance among film and cultural historians. See Lauren Berlant, "National Brands/National Body: *Imitation of Life*," in Hortense Spillers, ed., *Comparative American Identities: Race, Sex and Nationality in the Modern Text* (New York: Routledge, 1991); Marianne Conroy, " 'No Sin in Looking Prosperous': Gender, Race, and the Class Formations of Middlebrow Taste in Douglas Sirk's *Imitation of Life*," in David E. James and Rick Berg, eds., *The Hidden Foundation: Cinema and the Question of Class* (Minneapolis: University of Minnesota Press, 1996); Susan Courtney, "Picturizing Race: Hollywood's Censorship of Miscegenation and

Production of Racial Visibility through Imitation of Life," *Genders* 27 (1998), www.genders.org; Ruth Feldstein, *Motherhood in Black and White: Race and Sex in American Liberalism, 1930–1965* (Ithaca, N.Y.: Cornell University Press, 2000); and Lucy Fischer, ed., *Imitation of Life: Douglas Sirk, Director* (New Brunswick, N.J.: Rutgers University Press, 1991).

6 There are some important exceptions to this disappearance, most notably Brooke Kroeger's masterly recent biography of Hurst, *Fannie: The Talent for Success of Writer Fannie Hurst.* See also Abe C. Ravitz, *Imitations of Life: Fannie Hurst's Gaslight Sonatas* (Carbondale: Southern Illinois University Press, 1997).

7 Edward J. O'Brien, "The Yearbook of the American Short Story," in O'Brien, ed., *The Best Short Stories of 1916* (Boston: Small, Maynard, 1917), 377.

8 "Editor's Easy Chair," *Harper's Monthly*, May 1915, 958–961.

9 Ibid., 959.

10 Fannie Hurst, "Sob Sister," *Metropolitan*, February 1916, 27–29, 34, 40, 42–43.

11 "Review of *Every Soul Hath Its Song*," *New York Times*, November 12, 1916, cited in Kroeger, *Fannie*, 44.

12 Ravitz, *Imitations of Life,* 17.

13 Kroeger, *Fannie,* 42.

14 *New York Times*, May 4, 1920. Three years later, the *New York Times Magazine* did a front-page follow up story, "Eight Years after a Novel Marriage," December 9, 1923.

15 Waldo Frank, "Pseudo-Literature," *New Republic*, December 2, 1925, 46–47.

16 Hurst, *Anatomy of Me*, 242.

17 Robert Van Gelder, "An Interview with Fannie Hurst," *New York Times Book Review*, January 25, 1942, 2.

18 Archer Winston, cited in Kroeger, *Fannie*, 197.

19 "The Vertical City," *New York Times*, April 30, 1922, sec. 3, p. 14; N. P. Dawson, "Vertical City," *Literary Review* (*New York Post*), April 15, 1922, 579.

20 Thomas Schatz, *Hollywood Genres* (New York: McGraw-Hill, 1981), 246.

21 *Pictorial Review*, October 1932.

22 Fannie Hurst, "Women Who Lead the Way," *New York Times Magazine*, February 20, 1921, cited in Ravitz, 28.

23 For more general discussion of these issues, see, for instance, Christian Viviani, "Who Is without Sin? The Maternal Melodrama in American Film, 1930–39," in Marcia Landy, ed., *Imitations of Life: A Reader on Film and Television Melodrama* (Detroit: Wayne State University Press, 1991). For an excellent recent discussion of motherhood and its relation to U.S. race politics

in mid-twentieth-century popular culture, see Feldstein, *Motherhood in Black and White.*

24 For more on the use of Delilah as public icon for Bea's business, see Lauren Berlant's excellent essay.

25 For more on Aunt Jemima, see M. M. Manring, *Slave in a Box: The Strange Career of Aunt Jemima* (Charlottesville: University Press of Virginia, 1998); and Marilyn Kern-Forworth, *Aunt Jemima, Uncle Ben, and Rastus* (Westport, Conn.: Greenwood Press, 1994).

26 Predictably, given her history with critics, most reviewers in the mainstream white press failed to appreciate Hurst's vexed sentimentalism. Many reviewers complained about the novel in terms that dogged Hurst for much of her life. They critiqued the novel's narrative excess ("overlong and overwritten," according to one reviewer [*Christian Science Monitor*, February 25, 1933, 10]; "extremely emotional and overdrawn," writes another, who generously adds, "but not so crass in language and episodes as some of this author's previous novels" [*Booklist*, April 1933, 241]); and they suspected that Hurst wrote solely for the financial bottom line: "In *Imitation of Life* Fannie Hurst shows clearly the wear and tear of her determination to become the storyteller of the millions" ("Business Woman," *New York Times Book Review*, February 5, 1933, 7:4, 14:1). But there is also a sense, mostly among *Imitation of Life*'s women reviewers, that the novel has something significant to say, and that it does so in an unusually moving and powerful way. "Miss Hurst touches on a vital problem of women," Dorothea Lawrance Mann suggests in the *Boston Evening Transcript Book Review*: "How is she to meet the needs of her own feminine nature when she takes her place in the world of men?" ("Success — In Fannie Hurst's Own Style," February 4, 1933, 2). Mary Ross, in the *New York Herald Tribune Books*, celebrates the novel's portrait of "a woman singularly free from the kind of self-pity which seems to me unfortunately implied in the title of the book, a woman without need for self-dramatization, power and adulation" ("From a Waffle Shop to a World Wide Business: In Delilah Fannie Hurst Creates Her Finest Character Since *Lummox*," February 5, 1933, 4). And the *Christian Science Monitor*'s review leads to a more general assessment of Hurst that directly engages with the discomfort some audiences experienced with both her style and her political beliefs: "For many readers Miss Hurst's style stands in its own light. For many she is offensively outspoken in her discussion of human living. That she has seen and felt deeply, one has no shadow of doubt" (February 25, 1933, 10). Hurst could hardly have hoped for better than such an acknowledgment.

27 Ross, "From a Waffle Shop to a World Wide Business," 4.

28 "Of Women," *Cincinnati Enquirer*, February 11, 1933; "Successor to 'Lum-

mox,' " *Christian Science Monitor*, February 25, 1933, 10. The review in the *Chicago Herald Examiner* takes a more general celebratory view, calling the novel "one of the most human documents written on the race problem that is the penalty of slavery in a free country." Robert H. Wilson, "Speaking of Books," *Chicago Herald Examiner*, February 28, 1933.

29 In the decades that followed the publication of Hurst's novel there were also a number of films that dealt with the subject, including the two versions of *Imitation of Life*, *Pinky* (1949), *Lost Boundaries* (1949), and *Shadows* (1959). For more on the history of the term "tragic mulatto," see Werner Sollors, *Neither Black Nor White Yet Both: Thematic Explorations of Interracial Literature* (New York: Oxford University Press, 1997).

30 Perhaps because of the widespread popularity of the 1934 film adaptation of *Imitation of Life*, audiences found Peola to be a particularly exemplary character, so compelling that she worked her way into everyday African American culture: in her 1942 "Glossary of Harlem Slang," Zora Neale Hurston includes "peola" as a term meaning "a very white Negro girl." Zora Neale Hurston, "Glossary of Harlem Slang," in *Spunk: The Selected Stories of Zora Neale Hurston* (Berkeley: Turtle Island, 1985), 94.

31 According to Kroeger, Eden is modeled after Hurst's friend Elizabeth Arden, herself given to a thoroughly managed public image. Arden's name, *Fortune* magazine observed in 1938, was "an alias concealing many things." Cited in Kathy Peiss, *Hope in a Jar: The Making of America's Beauty Culture* (New York: Metropolitan Books, 1998), 79.

32 Hurst, *Anatomy of Me*, 141.

33 Ibid., 42. Virginia Eden, née Sadie Kress, is perhaps a nod to Hurst's relationship to her own Jewish upbringing.

34 Langston Hughes to Fannie Hurst, July 13, 1937, Harry Ransom Humanities Research Center, University of Texas at Austin, FH/151/1.

35 Zora Neale Hurston to Fannie Hurst, January 30 and February 6, 1940, Harry Ransom Humanities Research Center, University of Texas at Austin, FH/152/2. The question of the authenticity is one not unfamiliar to Hurston; in the late 1930s she and Richard Wright were engaged in a similar literary argument of their own about the rightful place of politics and "culture" in African American literature. He accused her great novel *Their Eyes Were Watching God* of being part of the minstrel tradition; she wondered in a review of *Uncle Tom's Children* if, given the book's use of dialect, Wright might be "tone deaf" (*Saturday Review of Literature*, April 2, 1938).

36 Robert Hemenway, *Zora Neale Hurston: A Literary Biography* (Urbana: University of Illinois Press, 1977). Hurst seems thoroughly, incessantly aware of race in her interactions with Hurston. Her preface to Hurston's first novel,

Jonah's Gourd Vine, published the year after *Imitation of Life*, betrays what seems a strangely unconscious relationship to Hurston's blackness. At one point, for instance, she enthusiastically writes about Hurston, "A brilliantly facile spade has turned over rich new earth." See also Hurston's glowing assessment of Hurst in her memoirs, *Dust Tracks on a Road: An Autobiography*, 2nd ed., ed. Robert E. Hemenway (1942; Urbana: University of Illinois Press, 1984). See especially 238–243 ("Two Women in Particular") and 310.

37 Fannie Hurst, "Zora Hurston: A Personality Sketch" (1961), reprinted in Fischer, *Imitation of Life*, 174–175.

38 For more on the relationship of Hughes and Hurston to *Imitation of Life*, see Jane Caputi's essay "Specifying Fannie Hurst: Langston Hughes's 'Limitations of Life,' Zora Neale Hurston's *Their Eyes Were Watching God*, and Toni Morrison's *The Bluest Eyes* as 'Answers' to Hurst's *Imitation of Life*," *Black American Literature Forum* 24, no. 4 (winter 1990): 697–716.

39 The review is reproduced in Fischer, *Imitation of Life*.

40 *Hollywood Reporter*, November 3, 1934, cited in Courtney, "Picturizing Race."

41 Cited in Courtney, "Picturizing Race."

42 Cited in ibid.

43 This racially inflected economic order of things is visibly manifested in all aspects of their world; when they say goodnight in their new mansion, for example, Bea goes upstairs while Delilah descends to the basement.

44 Delilah Jackson, quoted in Hinckley, "Rites of 'Passing.'" According to the *New York Amsterdam News*, Stahl's film caused "a sensation in Harlem" (" 'Imitation of Life' Provokes Discussion: Benefits, Evils of Picture to Be Argued at Symposium on February 13," February 2, 1935). For more on responses to the film, see Henry Louis Gates Jr., *Colored People* (New York: Vintage, 1994), esp. 23–24, and Donald Bogle, who calls the film "the first important 'Black film' of the 1930s" because of its "humanization of the Negro servant." *Toms, Coons, Mammies and Bucks: An Interpretive History of Blacks in American Films* (New York: Bantam, 1973), 57.

45 "Greatest Condemnation of Prejudice in America Seen in 'Imitation of Life,' " *Philadelphia Tribune*, February 14, 1935, 12.

46 Mercer Cook, "*Imitation of Life* in Paris," *The Crisis* 42 (June 1935): 182.

47 Sterling A. Brown, "Imitation of Life: Once a Pancake," *Opportunity: Journal of Negro Life* 12, no. 3 (March 1935): 87–88.

48 "The End of a Controversy," *Opportunity* 13, no. 8 (August 1935): 231. For examples of the debate elsewhere in community life, see, for instance, " 'Imitation of Life' Provokes Discussion," *New York Amsterdam News*, February 2, 1935.

49 Fannie Hurst, "Miss Fannie Hurst," *Opportunity* 13, no. 4 (April 1935): 121.

50 Berlant, "National Brands/National Body," 125. In her essay "Picturizing Race," Susan Courtney argues directly against Berlant's point; see especially n. 38.

51 "Sirk on Sirk," interview by Jon Halliday, reprinted in Fischer, *Imitation of Life,* 226–231.

52 Cheryl Crane with Cliff Jahr, *Detour: A Hollywood Story* (New York: Avon Books, 1989), 306–307.

53 Fischer, *Imitation of Life,* 237. Echoing his predecessor's take on the first film ("the most shameless tearjerker of the Fall"), the *New York Times* reviewer called Sirk's film "the most shameless tearjerker in a couple of years." Bosley Crowther, "Sob Story Back," *New York Times*, April 18, 1959, sec. 2, p. 18. The complete review is reprinted in Fischer, ibid., 241–242.

54 Rainer Werner Fassbinder, "Imitation of Life," in Fischer, *Imitation of Life,* 244–246.

55 In her insightful analysis of the film, Ruth Feldstein reads this moment as a failure for both Sarah Jane and her mother, who surrounds "her daughter with superficial symbols of status and raises a daughter who hates herself, is spoiled, and is disrespectful. . . . Sarah Jane can only reject discrimination, it seems, with immature self-hate and sexualized self-display, rather than with a developed political posture" (*Motherhood in Black and White*, 127).

56 It seems strikingly prescient regarding concerns that are still very much alive for women and men of the twenty-first century. Witness the uproar surrounding Sylvia Ann Hewlett's book *Creating a Life: Professional Women and the Quest for Children* (New York: Talk Miramax Books, 2002), which announced yet again the dismal prospects for motherhood among professional women.

57 Though the films, of course, sometimes helped boost the novel's sales: Kroeger reports that a new edition of the novel that accompanied Sirk's film in the late 1950s (which had Lana Turner and John Gavin on the cover) sold half a million copies.

· I ·

It struck Bea, and for the moment diverted her from grief, that quite the most physical thing she had ever connected with her mother was the fact of her having died.

She found herself, crying there beside the bier, thinking of her mother's legs. Such willing ones. They were locked now, as they lay stretched horizontally down the center of the parlor, in the rigidity of death. The bengaline dress, for which only four dreamlike weeks ago they had shopped together on Atlantic Avenue, now lay decently over those dear legs. Dreadful counterpane to the physical fact that Adelaide Chipley's breasts and loins and femurs lay dead.

There had been so little evidence, during her lifetime, of any aspect of her physical life, other than just the automatic processes of locomotion and eating and sleeping. Mother had never been the one to profess hunger, or fatigue, or warmth, or cold, but how those estates of being in others could concern her! Her legs had just carried her about through being wife to Evans Chipley, and mother to Beatrice Fay Chipley, and all things to the monotonous mosaic of little days in the little household.

True, it had repeatedly occurred to Bea to ask herself, following that day shortly after her fourteenth birthday when the physical fact of her coming of menstrual age had frightened her so terribly that she had sobbed all through her mother's clumsy attempt at explanation, how on earth it was possible to even imagine two such people as her parents ever coming together in a way to conceive her, their child.

Why, it was even difficult to visualize Mother as a young girl (how pretty she was on the old tintype) sitting in the parlor of her little home in Burlington, New Jersey, past which the railroad train thundered, awaiting Father on his Saturday night visits from Philadelphia.

I

They had always seemed too little acquainted even for that. Too—too remote, for the suggestion of passion. How could those two have begot child! They never even touched, except for the peck of the lips when Father departed and arrived, and Bea came in for that too, of precisely the same quality.

How then . . . ?

Following her mother's shockingly inadequate explanation shortly after her fourteenth year, she had fleetingly dared to ask herself that question over and over again.

How . . . ?

What secret and mysterious transformation could come over two such unintimate-appearing people as her father and mother, after they had closed the door of their bedroom nights? How account for their matter-of-fact exit from the quite inexorable matter-of-factness of life as it was lived on Arctic Avenue, between Georgia and Mississippi Avenues, into realms which begot progeny.

It was all immensely reasonable in the stuff of which the books she borrowed from the public library were made. *Janice Meredith. When Knighthood Was in Flower. Richard Carvel. Mill on the Floss.* But Mother and Father—how? Neither could it have been a matter between them that had solely to do with the first night, or the first months, of marriage. After her fourteenth year, Bea came to recognize, with her logic, that her mother's illness, the year before, had been due to miscarriage.

Almost equally strange was a high-school mate, Ferdie Leigh, getting a baby sister.

The Leighs lived on Mississippi Avenue, and Mr. Leigh, who had a bathing-suit concession on the Boardwalk, was elder in the Presbyterian Church. The Leigh children were not allowed to ride in street cars on Sunday. . . . Mrs. Leigh was quite old and ugly and narrow . . .

How . . . ?

How in the world did two people like Mr. and Mrs. Leigh, and more especially like her mother and father, ever become sufficiently well acquainted with one another. . . .

Life in the Chipley household was so crammed with just the daylight facts. Setting yeast. Stretching lace curtains. Fancy-work. Pickling. Carpet-beating. Ironing. Nice meals planned by Mother, around everyone's likes and dislikes, except her dear own. "The chicken liver at the end of the platter is for you, Mr. Pullman, knowing you don't eat rabbit." "Take plenty of floating island Bea; it's your favorite dessert." "Mr. Chipley, that is your kind of sweet butter." Life all cluttered like that, with littlenesses. Coming. Going. Sleeping, too, of course, but Mother and Father straight beside one another in bed, like her, Bea, in her own little room. And Mr. Pullman in his.

For a while, after she was fourteen, it had been difficult to keep her mind from sliding around to this mystifying riddle of the intimacies, that must, by very virtue of her own existence, have transpired between her father and mother.

Jeanette Clabby, another schoolmate, and who was a Catholic, would undoubtedly carry such thoughts to confession. If they possessed her. Did they? Nice girls would no more have discussed such things!

But the riddle of her parents would persist, privately.

Goodness! if she so much as entered the bedroom where her mother was dressing, she hastily threw a towel or a wrapper across her breasts. Her father, even in the years before they had moved to Atlantic City, from Philadelphia, and when the asthma was thick upon him, had not liked to appear before the small girl, Bea, in his undershirt.

What mysterious transformation was it could come over two such unintimate people . . . ?

And now in death, there was at last something physical about her mother.

The awfulness of thinking that thought smote her with something that hurt even more than her grief. How confusing to find ideas that bordered on the forbidden, mingling with the aroma of God which seemed to emanate from a face dead and dear.

How private she had been about her illness, delicate and secretive as she had been about everything else pertaining to what touched her most closely. And what a frightening, hurting illness! . . . And now God had folded those mysterious limbs into the sanctuary and still further privacy of death.

And to think that out of those dead loins had sprung life, hers— Beatrice Chipley's! They had been warm, yielding loins, and that crumpled figure over there in the corner of the darkened parlor, his back retching as he cried, had actually committed the act of sex. It made

3

mother's deadness somehow seem so young and inexpressibly heart-breaking.

All mixed up with this death of a mother from whom she had never been separated one full day in her life, was a kind of splendid grief she had experienced once, fleetingly, while reading from a high-school platform:

"I weep for Adonais, he is dead."

The words, as she recited them, had felt like wine, fizzing down into, and exciting and hurting her.

"I weep for Adonais, he is dead . . ."

I weep for mamma, she is dead . . . her arms and legs and breasts and her loins there, under the bengaline dress, are stiff and dead——

·2·

It was strange that in all the years of living in that small gray board house on Arctic Avenue, with the exterior staircase running down its flank like a ladder, in fact ever since she was six and they had moved from Philadelphia the year of the climax of her father's asthma, the things she, Bea, had taken for granted.

Things such as an always replenished stack of fresh handkerchiefs in her dresser drawer; clam chowder on Fridays; clean top sheets every Monday; face towels when you reached for them; and a winter's supply of coal in the cellar without anyone mentioning or reminding.

Management of even so modest a household as the one on Arctic Avenue was packed with a minutiæ of detail, of which, during the lifetime of her mother, she had scarcely been conscious. Then, icepans had never overflowed, nor laundry accumulated, nor windows grown thick with grime. There had been tape hangers always on towels, and unfrayed cuffs on her father's shirts, and new all-over-embroidery corset-covers in her dresser, without anyone seeming to give any apparent thought to them. They were just there, the product of Mother, sitting evening after evening, sometimes on a bench on the Boardwalk, or beside the Welsbach lamp in the sitting-room, at work with her indefatigable fingers.

Less than a month following her death, myriads of these hitherto unrecorded little items were to begin to stand out immensely against the all too brief span of each day.

Housekeeping for Father and Mr. Pullman, now that every detail of it rested suddenly upon her, was filled with tremendous trifles of which heretofore she had not even been aware.

To housekeep, one had to plan ahead and carry items of motley nature around in the mind and at the same time preside, as Mother had, at table, just as if everything, from the liver and bacon, to the succotash, to the French toast and strawberry jam, had not been matters of forethought and speculation.

Since her passing, Evans Chipley was somehow, to his daughter, looking so dwarfed. Almost as if he had shriveled into his clothes and hung in the middle of them like a spider close to the center of his web. Poor Father. Life for him must be made to proceed as closely as possible to the pattern she had woven about his fastidious little needs. There must never be any coffee lap over into his saucer, and his corn must always be cut from the cob for him, and socks must be folded away wrong side out, with the toe indented so he could slide easily into them, and on wet days when Father walked to his headquarters on the Boardwalk Pier, there must be newspaper in his rubbers against possible leak.

If Mother could carry these things around in her head without ever seeming to have them there, surely she, Bea, with her diploma from the Atlantic City High School fresh in its ribboned roll, must be capable of carrying on with at least equal efficiency.

True, during Mother's lifetime, it had been her pride that Bea did not often set her nicely shod young feet into the kitchen.

"Those things will come naturally enough when you get to them. I'd rather you spent the time practicing, or at your painting or burnt wood."

Darling Mother. How spared she, Bea, had been all those years, what with even Mr. Pullman's board money being chiefly diverted to provide all sorts of additional little luxuries for Bea and her father.

And now poor Father, deprived of those blessed first-hand administerings, was looking so dwarfed. This unintimate man, the mystery of whose intimacy with her mother still snagged her shameful curiosity, seemed to have touched life precisely in the manner he now inhabited his neat little dandified clothes; rather suspended in the middle, without contacts.

She must see to it that the taken-for-granted creature comforts of his life went on without the interruption to which hers had been so violently subjected. He had seemed so bewildered, not to say fastidiously offended, that night the little bubbles had appeared along her mother's lips when, without their realizing it, she lay dying. Mother's impulse, as she begged him to leave the room and let her suffer alone, must have been to spare him ugliness. The other evening when the icepan had overflowed and its contents had come creeping into the dining-room to their feet beneath the supper table! The mess of it was easily cleared, but to have had Father see and suffer, was the rub. His voice had actually cried, the morning he had come to her with a rent across his freshly opened pocket handkerchief. Mother had always tended that crying voice as you would a child's.

And now, just one month after she had taken up the reins that had been laid down in death by her mother, came the suggestion from Father as he offendedly, after one spoonful, pushed away his dish of ever-so-slightly scorched corn pudding:

"Bea, better see if we can't get Selene to come by the week."

She had been in the act of helping Mr. Pullman to some of the corn pudding, and now her hand hung with the spoonful over his saucer and made a little trembling motion as if it had been hurt.

And in front of Mr. Pullman, too. She began to press outward with her tonsils, with her whole body, in fact, in an effort not to cry.

"I'm sorry about the scorch, Father. The butcher boy came just as I was about to take it out of the oven."

"It's all right, Rome wasn't built in a day. Bah! bitter!"

Oh, oh, how that ground in! Rome wasn't built in a day. How subtly, and yet with what cruel benignancy, that ejaculation from Father summed up her inadequacies.

"Mr. Pullman and I can walk across the tracks to Selene's house after supper. This kind of thing won't do."

Now Father simply mustn't act like that. To begin with, he knew perfectly well that the black woman, Selene, who had helped Mother twice a week toward the end, had moved to Baltimore. If only he had come right out with, "Bea, child, you've scorched the pudding again."

He had no intention of taking on the additional expense of Selene or anyone like her. Except for the grace of Mr. Pullman's financial contribution, over and above Father's salary, there could never have been a Selene, even those last months of Mother's life.

Mother had once said that as a lad in Leeds, England, Father had seen better days. Perhaps, but certainly Aunt Chipley, the sole relative, who had lived with them in the Philadelphia days until her death, had given little evidence. Aunt Chipley, whose husband had been an ironmonger in Leeds and who, after his death, had followed her brother Evans to America, had drunk coffee from her saucer in great soughing movements and gone stocking-footed about the house. In fact, these constituted Bea's sole memories of her, except the tuberose smell of her parlor funeral, and the time she had yelled at Father that he was born a little clark, was a little clark at heart, and a clark would live and die.

It had worried her at the time because, first of all, you said "clerk," not "clark," and then besides, Father was not a clerk or clark. Even back in those days before the asthma, he had been city salesman for the great pickle-and-relish concern whose interests he now represented in Atlantic City.

Clerks stood behind counters. Father drove a buggy around town to the trade. Father wore spats. True, he drank out of his saucer, too, but without the soughing noise, and with his small white mustache lifted as if it were first fastidiously smelling of what it partook.

How small and neat and right he was. She felt now, with the entire pressing outward of her body, as it seemed to swell to resist all that was unspoken about the scorched corn pudding, the look she had so often seen in her mother's gray eyes. He was quite a relentless pattern of precisions, Father was. Such a little gentleman, that the rebukes lay folded into the custard of his manner. There was something utterly bewildering about the way his capacity for rebukes was whipped into his suavity. No getting at it any more than you could separate the flavor of the vanilla from the custard itself.

Strange that in all those years of seeing her mother's neck drop forward like a tired swan's, to the something that lurked behind the neat privet hedge of her father's mustache, that only now, when it was too late, she should find herself aching to hold her mother understand-ingly away from his small, scarcely perceptible cruelties.

Did Mr. Pullman, who had resided in the small bosom of that family ever since the move from Philadelphia, fifteen years before, realize any of this? He must know Father so well by now. It was through his business acquaintanceship with him that he had come to board at the house. To be sure, Mr. Pullman's work confined him to the Amusement Pier on the Boardwalk, where he demonstrated the varied uses of the varied relishes and gave out pickle literature and little stone pickles on stickpins. Father's connections, as city salesman, had chiefly to do with the Philadelphia office. Still, the Amusement Pier, jutting from the Boardwalk out into the vast curve of hissing surf which dances in against the flank of Atlantic City as it stretches quite beautifully between Absecon and Great Egg Harbor Inlets, was informal headquarters for every local employee connected with the pickle-and-relish concern.

Lucky for the Chipleys that it was, since it drew to them Mr. Pullman.

But how much better, this all-year-round "guest" arrangement, than every blessed year, come summer, having to move out, like the Leightons or the Doc Hansons, in an effort to catch up on the chronic national dilemma of living beyond their means, and then, nine times out of ten, renting the house to summer folks who had no respect for one's things.

Take the year the Hansons had rented to those four bachelor boys from Philadelphia who had dried their bathing-suits on the mahogany furniture and burned cigarette holes in every piece of bedding in the house. Or the summer the Leightons had rented to a Wilmington family who had ruined a davenport worth more than the entire season's rental.

Really, with Mr. Pullman, you scarcely knew he was in the house. One of those conservative New Englanders. So quiet, so considerate, so steady and church-going. Except for the cans of maple syrup, which he handled as a side line, arriving in consignments which he kept stacked in his room, you would hardly have known it was occupied.

Why, you could almost read the time of day by his orderly comings and goings, and really, in his frock-coat (lecturing, you see, at the Pier on the history and development of the tomato from the field to the jar), there was that about him that was as high-class as a clergyman.

Take your average unmarried man in a town like Atlantic City, where you only needed to walk three blocks from the house to the easily accessible gaieties of the Boardwalk. Wouldn't he just, though! Not so Mr. Pullman. Why, it was a pleasure, instead of a fear, to have a young girl growing up in the house with him. And goodness knows not many mothers in Atlantic City, who rented out, could say that. Perhaps it was the combination of his day-long work of demonstrating and lecturing at the Pier, and his noon-hour side line of soliciting orders from the big hotels for his maple syrup, kept him such a home-body, nights.

That fact, coupled with such nice house habits, such as reading or checkers, or one or two evenings a week a Sousa or Creatore band

9

concert on the Boardwalk, or a Saturday-night meeting of a local literary organization known as the Pleiades Club.

A gentleman, if there ever was one.

How often Bea had heard her mother sing this pœan of Mr. Pullman to a guest whose visiting-card, freshly released from a case of mother-of-pearl, lay newly uppermost on the hall tray.

Yet withal, even in his instance, the passing of her mother had revealed more and more her silent capacity for doing so many of the chores of life, too slight to be noticed while they were being accomplished, but suddenly, after her death, each one standing revealed as finite and exacting.

It was simply horrid, for instance, to have to go into Mr. Pullman's room, after his departure each Monday morning, and collect his laundry.

To be sure, as Mother had so often remarked, it was the income the renting of that room afforded made possible a laundress in the house half a day a week.

But just the same, to step into that room of Mr. Pullman's, Monday mornings after he had left the house, and assemble his seven handkerchiefs, two shirts, four pairs of cuffs, three collars, one nightshirt, one suit of underwear, one bath and two face towels, to be all tied into a wad for the washerwoman to carry down into the basement, was just terrible.

It was one of the things she had seen Mother do, almost without its registering, during the fifteen years of Mr. Pullman's tenancy of that room. One of those taken-for-granted, moving-about-the-house things. But picking up all these male personal objects of apparel herself, was quite another matter. Then too, quite unreasonably perhaps, there was something exasperating about the immutable precision of the listing. The two shirts into which he apparently must dive because the stiff white fronts offered neither entrance nor egress. The balbriggan socks, which it was now her chore to mend on those rare occasions when fine holes fell into them. The seven large muslin squares with the little tape insert in the corner on which was printed an indelible B. P. The precision, more than the chore itself, with which there were the two shirts, the four pairs of cuffs, the nightshirt with the red-taped border, was dull and exasperating business.

Apparently, when Mr. Pullman lectured to the visitors on the life history of the tomato from the vine to the ketchup bottle (contains no benzoate of soda or other artificial preservatives) he was particularly hard on the faille silk lapel to his black broadcloth coat. The buttonhole of it was in a chronic state of being pulled and frayed, requiring him to frequently breakfast in his brown velveteen house coat while Bea whipped around it with a fine black silk thread.

It wasn't even nice to think about, much less confess to herself, but just the same, the male aroma that hung over these rather intimate chores for Mr. Pullman made it horrid.

Father's things, which she jammed along with her own into a laundry bag, were one matter, but somehow these intimate rites where Mr. Pullman was concerned, even if he was up in his thirties, well, it was just one of those remote thoughts which made it not nice.

Did it, she wondered, ever occur to him, as they sat evening after evening around the supper table, that there existed between them the strange intimacy of her monitorship over his soiled handkerchiefs, night-shirts, and underclothing?

Of course it did not. Try as she would to keep them out, such ugly little bat-like thoughts must nest only in horrid minds like hers.

Mr. Pullman and Father discussing Free Silver, Dewey's candidacy for the Democratic nomination, the Gold Standard Act, Klondike, President McKinley, Galveston cyclone, trusts, had no subcellars to their minds. Why, Mr. Pullman was as invariable as her own father, about going through the halls from his bedroom to the bathroom in nothing less than a collarless shirt, and the bathtub he left after him was as bright as a new dime.

As Mother had so often remarked, Mr. Pullman was as tidy and as modest to have about the house as a girl, and so much less trouble.

Of course none of this occurred to Mr. Pullman any more than it must have occurred to him, even though he and Father were cronies, to sense Father's cruel capacity for rebuke.

He and Father would both of them continue to taste of their lips which were flavored with the slight scorch of their corn pudding, and then go for their stroll toward the quiet end of the Boardwalk. Or no, this was Mr. Pullman's evening at the Pleiades Club. Once Bea and her mother had accompanied him, when he had read a paper on Abraham Lincoln before thirty ladies and gentlemen who met monthly in the assembly-rooms of Second Church.

It had been quite terrible. Mr. Pullman, tall, sedate, his heavy brown hair, which waved away from a center part, looking more wig-like than ever, had cleared his throat and turned the corners of his mustache all through the vocal rendition of "Angel's Serenade," which had preceded the reading of his paper and, word for word, had been the copied substance of the article in *Encyclopædia Britannica*.

"You would think he would at least have changed the wording, Mother."

"Mr. Pullman isn't what you would call a highly educated man, Bea. Self-taught, I should say. But at least it shows his leanings toward the best. Another young man in his place might spend his evenings differently."

That was true. It was seldom he missed a Boardwalk, Creatore or Sousa band concert, and once or twice a winter he went by train to a Symphony concert in Philadelphia.

His interest in Bea's piano lessons with a local Miss Lee, had sometimes prompted him to sit by of an evening and audibly count, as her tendency toward accelerated tempo began to run away with her.

"One, two, three, Bea. Don't run away with yourself. That 'Turkish Patrol' is just fine! Now let's have 'Traumerai.' Slowly, Bea, one, two, one, two."

His regret had been so real when, of lack of volition on her part, those lessons had lagged and finally ceased.

"Knowledge is power, Bea."

"I know it, Mr. Pullman, but with all my home-work, I just didn't seem to get in enough practice!"

He was well informed all right, and in the days previous to Bea's graduation from Atlantic High, had not infrequently spent evenings beside the dining-room table where she studied, poring through her various textbooks.

Yes, particularly now that Father's arm was beginning to look more and more limp, it was good having him in the household, but perfectly horrid having to sort his linen.

·3·

About that arm. It was the winter following Mother's death that Bea first noticed it.

Suddenly it was borne in upon her that for days it had hung against his body as if pinned there from the shoulder.

"Father," she blurted out while helping him with his overcoat one morning as he was leaving the house for a canvass of the Boardwalk hotels, most of which carried far from negligible accounts with the pickle-and-relish firm, "your arm! What?"

"My arm, what?" he said, turning a face upon her that was chalky as the mustache itself.

"It's so"—she started to say, dead-looking, but faltered.

Father was such a little dandy. So full of pride in his neatly-shaven small square face, waved and cared-for white hair, precise shoes, gray spats and gray derby.

They said of him, at the Amusement Pier, that he approached the steward of a hotel as if stepping out from a bandbox.

And now suddenly this arm, dangling like a sign loosened by a gale!

Instinctively, and with vague childhood memories of his sense of outrage when asthma of a grave nature had made it necessary for him to request the home office to transfer him from Philadelphia to the more equable climate of seashore, Bea realized now that the subject of Father's limp arm must be handled delicately.

"Arms sometimes get neuritis, Father. I thought perhaps yours . . ."

"Blamed thing won't hurt when I pinch it," he said.

At that her heart gave a great jump. Father mustn't die, too! God, don't let him leave me alone. I'm afraid, as it is. That, of course, was sheer nonsense.

"Probably a little bad circulation. Hadn't you better ask Dr. Merribel?"

"See him dead, first. Whole bunch of them don't know enough to come in out of the wet. Your mother would be living today, if they hadn't cut into her."

No use getting Father started on that. His prejudice against the medical profession was one of long standing and long nursing. "They cut her to pieces," had been his bitter denunciation over the body of his wife as it lay dead with an inoperable cancer in it.

Bea felt that she knew differently, and that all that could have been, had been done, to save the darling existence of a gray-haired, gray-eyed mother, who had been all things to the small sheltered life of her child. But Father, ever since change of air, and not doctor's concoctions, had seemed to bring about the cure of his asthma, had been like that.

"It'll clear up," he said, pinching at the arm which hung in such peculiar isolation from his body, "and no doctor except Dr. Nature will get the pay or the credit."

The incident lay like a pall across the little morning in the little house on Arctic Avenue.

Was Father about to get paralyzed? People got their first stroke that way. Old Grandfather Vizitelli, whose son ran the grocery store next door, had first stiffened in one arm that way. Sometimes, come to think of it, Father's right eye did not seem to blink. An early memory of old Aunt Chipley dying in the Philadelphia house after months of an entire right side that would not so much as twitch, stalked across the retina of her memory.

Father was sixty-three. She had Mother's word for it, although, in view of his tiny-boned dandyisms and dapperisms, it was hard to believe.

But although Father would only admit to fifty-seven, he had inadvertently let slip, while Bea was studying one night for a history examination, that he had been born in Leeds, England, less than a dozen years after the Crimean War. That would make him in his sixties.

What a slim sliver of a fellow, this youth, then scarcely more than general handy-boy with the pickle-and-relish firm, must have been back in the days when he journeyed wooing, the fifteen miles from Philadelphia to Burlington, to call on Mother whom he had met at a church hay-ride. That, however, proved all to the good. Those small-boned, elegant little men were a wiry lot. Father, except for the asthma, had never been sick a day that she could remember.

Father ill would make the aloneness following the death of her mother quite too terrible.

Dispel the fear as she would, the limp arm did continue to cast its shadow over that morning of duties which she had suddenly inherited into a life her mother had so carefully kept immune from inroads of responsibility.

Mother's mock-regretful boast had been that Bea could not so much as darn a stocking or boil an egg, and here she was suddenly doing both and manipulating sixty dollars a month to cover rent, food, clothing, heat, gas, and the miscellany of all the suddenly revealed sundries of housekeeping.

The sixty dollars left Father only about fifty cents a day for accessories and, on those occasions when he did not get home to lunch, a bite at one of the better places. Father just had to do that, with his spats and all.

Father dressed so well. His work demanded it of him, in and out as he was of all the first-class hotels, where there were gala people keyed to the gala mood of an Atlantic City holiday.

It was easy to understand now why Mother had looked so gratefully toward the boon of Mr. Pullman's twenty dollars a month. Father's spats and derby hats and natty little shirts with their pleated fronts, ironed hard as a board, came under that budget, to say nothing of all the pleasant little fandangos, such as the unexpected ribbons, dresses, and accessories with which Mother had always managed to keep life happily expectant.

Easy to appreciate what the additional twenty dollars a month meant.

It meant, bless her, the accessories for Father and herself, a detached house, and no summer boarders to clutter up the place, hanging their wet bathing-suits across porch rails and window sills.

It meant, now that Father seemed suddenly such a frail link, something more than accessories. To one afraid of aloneness, the presence of Mr. Pullman in that all too deplorably depleted household, seemed all the more needed and staple.

What happened to girls thrown on their own resources? They worked, of course. If only Mother had not opposed the kindergarten course. A couple of the girls in the neighborhood worked for "pin money" at Clabby's bathhouse on the Boardwalk in summer, renting bathing-suits. Ugh!

It was considered all right to work for "pin money," although Mother had thought it made a girl mannish, like those Woman's Rights advocates. The salesladies at Braunstein's Department Store on Atlantic Avenue wore stiff collars and rainy-day skirts, but they looked nice.

It was considered all right, so long as it was for pin money and not through necessity, for a girl to work at stenography or teaching or salesladying, but the small house on Arctic Avenue with the front shades all drawn even, and the six neatly furnished rooms of oak furniture, mattinged floors, dimity curtains, and kitchen with a Pet coal-range and floor covered with bright oil-cloth, seemed suddenly a kennel with warm, close, protective sides.

"Thank goodness," Mother used to say, Bea was inclined to the home. No new-fangled ideas. It was good there, and sweet. Anyway, some girls were cut out for one thing and others for another.

Father's limp arm that would not hurt when he pinched it might mean nothing at all. Poor circulation. Had Mr. Pullman noticed the dead look to Father's side? No telling. There was no telling what anybody was thinking about in that little household. Father and Mr. Pullman could sit, or on mild evenings, stand, on the sidewalk in front of the house, and talk on subjects ranging from the maple-sugar industry in Mr. Pullman's Vermont, to Mark Hanna, Big Business, the *Maine,* Dewey, Panama Canal, "Tom Platt Silverites," G. A. R., Klondike, Battle of Manila Bay, Boer War, in terms of the utmost formality. "Mark my word, Mr. Chipley, the trusts are monsters." . . . "You just watch this rough-rider fellow Roosevelt, Mr. Pullman; he's the one is going to bust the trusts. . . ."

Why, believe it or not, Mother up to the last day of her darling life had addressed Father, at least in the presence of others, as "Mr. Chipley," and while Father spoke to and referred to Mother as "Adelaide," the name had seemed to set stiffly and precariously on his lips, like a saucer balanced there.

To be sure, once back in the Philadelphia house (what a row of them lay tattooed against her memory! Forty little identical houses with forty little identical faces and forty little identical mansard roofs), the day the doctor had ordered Mr. Chipley to Denver, Arizona, or Saranac, for his health, and they had finally struck the compromise of Atlantic City, Mother had laid her arm along Father's shoulder, there in Bea's presence, and said:

"Never mind, dear. On the grounds of ill-health, the company will be sure to grant your request for a transfer to Atlantic City and the sea air will do the rest."

"Never mind, *dear!*"

In the light of later ponderings, over the vast closed doors that somehow seemed to shut in the walls of her small world, it seemed to Bea that, had she been born following the orgy of this unwonted act of demonstration between her parents, it might have been easier to account for herself as the progeny of these two people, whose phenomenal act of begetting her at all was, for a time at least, to remain the subject of her adolescent bafflement.

No, there was no telling what Mr. Pullman thought about, other than in casual response to the disjointed series of acts, trivia, and events, which moved across the face of the days.

It made of people such strangers. Personally, Bea wanted to know if it ever privately occurred to Mr. Pullman to admire some of the bold beach girls in their knee-length bathing-suits, long, black-stockinged legs, or if he had ever kissed anyone, or been lover to a woman lying full-length in his arms.

·4·

Out-of-town people and excursionists were constantly saying, "Oh, how gay it must be to always live in Atlantic City! So much to do and see!" "Guess you just about live in the water. I would—and as for all the excitement—my, I just never tire of the Boardwalk!"

They seldom seemed to realize how casual a rôle the incandescent strip of hotels, shops, and amusements, except as source of income, played in the lives of those who had their daily being within the township proper.

To begin with, the Boardwalk, except to the holiday-makers who came pouring in on the Reading Railroad from Philadelphia and New York, or on convention or vacation missions from the Middle and Far West, was not the event it offhand might have appeared.

Occasionally it was pleasant, of a fine evening or holiday, to mingle for a time with the great stream of visitors upon whom, either directly or indirectly, so much of the city depended for livelihood, but there were weeks when Bea did not so much as set foot into its carnival of turmoil.

Mother had shrunk so from its high-tensioned entertainment, seldom venturing for more than an occasional hour, and then seating herself rather stiffly on a bench in front of Clabby's Baths, or on the Steel Pier for a band concert, or in fine weather venturing out, if Father happened to be about, to the end of the Amusement Pier, where Mr. Pullman, on his platform, traced the life history of the tomato from the vine to the ketchup bottle.

While not his headquarters in the sense that it was Mr. Pullman's, it was not unusual for Father to drift in there between periods of town and hotel canvassing, moving among the displays of tinned and bottled relishes, or watching the beach crowds toss balls, stretch limbs, or burrow themselves warm graves into the sparkling sands.

The Chipleys, all three, were fond of walking out to the tip of the bright new Pier, not infrequently, between lectures, Mr. Pullman, in his black broadcloth coat, and his lips smacking softly of the relishes he was fond of tasting, joining them.

All that was changed now. Without Mother, to whose apron string, in local phraseology, Bea had the reputation of having been tied, the trips to the Boardwalk were still more infrequent. Boys were quite rude to a girl in bathing alone, without a mother sitting embroidering on the sand, and once to her terror, a lock-stepping half dozen of them, indulging in the forbidden sport of appearing on the Boardwalk in their bathing-suits, had closed around her and tried to tease her down to their games in the sand. "Tell me, pretty maiden, are there any more at home like you!" Oh, how fresh!

Old before her time, a couple of the friends with whom Mother had used to sip an afternoon cup of coffee, and particularly Mrs. Doc Hanson, had warned her, "Join the young folks. . . ."

What had going to the Boardwalk to do with keeping young? Lots of young people, right there in the neighborhood, didn't go half a dozen times a year. Why, Mrs. Vizitelli hadn't been there in eighteen years, and not a gray hair in her head.

Down around the Inlet, or up at lovely Ventnor, was quite another matter. There the ocean, as it rolled in, full of lips that seemed to dump their mysterious chatter onto shore and then drag it out again untranslated, was not just part of the monkey-shine of carnival. There, uninterrupted by peanut whistle, popcorn smells, or shouts of bathers, one could stroll, perceptions succeeding each other with "perpetual flux and movement." This last phrase had stuck in her mind over an only half-understood passage from Hume across which she had stumbled one afternoon while thumbing through books at the public library. She had taken the book, *Treatise on Human Nature,* home with her, but had not been able to forge much beyond that point.

But the one passage, reminding her more and more of herself, had stuck. "There, mind is a kind of theatre, where several perceptions successively make their appearance, pass, repass, glide away and mingle in an infinite variety of postures and situations. . . ."

Oh, how true that was of herself! Bewildering emotions, themselves in perpetual flux and movement, seemed accelerated when she found herself, a speck, seated beside the salty crashing of the ocean or strolling the shore along the unpeopled waters that led to the Inlet. Walking with her mother, as she so often did, arms intertwined, a sense of shame of some of these private impulses which sped to her very finger tips would sweep over Bea. They made her alone, even from Mother.

How lovely and pure and simple and good was Mother's face as she strode ahead, with the clarity in her gray eyes and spray lying all along the fine lines of her face.

It made Bea secretly ashamed to be caught up in the inner turmoil this old ocean engendered. Old gray crocodile. Old gray devil-man. Old boiling cauldron of old wisdoms. . . . Old pain. Old, old joys. . . .

And yet once her very own mother had stood looking at that ocean with heavy lenses of tears across her eyes.

It had been a shock, and even a fright, and well Bea knew that it was her mother's hope she had not seen. They would no more have discussed it! The people in the little house on Arctic Avenue were locked securely one from the other.

And now, since Mother's death, the walks along the sand were more frequent and somehow even the sense of maelstrom a lonelier sense. Mother, now a part of the perpetual flux out there . . . .

One wanted so terribly to be happy. Bea remembered what her father had once said on the eve of their purchase of the second-hand upright piano which now stood in the parlor beside its floor lamp with the shirred pink silk shade that was like an open parasol: "Don't let them see how anxious you are to have it. Things always come to those who don't appear over-anxious."

Bea was over-anxious. Over-anxious for a tidy kind of happiness that would never be deployed into, the way the ocean deployed into the sanctity of land.

That was what made the little house on Arctic Avenue seem so gratefully like a snug kennel. Safety and security were as warm and comforting as the long-legged and long-armed woolen underwear she wore in winter. Parties, the fear of boys not being nice or interested, desire to please and impress, self-agonies, timidity, yearning for popularity, fear of ridicule, criticism, perspiring hands, were what one encountered outside the shelter of the four walls of Arctic Avenue. Mother had known the timidity which had kept the palms of her hands moist at parties and had frequently urged, as if it were not dearer just to have Bea loving to be at home: "Get out with the girls and boys, dear. You'll get confidence. You can't expect to be tied to my apron strings all your life." But it had been so right, there!

If only things could have gone on that way forever. Once, when she had expressed the equivalent of that, her mother's palm had pressed the words back against her lips.

"Child, what are you saying? It isn't natural for a young girl to stay around too much with older folks. Some day you'll want a home of your own."

That had meant that some day she would marry. Perhaps. That would mean a house of one's own. A darling one, she hoped. Curving white staircase, such as they were building into those adorable new Ventnor cottages. Bow window in the dining-room, looking out, over geraniums, at ocean. A bedroom with one of those mahogany dressers with a curving balcony front, Honiton-draped top, laid out with silver; wide brass bedstead with plenty of Honiton lace . . . .

Everywhere you turned at Atlantic City, during the crowded summer season of navy-blue nights, frosted with the light hoar of moonlight, were couples. Boys and girls, men and women, seated, small as mushrooms on the sands, in the shadows close to the ends of piers, along the lower reaches of the beach, their bodies twined toward one another like vines toward the light.

Poor things, Mother had said on one occasion, when these recumbent bodies on all sides of them as they walked became too thick to be ignored. Poor things, subject to every temptation.

What temptation? Most of the hairy, leggy, bodies of the men in their two-piece striped bathing-suits, were quite the reverse of tempting. For that matter, so were they when clothed in their navy-blue coats and "ice-cream" pants, yellow shoes, sporty collars and ties. What tempted girls to want to lie in the arms of men while they in turn pasted their cheeks against the cheeks or necks or breasts of the girls?

It was infinitely nice just to walk arm in arm with Mother—or Father. Or Mr. Pullman.

· 5 ·

What happened the day she was eighteen and Father's arm had already had the dead look to it for weeks, came not precisely as a bolt out of the blue, but out of skies soggy with her secret tears.

It was her first birthday since the death, and Father had not remembered. This fact, watered with tears, brought her no resentment, only heartbreak. Father would have been the first, had she reminded him, to bend down his neat white pate, as he did when guilty of small omissions and say, "Cut off my head. It's empty," and would have hurried to see to it that a box of Fralinger's salt-water taffy or a ball of Boardwalk popcorn was beside her supper plate.

The omission had not been a sin. Only part of the ineffable loneliness that washed over her like a lusterless tide.

Mother had always poked this day as full of little nonsenses as a pudding with currants. New hair ribbons; broad pink or white moiré bows, ready-made, which she wore anchored with a hatpin to the braided loop at the nape of her neck. Last year, on her seventeenth, just when Mother was beginning to grit her teeth through pain about which she had been so long silent, so that once Bea had exclaimed, "Mother, don't do that horrid scratching thing with your teeth" (oh, darling, forgive!), there had been the cutest little silver plaquet-pin, so your plaquet could never gape, and an Irish-lace jabot in a Wanamaker's box, and a hand-painted autograph album into which John Philip Sousa had subsequently inscribed. Such a pretty glove-box too, of conch shells, made by a neighbor who sold them to a Boardwalk dealer for five dollars apiece (one dollar and forty cents to Mother), a copy of that darling book, *David Harum,* and a pair of sterling-silver hatpins, also in a Wanamaker box.

For a while it had seemed to her (unworthily, she was to realize later) that Father was remembering and pretending not to. All through supper, a little crackle of artificial gaiety had flickered, in too frequent laughter, along his white mustache. Father was not naturally gay. Usually he crackled with the dry fire of this kind of forced levity when he was about to say something oblique or in the inverted fashion that for years had caused the back of Mother's neck to hang forward. Sometimes, too, this expression flickered when a little excitement, like the surprise years back, announcing the family's trip to Pittsburgh, upon the occasion of the employees' convention in the home-office city of the Pickle and Relish Company, was impending.

At that time, Bea remembered, he had been quite horribly gay, propounding riddle after riddle to his wife, to whom these moods were as embarrassing as their reverse could be painful.

The evening of Bea's eighteenth birthday, after propounding several, he leaned forward to pinch her cheek, taking the cool young flesh between his fingers.

"What's the difference between an elephant and an egg, eh!"

"Why — why, Father, that's a queer one."

"Mean to say you don't know the difference?"

Thank Heaven, Mr. Pullman did not either lend or withdraw himself from these moods, eating calmly ahead, his temples working beneath the smoothly parted, wig-like hair.

"No, Father."

Then on a little flash of forced hilarity his glance darting to Mr. Pullman:

"Don't know! Well, well, you'd be a good one to send out to buy eggs!"

It was here that he pinched her cheek. She could have cried of a curious embarrassment.

Even then, when immediately after the meal Father had disappeared alone on the rather surprising mission of a late business appointment, no portent of what was to come struck her. Tears were aching in her throat that day. That they would flow later when her head struck its pillow was something to which she could almost look forward.

Suddenly, as she drew back her chair with that immemorial gesture of a woman about to clear table, the figure of Mr. Pullman, risen, was at her elbow, breathing. It was the breathing which shot her through with a strange premonition of she knew not what. It was a man breathing under a kind of excitement that was immediately transmitted to her. There was something about that breathing that caused her flesh to rise and shudder a little, as Mr. Pullman was risen and shuddering.

"Bea," he said, and laid his hand right down on the risen nap of hers, "your father and I had a long talk, just before supper."

For the first time in her life a rushing consciousness of the contour of her body flowed over her. It seemed to her, in that startled listening instant, that her flesh was being pricked into awareness, pore by pore. Not exactly unpleasant. The sensation was related somehow to the appearance of a tall building, lighting up, window after window. The soft rush of his breathing pouring over her was what did it. She let gasp an inner shame.

"Bea, your father and I have had a long talk."

She felt as if she had just had a silly and unaccountable scare over she knew not what.

Long talk, of course! Father and Mr. Pullman were forever having long talks. Right in the middle of the sidewalk before the house. After supper. Politics. Business. Sometimes they sent her, since she was the quicker at reference volumes, to the *Book of Facts* to settle small disputes: President Harrison's years of office. Date of first ocean pier at Atlantic City. Date of opening of Philadelphia Bank of North America. Population of Mays Landing.

That hand on hers! It dawned upon her, with a recrudescence of excitement, that no man, except her father for his morning and evening pecks, had ever touched her. Oh yes, and old Dr. Merribel, once, feeling her bare back with his ear, when a cold had settled on her lungs.

"Sit down, Bea, I want to talk to you," said Mr. Pullman and pushed her so that she sank softly onto a chair, and began clearing his throat the way he had, during the vocal solo, the evening of his reading of the paper on Abraham Lincoln.

Gaslight from two Welsbach lamps, the kind that crumbled to the touch, spilled down on them, making prunes of their eyes and smearing their faces with pallor and their lips a faint purple. She had always noticed about him that his moist lips stuck slightly after each word, as a silence cloth under a too hot dish leaves an imprint on a polished mahogany table top.

Under the bright brown mustache, it was a very curving and very full mouth.

"Don't you want to know, Bea, what we were talking about?"

"Yes, Mr. Pullman," she said off her own cool lips. She had a way of blowing up her hair out of her eyes when it escaped her pompadour. It was pretty tan hair, with a deep natural wave that showed in each single strand. He liked it. She could tell, because he breathed faster, and watched her lips and the flying strands. It was the queerest experience, this coming suddenly aware of her teasing bodily self. The nape of her neck felt nice and long as she turned her head slowly on it. Under her shirtwaist, lovely white breasts, which, as they had developed, had filled her with secret shame, causing her to bind them down to flatness under towels and tight corset covers, seemed part, now, of that strangely exciting sense of her contour. It was not pleasant, but at the same time it was strangely exciting to behold his eyes seeming to want to undress something that she coveted, with a sudden exaltation, for her modest secret self.

"Now what have you and Father been talking about?" To her amazement, for the first time in her unaware life, she felt her voice taking on the curving sex quality she had noticed in girls at school when they talked with boys.

"About you," he said, the pupils of his eyes focusing and becoming smaller as she had observed them in poll parrots. "Your father and I have been talking——"

"What on earth . . ."

"Bea, the thing for this house—now that your mother is gone—is for you and me to get married."

It was curious not to feel completely surprised, or could one be too stunned for surprise?

"If we married—things would look better. Besides, you are what I want, Bea."

So this was it. These were the things those bodies on the beaches, twining toward each other like vines toward the light, must be saying to, and wanting of, each other. This was the answer to the mysterious

25

bafflement which had pressed against her curiosity. How had Father asked Mother to marry him? What had he said, when he proposed? A mainspring, so long concealed by the blank, clock-like face of her world of externals, was suddenly being revealed. She was being a woman.

"We figure it this way, Bea. It's not good around here, now. Your father don't feel it's good this way any more than I do. Never mind why. You're too innocent to understand. A man likes that. Innocence. A man likes innocence. A man likes innocence a lot. Anyway, a man like me, who wants a home with a wife in it. I'll make a good man to you, Bea."

She believed that.

"It will mean a lot to your father. He's not getting any younger. It will mean a lot to me. You see, we figured it out like this. You're alone now, Bea, except for your father, and him not getting any younger. . . ."

As if part of her secret fear about the arm were not bound up with just that frightening thought! She half moved to put out her hand to touch the security of his presence, but because of that something which thickened his gaze each time she moved, she continued to hold herself tautly away from his nearness.

"I don't pretend to be any better or worse than the run of us. Not good enough for you, but then, what one of us is good enough for a good woman? I can stand up straight in my church, and in my business, and look my conscience in the eye. There's not only my salary, five dollars larger than your father's, but you would be surprised what my little side line in maple syrup is beginning to yield. Cover three or four hotels in a noon hour and come away with an order or two every time. I've got a living to offer and I figure on promotion ahead. Only held two positions in my life. Brattleboro, and now here. Looks like I'm pretty steady, don't it? Same now. No changes around here, your father and I figure. Everything going on as usual, except us married."

Married! She would be married to this lean, rather unromantic New Englander, with his Adam's apple and brown wig-like hair, long lean body, and strangely contradictory, moist-looking lips carved heavily into his lantern-shaped face. There was no youth to him, even to his feet, which he wore incased in Blüchers with rubber gores, or the furry way he had of completing each word as if it tasted. All his little habits, such as standing in stockinged feet polishing his shoes in the kitchen every night before retiring, unwrapping the consignments of maple syrup and saving the paper and twines in neat stacks on his closet shelf, keeping his copies of *Brattleboro News* piled unopened on his table until Sunday morning, when he read them in rotation in the hour before leaving for church, were not young habits. Something told one that Mr. Pullman had never been young.

Marriage. Most girls, except spinsters, Heaven forbid! like the Miss Burl who made the conch-shell boxes, came to it. Mother had made no bones about saying: "Some day you will marry, but there is time enough to begin to think about that." Well, the time had come. With Mother gone, life was much as if some one had left open a door to a warm room and strange bitter and alien winds were suddenly rushing into security.

With Mr. Pullman, life would once more have to it that darling aspect of being safe. There would be that indefinable security which comes with a home of one's own. Not ideal, of course, the house on Arctic Avenue. But even that, temporarily, was pleasant to contemplate as one's own and then perhaps some day a bungalow in Ventnor, with a brace of bow windows that overlooked the ocean. Security! Her own curtains to select and hem. Her own place in the life of a man. Her own ability to provide Father's old age with a home. There would be babies—the part one understood so feebly——

Thus in the year when men were debating whether a college professor was of sufficient stamina for Presidency of the United States, Bea lifted her face, which intimated yes, for the betrothal kiss of Mr. Pullman.

·6·

The marriage was to take place under a white silk bell with a small stuffed dove head for a clapper. The glass eyes of the dove and the little beak hung downward on a strip of white satin ribbon. One of the stewards of the Hotel Dennis had loaned it to Father for the occasion.

Not that it was to be so much of an occasion. The odor of the tuberoses of Mother's death had lain too recently in the room which was to be the scene of her child's marriage to her boarder.

The sensing of this was unanimous between the three of them.

Unfortunately, though, the day, a hard bright 3rd of November, turned out to be one which pressed external excitements against the small clapboard walls of the little house on Arctic Avenue.

No one had remembered to reckon that this choice of date verged, with disturbing closeness, upon the mounting excitement of impending national elections.

For the two days preceding Woodrow Wilson's first election to the Presidency of the United States, the Boardwalk, to say nothing of the city itself, shook to one demonstration after another. "We want Teddy." "Down with the Steam Roller." "It's a Dem—it's a Dem—it's a Dem-o-cratic year! Wilson!"

Already, during the forenoon of the day of the wedding, the pouring of crowds, banner-carriers, and paraders toward the Boardwalk; the disgorging of the Reading excursion trains from Philadelphia which rushed along Mississippi Avenue up to the Boardwalk, emptying coaches as far back as Arctic Avenue, to say nothing of loaded incoming Pennsylvania trains as they came rushing in along Georgia Avenue, contributed tension and din.

It was one of those days when the all-year residents of the town whose incomes were not immediately derived from the demonstration, kept close to home and prepared to rent out spare bedrooms to the ''overflow.''

Was there ever such a town in which to live? thought Bea that day of her wedding, as the outdoor tensions began to invade her own. It was like dwelling in a hurdy-gurdy. Even on its comparatively quiet days, Atlantic City reverberated to brassy out-of-door music. Every time you peeped out of your window, there was a monkeyshine of one sort or another, pretty sure to be somewhere in view, and no telling when the next blare of mechanical music would burst forth. Mother used to say she got so she could stir up a cake or carpet-sweep to the rhythm of any old German band. Of all days, her wedding day, for the last big demonstration before elections! Mr. Pullman had been right cute, though, pasting a picture of ''Teddy'' in the parlor window and climbing out along the ridge of the porch in order to tack up a small American flag.

''Just to show them we appreciate their celebrating our wedding with a big parade and a brass band!''

Anything, of course, to cover up his nervousness.

As Mrs. Hanson, who was being such a help in the arrangements, remarked:

''Wouldn't it just blast you to see a big strong man like Mr. Pullman turn nervous as a cat over his wedding.''

It was really quite pathetic. Hoisted up on his cheek bones, like red balls announcing skating on the lake, were two rounds of unwonted color, and he could not sit still. Mr. Pullman just could not sit still, although he had decided to remain in his room the morning of that day of the wedding, and to appear down in the parlor at noon just before the arrival of his friend the curate, Dr. Aspern, of Second Rock Church.

It was certainly better so. Much more delicate. It occurred to Bea, after it was too late to do anything about it, that perhaps Mr. Pullman should have taken a room in the neighborhood, those twenty-four hours before the ceremony. Of course, Mrs. Hanson had practically taken possession and, with Mrs. Vizitelli from next door, in and out, it was all right—still——

It was impossible, not to be aware, even though he tiptoed on his journeys through the hall to the bathroom, of the unprecedented sounds of midmorning bath-water plunging into the tin tub, and the little snipping noises of his scissors came from his room as she sped through the halls on the feverish missions of that feverish day.

There were to be eggnog and angel cake served on the sideboard in the dining-room. Just a "snack." Mrs. Hanson, bless her, had baked the cake and loaned her cut-glass punch-bowl with the little glasses that hung on hooks from its brim. There would only be Mrs. Hanson and a Mr. Farley, a friend of Mr. Pullman's, who passed basket with him at Second Church on Sunday mornings, who would "stand up," and Father who would give away the bride, and Mrs. Vizitelli who had loved to dandle Bea as a child when her mother had taken her into the grocery store and who had repeatedly vowed she would see Bea as a bride. Poor dear, she would not hear of coming into the parlor, but insisted upon viewing the ceremony from the pantry.

A mere wisp of a wedding. Not even a veil, since Mother so recently had lain down the center of the room in which the ceremony was to take place.

Only yesterday, it seemed, Dr. Aspern, with his spectacles far down on his nose and their lenses horizontally bisected, had stood in this same room intoning the funeral oration over Mother's darling clay. . . .

To think that life had sped on so rapidly just these few weeks after her going, into channels that must have been undreamed of by her. Or had they been? Always, she had said, placing her hand with the almost chronic thimble on the third finger, into the warmth of Bea's hair, "Some day, of course, you will marry," but invariably with a sort of promissory note in her voice, as if against that some day arriving no sooner than necessary. Now suddenly it had become necessary. The loneliness and the sense of that door left open, admitting chill, had made it necessary.

The brass bands were quite terrible. "Hiawatha." "Mosquito Parade." "Jack Johnson Came Home." "Alexander's Ragtime Band." "Hackensack." "Bedelia." "John Brown's Body." "Where Was Moses." . . . They beat up around the house so and made her feel quite crazy with all sorts of excitements.

Mrs. Doc Hanson, herself harassed with overwork, kept admonishing her not to "run her legs off" and to lie down and rest while she and Mrs. Vizitelli and a fourteen-year-old black girl, Angie, in for the occasion, did the arranging.

But there were last-minute things galore to be done! That swap of bedroom, for instance. Father was to be moved out of the double bedroom he had shared with Mother, into Mr. Pullman's, and her own little room left temporarily empty, put to the use of sewing-room, spare room, or whatever disposition such excess space in the house of newly-wed folk was temporarily put.

If only Father would make haste about swapping rooms with Mr. Pullman. He moved so casually, emptying his dresser drawers and carting his ties and shirts across the hall, sorting and resorting his belongings on the wide double bed of the room he was vacating, just as if, in the brief remaining time before the ceremony, it did not have to be remade, and certain last-minute touches, preparatory to the invasion of a bride and groom, achieved.

Mr. Pullman, for instance, liked the north side of the room for his shaving light. She knew that, from the way he had dragged over the washstand in his old room. If only Father would hurry. She wanted to move the chiffonier to a position similar to where Mr. Pullman's washstand stood in the old room. She had some lovely new pillow-slips with B. P. embroidered on them which Claire Leighton, who had moved away to Oklahoma City, had sent, and which she wanted to have fresh in their places, and a box of flowers wrapped in cotton had come from Mr. Pullman's aunt in Bangor, Maine, which she wanted to arrange in the pair of vases on the mantel. The B. P. on the pillow-slips was done in French knots on a hemstitched border. Pleasant that in marriage she was not going to have to change her initial. But in a way she felt cheated of a thrill.

They were playing "Stars and Stripes Forever," as a Reading train, just disgorged of excursionists, was backing its way along Mississippi Avenue, coughing steam.

What a crazy town in which to plan a quiet wedding to follow softly in the bereavement of a dearly beloved.

One evening, according to what had been a favorite story of Mother's, about a year after they had moved to Atlantic City, a giraffe, being led to a Boardwalk exhibition, had actually poked his head in through the lace curtains of the second-story front window, as she had sat there rocking the child, Bea, to sleep.

What a town! What a wedding day. The—arm-ee—and—na-vee—for-evuh—three-cheers-for-the-red—white-and—bl-ooo!

The shaving soap smelled so. Mr. Pullman, with all his fixings, was making the house smell like a barber shop. It was nice, though. Bay Rum.

Her own blue silk wedding dress was being pressed by Mrs. Doc Hanson over at her house. There was a picture-hat of blue panne velvet to match. A wedding veil would have made her cry, terribly. It would somehow have suggested Mother, misty and remote in death. Besides the parlor was so small. . . .

Her long white kid gloves, stretched and powdered, were laid out on the bed. Mr. Pullman had gloves, too. Heavy new white kid ones. She had glimpsed him, sitting on the edge of his bed in his undershirt, trying them on.

It had startled her so that she forgot the mission which was sending her speeding along the hall.

Oh yes, her lovely new white dimity nightgown had come back from the seamstress with one row of beading accidentally left empty of satin baby-ribbon. She needed privacy for running that baby-ribbon. Suppose some one should stumble upon her, sewing on that particular nightgown.

She found her bodkin and a secluded place on the stairs leading to the attic trunk-room. Weaving the ribbon through the embroidery, her legs began to tremble. Here she crouched, quite alone, on the edge of her journey into mystery. Mother . . . ?

The silence of her mother, loaded and unrevealing, seemed to wind against her ears.

·7·

The outdoor demonstrations made Dr. Aspern fifty minutes late for the ceremony. It was all but impossible to get through the paraders as they clogged Atlantic Avenue, and while the bands blared, and the gold-fringed banners rode past the windows, the little party sat distributed through the house and waited; Father, in his Ascot tie, spats and small creased trousers, strumming his fingers on the table and drinking from the punch-bowl, until Mrs. Vizitelli carried it out into the kitchen, ostensibly to keep it on ice. Mrs. Doc Hanson, in and out between her home duties and the arraying of Bea and the house; Mr. Pullman, inside his room where you could hear him pacing and every so often opening the door to hold his ear to the crack for the sound of the arrival of Dr. Aspern.

It was quite dreadful, that little house, set there in the midst of din, waiting.

It was dreadful, because, now that the double room had been cleared and made ready, the chiffonier moved, Bea's new fineries and under-things laid out on the fresh paper in the dresser drawers, leaving free drawers for his, the new pillow-slips with B. P. embroidered in, fresh and snowy on the snowy bed, the pressure of a certain kind of silence, loaded and unrevealing, had time to settle in a sort of heaviness against her chest.

It gave time to think and shiver a little; shiver with one knew not what; shiver with the desire to be happy; shiver with dread and antic-ipation and ignorance.

Mr. Pullman in congress gaiters, moistening his rather moist lips, was not quite the dream of all the suppressed silent years. But perhaps marriage was.

33

Ever since she had played dolls, Bea had wanted, secretly, of course, in the little house of little secrets, to be married. To live in the security of one's very own home. To be Mrs. To sit opposite a man with whom one had borne a child. To fuss over and rear and dress that child as Mother had fussed over her.

Sitting there in brand-new kid slippers with their white soles, blue silk dress with its yolk of Irish lace and balloon sleeves, large blue velvet hat with willow plumes rising away from her gray-eyed, pleasantly wide-mouthed face, little, if any, of ridiculous innocence was apparent. On the contrary, although there was something tremulous and eighteen about her, there was at the same time something markedly mature. The rounded breasts lifted by whaleboned corsets were full fledged; so was the dimpled hand that occasionally she pressed against them, as if to still their tumult.

But her tendency to premature development which had caused her to bind her quite lovely bosom, as it matured, with tightly wrapped towels, and suffer secret humiliation over her tallness, were no longer to be worried about. Marriage freed you from the nervous concerns of girlhood, eased your sense of being an outsider to life, even where your very dear parents were concerned, once they closed the door of their room behind them. Marriage established you. Gave you a sense of security and being cared for in a special private way that meant everything. That is, if the dear close snug things mattered a lot. They did to Bea. The inside of a married woman's pretty house. The sight of a baby under a coverlet with a pink bow, in a perambulator. A husband unlocking the front door to his home. The silhouette of a housewife moving about her very own kitchen. Husbands and wives pairing off and going home together after a prayer-meeting or a concert or a eucher, or gazing together into a shop window, were something over which to feel wistful and somehow a little chilled.

From now on, in a very few moments, a husband would be caring if she got her feet wet or if other men ogled her. Or in that curious and possessive way that men minded certain things in their own women that were matter of indifference when they observed them in others, Mr. Pullman would be saying: "It's all right for other women to let their bare skin show through those thin net yokes, but I don't want my wife to do it."

34

That must give a woman a darling, cared-about feeling:

"You talk so much more of marriage than you do of Mr. Pullman," Mrs. Doc Hanson had blurted out on one of those few hurried days between the betrothal and the wedding. "Are you marrying marriage, or Mr. Pullman?"

Mr. Pullman, of course. Marriage was the symbol of Mr. Pullman.

That must be Mr. Pullman now, leaning over the top of the stairs. That was he, greeting Dr. Aspern! Ready now!

Marriage had come.

· 8 ·

Everything had gone very well, even with all the commotion out-of-doors and a section of the Reading train panting and coughing right through the ceremony and the strains of brass bands rattling the very window panes of the parlor as Bea and Mr. Pullman dropped softly to the floor cushion for the ritual of the marriage service.

The ring, balking ever so slightly at the knuckle, had slid on. There was something protective in the soft creaking noises and breathing of Mr. Pullman as he knelt. She tried to marshal her mind during the ceremony. Here she was in the midst of this most important moment, perhaps in her entire life. *Love.* Did her gown, as she knelt, properly cover up the new white soles of her shoes? *Honor.* Some one had left the kitchen faucet running! *And obey.* There was an imperfection in the weave of Dr. Aspern's striped left trousers leg. And now a kiss, the taste and smell and temperature of bay rum. . . .

And there wasn't even a young girl present to catch the bride's bouquet. Pink roses and baby's breath.

Later, Mrs. Hanson (in transparent navy blue voile over oxblood taffeta), Doc Hanson (dentist over Cuskaden's Drug Store), Mr. Farley, who operated a burnt-leather and shell-goods concession on the Boardwalk, Father, and the bridal pair had taken a hack for *table d' hôte* dinner at the Hotel Rudolph.

While this showy Boardwalk hostelry, catering as it did to a wealthy Semitic clientele, would not ordinarily have been first choice, it was all quite special, both Father and Mr. Pullman knowing the chief steward. And as Father had put it, Hebrews are so good to their own stomachs they will be good to ours. And indeed so it happened.

Black waiters in white coats and white eyeballs and white teeth, hoisted their trays and wound among the family-sized round tables of the vast dining-room.

An orchestra played behind a trellis of artificial autumn leaves. Prosperous-looking families, surrounded by wide assortments of foods, dined to the clatter of dishes, music, and surf.

The slap of bare brown palms against pantry swinging doors was part of the constant din, and even with the season well turned toward its decline, the aggregate of holiday diners was not inconsiderable.

Heavy-busted, Oriental-eyed girls in heavy authentic jewelry, dark men with blue jowls, stout children with chins rising barely above enormously piled plates, plump, pretty, clucking mothers, young love, still slim, seated tête-à-tête at the smaller tables for two, and din, din, din.

The table was in an alcove, and the chef had baked a small bridal cake with a pair of dolls in the center, and a bottle of Moselle wine was in a wicker cradle at Mr. Pullman's left.

Everybody stared when the wedding party walked through the dining-room, the slightly greasy lips of the stout and pretty young Hebrew mothers of unmarried daughters, parting. Bea, in her light feather boa, her hand on Mr. Pullman's arm, who carried her cloak, felt the rising tide of color rise and prick her face.

Hebrews were such artists about life, often bad artists, it is true, but walking in among the spice of those dark, lit, sometimes greedy, but strangely alive faces, it struck her that they must regard this groom of hers as so much oatmeal . . . unctuous oatmeal. . . .

"Look, there's rice on your beard, Mr. Pullman," cried Doc Hanson. Of course there wasn't, and Mr. Pullman had no beard, but it made them all laugh as two negro waiters drew back chairs and ice-water began to tinkle in their glasses.

"Mrs. Pullman," cried Mrs. Hanson, elaborately, "pass your *husband* the olives." That broke the ice of the occasion at the very start and Mr. Pullman pressed her knee under the table and Father, whose waning tipsiness, induced by the home-brew punch, revived with the second glass of Moselle, began to relate little childhood escapades of Bea's in the manner of one wanting to climb over his own mustache to get it said.

". . . and everything is as all right as rain, until her Mother, God rest her memory, gets to rockin' her to sleep and believe it or not, believe it ladies and gentlemen, as you prefer, right as rain, until her mother gets to rocking her to sleep and all of a sudden, as I'm sitting here, I've her sainted mother's word for it, right through the lace curtain, big as life, bigger, comes the giraffe. . . ."

Oh, it was merry enough, with everybody complimenting everybody and touching glasses at each sally, and sometimes there were naughty ones from Doc Hanson, such as "May all your troubles be little ones," and Mr. Pullman's knee nudging hers. . . .

That was being married, Mr. Pullman's knee presuming to touch hers! She let her eyes stray to him when she dared. There was something forthright and handsome about him, say what you would. His vigorous brown mustache and vigorous parted hair might have been painted on, and his legs, not slender and puny like a boy's, but thick toward the top, carried him firmly.

He would have made two of Father, and even Doc Hanson, who was thick-set, looked quite pudgy before the tall squarish figure in the frock-coat with the black binding, striped trousers, and white carnation in his buttonhole.

If anybody in that party looked the doctor, it was Mr. Pullman. As a matter of fact, there was a striking resemblance between Mr. Pullman and "Mahatma" on the Boardwalk, who dispensed Indian herbs and pamphlets on Vigorous Manhood.

Others had also remarked it, although it was not the sort of thing you would dream of observing to Mr. Pullman himself. Mahatma had greasy coat lapels and his parted-in-the-center thatch of too brown hair really was a wig.

Suddenly, with his air of rivaling Mahatma, Mr. Pullman pushed back his chair, cleared his throat terribly, and in precisely the voice of tracing the history of the tomato from the vine to the ketchup bottle, commanded a hush that instantly straightened the faces of the company.

"Friends," he said, and lifted his glass of Moselle, "to the memory of one who has departed us in the flesh, but is our loved guest here tonight in the spirit."

She felt as if she were going to faint, as if the evening were a drain-pipe through which she was slipping. Father was looking at her with his eyes dragged down like a St. Bernard's and his lower lip wagging;

her husband, seating himself, placed his hand over hers.

Mother. . . .

"And now," said Mr. Pullman, again changing the tenor of the occasion with his voice, "and now?"

"Say, Chipley," began the Doc. "You like riddles. Here's one. How long is a Chinaman?"

That broke the ice again, and it seemed to Bea that she came up from under it where she must have been fainting. . . .

Now, how long was—a—Chinaman. . . .

Everybody was lovely at the dinner, just as if nesting in the backs of their heads was not the consciousness that these two were beginning being married this night.

Doc Hanson was great fun, and dear Mrs. Hanson, to whom he was untrue, had rigged herself up in great state for the occasion. The poll parrot nesting in the voluminous velvet folds of her hat gave her an exciting and really quite crazy look. It dipped over one side, its black gums seeming ready to sink into her eyeball and somehow causing her very expression to match its own. Mother had liked this good-natured dear. Her third marriage—she had buried two, and not one of them any better than he should have been—had not violated that impeccable good-nature.

Mr. Pullman was being delicate as one could wish. With all the right in the world now, he had only kissed her once, following the one at the altar. That was when she had run upstairs to get her feather boa and they had met on the landing. It had been all right. Not a bit frightening. Only now—it was pitch dark outside and they were already at the ice-cream and coffee.

The next move, since they were postponing what was to be their honeymoon trip until Mr. Pullman's annual week's vacation . . . the next thing would be home.

Suddenly the ice-cream, as it slid from her spoon across her lips, simply would not go down. It lay melting for a long and uncomfortable while in her mouth, before she could swallow.

·9·

The gas was burning in the hall, and the scent of the roses and carnations, already going limp in their vases, crowded to the door, almost like a presence to meet them.

Mrs. Vizitelli and the little black girl had tidied nicely. (Had Mrs. Vizitelli seen to it that she had carted nothing away? This one was a great one for stealing laundry soap, and now, what with so much angel-food left over, and an unusually full ice-box—no telling.) The chairs were all back in place. The wedding bell wrapped and on a pantry shelf waiting for Father to return it. The little parlor table, before which Dr. Aspern had read the ceremony, in position once more between the windows, the shells, the small white moiré Bible, the china plate with the signatures burned into it of the east of the Alleghanies salesmen and their wives who had attended the Pittsburgh home-office week of the Pickle and Relish Company, back once more in their usual neat geometry.

Except for the scent, which had also hung around like a last reluctant guest following the funeral, it might have been any evening on Arctic Avenue, after church or Pleiades or band concert. The Hansons going their way; five houses down on the other side of the street; the magnified sound of late pedestrians' footsteps and laughter; the little pale patch of light which the corner street lamp threw across the lower half of the face of the house, making the keyhole discernible.

Father was unwontedly tired. The side of him on which she fancied the arm looked numb, hung half an inch lower. The tipsiness had left him quite limp, and his left eyelid drooped like a crocodile's, low and full of wrinkles. He always tired like that, exhaustedly and without the least reserve. Mother used to relate how he could undress with his eyes closed, asleep almost before he touched the bed. He went upstairs like that, his feet striking heavily, and his head directed toward the door of the old room he had shared with his wife. Diverting his blind steps toward the room he had swapped with her, made Bea want to cry a little. But Father was too tired to notice. The moment she lighted his gas, kissed him and closed his door, nothing was left of his little elegances but the desire to get rid of them as he sat on his bed edge, peeling off garment after garment with his eyes closed.

He let her go like that, on this of all nights . . . alone, pecking her on the cheek in his half-consciousness and actually suffering so with the weight of sleep that eventually he slid into bed with his shoes on.

She stood in the upper hall. Downstairs, Mr. Pullman, about to take his usual long glass of cold water on a single draught, was hacking ice.

She lit the gas in their room. It was immaculate. Matting freshly scrubbed, crisp lace curtains, long enough to be laid out on the floor like the train to a miss's graduating frock. Once the wedding party was out of the house, Mrs. Vizitelli and the black girl had moved Mr. Pullman, even to the stacks of undistributed cans of maple syrup, which now stood neatly on the floor beside his chiffonier. His razor strop hung over the washstand in a position relative to the one it had occupied in the old room. His slippers, too, brown felt, stood beside the coal-scuttle on the white-marble hearth, precisely as he had kept them in the other room, and on the mantel, between the two brown pottery pug dogs, was a small array of his personal objects. Framed photographs of an exceedingly narrow-faced pair of parents, deceased. One of quite an aged aunt, deceased. A framed program of the Pleiades Club, the one on which Mr. Pullman was announced to read his paper on Abraham Lincoln. And of all things! Dear knows from where, the black girl had unearthed a picture which must, in some way, have got mixed up with his other belongings. A horrid cabinet-sized thing of a woman, which Bea turned face down, in stockings and no clothes, trying on a man's high hat before a mirror. With what seemed actual malice, that picture had been propped up against one of the china pugs. Those darkies. . . .

The bed had been turned down, and on the side near the window on which her mother had slept, was the dimity white gown with the beading. Another pair of lives was about to begin moving through the secret places of experience, there in that room. But how? Now that the curtain veiling the unmentionable was about to be withdrawn, what was going to happen? To her? To happiness?

The hacking of the ice had ceased. She must hasten downstairs for fear he might think it was she who was waiting for him to come up, when suddenly, more than anything in the world, that was precisely what least she wanted.

As a child, when fear of dark hallways had sent her feet speeding, she now began to run downstairs, to where there was the lighted parlor and Mr. Pullman seated in a rocker with the water-glass, which he had just drained, in his hand.

He rose to take her in his arms, and began to place a series of large, slow, sucking kisses against her face and down along the Irish-crochet yoke.

"You're my wife now," he said into her flesh.

She wanted him not to smear against the lace which had been made by her mother and was of beautiful raised rose design, but would not have withdrawn for worlds. This was being married. He was very nice, too, and smelled of bay rum and those little scented black things he chewed. More than that, was the cold male aroma of his flesh as he held and desired her. "You're not afraid, are you?"

She sat on his knee and played with his cravat.

"No."

"I won't frighten you."

She didn't want to push his hands away from her face and neck, but she wished—she wished he wouldn't.

"You belong to me, now," he said, and it was fascinating to watch the pupils of his eyes become quite small when he said it. Fascinating and, in spite of her firm resolve to sit relaxed against his knee, a little frightening.

She drew an outline of his lip with her forefinger.

"And you belong to me."

At that he jerked her to him, his breath pouring down through the lacework of her yoke.

"Go upstairs," he said. "To bed. I'll come."

All the breathing and the beating and the commotion of her being seemed to stop at that. She felt more motionless than she had ever dreamed she could be, and still live.

"Why, yes," she said, finally, and, more to withdraw from the torrential avalanche of his breathing than anything else she could think of, began obediently to walk upstairs.

The gas, contrary to custom in a house where it was usual to turn it out after ever so brief an exit from a room, was still going, and there was her gown on the side of the bed near the window.

Well, one didn't stand and gape that way, at a gown. She began to unhook the plaquet of the blue silk skirt and then to climb with both her arms down toward the center of the back, at unhooking the basque.

When she knew him better, her husband would do that.

Her petticoats were so pretty. She took them off, the three, one by one, trying to concentrate on the sweet little handmade details she knew about each of them.

Unhooking her corsets, the wardrobe gave one of its habitual groans of creaking wood, and throwing her arms across her breasts, she leapt, shivering and appalled, to the corner of the room.

It made her cry of anger. Anger at herself. There was no hurry. There was no fear. She slid into her gown, closing it at the neck and at each wrist with a bow of white satin baby-ribbon, and, the color of maple syrup pouring from one of Mr. Pullman's pails, her hair came down below her waist and hung like a photograph of a waterfall. It was wonderfully alive hair that sometimes snapped and bit with electricity if you so much as touched it, and separate strands seemed to raise themselves up, each with a glow of life. It was syrup brown mixed and lightened by some of the ash color of her eyes. Beautiful hair, which, when twisted into its "horse's tail" at the nape of her neck and plastered over with a ribbon bow, suggested little of its wealth.

Standing in front of the mirror which she tilted to reveal her full length, it enveloped her like a domino. A face covered with a pallor, smooth as cream which, flowing around her features, seemed to obliterate everything except gray eyes plunged into by enormous black pupils.

Perhaps, since Mr. Pullman was a gentleman—Mother had always said it of him—he would not come up tonight. Would give her time—privacy——

Standing trembling, grateful for the security of the cloak of her hair, the overwhelming ridiculousness of her plight poured upon her. If only Mother had not left her without telling . . .

The Welsbach burner sang its whiteness down over her whiteness. There were things to do. Blessed little active things. The placing of her blue kid slippers in tissue wrappings in their box. Getting all her paraphernalia, corsets, underclothing, hair-rats, garters, out of sight. Hanging the blue silk dress wrong side out in the closet. In it now, dangling in rows, were the suits of Mr. Pullman. Two of them and his brown velveteen morning jacket and some odd pairs of trousers hanging upside down by clips. There were his shoes, too, strong Blüchers into which his strong feet on their heavy mature legs rested roomily.

As alarmedly as a hare takes fright, suddenly she banged shut the door, turned the gas jet, and was in bed, deep, trembling, and her skin dry as powder.

Mr. Pullman was a gentleman. But his breathing had poured so. Beasts in jungles were supposed to breathe that way. Long and deep and hot. He had been kind. He would be kind. His lips and the way they drew unto him. . . . That cabinet-sized picture, face down now, on the mantel. Mother, if you had only told. . . . Tomorrow things would be lovely. Bless him, after all, Mr. Pullman was not coming. Bless him. . . .

The door opened then, and precisely as the panther is supposed to do in the jungle, some one was breathing in the dark.

·10·

On Fridays Mr. Pullman had got into the habit of liking his Absecon oysters. A Mr. Wilson, with a fish store on North Carolina Avenue, saved her twelve beauties every Friday morning. It was pleasant in the crisp "R" months to take the longer route of walking over to the Boardwalk, as far down as Haddon Hall or Steeple Chase Pier, turn off into North Carolina Avenue for the oysters, and then home by way of Arctic Avenue, doing incidental shopping on the way.

Mighty pleasant when the ocean was just mild and curly and sails bobbed against a deep blue sheet of sky and the air was sharp enough to keep the white beach clear of shouters and bathers.

That was the ideal time, after the guest-ridden, excursionist-invaded summer season was over, to venture onto the Boardwalk, if you wanted to enjoy a sense of the vast beauty of a sea that remained so impersonal to the strutting parade of bathers, hotels, strollers, lovers, roller chairs, vendors, brass bands, banners, popcorn balls, horseback-riders, sand artists, fakers, youngsters, oldsters.

In July and August, when the excursion trains thundered in at the rate of dozens a day, disgorging holiday-makers in a thick stream that reached backward from the walk as far as Arctic Avenue, the ocean somehow became just part of the bedlam into which merrymakers plunged with no sense of its gorgeous miracle, beyond the last two or three breakers that came plunging in to tickle their none too ticklish sensibilities. They screeched when riding the waves, much as they screeched when the cave of the winds on the Steel Pier blew the girls' dresses up over their heads.

All five Fridays of April had been fine. Along the thinly peopled Boardwalk, wind and sun and salt seemed to pour in off the ocean,

45

painting and coating the body with one sensation of exhilaration after another.

It must be good for me in my condition, thought Bea, breathing in with every inch of her capacity during these Friday-morning walks after the Absecon oysters.

Ever since February, the "condition" had been almost as concrete as a presence, around which revolved every act and consideration. Even during the period of those dreadful mornings of facing each day wrung with nausea, when she had perspired of chill and rattled into chill through perspiration, it had seemed nice and right to be in the condition. A justification, in some way, for that sense of the passivity of things. The fears, the hopes, the ecstasies behind the veil had simply not been there. And neither, mind you, was she unhappy. Not a bit of it. On the contrary, it was all right being married to Mr. Pullman. Nice. Only marriage, the marriage part, was nothing mysterious at all. A clinical sort of something, apparently, that a girl had to give a man. It was a little terrible at first. Quite terrible, in fact, to have to feel so passive, so unstirred in the face of all the strange delights it was within her power to awaken in Mr. Pullman. After a while one's chief solace lay in just that. It was wonderful, it was beautiful, it was being a goddess, to be able to bestow, even though within yourself no fires were lighted, only the willingness to endure.

The *condition* was her compensation. It made the quite shocking sense of let-down merge readily into the not unpleasant routine of her marriage to Mr. Pullman. And do not for a moment think that quite a few of the compensations she had foreseen were not there. They were.

Marriage with Mr. Pullman had its problems, of course. But then, to quote Mrs. Doc Hanson, "Dear God, what marriage hasn't?" He wasn't a man you could handle so as he could notice it. Just a bit set in his ways about the little things (how he could pound a bolster to get the feathers distributed his way before retiring), but when it came to the big, always ready to give in at the end. The time she had wanted to order their new parlor set from Wanamaker's in Philadelphia, and he had believed in giving Braunstein's, a home concern, precedence. That was as it should have been, except that Wanamaker had such a lovely three-piece, rose velvet suite, not a bit more expensive than the green-and-gold velours set, really more practical, which they ultimately purchased. Of course, they had bought it at Braunstein's, because after he had given in about Wanamaker's, not for worlds would she have had it any but his way. And really the green-and-gold velveteen, splashed in flowers, turned out quite handsome in the end. But it just went to show what being married to Mr. Pullman meant. Knowing how to handle him in the big things and letting him have his way in the little. Take the time he had wanted to throw over the maple-syrup side line because Prynne & Company, the Brattleboro concern, had wanted to hold him to accept a shipment that had arrived in bad condition.

She had won out by taking a secret trip to the local claim agent in an attempt to force the railway company to do the adjusting, a solution which Mr. Pullman had claimed would be impossible, owing to faulty packing at the Brattleboro end having had so plainly to do with the leakage.

Just one of his stubborn fits which you had to learn how to handle, or there he would have gone and thrown over the tidy little side income that was precisely to her what Mr. Pullman's board money must have been to Mother.

It meant a lot of little addenda, that extra twenty dollars or so a month that Mr. Pullman earned by the comparatively slight additional effort of carrying a few gallons of the syrup around to certain of the Boardwalk stewards who took it regularly.

Everything in knowing how to handle a man.

Take this little matter of the Absecon oysters. Why, to hear him brag about it, one would think the Friday walk to Wilson's fish shop on North Carolina Avenue was miles instead of just this pleasant early stroll along the Boardwalk. Mr. Pullman appreciated little things like that. Loved for her to cream and sugar his cereal; insert the large gold monogrammed buttons into his stiff detachable cuffs. Pinched her cheeks over favors, and in the case of the Absecon oysters, inhaled each one, as if its flavor had a double meaning.

Oh, there were compensations being married to Mr. Pullman, and plenty of them, and life, especially now that those perfectly terrible spells of morning nausea were over, was good.

It was amazing what feeling secure did to the front one put up to the world. Striding along the Boardwalk in the nippy morning air; wife of a local man of impeccable standing; mother-about-to-be; motivating force of the small, well-kept home whose very existence depended upon her return from the fishmonger's into its sweet-smelling security—made a difference in the way you faced the world, the day, and the fishmonger.

The Bea Chipley of six short months ago had been a mouse, wanting in, as it were, and scratching feebly at the walls of life. She was in now. One soon learned to tune oneself to the more tempered actualities of marriage. The actualities, in fact, the darling little secure rows of days of tinkering and building more and more stably into the home, were what made the secret aspects of it endurable. It was not that they, these secret aspects, could not be quite terrible. But on the other hand there was this to consider. He was so nice. As considerate as you could expect! Mixed up in it all was not even disappointment, since her expectations had been as inchoate as her knowledge. The mystifying part of her relationship with Mr. Pullman was the sense of feeling external and non-participant to the spectacle of the supreme emotion flashing its strange, and she supposed sublime, impulse through so matter-of-fact a conductor as Mr. Pullman.

It seemed a lot to be able, through just the volition of being herself, to bring to him what seemed to be almost intolerable ecstasies of the flesh which, through the calm unruffled curtain of her own unawakened flesh, she could regard with almost clinical detachment.

Mrs. Doc Hanson, by way of immediate metamorphosis after the wedding day, which had transformed her from Mother's neighborhood friend into eager and intimate old-wife, had frankly out-and-out questioned her.

"Well, don't answer if you don't want to, but if you are inclined to be one of the frigid ones, don't let him know it. I would be a lot better off today if I had learned sooner how little to let my husbands know about me."

Did Mr. Pullman suspect she was—that? Profiting by the suggestion, she tried to make him believe she shared. . . .

That was why the coming of the baby, so rightly, so promptly, made it all comfortably all right and normal.

As right and normal as trotting along the Boardwalk this cerulean morning, her home standing solidly behind her, spick and span, after its morning cleaning, her purpose Absecon oysters for Mr. Pullman's supper and the purchase of Omega Oil for Father, who was complaining of pains under his shoulder blades.

A hack drew up at the curb simultaneously with her return to the house, laden with the carton of oysters and the package of Omega Oil. Stepping out of it were two *attachés* of the Seaside Hotel, where he happened to have been stricken, bringing Father home.

He had had his stroke in earnest this time, from which he seemed to recover later in the day, but which left his left eye, half of his mouth, arm and leg from thigh to toes, rigid as lumber.

· II ·

In some respects Father was easier to handle than she would have foreseen, and then again there was just no pleasing him.

He took to his wheel-chair with almost immediate docility, seeming to experience an actual pleasure in the fastidious selection from the three which had been sent from Philadelphia on approval, as well as in his place in the side yard in the sun, where, after a while, there was usually some one pausing to pass the time of day with him.

Elegance of a sort descended upon the chair-ridden old gentleman whose baby-fine white hair was always fresh and damp with the mark of the comb through it, and whose small immaculate clothing seemed never rumpled by his predicament of paralysis.

It was surprising how well he came to make himself understood out of the unimpaired corner of his mouth through which he had to crowd articulation. At least to Bea it seemed so. After the first two or three weeks, translation became a relatively simple matter for her: "Reem Sasheesho"—Read me the *Saturday Evening Post.* "Ray Mewsh"— Play the music-box. "Iwa Cough"—I want coffee.

On the other hand, Mr. Pullman never learned the knack of it, so that, no matter from what part of the house she heard Father's voice addressing him, down the stairs she flew in her "condition," to thrust herself between Mr. Pullman and this calamity which had descended upon their house.

It was as if she felt responsible. Apologetic. Needful of sparing him. Which, in justice to Mr. Pullman, was not the case, at least not until by her manner of apology she invoked it into being.

He must, of course, have foreseen the coming of the day when the Company could or would no longer continue to carry Chipley on its salary list. As a matter of fact, it was after the sixteenth week that, with a note of regret, the weekly remittance ceased. But even then, except for a discussion as to the wisdom of renting out Bea's old room instead of fitting it up as a nursery, Mr. Pullman, with delicacy, seldom alluded to the additional burden.

Here again, in the matter of the contemplated nursery, the small revenues from the maple-syrup side line helped meet the situation. Seaside Hotel, Hotel Traymore, and Pierrepont had all recently been entered into the little black book in which Mr. Pullman noted these accounts. The aggregate from these sources made it possible, even with what had befallen Father, to forge ahead with the adorable plans for that nursery.

Baby-bunting wall paper. Dotted swiss shirred around the cloth-basket bassinet. New matting and a gate for the head of the stairs. The gate somehow was the most exciting detail of all to contemplate. Protection against a child's adorable but perilous instincts to explore, it hung in her mind.

"We'll make out all right," Mr. Pullman had said into the stub of pencil point held against his lips the evening the letter from the Company regrettng discontinuance of Mr. Chipley's weekly remittance lay before them. "Those little rascals of maple-syrup accounts will do the trick."

He was right nice about money affairs, Mr. Pullman was. Generous and ready, just so you took pains to let him know you knew who, after all, was holding the purse strings, and dear knows, now with Father incapacitated, she was certainly doing that, and letting him know it was not only a duty but a pleasure.

No, it was little short of admirable in the way in which Mr. Pullman had stood up under the entire situation, except, and she felt base in letting the thought flicker against her brain, the change in Mr. Pullman's attitude toward Father, after that stoppage of salary, had been so lightning quick.

Nothing much on the surface, mind you, but far from the old attitude of cronyship that had existed between them, Father, almost from the day, almost from the hour in which he became financially dependent, became some one not to be answered. That hurt, that almost killed her. Far from even trying to interpret, or have Bea interpret for him, the misshapen words as they mushed thickly off Father's lips, Mr. Pullman not only no longer addressed Father, but no longer wanted him at table.

"This won't do. Bib him and feed him off to himself," had been Mr. Pullman's illy concealed dictum of disgust one night at dinner when spoonful after spoonful of bread soaked in chicken gravy (so nourishing) held coaxingly against her father's stiff lips by Bea, had drooled away from its destination.

Oh, that had not been fair of Mr. Pullman! To be sure, a man coming home tired, had a right to expect release from the exactions of a busy day, and the crowds which milled the pickle-and-relish pier could be exasperating, what with their sampling, sampling, and crowding about for the pickle stickpins without regard for Mr. Pullman's oratory. But stored up in almost every mind, she had observed, was a grudge against some one individual which it found hard to forgive. Mother's grudge against Father had been his never consenting to take out life insurance. Father's against Mother, in spite of the fact that the enterprise had died a total loss, was her one-time refusal to lend him two hundred dollars, her savings, for an investment in a Boardwalk concession called The Battle of San Diego.

To her dying day, with his admirable qualities to the contrary notwithstanding, Bea told herself she could never forgive Mr. Pullman his defection where Father was concerned.

To be sure, as an invalid, Father did immediately develop a querulous, exacting side that kept her really quite cruelly on the jump. Not that by sigh or word of mouth she would ever have let on to Mr. Pullman!

But you could never have conceived to what extent the hitherto more or less innocuous fastidiousness of the little man suddenly developed into querulous tyranny that sometimes brought Bea exhausted to the task of getting him to bed. Just as if the more she tried the more there developed her talent for bringing out a latent cussedness in Father.

All true enough, but a man marrying took his chances on life doing things like that to him. Why, just look at Doc Hanson, who didn't profess to be half the man Mr. Pullman was! Half? Couldn't even speak of them in the same breath, everybody knowing Doc Hanson wasn't any better than he needed to be. But the way that fellow toted around blind old penniless Mrs. Hassiebrock, his mother-in-law, just as if she were a queen, and her, as Father had once laughingly put it, her a "hellion on wheels" if ever there was one.

No, what with her "condition" and all, Mr. Pullman should not have made it necessary, along about the time for him to come home, for her to whisk Father out of sight as if he were some old kitchen apron.

Father, for all his naughtiness, was so terribly meek about that, urging his invalid's chair out of the front room by manipulating his good hand along the wheel and doing all in his power to have himself disposed of before the entrance of his son-in-law. There was something heartbreaking about it; something heartbreaking and infinitely puzzling. Father would actually hurl a dishful of his gruel or puréed potatoes down the front of her dress if she displeased him by its preparation or manner of tilting the spoon.

But to Mr. Pullman, who ignored him as if he were so much meal in a sack, Father presented an obsequious, almost fawning front, eager to be out of the way if that was what pleased most, pathetic in his desire to mumble forth to him the doctor's dictum that his speech seemed less thick, impeccable in his table manners if by any chance Mr. Pullman walked through the kitchen, where, likely as not, two minutes before, Bea had been having a bad time with him.

His deference to Mr. Pullman, even while they lightened certain of her trials with him, broke her heart.

On one occasion Mr. Pullman had entered the kitchen right in the midst of one of her father's most shocking instances of insubordination of her administerings. In trying to adjust his spats, which, along with every accouterment of his late dandyisms, he still insisted upon wearing, one of the straps had come loose. The ready beast of rage which seemed to crouch just beneath the surface of his dealings with Bea leaped at her then, and with his good arm Chipley lifted a rolling-pin which lay on the adjacent table and struck. It landed whack across her jawbone, horrifying him and causing her to cry out so that Mr. Pullman, reading his *Philadelphia Inquirer* in the dining-room, came hurrying out in his congress gaiters that clicked.

The scene that followed tattooed itself for life into her consciousness. She was to cry against it, as two months later she writhed in childbirth, mistaking it, in her semi-consciousness, for the immediate source of her agony.

"God damn you," Mr. Pullman had shouted, kicking the step of the invalid chair with the side of his huge Blücher shoe so that it spun halfway around on its rubber-tired wheels. "You house-devil, touch her again and I'll break every bone in your persnikkety body."

It was the first and last oath she was ever to hear come off those piously shaped lips.

It was grand to have him sweep his arm about her in the protective manner she craved, and yet, upon seeing her father cower into mute acquiescence, the kick and the oath were at that moment translated into secret and lasting unforgiveness for his brutality to a mealsack in a wheel-chair.

·12·

Mr. Pullman was not one who needed to be prodded about this matter of life insurance. He had doubtless heard years of the dickerings on this subject between Mother and Father. You could scarcely lie abed in one room in the house on Arctic Avenue and not overhear a conversation going on in an adjoining. A man can save without shelling out in premiums to insurance companies, had been Father's life-long contention.

"I know, but we don't seem able to get ahead of ourselves."

"We will."

Of course, they never did.

Bea knew for a fact that her father had even been hard pressed to meet the sudden exigency of her mother's undertaking and funeral expenses. She had used the circumstance to try and take the edge off her pain. After all, it was better, Mother's going first. Being left unprovided had been a chronic dread with her. Just had not ever been able to get ahead with savings for that rainy day. Being left "unprovided" had been a life-long dread with Mother. The fact that two or three of the girls in Bea's graduation class had gone into stenography, and that one, Ella Stanhope, had got her name in the papers as the first woman bank cashier in Atlantic City, had accelerated Mother's amazingly stubborn demands for life insurance. If, God forbid! the unexpected happens, a man must leave his women folk provided for. Mr. Chipley must see to that: Her one demand. Oh, it was better so, her going first. . . .

Yes, Mr. Pullman must have been well initiated into this ancient controversy between her parents, because, always now, he took care to see to it that discussions pertaining to that subject took place in

Father's presence, invariably causing him to wince a little with his good eyelid and then immediately simulate sleep.

Mr. Pullman intended to take out a two-thousand-dollar life policy, and "when baby came" just for the cute fun of it, start a little building association account in baby's name. Surprising how those things grew!

Surprising, too, how Mr. Pullman, who had formerly seemed such a detached person, his interest in the household so casual, had suddenly developed a whole string of the most intimate domestic interests. A little too much so. Why, he could tell, when he walked into the house at night, if a bisque figurine had so much as been moved from the mantel to the whatnot. And how pleasant it was, during the day, to arrange and rearrange. Nice, of course, to have a man interested that way. But really, Mr. Pullman took the cake. Didn't he just have to have his way about where the crib should stand in baby's room and about looping back the swiss curtains instead of letting them fall straight, the pretty way she had planned? And as for her appearance, well, sir, Mr. Pullman was certainly particular about the way her shirtwaists sat in the back, and concerned that her heels were properly low and broad and never run over!

Who would have thought he would ever turn out that way!

It was nice, of course, having him so interested. Didn't he rehang the lace curtain on the front hall door one morning on his way out, because the design was upside down? Only sometimes there were things a woman should decide. Those long infant's dresses, for instance. What difference should it have made to him whether she ran the tucks sidewise or lengthwise. It did, though, and sidewise they had to go.

Well, it was better than some men who thought women's cares beneath them. He was sweet about baby coming, not above speculative playfulness about its sex. Jessie was a good name to plan in advance. It had been his mother's. Also, and many a laugh they had, unless twins, it was a name to fit either sex. He humored her in these laughing bouts, cautioning her, though, against over-strain. All well and good for some smart-alec women of fresh ways to ride horseback and go in the surf when they were in that "condition." Nothing like that around here! Once every so often she went to her doctor's, nor was she allowed by her husband to do any heavy lifting, which must wait to be done by him evenings when he came home.

Then, too, there was this inestimable boon to these uncomfortable months, which she was reluctant to admit even to herself. Mr. Pullman was such a gentleman. He offered, which proved him one every inch, to have a cot put up in the nursery and transform it into his temporary quarters. It would have been—well, it would have meant a lot; but that she refused to sanction.

Meanwhile the days, full of not unpleasant realities and of dreams as well, moved on. The plan afoot for the new home, a year, or at the most two years, hence, was the dearest of all the dreams. The idea was to purchase one of those darling bungalow cottages they were beginning to put up around Ventnor, where there could be a sun porch for Father and the baby, and a view of the sea from the west windows.

There was a payment-down, rent-toward-purchase, arrangement which Mr. Pullman considered very fine. It gave the prospective buyer his chance both ways. If, God forbid! illness or unforeseen circumstance interrupted the gradual acquisition of the home, nothing but the initial deposit of something like two hundred and fifty dollars need be forfeited. It would be lovely, living down Ventnor way, removed from the growing din of the town and the proximity of Boardwalk activities, to say nothing of the inpouring excursion trains which intersected Arctic Avenue at two adjacent corners.

Mr. Pullman, who was not demonstrative outside the privacy of their own room, had kissed her right in front of Father the night they had planned this all out.

It made her blush, his doing that to her in her unsightly state. Honestly, it was a wonder he would even look at her. It filled her with a sense of shame to go about even in front of Father, who, so far as one could judge, continued ignorant of what by now had become such a conspicuous fact, causing her embarrassment even when she wrapped herself in her ''maternity'' cape and went out toward evening for marketing and shopping.

Father could not have known. He would never have dared, for instance, even in his poor old state, to have lifted the rolling-pin that time, or to grimace and make talons of the fingers of his good hand when she displeased him in the matter of food or dress.

He was sly, all right. Knew how to confine these paroxysms of rage to the periods when Mr. Pullman was not about, and then he could be mighty naughty. His exactness about his clothing made the laundry such an item, to say nothing of meals. He would calmly let food, not to his liking, flow away from his lips as she tilted spoonful after spoonful of carefully puréed vegetables or meats against them. Sometimes it would be necessary to prepare three or four varieties before the welcome feel of suction against the spoon would convey the glad tiding that his fancy had at last been reached.

Of course, nothing of this was ever allowed to get to Mr. Pullman. It was one of those lonely struggles in which women somehow have the courage to engage.

"If he was my father," Mrs. Doc Hanson exploded to her once, "I'd fold him over my knee and spank him or let him go to the house on the hill."

This was coarse of Mrs. Hanson, and Bea let her see that she thought so. It wasn't that simple with one's own. Besides, chances were that if Mrs. Hanson's old mother by some miracle should turn querulous, she would be the first to bare her back for the burden.

Bitterly, though, Bea thought to herself, if just an ordinary fellow like Doc Hanson could make the sacrifice, Mr. Pullman might be nicer to Father, for her sake.

Well, you can't have everything. Dear knows she was a lucky girl to find herself with a husband and home and coming child instead of having to brave that strange cold world out there into which girls were actually voluntarily venturing nowadays for such positions as stenographer, teacher, saleslady, or, as in the outstanding case of Miss Ella Stanhope, cashier.

A girl had to be cut out for that sort of thing. Yes, indeedy, there were worse fates than being married to Mr. Pullman. Worse fates! What a way to put it! There wasn't any bad fate at all in being married to him. Better say, very good fate.

It was a lush June evening that she prepared him his dinner with these thoughts running through her brain. A particularly good dinner (a New England one, for which he had great relish), because in the morning he was going on one of his rare visits to Philadelphia, to confer with the office there regarding a scheme he entertained for enlarging display space on the Pier. Also, from certain correspondence she had seen indicated on letterheads when he emptied his waistcoat pockets on

Saturday night for Sunday church, she felt sure that Mr. Pullman was conferring with the life insurance company there.

She hoped he would tell her when the time came to go through with the ordeal of his physical examination, but from something he had once said, she feared he might spare her this. A man had a right to want his wife by at apprehensive times like that, although, dear knows, Mr. Pullman was the picture of health.

It was on the trip to Philadelphia the following morning that there occurred the train wreck, remembered by many Atlantic City veterans, when four coaches and an engine went over an embankment into the Delaware River, killing outright eleven people, one of whom was Mr. Pullman.

·B·

She was having a premature baby. They could not keep her far enough beneath the ether for her not to realize that.

She was having a premature baby in a hospital room which every so often came down over the face like a mask and Mr. Pullman was kicking and spinning Father's wheel-chair, and when they started to try and amputate her legs by pulling them out from the sockets, she screamed, and there was the upper half of her separating from the something going from her. . . . Mother, or somebody with a white headache—they all wore white linen headaches about their brows, no, not headaches. Of course not!—Mother or somebody was telling her to press and relax, and a classmate named Freda Uhl, whom she had not seen or heard of for at least ten years, was shoveling coals into a furnace—the furnace of an overturned steam-engine which had spilled out onto Mr. Pullman, who was lying in the midst of it, the shape of a crazy old wooden cross. . . .

Stop that!

Relax. God or somebody was putting her together again. Flaming terrible legs which were being hooked onto the slashing knives of her pain. . . . Mr. Pullman was spinning that chair. . . . No, no, no! Stop that!

Jessie was born.

· 14 ·

An idea which must have been floating about her troubled subconsciousness suddenly awoke Bea, hitting against her brain.

It had happened like that frequently of late, an alarm of hope, usually false, routing her out of sleep.

But this! Curious, now, that she hadn't thought of this before. It seemed so obvious. It would have saved so much running about until the soles of her feet made the Boardwalk and the sidewalks feel like red-hot stoves.

There must be a box of the cards still in Mr. Pullman's upper chiffonier drawer! In all the weeks she had not yet found the impulse to go about emptying those drawers of the minutiæ of personal content. If only she had, the sight alone of those business cards might have saved her so much of what had been the almost vain travail of trying to persuade busy men around town to pause in order to see a woman hunting a job.

There they were! In their neat box.

```
+----------------------------------------------+
|                                              |
|                B. PULLMAN                    |
|                                              |
|    Iron Pier        Atlantic City, N. J.     |
|                                              |
|                                              |
+----------------------------------------------+
```

The accident of the initials made it all right. Beatrice or Benjamin Pullman could use those cards. If only she had thought to employ this device as a talking-point to the Pickle and Relish Company, on the trip she had made to Philadelphia to try and induce the office there to take her on in her father's place.

Of course she had gone about it all wrong. Naturally there was something strange and irreconcilable to a business man to have to contemplate a woman, her hands always loaded between hiking her skirts off the ground, her pocket-book, and her gloves, rushing about as salesman. (Those rainy-day skirts had sense to them!)

The two-hundred-dollar gift from the firm had been really a touching boon, considering the fact that so shortly before this calamity of the death of Mr. Pullman they had carried Father for twelve weeks. But what was that, compared with what the security of being permitted to carry along Father's position would have meant?

Mr. Pullman's position, of course, would have been out of the question. Demonstrating required the quite special talent of voice and presence. He had always said of himself, that people first tasted the command in his voice and then came nibbling at his products. That was true. Sensing the park-statue solemnity of him, they paused to listen, then just as solemnly to taste the chilli sauce and picca-lilli off the tips of small paper spoons provided for the purpose.

But Father's work was another matter, particularly since he had not been replaced and his territory was being handled, inadequately, no doubt, by two of the Philadelphia salesmen alternating on weekly visits to Atlantic City. Father's customers would be more than willing to carry on with his daughter. Of that she felt sure. But just try and convince a business firm of that! If Father's own concern could not see a woman in the strenuous rôle of city salesman, what could you expect of the firms to whom she was not the wife and daughter of erstwhile trusted employees. Regarding it from that angle, the two-hundred-dollar gift had been little short of good-riddance money. . . .

Why, even the men in Atlantic City, to say nothing of the canvassing tour she had made that day in Philadelphia when Mrs. Hanson had come over to mind her child and Father; some of the men, who knew who she was, would scarcely lend civil ear to her application.

"Don't let them get fresh with you," Mrs. Hanson had admonished. "In the nasty eyes of a lot of men a woman who is out to earn her own living a man's way is either a freak or don't mean any good."

Except in one instance (a deacon, mind you, right in her own Atlantic City) where she had been crowded up against the door and a pair of insinuating knees pressed against hers, from which she sped out into the corridors, nothing of that sort had even approached happening.

In most cases it was simply a matter of no precedent for women in the concern.

If only, thought Bea, on occasion after occasion after defeat, I had more gumption! They feel in me how worried I am! That's no good. I look a fright. Perhaps I'm dressed wrong. The shirtwaist and skirt are all right, but it might be a good thing to leave off the taffeta petticoat which rustles so. Felt right silly, talking to old Mr. Massingham of the East Jersey Title and Guarantee Company, seeing in the looking-glass behind him the way those blue plumes kept shaking so on my hat when I talked. One of those plain, short-back sailors, like the girls in the big offices in Philadelphia wear to work, would be more business-like.

And if only there were a greater variety of alternative positions. Not that there was any sense of emergency; even with the hospital and doctor's bills paid, there still remained, what with the Pickle and Relish gift and the railroad settlement, a seven-hundred-dollar residuum. But it just did seem as if one could not find rest on that slender time-ledge of security.

Salesladying and teaching and stenography seemed to be about the beginning and the end.

But positions as saleslady on and off the Boardwalk were at a premium. Braunstein's department store would have been an ideal berth, close enough to the center of town to be within easy walking distance to wherever she would ultimately have to install Father and her baby. The general manager there had known Mr. Pullman slightly. He would keep her in mind.

Besides the notorious case of Miss Stanhope, there was a white-haired spinster, a Miss Bogarthy, employed as bookkeeper in one of the hotels just off the Boardwalk. But inquiry revealed that she had virtually inherited the position from her father, whom she had helped out in his cage, back in the days when his eyesight and health began to fail.

The daughter of an invalided father and mother of an infant child herself, she could not very well contemplate the nursing of other people's children. Not but what, if some sort of arrangement presented itself, she would not grasp at the opportunity.

If only I had taken a Normal course or studied stenography! If only——

Standing beside the chiffonier in her long-sleeved, high-necked night-gown, the small box of cards in her hand, the thought which had awakened her spread, warming her brain into the wakefulness which was coming more and more to eat into her nights.

Perhaps if she could establish a mail contact with some firm under the name, "B. Pullman." Men often worked for firms, handling their products, without necessarily having personal contact with the home office.

Take Mr. Pullman and the maple-syrup side line! (Ah, the pity! They had planned the honeymoon trip to Brattleboro, Vermont, that summer.) Mr. Pullman had never so much as laid eyes on anyone connected with the little maple-syrup firm with which he did business.

There had come two letters from Prynne & Company Sugar Mart, still apparently ignorant of his death, reminding Mr. Pullman it was "some time since they had been favored with an order." She had not found the opportunity or heart to reply or even to inform a remote cousin of his in Rutland, who had sent them a quite horrible hand-painted piano-scarf for a wedding gift.

She had delivered the six or eight cans of post-mortem syrup according to the careful data found in Mr. Pullman's black notebook, lugging the heavy cans herself, after dark, in the immediate weeks before the premature birth of her child.

The idea, spreading by now in her brain like the ink spot from an overturned bottle onto a blotter, took pattern.

Why not! The name B. Pullman, to the firm in Vermont, was just that, nothing more or less. It was fair to assume that the hotels to whom the account was an old one would continue. New ones could be approached by mail. However small the beginning, it would relieve the strain of what were threatening to be these tormenting nights.

Well and good to regard with equanimity, up to a certain point, the cash of over seven hundred dollars which she kept wrapped in the thickness of two handkerchiefs in the bottom of a locked trunk. The fact which remained however, to be constantly borne in mind, was that between her, her father, and her child, and the peculiar exigency of no funds, were not more than six or seven months' security.

The five-hundred-dollar check from the railroad company had been a godsend, but at the same time had branded her guilty of serious tactical error.

If only she had not accepted the settlement money from the agent who had appeared one of those horrible days immediately following the plunge of that fateful train! Proper lawyers, she had subsequently learned, might have helped her to recover many thousands. That would have been repugnant to her, bartering for payment in return for the life of Mr. Pullman, but no question about the validity of such a claim.

Defective steel in the shaft of a speeding engine had sent the sole support of two adults and a coming child to his death. Small doubt but what families of some of the other victims of this wreck were recovering at least the solace of financial restitution for the tragedy of human loss.

"It is one of those things," the irreconcilable Mrs. Hanson would reiterate until, listening to her, the senses tottered, "makes me want to jump out of my skin! To think Doc and I had to be in Philadelphia the day you settled for a measly five hundred!"

But little use to cry over the spilled milk of that, now. She had accepted the check, gratefully, from an agent who carried his penpoint wet and ready.

Surprising how high Mr. Pullman's funeral expenses had managed to pile themselves. Far beyond what she had anticipated when, only half heedingly, she had agreed to the various bland suggestions of the undertaker.

As revealed by the still mounting minutiæ of the various bills as they continued to come in, the coffin, it seems, had been tufted, camp chairs had been brought into the parlor, where there were far too few present to occupy them, and the carriages, according to the surprising details of the various statements, had been double and rubber-tired.

The large spray of carnations "With deepest sympathy" from the Iron Pier Associates must have covered up the tufting, or perhaps it had been concealed because Mr. Pullman, in violent death, had not been in a condition, even after the tinkerings of the undertakers, to be gazed upon through the small window of his casket, as Mother, who looked beautiful in her last sleep, had been.

The condition of his "remains" had been carefully concealed from her "condition." Sometimes, in spite of herself, quite a cold sweat would break out all over her because her mind skidded onto that forbidden thought. How must Mr. Pullman have looked to the embalmers? Perhaps he had had no face left. To think that anything so orderly as a face like Mr. Pullman's could instigate God to tear it out of existence that way.

It was blessedly better, awakening as she did to the spur of an idea, than to be torn out of sleep shuddering with the forbidden conjectures of what had remained of the lacerated clay of Mr. Pullman.

Here was a glimmer, through her growing terror, of something hopeful.

To the small distributing firm known as Prynne & Company, Brattleboro, the demise of B. Pullman could be a matter of little note.

It was a common thing for businesses to go on functioning under the original trade name, after the death of the founder or after it had passed into other hands. Business went on as usual. In all probability Prynne & Company would never bother to question one way or another, particularly if she were careful to form a habit of signature not dissimilar to the late B. Pullman.

B. Pullman, for some reason with the "B" bisected, had been his habit.

The value of B. Pullman lay in its entrance wedge. You sent in your card. B. Pullman. You got at your man.

You signed letters to customers who need never lay eyes on you. B. Pullman. They made cards on the Boardwalk while you waited. One hundred for ten cents. B. Pullman.

It was as B. Pullman that she sold that week, by the device of leaving stamped, addressed envelopes and samples from a quart tin which she had on hand, at several hotels not entered in the black book, eleven gallons of maple syrup.

Further, the black book revealed this to be one gallon over and above the best week achieved by Mr. Pullman.

But, as opposed to the period of his noon hour given over three times a week, she practically tramped, or rode street cars, the day through, a schedule complicated by the need to report back, every hour or less, to the house on Arctic Avenue that contained her father and child.

· 15 ·

Years later, she was to relate to a national group of business and professional women convening at Hotel Commodore, New York, that the tide of those days turned for her on a pail of syrup and a flight of stairs, the latter enabling her to let the three upper rooms of the house on Arctic Avenue for a sum that to the penny paid her monthly rent.

This flight of stairs, which was an exterior one, led up the flank of the house into what had once been Mr. Pullman's room. Theoretically, because it gave entrance in a private and detached manner that did not necessitate passage through the lower floor, it was ideal for the lodger.

That Mr. Pullman had never availed himself of it had been, in Mother's eyes, another commentary upon the impeccability of his virtues. Just fancy what getting the wrong person into such a room might have meant in vagrant comings and goings, to say nothing of possible goings-on! But the turning of his key in the lower front hall, almost to the daily second, was something that belonged to the stability of Mr. Pullman.

He and those stairs would have made one another ridiculous. So much so that during the lifetime of Mrs. Chipley it had been Mother's contention with a landlord who protested, that he remove the stairs, which required weekly scrubbings, from their position of undue conspicuousness against the flank of the house.

It was the advantage of these very stairs, however, which now caught the fancy of the first applicants, a Mr. and Mrs. Tannehill, who responded to the small advertisement in the *Atlantic City Press:*

For Rent, furnished: Three neatly furnished rooms. Share kitchen and bath. Twenty dollars a month.

The privacy of the exterior staircase had appealed at once to Mr. Tannehill, who, along with his wife, conducted a photograph studio on the Boardwalk, near Georgia Avenue, and who, as evidence of good faith, paid an immediate deposit on one week's rent and left an umbrella.

It crowded up things pretty badly. Father on the divan in the parlor, herself and child in what had once been the dining-room. But the proportionate peace of mind was worth it.

Fortunately, Mrs. Tannehill and her husband alternated at the studio, so that there was a fair amount of certainty that one or the other of them would be usually in the house, a circumstance which helped the quite terrible unease occasioned by being obliged to leave a semi-helpless old man and a helpless infant alone there even for the inter-mittent periods of absence she allowed herself. Also, the sense of her lodgers' presence there at night helped.

The Tannehills were a pair, it later developed, who had never been married at all, but had rented her second floor in order to live in a domestic brand of sin the like of which stunned her more than the fact itself.

It was not only a domestic brand, it was of an orderly and mundane routine, which even during the period of her innocence of the actual relationship, or lack of it, between this pair had caused her sometimes to wonder if its regularity did not irk Mrs. Tannehill, who was a large blond woman of exactly the consistency of the crab-apple jelly for which Mrs. Hanson was quite famous locally.

In her mother-hubbard, with a yoke that struck her just above her large breasts, her yellow-and-gray hair in a leaning psyche on the top of her head, her fleshy hands mushing up softly around an array of turquoise rings, she flopped about those upstairs rooms, doling out the most menial services to Mr. Tannehill, himself of soft, rather sybaritic flesh to which he applied scents that clung to upholstery and stairs: Sunday mornings you could hear the clip of her scissors trimming his nails. Late evenings she washed out his light-blue underwear and hung it on a line she had improvised in the bathroom she shared with the lower half of the house.

It was revolting to need to dodge the soft dangling legs and shirt tails of Mr. Tannehill's drying garments, but the blessed boon of the solution of her immediate rent problem offset even the many disadvantages of this bizarre couple, who permeated the house with a strangely assorted odor of drying underwear, sen-sen, eau de lilac, and the smell of banana which seemed to emanate from a gilt wicker chair which Mrs. Tannehill apparently carted with her for the purpose of removing the sting from the impersonal cold shoulder of the furnished quarters through which they wandered as the seasons shifted from Atlantic City to Miami.

It was reassuring to come home and find the odor of stale sen-sen hovering over the garments of the child. It meant that Mrs. Tannehill had been in and out during Bea's absence. Her love of children took a form of fine, if unæsthetic, frenzy which had the unfortunate tendency to frighten. "I love it to death. I could bite a piece right out of it. If only I could chew that darling pink toe." All this through Mrs. Tannehill's gold and gritted teeth as she snatched up the infant, burying her scented face into its face and hair.

Invariably the child set up fast and frightening crying, struggling away from the deluge of pleated cheek and sound of Mrs. Tannehill's gritting teeth, but her violently restrained pinches traveled along the tender flesh, stiffening the tiny body against the imminence of the occasional stinging pinches which escaped her control.

Father, too, shuddered fastidiously away from the well-meant ministrations of Mrs. Tannehill. Her breath blew his hair when she talked, and to avoid the warm sen-sen gale of it he would operate his wheelchair rapidly as possible backward and away. Her easy sympathy made her garrulous in quite a terrible way. Since she could understand no more of Father's thick utterances than she could of baby's gurglings, her next best was to resort to blabbing through lips spread to achieve some sort of perverted vernacular which she fancied equal to the occasion:

"Does bad ole sun shine in him poor ole eyes? Here, muvver roll him into kitchee 'till preety Miss Beebee come home with big boxful goodie-goodies for her daddy."

Father's sack of a body, in its dandified suit, could not withdraw all the way from her touch, but his eyes, old as a crocodile's, and somehow, since his second stroke, as evil-looking, would roost, with a sort of hate, upon her.

It was extraordinary the agility Father had been able to cultivate in that part of his side which the second stroke had left uninvaded. He could lift his grandchild out of the wash-basket crib which stood at a certain angle beside him, ride himself to the kitchen stove for the prepared bottle of milk which also stood at a certain angle in its pail of warm water, and even perform the service of change, with minimum of infant discomfort.

Sometimes in the midst of her intermittent but practically day-long traipsing in and out of the trade entrances of hotels and boarding-houses, the flashing vision of that small house on Arctic Avenue and its helpless inmates would fill her with premonition that would send her scuttling home, even though her last look-in might have been but a half-hour previous.

Her impotent father operating himself on the wheels of his invalid chair, trying to administer to her impotent child, whose twelve-weeks-old back was still too soft to sustain itself without the brace of a palm held against it!

Fire! It was as if hourly she knew by heart what must be by now the precise positions of the smoldering coals so carefully placed within the range.

Stroke! When doctors said it might mean a matter of hours or a matter of years before the second or third, usually it meant the former. Her dead father might be sitting there now beside her alone child!

Once, after she had sent in her card to the manager of a large new restaurant which was opening on Atlantic Avenue, this clap of thunderous apprehension boomed so across her peace of mind that, without waiting for a long-coveted interview, which was just about to be granted her, she started running the ten blocks back to the house on Arctic Avenue, which twenty minutes before she had quitted.

It made nervous apprehension her running-mate. It made the slamming of a door strike terror, and the sound of the sea ran through her constant unease like foreboding rhythm.

What if!

What if the carefully banked coals in the kitchen range should suddenly collapse onto wooden flooring? What if she had weaned her child too soon?

What if! What if paralysis should suddenly race into the unimpaired arm of her father, causing her child to roll like so much logwood to the floor?

What if croup or convulsion or any of the catastrophies of infancy were to swoop upon the bundle of helplessness that lay committed to the feeble care of another bundle of almost equal helplessness?

What if she, hurrying along with the twine of a can of maple syrup cutting so into her fingers, were suddenly to be run down by a horse and buggy or stricken suddenly by one of those unfathomable acts of God which, one after another, had so recently descended upon her house? Acts of God. Why were only calamities referred to as acts of God?

"What if," and "if only!"

If only, of all possible days, Mr. Pullman had not chosen that one! If only, due to a suddenly detected flaw in the doctor's license to practice dentistry in the state of New Jersey, the dear Hansons had not, overnight, as it were, up and departed for Montreal. If only Mrs. Vizitelli were not so tied down by the demands of a large family and the grocery store. If only Father—if only destiny—if only life. . . .

Now, now, life was making out nicely. The first six months of her back-door assault upon every hotel and boarding-house within the broad pleasure belt had yielded her an average of ten to twelve dollars a week, although it was the last six weeks of those six months which succeeded in jerking her average up to its level.

The tins of syrup were arriving at the house on Arctic Avenue in considerable assignments, and evenings after dark, when she could get Mrs. Vizitelli or her daughter Nettie, or Mrs. Tannehill, in the event that it was her evening home from the studio, to remain in the rooms, she set about their delivery.

Fortunately, the summer, approaching its peak, was the force that augmented her sales of what Mr. Pullman had handled chiefly on the basis of its being a winter product. Evenings now, a solid front of illuminated hotels, going full blast, formed a dazzling sea wall of movement, energy, and carnival, behind which the city streets, ships, smaller hotels, and boarding-houses achieved something similar to that movement, in a reflected, if somewhat shoddy, glory.

Pianolas, peanut-stands, billiard-halls, dance-pavilions, penny arcades, weinie-stands, photograph and shooting galleries, clam-counters, salt-water-taffy emporiums, saloons, shore-dinner resorts, ice-cream parlors, fortune-telling concessions, astrologers, tamale-hawkers, operated not only along the Boardwalk, but corroded a brassy trail into the side streets and along the main arteries of midtown, creating a sort of small summer madness along streets that in winter, with a stiff wind howling in off the ocean, were those of a village with its head tucked under its wing.

Boarding-houses with buzzing verandas spilled their commotions from lighted windows and crowded stoops. The knee-high swinging doors of saloons slapped inward and outward and family entrances were the scene of constant comings and goings. Greek restaurants poured greasy odors, kosher hotels buzzed with the activities of stout matrons in machine-stitched wigs. Nationalisms flared along these side streets, each country to its odor, complexion, and often as not, its hoisted flags.

There were certain streets along which Mr. Pullman would no more have walked with her, much less have permitted her to walk alone! Still more streets along which she had never ventured, even in Sunday-afternoon walks with her parents, and, for that matter, streets whose existence she had never before realized.

They were the streets she traversed frequently now, the narrow ones honeycombed with lodging and boarding houses; also the wide boulevard of Pennsylvania Avenue with its line-up of pretentious "guest homes" and small hotels, and then, of course, those side streets which led up to the trade entrance of the Boardwalk hostelries.

"Lead me blindfolded through Atlantic City," she would tell her father, hopeful that some of her tidbits of conversation reached him, "and I can tell the streets by the smells. I can tell Jewish garlic from Italian."

Had it ever occurred to her to question why, in these multifarious lanes, she remained unmolested, a glance at her reflection in the mirror might have answered.

It was at that period in her life when the youth of her seemed to have passed behind the dark cloud of a dowdiness induced by frantic haste. It was as if she could scarcely wait for each day to begin in order to do something about it. To relieve a fright. To cram what had seemed such a well-behaved, well-meaning destiny back into the groove from which it had slipped.

The haste, the frenzied sense of needing to do many things at once, the weight of the syrup tins pulling at her arm sockets and cutting into her fingers, the anxiety of doubts that always existed between the taking and the delivery of an order, were out in a tense grimace over her face.

Hurrying along on her nocturnal errands of delivery (she could never bear to sleep between an order and its execution), her gray-eyed, wide-featured face, with its somewhat Maltese feline quality, was drawn in at the lips until they stretched across her dry teeth in a grim harassed line. Her sailor hat, too, had a habit of riding back on her pompadour, enhancing her air of almost painful concentration upon her destination of back doors.

Loitering men in lighted doorways or on street corners looked after her, but did not follow up with more than the occasional half-hearted accostings which they subconsciously expected of themselves at the passing of an unaccompanied woman.

It is doubtful if Bea, her face twisted with purpose, ever even heard.

Maple syrup and delivery mattered so terribly. It actually gave one little time, beyond an obsessing concern for its creature well-being, to realize one had a baby. Countless little budding impulses seemed to have been nipped in the frozen garden of her expectations. Babies must live, and so the struggle for, rather than the fact of, its existence became paramount.

It was at the end of about the fifth month that it occurred to her, in the light of the increasing orders, to write and obtain from Hiram T. Prynne, of the Sugar Mart, an additional five-per-cent discount for cash. It was also at the end of these months that her hypothetical forebodings of, "what if," resolved themselves into a happening that potentially, at least, was fraught with tragedy.

She returned home one afternoon to find her father seated rigid and unseeing in his chair, her child, as it had rolled from his unretentive lap, dangling and howling head down over the side wheel, where it hung precariously suspended by the lace hem of its dress, which had providentially caught on the lever by which Mr. Chipley propelled his chair. Except for her return, either the child would ultimately have tumbled to the floor or hung there head downward until its cries attracted the possible attention of Mrs. Tannehill, or ultimately ceased in suffocation.

The state of unconsciousness from which her father then emerged, without having been aware of his lapse, was the forerunner of a series to which he was to become subject. But the first was sufficient to stun

Bea into the realization that never again could these two be left there alone in this state of their mutual impotence.

The much-mooted problem of a servant became no longer controversial. The crime had been in daring to makeshift so long.

The boon of the additional discounts in her dealings with Hiram Prynne would go a little way toward meeting the additional eight or ten dollars a month the hiring of a servant would entail, and besides, she was about to be initiated into the technique of raising money by way of the pawnshop.

There was one on Atlantic Avenue with the three balls over the doorway. Unbeknown to Mr. Tannehill, Mrs. Tannehill carried on quite a constant series of negotiations there.

The solid silver nut-bowl on the sideboard was reassuring reminder. Her mother's dozen sterling-silver knives and forks and spoons. Her own pathetically new bridal outfit of prettily engraved silver fish set, dessert spoons, ramekin-holders and bonbon dish. Her graduating gift of a blue enamel watch with its fleur-de-lis pin to match. If need be, her mother's gold watch with its chased gold case and long gold chain. If need be, too, yes, if need be, the gold horse-head with a tiny diamond eye which her father wore daily even now in his cravat. She would substitute an imitation one, slyly. What Father did not know would not hurt him. He knew so little. Sometimes she wondered if he knew of the death of Mr. Pullman. But in any event, life must go on. . . .

A visit across the railroad tracks to the shanty district where Selene had dwelt, revealed no one else in that particular house who was available for a position at general housework, "sleeping in."

There was the difficulty. Sleeping in. Most of the female domestic help, wives, sweethearts, or what nots of the thousands of negro waiters, chair-pushers, and miscellaneous helpers about town and the Boardwalk, demanded the freedom to return home evenings.

"No, ma'am. I cain't take no job at sleepin' in. I got a husband waitin' table at de Seaside Hotel, and three chillun needs me to put 'em to bed."

"No'm. I got to sleep home. I's married."

"Sleepin' in? No, *ma'am!*"

It was on her disgruntled and discouraged way homeward across the railroad tracks, as she was mentally framing an advertisement to insert in the *Press,* that suddenly she emulated something she had seen her mother do. In fact, it had been the method by which she had secured the services of Selene.

"Do you know of anyone who wants a position for general housework, sleeping in?" she inquired of the enormously buxom figure of a woman with a round black moon face that shone above an Alps of bosom, privately hoping that the scrubbed, starchy-looking negress would offer herself.

"I sho does, miss, and dat's me. But I's got a three-month-old chile, honey. You white folks ain't got no truck with a black woman wid a chile. I's learned dat, walking my laigs off this mawnin'."

"You mean you would want to bring your baby, too?"

"Honey chile, I'll work for anything you is willin' to pay, and not take more'n mah share of your time for my young un, ef I kin get her and me a good roof over our heads. Didn' your maw always tell you a nigger woman was mos' reliable when she had chillun taggin' at her aprun strings? I needs a home for us, honey, and ef you wants to know what kind of a worker I is, write down to Richmon' and ask Mrs. Osper Glasgow, wife of Cunnel Glasgow, whar I worked since I was married . . ."

"You have a husband?"

"Died six months ago in the Atlantic City Hospital of a lung misery that brought us here from Richmon'. A white nigger, miss, that you'd never think would've had truck with the likes of me. God rest his soul. It wasn't 'til after de Lawd took him dat I learned it was a bigamist's soul. Ef you doan' believe I kin housekeep, miss, wid a baby under my arms, try me."

Why not! The child would insure this woman's permanence. In a town with nine thousand colored population, reliable houseworkers were nevertheless difficult to obtain. With the wives of waiters themselves veering from general housework and angling for the less confining duties of waitress or chambermaid, domestic help was what it had always been in Atlantic City—a nomadic procession of women with home ties of their own, or of slim young blackbirds with no stability whatsoever.

"Is your little one healthy?"

"The purfectest white nigger baby dat God ever dropped down in de

lap of a black woman from Virginie. Her pap didn' leave her nothin'
but some blue-white blood a-flowin' in her little veins. 'Twas de ruin-
ation of her pap, dat blue-white blood. 'Tain't gonna be hern. We's
black, me and mah baby, and we'd lak mighty much to come work for
you.''

So, Delilah and Peola.

·16·

Sometimes it seemed to Bea that, operating her business on no capital, and paying back into her small enterprise most of her profits, she was running her house on a minus sign.

A hospital and two clubs now enriched her list, and there was still the unexplored area of private homes to be canvassed, but the expensive sunlight treatments for Father had seemed one of the things she would never have forgiven herself for not trying, and if you believe that five can live as cheaply as three, try bringing into the house, even at the driblet wages that satisfied Delilah, a buxom negro woman who, with the best intentions in the world, swelled the food budget so considerably.

There was a time, there the first months after the advent of Delilah and Peola, when the nights, what with the four of them, Father, Jessie, Delilah and hers, breathing peacefully in the small area of crowded first floor, practically amounted to a session in mathematics. Either lying in bed or crawling out of it to work on the kitchen table, there was figuring to be done, on the backs of used envelopes, on scraps of old paper, which could not be accomplished with the hard bright day full upon her, when the phenomenon of living on a minus sign seemed less fraught with danger than it did at night. Worries that kept themselves at half-mast during the busy days seemed, at night, to creep out of the corners of her restlessness and with enlarged heads, grotesque torsos, and frightening grimaces press the seriousness of her predicament full upon her.

The electric baths for her father, which he seemed to enjoy, were now a matter of one a day and of heavy cash drain. The Tannehills were not all that could be hoped for in the matter of promptness at paying rent, frequently falling one, two, even four weeks in arrears, and then meeting her timid pressures with installments. The amazingly pale-tan infant of Delilah, with its fierce black Indian-looking eyes and straight glossy hair, developed a rash which required four visits from Dr. Merribel. Much of her worry there had been fear of possible contagion or infection, but nothing beyond a small skin irritation developed, and tucked into the end of the wicker perambulator, which against a deeply rooted prejudice planted by a mother to whom the system had been anathema, she had purchased on installments, rode the small nub of Delilah's rather astonishing anomaly, a black-and-tan little masthead to the ship of state which carried the blue-and-yellow porcelain of Bea's child.

Daily, in fine weather, you could behold Delilah, the vast moon of her face shining above the alp of her bosom, manipulating her three helpless charges, the two infants in the perambulator and Father in the wheel-chair, toward the beach, three long blocks to the west.

All to the good, for the growing peace of mind that permitted Bea to work now in two long half-day periods, without that flaying sense of the need to rush home. Delilah might be said to have risen like a vast black sun over the troubled waters of the domestic scene, laying them and the hordes of fears, large and small, that had dogged her heels all day.

Delilah, with a radiance that emanated off the polished disk of her face and off the impeccable fortification of her huge gingham aprons, had placed something as horny as the hand of a crocodile upon this uneasy household and brought it somewhere akin to a going concern.

But it cost to feed Delilah, who not only had the palate and the capacity of the gourmet, but the grand old Southern skill to prepare dishes fit for a daily company of them. Her breakfast bacon, fried to its cunning turn, tickled the senses awake. There just never were griddle cakes like Delilah's. Her crullers doused into boiling baths of specially rendered fat that cost so, swelled to a perfection which she sprinkled with powdered sugar and served piping hot.

In fact, everything cost to such an extent, that one night, seated in her nightgown, barefoot, figuring on the backs of envelopes while Delilah's breathing blew through the rooms in a small gale, she wrote out the following for the printer:

B. Pullman is forced regretfully to announce the following slight increase in price schedule, to become effective after October first:

Ten cents per gallon on every purchase amounting to five gallons or less.

On purchases over that amount, five cents per gallon.

Orders received before the above date, accompanied by check or money order, will be filled at present prices.

It worked! Not only were there no lost accounts, but quite a few stewards of the larger hotels took the opportunity to accomplish the slight saving by ordering well in advance. Checks came in covering not only immediate orders, but future deliveries.

For the first time since Delilah's initial month of service, Bea was able to pay her a portion of the arrears. This she refused with such loud ejaculations, stretchings of the orifice of her mouth into a very red and very white cave of long-drawn winds, that meekly she was forced to restore the money to her purse.

"We's partners in dis heah shebang, Miss Bea. Nevah did have no truck wid money-suckin'. We got our chillun to think about before we go squanderin' de fust spare money dat comes in on no-'count suvvant's wages."

The major dispensation of this experimental period would have summed up into one single noun—Delilah.

Into every cranny and crevice of the strangely placed household there poured the red, black, and white personality of this immense woman. The red of her easily-hinged large mouth, packed with the white laughter of her stunning allotment of hound-clean teeth; the jug color of her skin with the gold highlights on cheekbones; the terrific unassailable quality of her high spirits, Baptist fervor, and amplitude reached and encompassed two infants and an infantile old man, who turned his cold old bones toward her warmth.

The household, sleeping in what segregation the cramped quarters allowed, Bea and her child in what had been the dining-room, Delilah and hers on an improvised cot in the little "reception" hall, the old gentleman upright in his chair or on the leather sofa in the parlor, awoke nowadays to the tease of sizzling bacon, steaming mountains of griddle cakes of fluff and no weight, which presently, with her enormous prodigality, Delilah would smother under some of the household supply of maple syrup. Coffee that Mrs. Tannehill declared wound upstairs to her, causing her to yearn like a drunkard, and a porridge for the old gentleman which he took through a glass tube, with the greedy suction of a child.

There was no suppressing the enormity that was Delilah, nor was there the desire to suppress it. Her table might appear frighteningly lavish (how she loved the board that groans), but she had skill immense as it was consistent, in utilizing breakfast's left-over bacon into luncheon's coleslaw served with sizzled bacon cubes, and there was no such thing as too many griddle cakes, because once Delilah herself surrounded them, the golden syrup began to pour down their diminishing flanks to form engulfing pools into which she dove with an exaltation not dissimilar to the white-eyed ecstasy with which she soared into her frequent outbursts of Baptist fervor.

So it was from a going household of Delilah and three babies that Bea plunged every morning, into the territory for the day, and the special calls for solicitation and reorders which she had jotted onto the small silver pad she wore on a chatelaine at her waist:

Call Hotel Fassio (ask for Elkus). Hotel Lurray. Hotel Traymore. Albrecht's Hotel (Jones). Rhode Island Avenue. C. K. Mistrial, Caspain Avenue. (Recommended by Stahl.)

She used to insist that, according to actual measurement by one of the Boardwalk penny devices, she had become taller during this period. Be that as it may, or whether the amount of walking as it hardened and slenderized, might have been accountable for the undeniable look of stature and added length of face, the look of new height was there. And it was a leaner face, an obsessed face, that strode ahead of herself those days of the first years of her bird's-eye canvassing of Atlantic City, a quality of straight-lipped concentration out in it that must have immunized her not only from street loiterers of a carnival city, but from the men upon whom she thrust herself, once she had cleaved her way through to them by the little device of the business card.

After that it was simple enough, so simple that sometimes, secretly and half ashamed, she was moved to contemplate her reflection in the mirror. Even with her vigorously honed-down contours, marriage or maternity or disaster, or all three, had brushed her with the light and quite lovely pollen of slight maturity.

Withal, the alleged perils, so vividly anticipated by Mrs. Hanson, who had always worn an extra enforcement of petticoats against an ever-potential Jack the Ripper, of a woman venturing into the ice-fields of business, had not dawned upon her experience. Men registered surprise at the sight of a woman as follow-up to that card, some a passing annoyance, a passing facetiousness, others a rather disgruntled refusal to permit her to even recite the virtues of her product, but few seemed to find in the unusual spectacle of a woman salesman, a purposefulness that was enticing, or more than casually to be noted.

To be sure, a steward of a hospital, himself a staff physician, had asked for a kiss in return for a filled-in order blank, but at her refusal had gone through none of the alleged rigmarole of withholding the order, or, for that matter, had scarcely bothered to register disappointment at her refusal. "As you will, sister."

The resident buyer for a local firm of wholesale grocers had pointed a more or less immediate way out of the untoward predicament of a woman engaged in this strange traffic in maple syrup, but had seemed content with her curtness for his pains. After the rather mild and easily rebuffed advance, men occasionally were men, but in the main they had merely been friendly and in some cases where her sex entered at all, it was to the extent of influencing some male to give her an order, where, except for her being a woman, none would have gone.

But the women! The woman superintendent of a hospital brought her to the verge of what was to her, at the time, a most serious money involvement, by throwing back on her hands a very special consignment of maple sugar in the loaf, after the Brattleboro people, who did not handle the product in this form, had gone to considerable pains to obtain it for her.

Time after time, her defeats, her snubs, her humiliations, her failures, were to descend upon her from the women executives of hospital diet kitchens, hotels, and from the women along the Boardwalk who conducted eating establishments, who would have thrown their patronage to the male had the alternative presented itself.

"Miss Bea, honey, you ain't got enough flirtatious ways wid de men and enough 'onery ways wid de wimmin. Make up your mind you kin fool a man and he'll like it, and you cain't fool your own kind and dey doan' like it. Treat 'em both de way de Lawd fashioned 'em, and He sho did allow more fool to a man and more foolin' to a woman——''

How this vast monument of a woman stood behind the flat, prairie-like quality of those days! To open the door to the boom and the roar of her was to stumble into a household warmed by the furnace of Delilah. Her huge smile was the glowing heart of that furnace into which, sore and weary, Bea nightly dragged herself, wanting to be enveloped into the limitless reaches of its warmth.

"Gawd bless mah soul if it ain't mah honey-chile! Clean dead-beat to de bone. Off wid dem dar stockin's. Let Delilah rub up dem white little dead-beat feet. Look what Delilah's got heatin' for her dead-beat honey-chile. Hominy what I found in de market and dat you up heah don't know nothin' 'bout. Doan' you wake up mah babies. All three of 'em sleepin' after de very ole debbil in each and every one of 'em sense you left dis house dis mawnin'. Miss Honey-Bea, what you think that pap of yourn et for supper? Cracklin', honey, may de Lawd strike me dead if he didn't. Cracklin' dat I fed dat little Englishman, between de lips lak he was a little chippie, an' he smaked 'em lak I had fed him an-gel food.''

The untold relief of those warm pale-palmed fingers kneading and soothing and cooling the tortured soles of her feet.

"Miss Honey-Bea, jes' ask me if dem two little bratses didn't get up out of deir washbaskets dis mawnin' on de wrongest side you ever heard of. Crainky ain't jest sayin' it. Did mah white chile quit bawlin' 'til I tote her, mah wash a-boilin', every inch of dis mawnin' in mah arms? Did mah black chile make her maw so spankin' mad she spanked her li'l' backside?''

How cooling to burning shoulder blades, Delilah's fingers kneading as if into dough that under her fingers became fluff.

"Honey-chile, what you think?''

"I can't think, Delilah. It's too delicious just lying here getting rested by you.''

"Honey-chile, your young un gonna sprout a tooth! Two weeks younger dan mah 'onery one, and sproutin' fust!''

The naughty, kindly, and limitless capacity of this Delilah for rubbing in the salve of unctuousness. For weeks, while Bea had been vainly running finger along the stubbornly sterile gums of her child, the offspring of Delilah had been fretting away at two tiny white specks forcing their way like crocuses through the flesh of her little gums.

What a woman! Even her insincerities were so palpably sincere!

"Mah chile doin' all de squallin', and yourn walkin' away wid de teeth. Ain't dat de cussedest, Miss Honey-Bea! Like her pap, all big noise and no big doin's. . . ."

In every matter of precedence, including teeth, was the priority of Bea's child most punctiliously observed. The duet of their howling might bring her running intuitively to her own, but the switch was without hesitancy to the white child, every labor of service adhering rigidly to that order.

But her emulation of everything pertaining to the bit of pale porcelain which contrasted so oddly with her own, was as slavish as her adherence to the rule of precedence.

Within two months after her arrival, drawing upon who knows what mysterious source of scraps, Peola's colorful and fantastic little wardrobe of checks and bright calicos had been replaced by a coarse replica of the sheer and dainty one which had been concocted during the lifetime of Mr. Pullman, by Bea's waiting fingers.

Even in the matter of feeding, Delilah's child, who the first weeks of her life had thrived on a hit-or-miss system of nobody's formulating, now conformed meticulously to Dr. Merribel's carefully devised scheme for the white child.

Over this precedence in teething, Delilah had gone so far as to secretly attempt to ward off Peola's threat of triumph, by boiling up a concoction of frogs' legs in lieu of mole-feet, and standing over its boiling fumes, secretly adapt an incantation she remembered hearing her mother chant against wakeful pickaninnies:

> "Doan' talk—go ter sleep!
> Eyes shet an' doan' you peep!
> Keep still, or he jes' moans,
> 'Raw Head an' Bloody Bones!'"

"Miss Honey-Bea, if you doan' believe me, come right on over to whar your baby chile is sleepin' an' lemme show you de fust liddle debbil-tooth dat has sprouted in dis heah house, and yourn's two weeks young'n mine!''

Oh, Delilah! Darling rogue.

·17·

The idea of the maple-sugar hearts was really Delilah's, although it was Bea who, on the impulse of one of her flashes, sprang out of her bed again one night with the sudden impact of a scheme.

Tireless at humoring Mr. Chipley, Delilah had taken a block of sugar from the consignment which had been so worrisomely rejected by the woman superintendent of a hospital, boiled it down, and by aid of cooky-cutters, produced little heart-shaped lozenges which she stuffed with a cream filling and with which she surrounded Father's dinner plate on Valentine's Eve.

Why not cream-filled maple-sugar hearts, of the very peculiar tang which Delilah somehow achieved in them, done up in pretty boxes for the trade!

Under Delilah's touch, and recipe of her own concocting, they became curiously and teasingly flavored.

The hand which could take an ordinary flank steak, roll and maneuver it into a roast stuffed for a king, or, with scarcely more than a dash of milk, sugar, and butter, fluff up muffins that rose out of their pan the shape and magnificence of the chef's crown which Delilah wore on her head during these operations, wrought perfection in the making of these hearts.

Why not? The consignment of sugar dumped back on her hands just at a time when the Tannehills were beginning to fall heavily back in their rent had been a budget tragedy of terrible concern.

To one whose margin of profit was something to be fearfully worked out each night on the backs of envelopes and oftentimes while riding home in street cars at the end of a long canvassing day, the very sight of those boxes of rejected maple sugar, standing in a pile beneath the hall staircase, was to invoke memories of tragedy.

One pound of the maple-sugar hearts, in the white glazed paper boxes that would dress them up so, if her guess as to the cost of these boxes was anywhere near right, counting lace and waxed paper, and cord (gilt), could be sold, at profit, for twenty cents more than the actual cost of the sugar. At least there would be little to lose in using up the consignment on that experiment.

Perhaps the Candy Corner on the Boardwalk would display a few boxes on a commission basis. Delilah's Hearts! Why not Delilah's photograph, in her great fluted white cap, and her great fluted white smile on each box? Delilah, who, though actually in no more than her late thirties, looked mammy to the world. . . . Delilah beaming and beckoning from the lid. . . .

Well, no use crossing those elaborate bridges until they were reached. Photographs cost! But the hearts, in plain white glazed boxes, were another matter. Twenty to start with, or perhaps forty-eight . . . if only, right from the start, the boxes could be enhanced by the novel addition of the black photograph of Delilah against the white!

Why not Tannehill! Tannehill would take a photograph of Delilah. Genial and amenable at best, the matter of the arrears on his rent would make him more than ordinarily so. He had taken some of Bea the month previous. Cabinet photographs showing her shoulders and bodice with its high collar and Irish-lace jabot, her head turned slightly to reveal an ear and the hair rising away from it to its wide pompadour. Also some of her naked child, swimming on its adorable stomach, through a fur rug.

Occasional photographs such as these would be records. . . .

Would Delilah, ridden as she was with lore, superstition, and taboo, trump up some reason identified with the light of the full moon, the shank bone of a mule, or the rabbit's foot she kept dangling from the side of her child's crib, why she should not pose before the camera? There seemed no limit to the extraneous influences, tides, hog teeth, buzzard feathers, china-berries, red heads, black cats, spilled salt, white horses, voodoo, which could determine or prohibit her slightest action.

"Never bathe a baby wid your back to de window. Hop-toads'll jump in de water and wart up your chile something terrible."

"Step on de forepaw of a northbound black cat, and misery'll git you sho as heaven."

"Sweep de baby's feet wid broom sedge every mawnin', or he jes' won't grow."

"Pulled teeth should be put away in a stockin'. If a dog should walk on one, de chile will have a dog's tooth in its place, sho as heaven."

From her cot in the reception-hall, where she lay beside a festooned washbasket containing Peola, came the heavy sleeping noises of Delilah, roaring through the silence.

No use, out of her consuming impatience to get started on this project, to try and awaken her. Once her head struck pillow, nothing short of the cry of one of three babies could tear Delilah from the thicket of sleep which closed around her.

Besides, why? There was nothing about the idea of the forty-eight boxes of candy hearts, flavored so slyly, to be done up in white glazed boxes, splashed with a photograph of Delilah, and tied with gold cord, that would not keep until morning. But just the same, until then, with an envelope propped against the Welsbach to shield the light from possibly scratching against the lids of her sleeping child, she virtually waited through the night for Delilah to awaken, sitting beside the window, scribbling on the backs of envelopes, adding, subtracting, looking out and looking out upon a backyard scene of jet-black woodshed, jet-black plane tree and the miracle of a full moon not succeeding in white-washing them.

The matter of the photograph was managed, after all. Mr. Tannehill took it one Sunday morning in the side yard, with Delilah as fluted and as irate as a duchess.

"This heah ain't no rig for to have your picture taken in. Maybe you doan' believe it, Miss Honey-Bea, but I's forgot moh about style dan de niggahs in dis heah jay-walkin' town ever knowed. Please, Miss Bea, honey, ain't you gonna let me wear mah hat dat ole Mrs. Wynkoop down in Richmon' give me for to git mahself married in? I want to keep record for mah chile of how her mammy looked——"

The photograph of Delilah, however, turned out to be one of those rare accomplishments of a face choosing the moment of the clicking of the camera to illuminate and reveal. Breaking through a white background, as through a paper-covered hoop, there burst the chocolate-and-cream effulgence that was Delilah. The heavy cheeks, shellacked eyes, bright, round, and crammed with vitality, huge upholstery of lips that caught you like a pair of divans into the luxury of laughter, Delilah to the life beamed out of that photograph with sun power!

It took three weeks to succeed in placing, on commission basis, the first forty-eight boxes. Twelve at Connie's Candy Counter. Twelve in the lobby of the Pierrepont Hotel. Twelve in Cuskaden's Drug Store. Twelve in the Atlantic City Novelty Shop.

Four weeks after that, to the day, came the first two reorders. One for five boxes from the Candy Corner. The other for twelve, from the Pierrepont. Reorders which became the occasion of the first trip to Philadelphia in two years.

There was not a copper kettle adequate for candy-making, on even a semi-professional scale, to be found in all Atlantic City. Besides, it began to seem desirable to set about ordering the white one- and two-pound boxes, with the effulgence of Delilah bursting through the cover, in considerably larger numbers.

Neighbors began to complain benignly that the smells emanating from the small dun-colored frame house made their mouths water. Bill Vizitelli, after school hours, covered the dirt floor of the woodshed with pine boards upon which were mounted two new copper kettles. The larger new consignment of candy-boxes, of outlandish bulk and no weight, crowded up the space under the stairs in the reception-hall. The business of sorting lace-paper mats began to be something which Father could manage from his wheel-chair.

A little timorously, to the impetus of the first two or three reorders, then a couple more, and still a couple more, and Delilah's Hearts were on the market.

·18·

After the Tannehills went, walked out, virtually, owing the last six weeks and leaving behind a trail of solicitors and collectors who dogged the house for months after, it seemed logical to once more attempt to rent that upper floor.

Except for Delilah.

"Miss Bea, honey, I cain't have mah cookin'-floor all cluttered up wid mah three babies. Me and mah hearts need privacy. De Lawd needed privacy dem days befoh creation or He couldn't have thought it all out de way He did. Jes' look how He reckoned Sunday following Monday and all. My hearts'll make up dat dar rent money, honey, if you give me peace and quiet to make 'em in."

Up to date, the reorders had been real enough, continuing and increasing. Thanks to the genial offices of a Mr. Marks, one of the late Mr. Pullman's colleagues at the pickle-and-relish pier, the Belvedere Hotel in Philadelphia had taken a dozen one-pound boxes on consignment and reordered, but the margin of profit continued to baffle and elude. Somewhere in that strange interlude between each finished pound there occurred the discrepancy between profits on paper and actual results. Discounts, spoilage, exigencies, such as the two dozen boxes which she herself, aided by little Bill Vizitelli, had delivered to the Royal Palace Hotel, only to have them topple over, as they were being carried by a bellhop, into a vat of boiling water. Not her fault, but, to save the terrified lad dismissal, a loss which managed to keep her calculations on the debit side.

Each evening, after a usual session of attempted entertainment of her Father, who could be so irate with her, and after moments with her child, whose bedtime usually overlapped her return, the figuring, once

89

her household was in bed, began. The profit, gross, of each pound box of candy, multiplied by the number of boxes sold. From this total, deduction of daily expenses. Result, almost invariably, a minus quality that sent her to restless bed, tortured with the need and yet the inability to provide the necessities of that household.

There were three babies, two of them beginning to crawl, and one of them practically having ceased to move, for whom nourishing food had to be provided with militaristic regime. Herself and Delilah might make gratefully out, for four or five consecutive meals, on one of the stuffed flank-steak roasts that Delilah could maneuver out of almost any old cut of beef, and wonders could be accomplished by that black crocodile-like hand in providing dishes that were not only tasty, but toothsome, out of anything from barley to tapioca. But milk and cream and white meat of chicken and dainties for the exacting palate of a paralytic who could not feel a pin stuck into his flesh, but whose palate could recoil from the slightest flavor not felicitous to it, were imperative.

The creature-lives, for which incredibly she was suddenly and solely responsible, of five human beings had to go on; had to proceed and thrive on profits squeezed from her manipulations of a not highly important food product known as maple sugar.

It was strange that so casual a commodity to human needs as the sugar could suddenly have become the centrifugal force of her universe.

It mattered to her with an intensity which, while it was privately embarrassing to herself, must in some measure have helped produce the ultimate results, just what decision took place in a steward's or housewife's mind concerning maple sugar. Often, waiting for that decision, her finger nails sank deeply into her palms to the rhythm of a quickly reiterated prayer which ran under her silence: "Please, God, make him. Make him order. Make him. Make him."

There had once been a girl in high school, quite a beauty, named Erna Ponscarme, who had been able to desire the immediate thing in that passionate sort of way. Almost invariably unprepared when called upon in class, she had the habit of clutching violently at the arm of her nearest classmate and hissing under her hot breath: "Tell me. What is the answer? Tell me. Please! Please!" Almost immediately following graduation, Erna, daughter of a chef in one of the larger Boardwalk hotels, had married the proprietor and now occupied a suite in the same hostelry where her parent, once of the kitchen, was now maître d'hôtel.

Apparently, there was something to wanting as passionately as did Erna. It had kept her a sort of laughing-stock with her classmates, but in the end it had got her there. Graduation with honorable mention and subsequently the most spectacular marriage of any girl in the class.

Perhaps the laugh was now on the girls who had lacked Erna's impolite gumption.

Digging her nails into her palms, prayerful under her silence, time and time again, something about the spectacle of herself reminded her of the terribly eager Erna, pinching her classmates as she hissed: "Tell me. Please! Please! Martin Luther's dates."

Wanting passionately had got Erna there, all right. On the other hand, Bea's was not a matter so much of wanting passionately as needing passionately. Mouths to be fed.

There was something that got at her emotions about the spectacle of her child, pulling with remarkably strong lips at the nipple of a bottle which contained the good and proper nourishment of her own providing. Different emotions, perhaps, than she had stored up in her anticipation.

Motherhood had turned out not to be a matter of nursery prettiness, adorable pastimes over a layette, hours beside a perambulator on a sunlit beach, or retailing baby anecdotes to Mr. Pullman.

There had been so little time for anything more than a hurried realization that here was a mouth whose first quiver and howl had shaken the world with imperious demand to be fed.

The fact that it had mattered, that call, more than anything else had ever mattered before, must, in some ways, she felt sure, be part of the compensations of motherhood which she had been taught to expect would be hers.

But up to now there had been so little time for self-analysis. It was unceasingly wonderful that the little creature was beautiful and whole. All there. Proper assortment of twenty fingers and toes. Pink ones! Yellow down for hair. Small pink zero of a mouth that had to be kept wiped. Oh, one had moments, of course. Such as when the doll-like creature, starched and white, was placed in her arms by Delilah. Or when she found she could hush small cries emanating from the enlarging zero, by pressing these cries, that seemed strangely hers, into her breast, or when she beheld her own, riding in the huge crotch of Delilah's elbow, opposite the pale and black bit of fierceness that was Peola.

But more usually, the twenty-six inches of life for which she was so suddenly responsible was something, along with a myriad of other concerns, about which to dash through the days, engaged in what was becoming the more and more engrossing occupation of livelihood.

Some day, she told herself upon these occasions when the pangs of the not realized sense of her maternity were upon her, there will be time for the old dreams of hours in a nursery; beside a child on a beach; or on the veranda of a yet-to-be-realized cottage in Ventnor; doing the fine head-tuckings and engaging in the lovely pastimes of sewing for her young. Hours that were not to come.

But the quaint dream of them, from a girlhood that was already taking on some of the contours of having itself been quaint, was what impelled her, finally, to risk not attempting to once more rent the second story of the house on Arctic Avenue.

Thus the little nursery up there would come into its own, to be shared, during this period of sublime democracy of childhood, with the dark child, who, except for the contrast of the whiteness of Jessie, might have passed for white herself. Father could be comfortably manipulated upstairs to a room of his own, there to sleep with his open door facing her own open one, leaving Delilah a free hand on her kitchen floor.

In spite of the stubborn persistence of the minus results on the backs of envelopes, the list of maple syrup reorders was half again its original length and Delilah's Hearts were moving.

It was worth taking the risk, at any rate for a month or two.

It required her nerve, all of it. But sleeping upstairs again in what had once been her marriage bed, with the remainder of her household normally quartered and grouped around her, was a blessed reinstatement which must somehow be made permanent.

That was the summer, one of flaying heat and unprecedented prosperity for the resort town, that the pattern ran something like this: eight hours of day-by-day, door-to-door canvassing that covered three out of Atlantic City's four wards as well as Ventnor and Longport. Weekly and often bi-weekly tours of the Boardwalk hotels. Evenings devoted to delivering, sometimes with the aid of Bill Vizitelli, the heavy bulk of candies and syrups which had been assembled, ticketed, and wrapped by Delilah.

The twine-bites from these luggings were to remain across the insides of her fingers, irradicable evidence to months and miles of carting through the streets of a city that, even in its byways, put up the bold, raucous, penny-whistle front of carnival. Scarcely a lodging-house or cheap hotel but poured its kitchen odors upon her as she passed or sought out trade entrances. Stench from fish-frys, shore dinners, hamburger-wagons, of bathing-suits as they dried over porch railings, roasting peanuts, sour alleys and streets where the poor, in a dreadful kind of finery, aped the Boardwalk, seeped into her clothing on those days when her route carried her away from the translucent, spangled air of the ocean front, into back streets, to such an extent that Delilah, waiting to peel the shoes and stockings off her tingling feet and the wilted clothing off her shoulders, would sniff with her great flaring nostrils.

"Fish in dis jacket. Weinies in dis waist. Clam chowder in your hair. Been back-streetin' today. I kin tell de smell of a white-trash fish-fry wid mah both eyes shut. Better not go near mah old gemmeman wid chowder on your hair. Dat ole man's got fas-tidousness."

But even if much of that summer stank of fetid back doors and the glare of the long tramping days was like sheet tin before her eyes, and her corsets at night, when she removed them, were streaked with rust from her constantly perspiring body, there were compensations.

Except for a temporarily disastrous tendency of Delilah's Hearts to melt and glue together under mounting temperature, a difficulty quickly overcome by waxed paper cups, the candy, there for a time during the peak of the summer season, did nip and tuck with the syrup orders, multiplying until Delilah took it upon herself to engage, at twenty-five cents a week, the services of small black Jake, aged nine, who came in after school hours to assist in everything from scraping copper pots to wheeling an irate old gentleman who, to the youngster's

93

strange delight, struck out angrily with his cane at whatever did not please him.

And how much did not please him! The slant of sun, the angle of his chair, his rug, the sweetness or lack of it of his lemonade, the falsetto howling of Peola, the temporary absence of Delilah in the kitchen at her ironing, the lateness of Bea, the earliness of his bath, the warmth of his coffee, the chill of his milk.

"Ole gemmeman, dar's a debbil sitting down dar inside your fastidousness, dat de Lawd has got to pluck out wid a pair of tweezers if He's gwine to let you into heaven. If you doan' quit dat bangin' around wid dat doggone cane of yours, sho as black cats has stick-up tails, 'Lila's gonna spank.''

And in just the proportion that her day-long mouthings, effusions, invocations, incantations, and threats mounted, did her indulgences mount with them.

"I'm gonna spank mah bad ole gemmeman if he doan' quit his pesterin', sho as dar's wool on mah head," was her king of acquiescence to heating his milk, cooling his coffee, changing his coverlets, to his slightest whim. "Ain't dat de cussedest, dough. Three times me a-heatin' dis coffee lak dat's all I had in dis world to do. Lemme drop a little piece of ice in it, honey; maybe dat's what you're wantin'. If you touch Delilah wid dat dar doggone cane of yours, she's gonna break it spankin' you. 'Onery, dat's what you is, pore ole Delilah's big baby.''

On and on, hours of it, days of it, months of it. "Declare to goodness Miss Honey-Bea, wonder dat ole pap of yourn ain't druve me clean crazy."

Nor was that anything near the wonder of this woman, whose laughter shook the days, as the trains which rattled by the corner of Georgia Avenue shook the house.

"Gimme one belly-laugh and three meals of belly-warmin' vittals and one belly-prayer a day, an' I kin keep misery outside mah door, like it was a cat."

Yes, even to that glaring circus of a summer, when Bea used to crisscross the soles of her feet with adhesive to keep out the burn, were the compensations of Delilah and of late walks home along the Boardwalk, when swept of crowds, lights, wheel-chairs and venders, the sky, bending like the bowl of a spoon, seemed to scoop ocean landward in lovely soft hisses at her feet.

During such walks the mind cleared, revived, and bristled. Tomorrow became something more than just a blur across eyes that smarted even behind dark-blue sun glasses. Tomorrow became a deck, cleared for plans which came tumbling across it like spirited acrobats. Hurting twine-bitten hands and adhesive-bound feet took flight from the body which dragged them all day. The dome of heaven, salted with stars, seemed anything but its hard, daylit self.

Tomorrow, during such walks as these late homeward ones, became a theater of the kind of success that lay most immediately in her vision. Leisure to be with her child. A modest little rubber-tired trap or solicitor's buggy, in which she could drive about town on her canvassing tours. A cottage in Ventnor. Life insurance. A nest egg against her child's education. Helpers for Delilah. Larger wage for Delilah. Gadgets for her Father. Fine linen for her child. More income and more leisure.

They would mean hours in the nursery. Afternoons on the beach or on a Ventnor veranda, sewing for a child who romped as she stitched. Father in the very last word in wheel-chairs, sunning himself. Evenings of sewing tucks into the prettiest little-girl dresses in Atlantic City. . . .

For the moment life might be a matter of maple sugar, but it must not remain that. It needn't. It wouldn't. Maple sugar must be made to yield the belated reality of a home worthy of Mr. Pullman's widow and child.

A more or less assured market, say for fifty pounds a week of Delilah's Hearts and as many gallons of syrup, might, if contemplated during a leg-hurting day of high mileage and low sales, seem dishearteningly remote, but dreams came out brightly during nocturnal walks, especially at that shank of the evening when there was still plenty of evidence of human life about.

As the big hotels began to appear and the shops and the lights and the crowds and the magic of Sousa's brass band, or Creatore's, came crashing through the throng of visitors, such success as she craved seemed not only real, but within easy grasp.

95

In a world wanting so passionately to play, there was place for Delilah's Hearts. These big, good-humored salesmen with black cigars and Panama hats and stout wives; the rows of roller-chairs filled with self-indulgent-looking women and indulgent men; the brilliantly lit façades of shops, piers, and hotels, candy-and-amusement emporiums; the streamers of music flung like colored moiré ribbons across the scene; the sea applauding and booming; the smell of popcorn, taffy, roasting coffee, sea salt, festive women—gave sense of demand and supply.

It appeared so simple, trotting along invigorated, in her big hat, wide sleeves, and Spanish-flounced skirt whose brush-braid just cleared the walk. The dream of twenty dollars a week seemed, God willing to spare her health, something actually within easy attainability.

It was at times like these that the widow of B. Pullman bared her teeth while walking, in the grimace of intense desire.

·19·

Mr. Chipley had become wizened and incased in a tough skin that fitted him like a suit, several times too large, of loose old crocodile leather.

" 'Clare to goodness if de biggest baby in dis house ain't turnin' into his 'Lilah's ole alligator. Put dat arm into dis heah coat, or sho as mah name is Jack Robinson, Delilah's gonna spank. Lawd A'mighty! did I ever see anything like mah ole gemmeman, turnin' jes' as fast as he can into hide for somebody's valise."

One day, even the children, fascinated by the roomy old domino of skin, were discovered in the covert act of sticking pins into the loose wattles about the wrists, Mr. Chipley partner to their hilarity at his imperviousness.

Into the morbid silence, with the splashed fury of a hurled tomato, there burst the descent of Delilah. "Who's dat makin' all dis heah stillness? What you three young uns doin'? For de love of Gawd Almighty! stickin' pins in mah chair-baby! De Lawd bear witness. De Lawd shine down. It's a miracle de like of walkin' de Red Sea or may mah eyes bug out. Mah chair-baby's above feelin' de stick of pins! Angel skin is on him. But angel skin or no angel skin, Delilah's gwine to lam' down on dese bratses for a-stickin' him. Gimme dat white ear, Jessie, for to twist. Gimme dat yaller ear, Peola, for to twist. Stop pushin', Peola. You cain't git your ear twisted befoh white chile has had her'n.

"Jes' you two bad ones wait'll somebody comes home dis evenin' dead-beat and needin' rest and two liddle good angels. What's she gonna get? Two liddle debbils what stick pins in folks. Two liddle mean oneses to make her suffer moh when she's so dead-beat from earnin' 'em bread and milk and salt-water-taffy dat her laigs won't carry her no moh.

97

Gawd's going to put it all down in His pearl-and-lace book, every single one of your meannesses.''

Extraordinary the consistency of reaction to this thread-bare threat. The stoic little mouth of Peola hardening against tears; the fluted ripple of Jessie's lips wanting to widen into the orifice of a howl, but settling, with what grimness it could muster, into something resembling the hard little heartbreak of Peola's.

The proportion of occasions upon which Delilah carried out these threats to retail to the pale-faced tired young woman who came hurrying home, almost invariably after dark, bundle laden, was shrewdly sufficiently large to occasion apprehension and despair.

"My mamma won't care! My mamma likes for me to stick pins in Grampa.''

"My missy won't care. My missy likes for me to stick pins in Jessie's grampa.''

From her very infancy, Peola, quick as any child to ape, was nevertheless careful to avoid replica of her parent's diction. Where it did make way into her speech, it crept there from Jessie, whose drawling idiosyncrasies were to play an important rôle in her mother's ultimate decision in favor of boarding-school.

"Your missy likes for you to stick pins in Jessie's gramp,'' mimicked Delilah. "If I couldn't smack dat chile, Peola, right dis minute befoh her missy comes home. If dat ain't de low-downdest. I'm a-tellin' you de Lawd will come right down here on Arctic Avenue after you two if He finds a single pin in de ole gemmeman when He gits him up to heaven. 'Mamma likes for me to stick pins in Gramp!' Jes' you wait and see when your blessed mammy, her feet burnin' her like hell's asphalt, comes home tonight. Peola, come here and get yourself smacked!''

This was one of the occasions when Delilah saw fit to make good her threat, standing foursquare against the appalled retreat of the two young miscreants, who measured, respectively, the identical heights of three feet and one inch.

"... Sure as Moses writ de laws on marble stationery, Miss Bea! Me out in de kitchen in a big batch of Hearts and what does I hear? Nothin' is what I hears so loud it would crack your ears. I says to mahself, I says, dis here house is too filled wid de sound of nothin' to mean any good. I tiptoes, an' what does dis pair of eyes give me by de Lawd see? Something He never ameant me to see wid 'em. Two of God's chillun, Miss Bea, wid faces lak angels and souls lak tar, a-stickin' pins into mah ole gemmeman lak he was a mule's tail.''

There they stood, the two of them, before the enormous tower of Delilah, to whom they measured knee-high and less, as they drooped with chastisement. The small brightly gold Jessie, the small straight-mouthed Peola, whose pallor, the color of a pealed banana, lay over slim Caucasian features, coined out of heredity knows where.

There was a deep damp rim across Bea's brow, due to her hat pressing down all day. The sockets of her arms, from last night's lugging after dark, felt exactly their shapes.

The Moses Frank Hospital in Ventnor had a new dietitian who had struck maple-sugar products off its list. Her erstwhile schoolmate, Erna Ponscarme Sperwick, who had married the proprietor of the Boardwalk Hotel, who in turn was one of her best customers, had made a request which, coming from her, amounted actually to command, for a maple-sugar booth at an impending church fair.

Oh, how one needed to arrive home to that grateful moment of slumping into bed, drawing covers up around a body singing and sting-ing of fatigue, and drift off into the all too brief hours of immunity from the sense of peril to herself and hers, at every turn of the day.

And now here, as if to add to her sense of alienation from a household into which she longed to remain riveted like a fungus to its walls, were two children standing huddled away from her and into the very shadow that was betraying them. Jealousy of Delilah smote her, dying instantly, as it always did, of self-loathing.

The lightning intuition of Delilah, who was a lyre responding to the lightest breath of an emotion in Bea!

''. . . doan' stan' heah, you two, hanging on to 'Lilah, a-pretendin' youse don't want to fly those arms aroun' Miss Honey-Bea's neck. Declare to de Lawd you won't believe me, Miss Honey-Bea. Dese two liddle house-debbils been stickin' pins in mah ole gemmeman for to see him not hurt. Lawd strike me dead, Miss Bea, if dey wasn't.''

Dr. Merribel repeatedly had run a needle along the surface of Father's flesh, pricking into it now and then for symptoms of response or lack of it. The children, playing about, had doubtless observed that. In spite of herself, a grim kind of laughter shook her inwardly.

"No, no, Delilah. You don't mean our Jessie and our Peola. You must have them mixed up with some other dreadful little girls."

"I mean ourn. Look at 'em! Steeped in sin before their Lawd who has give 'em nothin' but love. Dat liddle yaller-headed one of yourn is no innocenter than mah black one, only mine might as well begin learnin' herself now, that what's jes' naughty for a white chile, can be downright ag'in' de law if a black one does it. 'Tain't no use mah chile tryin' to get herself raised on de idea all men is equal. Maybe dey is in de eyes of de Lawd, but it's de eyes of man I's talkin 'bout. Law! jes' to look at my Peola. Makes mah palm itch for to give it to her standin' up, whar de Lawd made it for her to sit down."

"Jessie, come here to Mother."

"No, no, no-no-no."

"Go to your maw, white chile!"

"Come here, Jessie."

"Go 'long, honey. Your maw won't lambast. Her'll jes' be sorry. Go 'long. Dat ain't no way for mah white li'l' pear blossom to treat her maw when her comes home dead-beat from work."

It wasn't, and Bea could feel the tears press against her tonsils and pangs of something bitter and hurting at the sight of the small tight fingers of her child curling around the horny ones of Delilah.

"Come to me, Jessie. Why did you stick pins into Grandfather? Don't you and Peola know that is a cruel sin? Come to me and tell me about it."

What a darling, straight, defiant little stick she was, to stand off there in the shadow of the bulwark of Delilah, her fluty mouth held straight and cold.

"I'm sorry, Miss Bea, even if Jessie won't be."

"Peola, will you stop bein' sorry before Jessie is sorry? Ain't you got no way of keepin' yourself in your place?"

"I know you're sorry, Peola, only I don't want you to be sorry before Jessie is sorry, because she probably put you up to it."

"Put her up nothin'. Nobody can put mah chile up to a meanness she ain't thought of fust."

"I did put her up to it."

"Well, you don't need to go cuttin' off your own haid before your own maw."

"You cruel little girl!"

"Oh, no'm, now, Miss Bea, her ain't cr——"

"Delilah, keep out of this. Jessie, come here."

"I won't."

"Jessie."

"I sticked pins, Miss Missy."

"Peola, hush. Jessie, come here."

"Won't."

Here was the decisive stuff, in this tiny crisis, which was to establish the basis of her relationship with the small gilt spar of a twenty-eight-inch girl standing so defiantly before her. Mothers with their wits about them realized that on such moments as this could pivot the delicate mechanism of status between themselves and their children. Jessie, a wild, elusive little bird where her mother was concerned, who flew out from under her caresses, who danced lightly away from her advances, must be captured, held, disciplined.

"Did you hear what I said?" There now, that tone would jerk this bit of porcelain, so strangely, so beautifully hers, to discipline.

"Yes."

"Then come."

"Won't."

"You cruel little girl, must I force you?" How could she have said that? She was her dear darling of a straight little jonquil, so sunlit, far too incredibly covered with sheen and the strange frivolity of beauty ever to have sprung from so staid a union as her own with Mr. Pullman. She was something bright and elusive as a hummingbird, that had to be captured in a tender gesture too quick for it.

Bea had never succeeded in that gesture. The spectacle of her child lingering away from her in the vast shade of Delilah was the cruel result of the necessity of too often leaving the house early mornings before the lids flew back from those very blue eyes and returning to it long after the child slept. Jessie, holding shyly away from her. Jessie, bright and wary-eyed as a robin, peering at her from behind the starchy barricade of Delilah's apron. Jessie standing stiff, as now, her fluty mouth held straight. Oh, you could not be hard on a child so placed that Mother was more of a boarder than even the average

father who left his home daily, returning late. What could she know?—
Still, regardless, here was one of those situations that had to be gone
through with.

"Why did you hurt Grandpa?"

"It never hurted."

"It might have."

"But it didn't."

"Well, if it didn't hurt Grandpa, it's hurting me. Hurting me
just terribly. Just as you standing there disobeying me is—hurting
me——"

To her own amazement, with every word she felt her voice slipping
upward into tears. A small explosion of them came down, wetting her
tiredness. She, who so seldom cried, was standing there quite foolishly,
hat toward the back of her head as she was accustomed to wearing it
from too weary a sense of it clamping her brow all day, bundles slipping
unheeded from her hands and the taste of dust along her lips.

"Gawd Almighty, mah Honey-Bea missy's cryin'!"

She was. Just standing there as she put it to herself, bawling, through
misery of the sudden impact of sense of impotency that was overtaking
her before the three feet of tight-lipped, blond aloofness, facing her
from the background of Delilah's apron.

What was the use? The struggling to keep together body and soul
and the small institution of this home, in which except for the blessed
expansiveness of Delilah, she mattered little, if at all.

Why, it was not even unusual, when she came home, to have Father
crouch sullenly in his chair away from her kiss, or bestowal of small
gifts of lollypops, spats, violet-colored liquor, or tiny bottle of a drug-
store perfume.

It didn't mean a thing, this turning away from those best beloved.
In fact, it was often characteristic of atrophying minds, Dr. Merribel
had again and again assured her. Father, quick to the extent of unre-
strained anger if she erred in her calculations respecting his wishes by
so much as the fraction of an inch regarding the position of his chair,
his cravat, his medicine-dropper, and who could really be quite night-
marish with her, must not be held responsible.

Impotence in this household seemed to reside chiefly in its reigning spirit, who left it each morning before father or child were awake, and returned evenings to find a pair of sleepy hostile strangers who needed to be wheedled.

It was terrible to stand there crying, like a child before the calamity of broken dishes, and the ridiculous part of it was that she could not stop either distorting her face or tasting the salted dust, or keep her hat from sliding backward, dangling ridiculously by the pin and hurting.

But even before Delilah, to whom life was largely a wail to which she must fly in order to administer, could reach her side, this bright miracle happened—straight as a dart to her there flew Jessie, wanting and needing to be held.

· 20 ·

Mingling with a certain consternation at the prospect of the maple-sugar booth which the former Erna Ponscarme had asked her to contribute to the First Church Fair, to be held on the Steel Pier, was something akin to gratification.

Aside from her business obligation to conform with this request, coming as it did from the wife of one of her first and staunchest customers, something of a first awareness of herself as enough of a local entity to be reckoned with in the community stirred within her. Participation in this event, under the auspices of this particular church and this particular occasion, stamped her growing repute. The implication moved her pleasantly.

A gesture of civic coöperation was expected of B. Pullman, business man.

The way to whet Delilah into a lather of enthusiasm was by way of the tried and true device of simulating opposition.

"I am simply going to explain to Mrs. Sperwick, Delilah, that much as I would like to have a booth, I cannot afford either the time or the money, although, of course, the church will pay the expenses of the carpentry and buntings. Besides, it is too much work for you."

"Lissen to dat chile talk! Jes' lak folks was invited every day to show off on de Steel Pier. Why cain't you afford it? You talk lak you ain't got no 'Lilah to help you manage."

"Yes, but——"

"Dar ain't gonna be no holdin' back from dis here corporation. Servin' de Lawd on high and advertisin' your wares on de Boardwalk is killin' two birds at one shot. May de Lawd Almighty, who I love, forgive me for what I jes' said, not a-meanin' thataway. De Lawd is no bird except a great white heavenly host bigger'n any white horse you ever seed, but de Lawd don't wear His wings showin' lak de angels does.''

"It is well and good for you to insist, but how will we manage, Delilah? Somebody will have to preside at the booth and I can't take two days off.''

"Somebody's a-goin' to preside at dat booth if I has to do de presidin' myself, an' de Lawd is going to be praised and our business is goin' to git itself advertised and like it.''

"But, Delilah——''

"Ought to see, honey, how de kids call after me when I rolls out mah baby. Dar goes 'Lilah. I's a walkin' trade-mark. Candy-box 'Lilah. Dem kids know me already from the candy-box—if it ain't a shame de way you made me get mah picture took for it, widout a-dressin' me up.''

It was stuff out of that remark which sent Bea out of bed to her feet at three o'clock of the morning following this encounter, with the full-grown conception of a plan seeming to spring from her sleep.

Why not Delilah, in her shining fluted cap, which no amount of indoor drudgery could seem to wilt, presiding over waffles and maple syrup at the booth?

The ladies would enjoy her fluffy, delicately turned waffles, as only Delilah could turn them. The ladies, and their husbands, too!

To the tune of this rag-and-bone of a phrase, "If I has to do the presiding myself. . . . I's a walkin' trade-mark,'' was born of *papier maché*, beaver boards, fifteen yards of yellow crêpe tissue paper, four small square tables, a waffle iron, and a glass counter for containing candy-boxes, the first B. Pullman.

B. Pullman's waffle-booth. Or just B. Pullman. Waffles. Why not a Pullman car? That would be cute! A little booth rigged up like a Pullman to match the accident of name. Not exactly a Pullman. You didn't eat in Pullmans. Rig it up like a dining-car! There were always brilliantly polished dining-car windows revealing snowy napery, shining silverware, and white-coated, white-eye-balled rows of dark-skinned waiters, flashing by the corner of Mississippi and Arctic Avenues as the Philadelphia and Reading trains sped their noses up to the very flank of the Boardwalk.

She had eaten in one once, when her father had managed to get them free seats on a special delegation train to Philadelphia. "They certainly don't know how to fry ham,'' he had complained, making a finicky mouth as he turned his over with his fork. But to Bea, with the scenery flying past and the white napery so heavy and glossy, it had seemed the best food she had ever tasted. And that trip to Pittsburgh when the sale's staff and families had attended the convention of employees of the pickle-and-relish firm. To find yourself seated beside the wide flashing window of a dining-car, unfolding stiffly white napery, jotting down, because your eyes were better than Mother's or Father's, the order for food that by virtue of the movement, sense of journeying, smell of leather luggage, train smoke and propinquity of kitchen, seemed flavored with romance!

Delilah in her fluted cap, cooking waffles at one end of a little booth designed after the interior of one of those dining-cars that you associated with Pullman Service! Why not!

Would Delilah? How soundly she slept, her huge body shaped like a cave around the form of Peola. Alert to the faintest cry of a child or sound from Mr. Chipley, a dining-car itself might have thundered through her bedroom without awakening her. How soundly the entire household slept, just as if, full-grown into the night, had not sprung this B. Pullman idea, wanting to be set into motion.

Who is this B. Pullman? she would start them asking. Mighty clever little idea of his. B. Pullman. Any relation to the railroad Pullman? Well, anyway, mighty clever idea. Snappiest booth in the place. That mammy certainly can juggle waffles. Guess I'll take some of those Hearts back home to the wife. Put your card in there, Mammy, so we can reorder on them, if they are as good as your waffles and syrup.

Oh, and why not darling little souvenir paper fans, like they gave away at the Steel Pier, with Delilah's picture!

If Delilah would only stir out of the deep draught of sleep which caused her breathing to whistle against her teeth and periodic groans of her complete abandonment to emanate.

—perhaps painted panels of some sort could be trumped up to be hung against the windows to simulate scenery—and copies of the little lighted lamps on each table that made the dining-cars glow so as they rushed along Georgia and Mississippi Avenues.

Impossible to return to sleep in a night that had thus been punctured with an impulse which had brought her awake tingling.

Outside, an evening the color of watered milk flowed over and seemed to immerse Arctic Avenue in bluish pallor. A wavy moon lit the car tracks along which the last "Owl" had passed. That strange pungent Atlantic City smell, from off a scene still hard at roasting its popcorn, chewing its taffy, pressing its sea-damp lips together, relaxing body-deep in sands, frying its fish, lying full stretched on white beach under the watery moon, undressing in hotel rooms, scuttling down side streets to brothels, lolling on spacious ocean-front verandas, under enchantment, sweating in mean rooms over saloons, rolled down the side streets and against the nostrils.

Standing at her open window, with the cool June air lashing her nightgown softly against her body, Bea could sniff it, taste it, feel it.

Even tied up in the cheap tinsel of beach love-making and Atlantic City brand of romance, the something that she had missed was going on out there. She knew that now, with the orderly memory of Mr. Pullman stored away in her mind in an orderly kind of grief.

Contact with the business world, in which, strangely enough, her sex seemed to have played no part, had taught her that. Something had passed her by, all right, without leaving her the leisure to more than fleetingly comprehend it.

There had been a girl, late one evening, as she was returning from deliveries, standing on the corner of Georgia Avenue and the Boardwalk, crying, and looking up at a youth in a checked cap who had slapped her face and walked off.

The stream of that girl's tears rose in wild, mountainous, grand places of the heart of which she, Bea, knew little, if anything! Something stale in the flavor of her entire life, and hitherto unsuspected, became for the moment suddenly uppermost, almost immediately passing out again into the limbo of her unawareness.

A man in the office of a fancy-grocery concern, where she had been soliciting a maple-syrup order, had picked up the receiver of a ringing telephone and said, "Hello, sweetheart," in a manner that gave her the strangest nostalgia for something she had never known.

Atlantic City, smelling of carnival and free-for-all love, did that, too, but so fleetingly that scarcely the wing of her desire brushed her consciousness.

Activity was the lid to the jack-in-the-box of a heart that hurt of some sort of deficiency; activities that flowed across the surface of her days, making maple sugar matter. Even now, remaining inert within four walls, after she had been awakened by a plan that pressed to be put into execution, irked too much for endurance.

A cape she had worn during the days of the coming of Jessie, thrown hastily on over a skirt adjusted on top of her nightgown, was scarcely attire to make a midnight stroll on the sands seem invitational or indecorous.

It would be easier waiting for the break of day, out there along the sand front of a carnival city that did not want to go to bed. The mind worried so at the little idea of the booth. The napery must be the snow white of Delilah's inimitable laundry-work. Her own Delft blue-and-white salad plates—there were eleven—could be used for the waffles, and coffee-cups to match. Four tables seating four each. About three gallons of syrup. Twenty boxes of Hearts. . . .

B. Pullman. Dining service.

Out along the white sands, the sense of the night a big frosted grape was even stronger, because the piers had darkened and only the hotel lights hung like cats' eyes.

Along the sands, beneath the piers, within black shadows, were crouched the immemorial lovers, as if carved out of the substance of the night itself. They belonged to it, as figures emerging in bas-relief are only half torn out of the marble. At streak of dawn their passion, born of this night, would flow back into it.

Cheek to cheek, lips to lips, and youth to youth, they lay.

To walk through them was literally to walk through love.

Bea, who was nineteen and had missed its meaning, strode through the familiar spectacle, her cape flying backward and her eye trying to keep ahead. . . .

What in all this prone youth was there that she had never captured—the languor in the whispers of these girls—the fuzzy male voices that vibrated? Her love had worn congress gaiters and had been unyoung——

Just the same, life was a full and going affair—four tables seating four—about three gallons of syrup. . . .

·21·

The trick of mind which made it habitual for Bea to trace back a chain of circumstances to its first link, fastened on the deluge of dull cold rain which poured uninterruptedly throughout the two days of the First Church Fair. . . .

Had it not been for the unseasonable and marrow-chilling weather, the B. Pullman might not have been the success that it was.

There was something downright soothing, to people blown in off the wind-swept ocean front, about piping-hot waffles on which the butter melted into little diamond-shaped pools, and coffee that lifted its aroma from a boiling, nickel-plated pot.

"Folks jes' nachally goes hot-waffle in a storm," proclaimed Delilah, twirling her irons and the whites of her eyes. "Something cozy as a blinkin' cat about a pipin'-hot waffle, wid de right blend of drip coffee to wash it down."

She might have added that there was something cozy as a cat about the enormous Delilah, fluted and starched to perfection, dominating the narrow confines of the rickety cross section of dining-car.

It was not much of a cross section. Except for the two wide windows flanked by small tables which looked out upon a painted drop of landscape, the dining-car idea had not quite managed to emerge. It was upon a trumped-up rear platform, railed in with a brass gate recruited from the railroad yards and personally lugged by Bea after dark, upon which most of the illusion rested. A small red signal lantern, a brakeman's red flag, and a screen door were contributing properties to the effect.

"A porter walkin' in here would jes' nachally swing a laig on board," had been Delilah's elated comment the morning she arrived, paraphernalia laden, for her first day.

That was scarcely true, but there were those who, sniffing through the golden aroma which filled the booth, not only perceived, but applauded.

"Fixed up like a little dining-car, isn't it? Right cute idea. Say, Mammy, don't care if I do have another order of those waffles. Lordy! they tickle the spot." QUART-PAIL-OF-DELILAH'S-MAPLE-SYRUP-MAILED-TO-ANY-PART-OF-THE-UNITED-STATES-AND CANADA. POSTAGE PREPAID. "Let's send some down home, Texas being a pretty large part of these United States. Couple of boxes of those Hearts, too, Mammy, while you're at it."

So, despite the conspiracy of two days which blew tatters of wind and rain at high velocity along a Boardwalk constantly bombarded by a swollen sea that sprang in angry spurts up through the cracks, the little fair, netting the church three hundred and eleven dollars, ninety-six of which was credited to the B. Pullman, topping the next runner-up, the grab-bag booth, by fifty cents, was a pronounced success.

The secretary and treasurer of the Ladies Auxiliary wrote a letter expressing appreciation of the splendid effort of Mrs. Pullman in behalf of First Church. The pastor called and made a bid for Jessie when she matured to Sunday-school age, although Bea's lapsed membership in Second Church was the one she intended to resume.

Erna Sperwick, whose growingly important rôle in the social columns was never to cease to excite the wonderment, not to say risibilities, of her erstwhile classmates, sent her a rubber plant in a jardinière.

A Mrs. Alex Grenoble, president of the First Church Ladies Aid Society and wife of a retired Philadelphia banker whose Atlantic City all-year home was a show place, called and left a card, which Delilah kept dusted and conspicuous on the hall table for months.

This call, after worry and speculation, Bea returned, choosing a time when she figured Mrs. Grenoble would be out and leaving a visiting-card, especially engraved for the occasion, with the first butler in uniform she had ever seen in the flesh.

Nothing more came of it at the time, but it all gave to Bea a sense of somehow being part of the citizenry of a community in which she had hitherto moved without contact.

Besides, where there were children! You owed it to your little daughter to screw up courage to return this visit of the wife of one of the wealthy and socially secure men of the town.

You could never tell when such a connection would prove valuable. Later, years later, one faint repercussion of this incident was to prove just that.

The boon of the small circumstance asserted itself in her canvassing manner, impelling her to scratch down into new territories which she had hitherto discarded as barren of possibilities. Why not the drug store? The railway station? Or, for that matter, Wanamaker's in Philadelphia?

To that firm she wrote a letter, sending along with it a sample box of Delilah's Hearts. Her proposition to place a consignment was rejected, but it brought her a courteously considered refusal.

> B. PULLMAN, ESQ.
> DEAR SIR:
>   *Replying to your favor, with sample, of June 29th, beg to inform you that we are not at this time open to your proposition, but trust that future opportunity will enable us to handle your attractively presented product.*

Into the shoe-box which she used for a letter file she inserted a new folder—*Wanamaker*.

If, in the end, as she reckoned the cost of carpentry and cartage, for which she had never found courage to present a bill, the First Church fair had netted a personal loss of thirteen dollars and eighty-five cents, it had also netted a strange profit.

Even while confronted by one of the periodic and always frightening crises in her budget affairs, she hurried with her pearl-and-diamond engagement ring to one of its temporary lay-ups at the pawnshop on Atlantic Avenue, the tiny nucleus of a perfect resolve had already formed in her mind.

A one-hundred-dollar capital and an advance payment of one month's rent would make it possible to establish a small B. Pullman on the precious frontage of the Boardwalk.

B. Pullman, Delilah's Hot Waffles with Genuine Golden Glory Maple Syrup. Delilah's Famous Egg-shell Drip Coffee. Delilah's Maple Sugar Hearts. Mail a pound box, postage prepaid, to the folks back home.

You do not know the real Boardwalk until you have eaten Delilah's hot waffles in the famous B. Pullman.

Such a concession, properly conceived, properly managed, might be a way out of the grilling routine of canvassing the back doors of the hotels, boarding-houses, private residences, hospitals, and drug stores of the city.

The stench of the days became not so much that of the kitchens, unsavory approaches to rear entrances to shore-dinner restaurants, stale popcorn, sweating negro bodies, as the odor of nostalgia which permeated her long tramping hours; nostalgia for that small kennel of home where her daughter was already racing on vigorous legs; where the sun lay cozily in the front rooms of forenoons and in the pleasant kitchen for the remainder of the day. Even in such a rickety sort of house, one who loved the security of walls could sit at the doing of secure indoor things. As a wife she had known briefly and sweetly of that security.

Each morning now, that she left the house, was a matter of bracing herself for a plunge into cold alien streams that were perpetual shock to her. The hanker in her was for the doing of little and tidy things. To stack spiced cookies into a painted jar for the cupboard. To hem the dotted-swiss bathroom curtains, were nostalgia indeed, that set in no more than she had left the house with its domestic doings for which she yearned.

It pressed on the idea of the B. Pullman like a hurting shoe. With Delilah presiding at the waffle-iron, and a black boy in a white duck coat combining waiting table with dishwashing, how easily conceivable that the miniature idea of a miniature dining-car might amuse the general public as it had the special public of the fair.

Just see what had been accomplished in that little ten-by-twelve church booth! Twenty-five dollars a day, and ninety per cent of it profit. Excellent point to develop in the attempt to raise the two hundred dollars capital toward a Boardwalk B. Pullman.

That attempt, had she foreseen it, was to cover a period of eight months, during which time, as Delilah ejaculated over trash-baskets, more figures had gone onto the backs of envelopes than chicken feathers into a nigger's sack.

Eugene McVickers, president of the town's second largest bank, whom she finally reached through the device of appealing to the Pittsburgh head of the pickle-and-relish firm, listened, at the point of her fanatically focused eyes, and advised her gently that her plan was not practicable.

How well, even rushing in to anticipate them, she knew the vulnerable points to her plan. No, Mr. McVickers was wrong, a larger capital than the two hundred would not be required. No, the waffles and maple syrup were not too wintry and seasonal for a summer resort. Hot waffles and maple syrup were a national dish. Delilah's hots would know no season. Besides, even assuming such to be the case, they were already experimenting with a delicious frozen-custard summer combination with the waffles. Yes, of course the rents were prohibitive along the Board-walk, but not when you had a popular novelty. Just see how the souvenir concession, which trafficked in sea shells and burnt leather, and the salt-water-taffy stands were multiplying in numbers! Yes, to be sure, seasons were short, but wasn't there an emphatic movement afoot to make Atlantic City a year-around resort.

Like clockwork the local business minds tick-tocked to her project.

No, no, you can't swing it, sister, so spare your energy. I've seen too many of them come and go. No business man will risk even a couple of hundred on a winter concession for summer-resorters. What you want is some Eskimo to back you for a North Pole enterprise.

The president of a large paint concern, who had known her mother as a girl in Burlington, made short work of their interview. "The place for a woman who has got to earn her living is behind the typewriter or the counter or the school-ma'am's desk. I wouldn't turn a finger to help put the best woman on earth into pants. What's the world coming to, with women wielding hatchets like Carrie Nation and crying out loud for the vote?"

Sperwick, the husband of Erna, had gone, most shockingly of all, to the point. She had never dreamed she could feel so smeared by mere words, every one of them usual ones from her everyday vocabulary yet suddenly arranged in a juxtaposition that made them shock her.

Nothing so brutally frank had she ever heard put into phrase before. Sperwick, a little black-eyed, dandified Italian with a turtle-like neck, had darted it at her, declining the plan in terms that made that fact seem secondary. "Only customer for crazy idea lak that is some fella who lak to sleep with you. Fine woman lak you—fine—strong—gooda busts—high. Beezness no place. Jeez Christ He makka woman for love. . . . ''

All her outraged senses of chastity rose like a row of good little girls, as if to form a ring-around-of-rosy against the sullied phrases. What a vile man! At what price must Erna have achieved her suite in the Boardwalk Hotel! What kind of a person dared he think she was? A nice, decent schoolmate of his very own wife's, she'd have him know, and a hundred times less fresh than Erna, who had been known as a ''boy-kisser.'' Just went to show, the flyer a girl was, the better the men liked her. Nerve! Men didn't breathe the mention of such parts of human anatomy as busts in the presence of a good woman, to say nothing of his allusion, in words of no evasion, to the act of sleep.

Italians were that way, about love and sex and nature. Her mother had always said, ''Never have anything to do with Eyetalian boys'' (dear darling, her sole and apparently insurmountable error of pronunciation). ''They aren't nice in their ideas about little girls.'' Nice? They were loathsome! Why, there were certain aspects about love that were never mentioned, because all decent-thinking people pretended they never existed. Imagine Mr. Pullman ever letting on!

It seemed to her that the incident must somehow be a reflection upon her own innate niceness. How dared he assume that she was the sort of a woman to whom such talk was not shameful.

''You're too nice a woman,'' the head of a realty firm told her, ''to be out after fish of this fry. Go get yourself a husband or a lover. Or at least a job behind somebody else's desk.''

For over a period of months these incidents actually proved a deterrent that kept her to the narrow routine of adhering strictly to her accustomed rounds. Apparently, to the men she approached, it had seemed either freakish or female of her to entertain the idea of a small business that would require even the small capital she sought.

Try and make the rather curiously focusing eyes of the men believe that her major idea was to achieve the security of life at home with her child. To the male mind, snooting about as if among the garbage of her motives, there was something neither savory nor welcome in the idea of a woman getting creative about this matter of business. Has been done, was being done, would be done, of course. There were enough of them already talking their women's rights, and God knows the spectacled kind of females that wanted them were welcome to them. But a woman with a pair of busts and a curve to her—get a man, is our solution. Or if you won't do that, be a man, then, and stand on your own.

After the incident of Sperwick, at least a percentage of them seemed to say just that with their manner or unminced words.

It was almost Christmas, following an ebb tide in her order-book that was without precedent even for off season, that she awoke one chilled December morning as much stunned that the thought had not come to her sooner, as with the impact of the idea itself, and still in her nightgown began composing a letter to Mr. Hiram Prynne, Maple Sugar Mart, Brattleboro, Vermont, submitting her proposition for opening a B. Pullman on the Atlantic City Boardwalk under the auspices and benign beneficence of that company.

Two weeks later, a reply from H. Prynne, Esq., stated that B. Pullman's favor of such and such a date having been under advisement, Prynne & Company Maple Sugar Mart, given proper assurances, would advance the sum of two hundred and fifty dollars for enterprise described in letter of such and such a date, provided B. Pullman would agree to certain specific considerations of Prynne & Company Sugar Mart, as follows. . . .

On an Easter Sunday that poured sunshine and broke a ten-year Atlantic City record for crowds, a B. Pullman, located just two blocks below the Chalfonte Hotel and rather shyly placed in the fifteen feet of width between an astronomer's booth and an Irish-linen shop, opened its new door to reveal the enormous face of Delilah, under its sunrise of headdress, presiding at the altar of the waffle-iron.

·22·

Mrs. Vizitelli, who for twenty years had conducted the grocery store at the corner of Arctic and Mississippi, used to say of her second boy, Vincenzo, that out of her turbulent brood of five, he was one who, by both nature and circumstance, had never given her an hour's trouble from the day he was born.

In a measure, Bea felt that same to be true of her first Pullman. Come what subsequently might, there was something of the determined normalcy of Vincenzo set in the brood of difficult Vizitelli children, about this Boardwalk enterprise which opened its brightly-polished, crisply-curtained eyes to the perfect beatitude of that thronged Easter morning.

If an almost too propitious beginning was destined for a sharp aftermath of decline, the average performance of this first-born was to continue to strike pride in its owner, similar to Mrs. Vizitelli's in her second born.

No measles, no paroxysms of naughtiness, no retarded growth, no rickets or bad reports of juvenile delinquencies.

Links in the chain, of which the Boardwalk B. Pullman was to be the first, were some of them to be strong, some of them weaker, but virtually from the start this pioneer B. Pullman showed a sustained and seldom faltering margin of profit.

"It's mah fust baby-chile," Delilah was wont to declare, in the sequence of years that took her to the inaugural procedure of launching new B. Pullmans in so many of the sizable cities and resorts of the country. "An' ain't a mother livin', dat doan' jes' nachally dote on her fust-born. You kin have all your Michigan Boulevard, Fifth Avenue, and Palm Beach Pullmans, but I'll take mah fust little Boardwalk waffle baby ovah and above even de new one dat's goin' into de skyscrapin' building that's givin' dis heah New York crick in de neck.''

But despite, or perhaps because of, a beginning so propitious, immediate and attendant complications piled fast and high.

With all the good intentions in the world, it remained impossible for Delilah to solve the corporeal problem of being two places simultaneously.

Even on the anti-climatic Monday following Easter Sunday, the Pullman tossed its waffles practically without interruption from morning until late midnight. It meant the presence of two climbing children and a wheel-chair in the small kitchen and back porch of the B. Pullman, where dish-washing and coffee-percolating were taking place, or the presence of Bea in the house on Arctic Avenue, in frenzied relief spurts between her canvassing rounds and presence at the Boardwalk scene of Delilah's activities.

For the first day or two it was well and good enough that two highly excited children and the old gentleman be carted along in a general morning exodus to the B. Pullman. After all, there was the little rim of back porch, which, while it did not overlook the sea and was cluttered with the sound of carousel music and the back-door smells of neighboring concessions, nevertheless was drenched in strong salt-laden sunlight and strongly inclosed against the truant impulses of two small girls. But even on the first day, the nervous, overwrought cries of the children had percolated into the diner, causing Delilah's eyes above the waffle-iron to roll in anxiety, while the old gentleman found the beach noisy and bewildering, and the constant scraps of adjoining musics irritating. Any way you looked at it, the arrangement at best could only be a temporary one.

What happened eventually was a shift system between Bea and Delilah in the house on Arctic Avenue, aided and abetted by the after-school services of the small sister of the helper at the B. Pullman, who for fifty cents a week tended two small girls and the chair.

That tended to alleviate, but did not solve, the rather curious dilemma already presented by the child Peola in her propinquity to the child Jessie.

Sooner or later, Bea kept telling herself, this situation was going to develop itself into a concrete problem. But why anticipate?

Delilah did.

"Some day dat chile of yourn is gonna wake up an' find my Peola black. Den what?"

"No use crossing that bridge until we come to it."

" 'Tain't our bridge to cross, honey. It's yourn."

"People are broader-minded about such things than they used to be."

"Yas'm. Broad-minded as mah thumb nail."

"I don't believe in making an issue of it."

"Neither did de good Lawd when he made us black and white, an' look what's been issuin' ever since. De glory in bein' black, honey, is dat de Lawd willed it so. Mah man grieved his heart out wantin' to pass. Dar ain't no passin'. When de time comes for mah Peola to stay on her black side of de world and yourn on her white side, we won't have to decide it, Miss Bea. Some day, jes' a little word lak nigger'll creep in, an' everything will be all right except nevah de same as befoh. Won't be your fault, won't be Jessie's, won't be ourn. Maybe it'll be de Lawd's, but only for bein' so holy an' good hisself, he couldn't figure out de meanness and misery was goin' to come from makin' dis a two-tone world. Glory be to Gawd, I's glad I's one of his black chillun, 'cause, sho as heaven, his heart will bleed fust wid pity an' wid mercy for his low-down ones. . . ."

"Delilah, Northern negroes don't feel that way any more. . . ."

"Northern niggers! Scratch one of dese heah North niggers an' dey'll bleed Alabama blood. It may be mixed up wid plenty of white blood, lak mah man was, but thin out chicken gravy wid water an' it remains chicken gravy, only not so good. Every day of mah life I's gonna rear mah young un to know de glory of bein' born one of de Lawd's low-down ones. I seen her pap suffer tryin' to pass. Lord'll gimme strength for sparin' his chile dat sufferin' an' pain. De Lawd never made no bones about makin' me . . . he certainly kinda done lost his nerve makin' Peola and her pap. Ain't dat de way, though? All dese pale Northern niggers spendin' their las' pennies to git Gawd's kink out of dat hair, and all de white ladies spendin' dars to git Gawd's kink into thars. I's seen too much white-nigger heartache in mah time. I wants mah chile full of nigger-love and lovin'-to-be-nigger."

Certainly in the narrow, tan little girl of level, soot-colored eyes and straight-banged, soot-colored hair, resided none of her maternal parent's rambunctious capacity for devotion, one way or another. You needed to earn your way into her carefully dispensed graces, and at the slightest intrusion of Jessie into the world of her rights, to watch, not without apprehension, for the danger signals of the flanges of her small straight nose beginning to quiver and turn faintly green.

" 'Clare, if it wasn't for dat chile's takin 'so after her pap, I'd swear she'd done been changed in de cradle on me. Dar don't seem to be no pickaninny in dat young un. Her's a little squaw."

"Are you sure, Delilah, there wasn't some Indian blood in your husband?"

"G'wan, honey. Not but what he wasn't Indian-giver—biggest you ever seen for givin' an' takin' back again, but dar was mostly nigger in mah nigger, no matter how high-toned he tried to be ovah the black wife he took hisself. Me that done the slavin' for him ought to know."

"She's so—why, almost dignified, Delilah, in a strange Indian manner."

"Indians. Dar wasn't nothin' any more Indian than a cigar-store Indian anywhars near fifty miles whar her pap was born of two Virginie darkies, which ain't sayin' dar mayn't have been plenty of white blood in him, down dar whar white blood in nigger veins comes cheaper'n moonshine whisky."

"But your Peola is so exceptionally light, Delilah."

"Accident, honey. And style. Her pap jes' had style mixed in, I guess, wid a teaspoonful of white blood back somewheres, an' it got him through life an' three wives widout ever turnin' them lily-pink palms of his. Style, but not a half-moon to his finger nails, and doan' you forgit it. Give a nigger style an' his blood stream is filled wid gold nuggets. Peola's got style, an' you jes' wait and see if her mammy ain't gonna work her hands to de bone for her and lak it, jes' lak some man is gonna do after dese hands of mine have gone to join de Almighty who dey loves."

"Peola darling, why aren't you a little sweeter to Jessie? Just see how she wants to love you and you won't have anything to do with her."

"Black chile, go over dar as fast as dem laigs will walk you, and make up wid dat yaller-haired angel-chile."

"Don't force her, Delilah. They play nicely together. It's only that Peola seems almost resentful of Jessie."

"Shall I tell you what's eatin' out her little heart? Sure as her pap's in de arms of a forgivin' Lawd. It's a curse on her already, lak it was on him. Mah baby hates to be black. Ain't that terrible, Miss Bea—ain't that heart-breakin'? Shamed to be what de Lawd made her. Oh, mah baby-chile, come heah to yoh mammy, an' let her kiss some of de ache out of dat sweetheart face. Dar ain't nothin' but glory in bein' black, baby mine, if you can look at it as bein' de will of de Lawd.''

"Delilah, as if that child realizes!''

"She do, Miss Honey-Bea. Her little heart's scarred wid it, lak her paw's before her. De Lawd help her an' her mammy help her! An' dat's what I'm put on dis earth for to do. Help mah baby find de will of de Lawd and glory in bein' what she is. Go make a fuss over dat white chile dis minute, if you don't want me to spank your little bottom-round.''

To Bea there was something that seemed actually to hurt her physically around the heart, to behold the eager receptivity with which her blond Jessie welcomed the slightest show of advance from Peola. And more than that, a twinge of jealousy.

"Mother had better take lessons from Peola, darling. My love comes too cheap.''

Repeatedly she found herself realizing her mistake in mauling and kissing at the small face of her daughter, which was to her so flower-like. The child almost dodged these fierce caresses, or cried out under a kiss that ground too deeply against the tender flesh, or wriggled out of an embrace that confined too closely. But, somehow, it remained quite beyond her not to snatch the yellow loveliness of this youngster greedily to her during the all too brief periods she spent with her at home during her waking hours.

"Mother loves you so, Jessie. She sees you so seldom. She knows she is rough, but it is because she loves you so.''

The old gentleman, who no longer spoke, or even attempted it, had invented a game which at first had repelled even the children, but upon his pantomime insistence had come to be a favorite.

Across the dead wood of his lower limbs a small plank afforded seesaw. This the little girls had learned to use at a lickety-split pace, their shouts rising with the old gentleman's apparent zest for play.

Then usually it petered out into a curious and stilly game carried on between Peola and Mr. Chipley, which Delilah declared gave her the "shimmy-shivers."

These two, across the chasm of years and color, could go into the trance, without the trembling of a lash, of staring at one another for periods that gathered silence and usually ended by the small and overstrained little Jessie, as she viewed the contest from the side lines, bursting into tears.

Delilah was intuitive about these endurance tests, darting into the room if the sound of silence irked her.

"It's dem two holding deir breath ag'in wid deir eyes! Peola, stop pasting your look onto de ole gemmeman's dat way. 'Tain't nice. What does mah chair-baby mean by letting his ole eyes get revited on mah young un's dataway? Stop it, both of you, or 'Lilah'll paste dem eyes bang up against one another for keeps."

"I declare, Miss Honey-Bea, it's like mah young un was tryin' to read in de ole gemmeman's eyes de reason for why de Lawd sent some into de world wid light and some wid dark skin, seein' He wanted 'em to be born equal."

"Delilah, you're fanatical on that subject."

"Maybe I is grammatical on dat subject, but you see, honey, I knowed her daddy."

·B·

The beginnings of the idea for the Philadelphia B. Pullman grew out of the waning of the Atlantic City season, in those days before the idea of its winter-resort possibilities seemed fully to have dawned upon the spangled brain of this playland by the sea.

With the autumnal thinning of the crowds, the passing of the excursion months, the boarding up of most of the gaudy faces of the Boardwalk pleasance, and with the hibernating activities of the majority of the major hostelries, the death rattle to the summer season was something a little ominous in its finality.

During the lifetime of Mr. Pullman the closing of the Pier for the winter months had made little impression into routine, because the duties of the staff were transferred to offices which the company kept operating inside the Pier building.

But now, come November, cold, salt-bitten winds whirled under the thin wooden floors of the concession structures, ballooning Delilah's wide skirts as she stood at the waffle-iron and rattling the little edifice on its high stilts, until the dishes teetered on their shelves and the wooden edifice rocked like a frail bark at sea.

It was when the need for boarding up the bright dining car windows and unhinging the striped awning became imminent, that the picture of a smartly equipped little B. Pullman in or near the busy, snatch-a-bite atmosphere of a great city's railway station began to etch itself sharply against her brain.

To be sure, the seasonal slump would release Delilah to the growing requirements of the kitchen in the house on Arctic Avenue, now that the demand for Hearts quite suddenly seemed to attain a new high level and hold it.

But as Bea wrote once more to Hiram Prynne of Sugar Mart, this time secure in the precedent of having successfully met the demands of the previous obligation:

> ... *my little project has proved itself. Are you disposed now to advance me a loan double yours of last year, terms identical, based on the following? ... Judging from the public's warm response to my Atlantic City enterprise, I am now of a mind to attempt to procure a lease on a desirable Philadelphia location, preferably near the Broad Street Station, or adjacent to the heart of the shopping district——*

A trip to Philadelphia, taken nervously while she awaited reply to this letter, revealed, in the day's shopping among realty offices, that twenty feet of frontage in proper propinquity to Wanamaker's, or the Broad Street Station, was a matter of larger monthly rental than she had counted on for the year.

But stubbornly, the newly generated enthusiasm for the scheme kept raging like wildfire up and down her brain.

Set into one of these flanks of gray stone that lined Market or Chestnut Street, the warm bright look of a B. Pullman, glowing into the drab fog of a typical downtown winter day, was something to bring, in the way of inexpensive comfort and cheer, to all this gray hurrying humanity, with its gray face tucked into collars and its shoulders hunched against chill.

On one hand, the restaurants with palms in the windows and ornamental balconies with orchestras, and on the other the bedlams of the quick-lunch room, met the creature demands of all the anonymous figures, but in an impersonal way that had little in common with the certain kind of achievement she had in mind for her new B. Pullman.

To some extent, the Boardwalk diner had smacked of it. Patrons had told her so. You relaxed in the B. Pullman. None of that lettuce-leaf, muffin-and-too-trimmed-lamb-chop, reduced-gentlewomen-from-Virginia, tearoom feeling to it. Delilah, starched, fluted, immaculate, at her iron, was something to set the juices of anticipation running, as the soft warm smells rose off her griddle. The dishes, the thin china blue-and-white ones from the house on Arctic Avenue, had given off no clatter. Toward evening, a candle with a bow around its neck like a kitten's, burned on each table.

This last to Delilah's ill-concealed scorn.

"Caindles! What for caindles, when you got de electricity going anyway. Caindles! We stuck 'em in bottles on soap-boxes where I was raised. My ole one-eyed granny would have give her right eye to have electric light for to do her ironin' an' eat by. An' dats jes' what she had to do, give her right eye dat went blind from tryin' to work by caindles. Caindles! I 'clare, 'tain't no wonder de Lawd gits scared and shimmies with earthquake when He looks down and sees some of the nonsense goin' on down on dis heah earth."

But the candles proved themselves to be part of the amber coziness at dusk, combined with the amber smells of waffles off the iron going faintly and just rightly soggy under inundation of melting butter and Vermont maple syrup.

You could do something mellow as that right into the hard metallic bang of these bat-colored city streets and these bat-colored city people. You could soften a moment, warm a chilled hour.

For a little pocket change, a delicate-lipped cup from which to drink good coffee; soft light, amber atmosphere of indoor security, which, however fleeting, was respite from the duress of that strife and stone and steel out there; the something she yearned to create was akin to the kennel warmth and brightness she so passionately wanted to pour around herself and little family in the house on Arctic Avenue. Here was opportunity or the equivalent of what life had started out to be with Mr. Pullman. Warm, amber, indoor security. Candle-light flickering on cozy inclosing walls. Culinary smells of indoor women, to whom homely chores were homey. She would shirr yellow curtains at the windows of this B. Pullman. Daily papers and a few of the better-grade magazines mounted on holders the way they arranged them in clubs. Menus the shape of dining-car bills-of-fare with Delilah having her laugh on the cover. A dish of Delilah's Hearts to be passed gratis with the coffee. Some day, perhaps, there would be a way to work out a scheme for an open fireplace . . . now that would be a pretty monkey wrench into the dining-car idea, wouldn't it! But no use adhering too rigidly to that. Once let the public get the general feel of a B. Pullman— all there was to it. Lonely young fellows away from home might feel impelled to forgather where there was inexpensive cheer. . . .

There were troops of boys marching through cold city streets these days, on their strange embarkations for war. Something as remote and outside the pale of interest as of understanding, as a war was happening. For months, like a monster from afar, the situation had been breathing, as it were, on the neck of American business, creating an unrest and an unsureness all along her territory. And now the American glove, a gauntlet of mail and steel, had been flung into the fracas. Something that had hitherto belonged to the pages of textbooks and school orations was going on all around. Boys with packs on their backs were marching. The calamity of this half-understood spectacle seemed less real than the not unecstatic hysteria of departure. Herself only negligibly older than the majority of these boys, younger than some, she had come unconsciously into an air of maternalism with them. As college students, week-end vacationists, playboys, they had frequently stormed the Boardwalk B. Pullman until it teetered on its stilts. She knew and liked their outrageousness, so exuberant and yet so easily held in check. Once, to Delilah's immense remonstrance and good humor, they had formed a hand-basket and pranced her, in violent pantomime against the outrage, up and down a bit of Boardwalk. "Good old Delilah! Hurrah for Delilah! Hip, hip, hurray! Good old Delilah!"

These same nice boys were marching now. Logical to assume that the war-bound youngsters who were beginning to be so terribly in evidence around city streets and stations would likewise assail the toothsome and inexpensive products of Delilah's magic irons.

That was precisely what did happen, although not immediately in Philadelphia, because it was five years before the brightly caparisoned and by then standardized dining-car was to flash its polished brass railing along that section of Broad Street she had so tirelessly explored pending the reply to her letter from the Sugar Mart, Brattleboro.

When that letter did come, it was curiously not what she wanted, non-committal up to a point, and yet in no way to be regarded as an out-and-out refusal. Sugar Mart regarded Philadelphia as too conservative to respond readily to the small novelty, but suggested the larger field of New York, where Hiram Prynne had a brother-in-law, an executive in a midtown realty firm. "In the event that through the offices of Mr. Fields you find premises there which you consider suitable to your purpose, as outlined in your recent favor, our firm will then take up the suggestions contained therein.''

New York! The thought flooded her with a certain dismay. If Philadelphia offered almost insurmountable rent difficulties, what was to be hoped for in the most notoriously expensive and overcrowded city in the world.

She had often heard her father and Mr. Pullman discuss how in some of the New York restaurants you paid extra for a portion of the pickle-and-relish firm's famous condiments, which in other cities throughout the country were served gratis with the meal.

''Those fellows down there can get away with anything. New Yorkers love to be bilked.''

Well, perhaps by that very token her venture might be ventured there. You paid more—you charged more—you earned more. But there again, that need in itself threatened to defeat the impulse so strangely growing behind all this. Business was business, of course, but there was something about the idea of the fragrant, amber-colored interior, tired faces getting ironed out as they relaxed to well-being which she had provided for them at fair prices, that had the same quality of satisfaction to it she had found in lining the nest of the house on Arctic Avenue to meet the creature-satisfaction of the man who for so brief a while had come home to it at night.

People sank gratefully into a B. Pullman because of the genius of a certain quality that had got itself born into it. On week-end days they had sat too long over their refreshment, while little pools of standees waited. Young fellows, for whom many of Atlantic City's far different resorts were primarily planned, found pause here. Sons brought mothers. Mothers brought sons. Post cards addressed ''Delilah,'' Atlantic City, from vacationists, mostly young ones, who remembered, were already quite an array, in a wire rack in Delilah's room. ''Hello, Delilah, from the Akron Boys who won't ever forget Delilah's Red Hots!'' ''Dear Delilah, wish we had some of your Hearts and Hots down here in Chattanooga. I'm the little red-haired girl you called Honey an' M'lasses.'' ''Dear Aunt Delilah, I voted to hold the Woodman's convention at Atlantic City again next year, just so we can sit in B. Pullman and gather round the finest hot waffles I ever seen flapped on land or sea. George Ryan of Bangor, Maine.'' ''Best regards to my seat in the little B. Pullman. P.S. Remember the little cock-eyed fellow who ate you out of five orders of waffles!''

The major need was to succeed in duplicating the genius of that certain quality which had got itself born into the first B. Pullman: Delilah's savory coffee, Delilah's hot waffles, Delilah's Hearts, Delilah's smile, Golden Maple Syrup, candle-light at dusk, thin china dishes, odors, the little pampering something that came so readily from Delilah. Prices within almost any tired shopper's range.

Some people have talent for writing poetry or building towers or singing arias. Mine must be to surround people for a few moments out of a tired day, with a little unsubtle but cozy happiness of body and perhaps of mind.

Well, why not? We can't all build empires and sonnets. How fortunate to have discovered talent for anything at all, even if for nothing more than the ability to provide people with a few moments of creature enjoyment. The B. Pullman did that. A feat not so simple as it seemed, witness the high mortality among Boardwalk concessions which, for one reason or another, were not able to keep head above water.

It was wonderful, having found a talent. Yes, it was that! Why, a woman patron from Oak Park, Chicago, had taken the trouble to come right out into the kitchen to proclaim it. ''My dear, this little place is a real stroke of genius! Such atmosphere! That adorable mammy! Such coffee! My dear, you've got something here. Wish there were something like it out in my town.''

Philadelphia, yes. Even Chicago, remote as it seemed. But New York! That was a different and a terrifying matter.

A day spent there as a child, with her mother, on one of those dollar-round-trip excursions from Philadelphia, remained stuck in the memory. Her fingers had been glued together most of the time, from clinging so to the tight clutch of her mother's hand as they darted across streets, between street cars, and beneath the hooves of horses.

Such irrelevant bits of recollection of that trip clung!

The din as they stepped off the ferry. New kid gloves at Lord & Taylor's fine emporium. A ride on the elevated railroad, and a visit to the strange wax morgue of Madame Tussaud. Curb venders selling polly seed to dirty-faced street children who gobbled them. A horse-car ride to the humble room of a white-haired trained nurse who kept imparting to Bea the strange information that she had helped bring her mother into the world. A trip across Brooklyn Bridge to visit a friend of her mother's who dwelt in a row of identical houses, as in their own Philadelphia, except that, instead of the two-story boxes that lined their street were lean, narrow, brown-stone buildings with hallways that smelled of cold boiled potatoes. The furniture had been slippery horse-hair, and poised on it, she had been given a pretty pink pastry, the inside of which proved to be cocoanut, which she loathed, and which Mother with the tail of her eye had forced her to eat.

Then brown button shoes, with tassels, at Stewart's. Some balbriggan socks, at a counter where the stools whirled, for Father. Finally, while waiting for the ferry to carry them the first homeward lap of the trip, fried-egg sandwiches and a little pyramid of ice-cream in a thick-lipped dish, her mother, already sickening of headache from the violent day, sipping hot water from a glass.

New York. To even so much as put foot into that cold swirling maelstrom would strike chill to her courage. If the business men of a community the size of Atlantic City had kept turned consistently cold shoulder to her business enterprise, what could be hoped of the steel-and-iron anatomy that was New York.

New Yorkers, as they poured into the beach resort, well-dressed, easy-spending holiday crowds, seemed cocksure, shellacked with so-phistication, free enough with money, but fastidious in demands.

You could spot them. The women almost invariably with something in the way of a skirt or a feather which you were seeing for the first time; the men shaved until that bluish cast came out along the jowl, more curt in their demands and paying a bit more generously and ostentatiously for services received.

It was surprising, though, how superficial the badge. Take them, for instance, as they came into the B. Pullman. They all boiled down into "general public." Underneath the skin, pathetically close to the so-phisticated surface of a blue shave or a rouged cheek they were merely Albuquerque, Altoona, Atchison, Arlington, Amityville, or Astoria.

New York itself might prove to be like that. Delilah was doubtless right. "Scratch any one of 'em all de way from New York to Alabam' an' watch 'em bleed God's red."

·24·

"If any one," Bea used to say after a habit of looking back over years that kept their quality of remaining perpetually amazing to her—"if any one had told me that at twenty-six I would be running two businesses and carrying my syrup and candy lines on the side, I would simply have said they were crazy."

She had an oracular way of stating this, as if no one had ever said this sort of thing before. It clouded up her eyes with a fierce sort of gray mud. It flashed across a face which had matured too young and which now looked actually younger than it had five years previous. A face upon which had settled the subtle mask, woven of the stuff of incipient self-confidence.

Not that the second B. Pullman had made anything resembling the propitious start of its Atlantic City predecessor.

Her initial ideal of a sliver of precious space within the corridors of the new Grand Central Station itself; corridors with sleek marble sides and tiled runways that were kept polished by the commercially precious tread of hundreds of thousands of daily feet—had almost immediately to be abandoned.

Every inch bordering the priceless thunder of those passing feet was worth its width in gold. There was one tiny frontage, its cement scarcely dry, that seemed almost diabolically designed to meet the requirements of a B. Pullman. Long, narrow, shaped like a car, it stood waiting to be caparisoned. Twenty-eight hundred a year. Thereupon ceasing to be a possibility, it became a defeat, that made additionally bitter her ultimate compromise on premises across the street; premises which were to prove so disastrously on the wrong side of the street.

She was long to remain a little mystical about the decision which prompted her to sign lease on those twenty-feet frontage of East Forty-second Street space. Some inner driving force, she always insisted, that was stronger even than her inherent distrust of that side of the street; the dark narrow interior, and the shabby old building which contained it, had determined her. Every judgment shrank from the choice. Even with paint and caparisons, there was really little to hope from those moldy old walls, although much could be done to dissipate their gloom.

At any rate, once the die was cast and her pen had made its trance-like motions in placing her signature to lease, the strangest kind of buoyancy rode high. Aided and abetted by what turned out to be the professional optimism of Fields, the brother-in-law of Hiram Prynne, the new venture managed to get itself conceived in a whirlwind of accelerated energy.

Why not! The Sugar Mart had confidence in their man, Fields. To return to Atlantic City without having closed with him on some plan or other would be to admit defeat. Here was backing. Here were premises, if not by any means ideal, at least they lurked across the street from the ideal. A miss, alas, that was to be as good as a mile.

To begin with, even regardless of the wrongness of its side of street, no more the lease was signed than the slit of space wedged into the shadow of the new Grand Central Railway station, began to develop undreamed-of, and undreaded disadvantages.

No sooner was the small gas stove behind its partition set going, than ventilation in the little one-window aisle of space became such a pressing problem that, two days after formal opening, the premises were obliged to undergo installation of an air-cooling system that not only closed the newly opened doors for three days, but swept away, at one stroke, a tiny reserve budget of eighty-three dollars.

That initial calamity and the all-too quick realization that manifold, if not on the surface readily apparent, were the reasons for what had appeared surprisingly low rental.

It was fair to assume that even Fields, whose high-power sense of salesman technique obliterated his sense of brother-in-law-ship to Prynne of Brattleboro, was unaware of the strange circumstance of a subway rattle, which, due to the rushing of trains underneath the building, swept the little interior every few seconds with a chill of rattling dishes and gittering of everything movable, that was finally subdued, but never conquered, by application of heavy felt to all flat surfaces.

It became, too, quite immediately apparent that not only was the handicap of that particular side of the street even greater than had been anticipated, but, by virtue of a small platform of safety erected at the street-crossing, the actual week the B. Pullman took possession of its new quarters, at least two-thirds of the pedestrians hitherto calculated to pass the B. Pullman were suddenly enabled, just twenty yards before reaching it, to make a comfortable short cut to the opposite side of the street.

All of which meant that, literally facing the grand façade of one of the busiest junctions in the world, the small B. Pullman, tucked into an ancient brick edifice in a city where old buildings, like old people, are quickly scrapped for new faces and new façades, began, from the very day of its inception, its fight against anonymity.

So near and yet so far, she was to think in moans to herself as she stood watching the tide slip her by, while empty moments and hours in the busiest heart of the busiest city in the world ticked themselves cruelly and expensively away.

Even though so large a proportion of the renting optimism had been Fields', it had all seemed quite different to her as well, during the period of the decision regarding that lease. The scene past the door had been one of such thundering activity. The plan of the long, narrow little premises had seemed to lend themselves to requirements. After all, even with the disadvantages of the wrong side of street, frontage at its worst, on so terrific an artery as this, was not to be winked at.

Why, if any one had told her, a twelvemonth before, that she would even be daring to consider any sort of New York frontage!

And now. For the first four weeks of the Forty-second Street B. Pullman the backs of envelopes, covered over with inexorable subtractions and additions, showed the kind of deficit that struck almost an insanity of terror into her already appalled and regretting heart.

If this continued, she could actually wipe herself out in no time.

Why had she dared it? How had she dared it? To think that only a few short weeks ago she had been in the unequivocal position to let well enough alone, yet, spurred by the desire of forcing her small success to succeed more grandly, had not quite dared.

If only . . .

Tucked away in that Atlantic City house on Arctic Avenue were, at the moment, responsibilities which, from the very beginning, should have dictated against, rather than in behalf of, this hazardous and by now, almost calamitous step.

What mad housing impulse, hers! To house herself and hers in a cottage in Ventnor. To house the impersonal harassed faces that would not even glance her way, in the golden glow of a Pullman of her providing. To house the future of her child in a sort of security to be had at the purchase price of this harried and harassed pressing forward.

The well enough to have let alone was back there in that house on Arctic Avenue. False as that security might seem, at least there was freedom from this kind of harassment, with which so little in her make-up seemed adequate to cope.

To some, all this might seem part and joy of the battle. But to one who so passionately longed for the sweet if small fruits of security, the waves of conflict beat cold and high and bone-breaking.

The pleasant little sounds of little success, like a cheeping of a new born chicken from its egg, of the Boardwalk B. Pullman had been one thing. This matter of cheeping away through the incredible din and clatter of this vast city, another.

How—how had she ever dared? As a matter of fact, she had not. The idea, top heavy, had been superimposed upon her originally modest one of a small Philadelphia adjunct to be operated as complement to the closed season of the Boardwalk.

Actually, come to analyze it, the entire folly, the whole madness, had had its beginnings in little more than the idea of a warm and appetizing smell, a glow of amber cheer against the stone flank of a city, a bit of warmth for those young troops marching toward a war about which she knew so little and comprehended less.

To be sure, mixed up in the small immediate reality were the needs and dreams for a growing child. On every hand, now, girls were going to college. Bea, it so happened, had never personally known one who did, but hers should. To one of the large high-sounding girls' colleges or to finishing-school in Switzerland, and there would be pennants of Smith or Vassar on her walls, and crossed tennis racquets and shelves of books and all the happy paraphernalia of happy girlhood. A home to which she could be proud to bring her friends. Bea had never been able to feel exactly proud of the house on Arctic. A bungalow at Ventnor, with the sea less than a block away and those handsome-shaped hedges inclosing Jessie's lawn and a side yard swing under a striped awning . . . and now . . .

For three weeks following the departure of Delilah, who had journeyed to New York to show her fluted sunrise of a face over the waffle-iron the opening day of the New York B. Pullman, leaving, to carry on in her place, a large handsome negress, trained in the Arctic Avenue kitchen, a thoroughly appalled young woman returned evenings to lodgings in a Lexington Avenue brownstone front, there to contemplate, half the night through, the brown wall paper of her hall bedroom, as if to wrench from its chromatic pattern oracular way out.

Back in Atlantic City, a little household was day by day, hour by hour, eating its way into the slender funds deposited into the horny palms of Delilah. Any day now might come the dreaded demand for more. Even with Delilah's magic in stretching the dollar beyond its conceivable ductility, her continued silence regarding Bea's questionings about funds was almost more worrisome than would have been the dreaded announcement of depleted exchequer.

Daily her postal cards, previously addressed by Bea, arrived, announcing in chirography fearful and wonderful the well-being of the little group on Arctic Avenue. But there were mouths to be fed there, the kind of nourishment that could bear no retrenchment; an old gentleman whose fastidiousness Delilah would be the last to deny; rent; osteopathy for Peola, who, strangely for a child, had developed a sciatic nerve; a helper to be paid for deliveries of what casual syrups and candies could be managed during Bea's absence from her territory.

But even reckoning with the temporary miracle of Delilah seeming to walk the seas of their dilemma, what next?

By the miss of not more than two hundred and fifty yards, of that she felt so sure, the B. Pullman, as if standing discreetly aside to let its success pass it by, was literally dying in its new tracks. To close it and run! A dozen times a day and night the impulse swept over her. There seemed so little hope. A child had been still-born. To somehow barge her way behind the granite which inclosed New York's money powers, for the additional loan which she dared not ask of Sugar Mart, would make it possible for her to get tenancy in that narrow mocking sliver of space across the street. Of local banking contacts she had not one, a corner branch of a Corn Exchange refusing her a checking account because of the inadequacy of her initial deposit. But one cold November evening, and be it admitted to her own actual self-embarrassment at the futility of her act, she walked three or four times around the block containing the vast edifice of the Madison Avenue residence of J. P. Morgan. By the lifting of a finger, he could! No, unless you were as insane as she suspected her prowling around this residence to be, you did not go up and ring a doorbell and ask a butler to be admitted to a man richer than kings, in order to accost him for a loan of what was to him less than pin money and to her ransom enough to buy her a universe.

No, you didn't do that.

It was as if she was in some sort of tranced race, sweat running, the muscles of her legs pulling, and yet, with all the hallucination of running, actually she was not making a move.

The heart strained, the eyeballs bulged. Two hundred and fifty yards. There were veins in her neck she could feel rise and throb. Hot prickles flashed over her body. Each time she swallowed, a contraction of fear seemed to sink into the strange vacuum of her body. . . .

All day the waffle batter, taking on the sickly odor of stagnation, stood cloying in its bowl, while the face of the imitation Delilah nodded over its lack of task, and the black boy in the white Pullman-porter coat dozed among the unaccumulating dishes and, scenting disaster, ran his finger up and down the Help Wanted columns.

Mamma—Mr. Pullman—why did you leave me——

It was on the thirty-first day, when the day's business had dropped to the new low of exactly one dollar and twenty cents, that a man named J. S. Squibb, whom Bea had never seen before, and was never to see again, walked into the B. Pullman and, in the name of a corporation that was negotiating to purchase the building that contained her premises in order to make way for the invasion of a skyscraper, offered her a three-thousand-dollar cash bonus for her lease.

·25·

Since the armistice, rents had gone soaring.

It was something, indeed it was a great deal, to be in a position to sign a lease on Central Park West near One Hundred and Third Street for the six rooms and two baths, at one-third more than the sum for which they could have been procured during the early days of the war.

They were such infinitely superior rooms to the four stuffy little ones on West One Hundred and Thirteenth Street and Amsterdam Avenue which she had rented when the move from the house on Arctic Avenue had finally been decided upon. So superior in fact, that there was no reality at all about the whole business of this move, just as there was none too much reality about the quick sequence of the years.

Two of the rooms, the square living-room with its bright-yellow hardwood floors and white woodwork, and the old gentleman's bedroom, actually overlooked Central Park. From only the second floor of a ten-story apartment building, it is true, but just the same, there, spread before the gaze, was the vista of reservoir, equestrian paths, driveways, traffic-polished roadways, and at dusk, pop-pop-pop, as the children loved shrilly to shout with their palms spread against the window panes, out came the lights, festooning the scene as you might festoon diamonds across Delilah's black and shining bosom.

The remainder of the rooms, Bea's and Jessie's, the dining-room, kitchen, and offshoot of a tiny chamber occupied by Delilah and Peola, looked down onto the tops of delivery wagons, parked automobiles and the light pedestrian traffic of One Hundred and Third Street.

Previous to this move there had been weeks of literal house-hunting. That ultimate house, with its upstairs and downstairs and surrounding green, standing foursquare, was still passionately the dream and still stubbornly the elusive. But in New York City, where apartment-dwelling was generally the rule, the private house was fraught with complications. Present scheme of life and routine and requirements of practicable living made the small suburban home out of question. Scraps of mornings and evenings, fleeting moments in the heart of the household, were too precious and too transitory to be spent on trains. Meanwhile, the cottage in Ventnor, the castle in Spain, the house with a garden, remained the compromise of six square rooms set into brick, bordered in asphalt, but within precious view of a Park that performed quite lovely seasonal antics in color, under the square eyes of the living-room window.

Next to having a house, with its upstairs and downstairs and surrounding green of its own, it was pleasant and easy to rig up this apartment with certain very dear accouterments of home. Nothing of the ''McKinley era,'' thank you, in the new furnishings of these new quarters. Of all the terrible effects to which for so many years she had been immune in the house on Arctic Avenue! That velours set, all splotched, which she had purchased and, if not actually liked, at least had not minded. The brass bedstead which, be it said for Mr. Pullman, he had tried to talk her out of. Those hideous lace curtains which with such pride she had purchased, starched, hung, and laid out on the floor like a girl's train. Live and learn. Even back in those days, allowing for styles, the right kind of houses had not been done in the key of the one on Arctic Avenue.

Although practically devoid of the experience of a social life which would carry her into homes of others, glimpses of apartments through open doorways, window and floor displays of the shops, hotel-foyers, offices done in the better manner, women's magazines, created their slow revolution against the van-loads of household furnishings that had been transported from the house on Arctic Avenue. A comic strip of her early environment should not be plastered against the mind of her growing child, as the memory, for instance, of the golden-oak sideboard, with all the little fretwork balconies containing the pressed-glass vinegar cruet, bisque shepherd, and beer-stein shaped like a fat monk, was riveted into Bea's.

With one stroke, preceding this last move, over loud lamentations from Delilah, the major pieces of the Arctic Avenue period had been carted away to a neighborhood dealer, who had a basement store and exhibited most of his wares on the sidewalk.

"Jes' breaks mah heart to go marketin' over on Amsterdam, Miss Bea, an' pass by dat furniture cellar and have to see mah ole gemmeman's little old carpet hassock, an' dat dar taboret of ourn what used to have the knick-knacks on, standin' out dere on de sidewalk, waitin' for to be sold like any ole nigger slave. I loved dat ole hassock, and you done gone and pulled it right from under mah feet."

"I'll get you a new one, Delilah."

"New one! Ain't a hassock made lak dey used to make dem ole ones. Call dat new little ole footstool a hassock? Dat's nothin' on God's earth but a floor pimple. An' dat dar dining-room buffet. Gimme a sideboard every time. Maybe the drawers of our ole sideboard wasn't lined in velvet, but dar was a place on top whar to stand de fixin's dat was made for God's own dining-rooms. You kin have your buffets . . . jes' lak you kin have your dive-in-ports instead of de good ole slippery leather sofa you might have give me for mah room."

"But, Delilah, it would have ruined the effect of your nice new bedroom set."

"Nothin' cain't ruin no effect for me, jes' 'cause somebody tells me a fashion. I loved dat ole slippery sofa. . . ."

So did Bea, the new trappings of the apartment on Central Park West, with its powder-blue Chinese rug that caught your first footstep into the hallway, and the neat geometry of a console table with a Hawthorne vase on its teakwood base. It was a copy, that hall, even to the unframed, scroll-shaped Chinese print, of the hallway of another apartment in the building, the open door of which she often passed on her way to the elevator. The living-room, a replica of a first-class department store window-display, had been carried out by the "department" even down to the blue brocade drapes at the windows and the pair of onyx and lapis lazuli candelabra that balanced the mantelpiece. The assembling of that interior, snatched from odd and ill-spared moments from her overcrowded days, was labor of the kind of love that knew not fatigue. The delight of feathering the nest in that gate-leg table, with the lovely and symmetrical device of drop leaf, of which she had never even heard until achieving one! Windsor chairs, just the ordinary wooden sort, not unlike kitchen ones, unless you knew their correctness, in dark rich mahoganies, standing about the living-room. Divan of old-blue velvet (oh, the splotched horror of a sofa with which she had once been content!) with an overstuffed chair to harmonize (not match). End-tables for the couch, with each a Chinese jade lamp and old-blue shades. The pair of lamps alone had cost one hundred and seventy-five dollars, over which, from the point of view of budget, she had not even needed to hesitate. There was just no getting used to the idea. A beautiful octagon-shaped mahogany dining-table to match the buffet and six fiddle-backed chairs with cane bottoms. A painting of some oranges and Malaga grapes and a ripe red banana with the peel half back, just wonderfully natural, for over the buffet. The nice and obliging girl salesman in the furniture department had suggested it and gone all the way over to the picture department with her for the purchase. It warmed the dining-room beautifully, that picture, hanging in all its rich oranges and browns above the buffet and against the tan wall paper. Good masculine-looking oak furniture for Father's room.

There had really been no need for the bed. For more than a year, now, Father had been finding it easier to sleep upright in his chair. But it was wonderful to be able to provide him that set, complete, with a chifforobe of smoothly planed drawers that catered to every whim of his personal fastidiousness. The bedroom which she shared with her young daughter was really quite frivolous in its furnishings of a lovely new kind of wood called curly birch, with its twin beds, balcony-front dresser and dressing-table, blue silk scarves, curtains, and upholstery for the low boudoir chair and window seat. The master bathroom delighted, too. Its frosted-glass window set high in the wall. White mosaic floor. A fine white medicine-chest over the washstand that went right with the apartment; and then all the amusing nickel accessories that she stole the time to purchase, rushing in between appointments to shop the soap-dishes, cute sponge-rack to hook on over the bathtub, and a little white-enamel stool for Jessie, who by now could stand on it and reach the spigot of the stationary washstand for her own adorable little ablutions.

You just couldn't believe, the joy, between business negotiations of proportions that never ceased to bowl her over by their growing scope and importance, of this shopping for gadgets. The day of one of the important lease negotiations of her career, she stopped between lawyers' offices, to dart into Stern's for the purchase of a shower spray small enough for a child to manipulate in the bath. She was boastful of the fact that she believed she had started the craze of color kitchens in New York, inaugurating into her own all sorts of red-enamel pots and pans and red-checked oilcloth and a bright linoleum.

It was a complete enough little household of a pathetic kind of conservatism mixed in with a small quality of daring such as the bright kitchen and a gay piece of India print which she bought for its color and nailed up against the wall to brighten a dark bit of hallway. All her very own, as, warmed to the core, she looked about it, yet so little hers. Rather, Delilah's, upon whose terrific and willing-to-sweat shoulders rested so much of her success. Indeed, if you looked at it in a certain way, much of this well-being, this warm, good nest, was the gift of those boys, or rather what was left of them, who had packed the returning transports from Brest, as they swung up the harbor to be greeted by Mayor Hylan's Committee of Welcome.

These same doughboys, with body scars and deeper, more subtle scars deep down in the wells of their eyes, had, during those strange days of the strange orgy of going off to war, literally rioted her B. Pullman into prominence. Overnight, as it were, they had transported it to the priceless vantage of the front page of every metropolitan newspaper:

TROOPS STORM DOORS OF WAFFLE SHOP

SMALL RIOT IN GRAND CENTRAL STATION AS DOUGHBOYS, LED BY ALLEN MATTERHORN OF SEATTLE, VIE FOR SOUTHERN MAMMY'S OLD-FASHIONED WAFFLES AND MAPLE SYRUP.

Doughboys with lusty voices and still lustier appetites, passed up the beck and lure of the Great White Way last night and chose to bombard the portals of a newly opened refreshment novelty in the esplanade of Grand Central Station, known as B. Pullman, where, for fifteen cents, hot waffles, such as mother used to make, steaming coffee, all presided over by a grand old black woman in starched white. . . .

Actually, the boy, Allen Matterhorn, of Seattle, the youngest of them all, and with a sprinkling of freckles in a milky way across his nose and cheekbones, had eaten seven portions that gay mad night, his tan-colored curly hair standing up in shock from its constant tousling from the others.

"Dat boy shore did know how to git on de outside of a waffle better'n anybody I ever seen. Dar's a boy after mah own heart. Lawd help de mother dat's havin' to give him up—dar's a boy wid a grin into his face after mah own heart."

He had sent Delilah a pair of post cards through twelve months of days that shook the world, the first, a flamboyant word of greeting from Nantes in a bold boyish hand; the second, months later, in a strange small scrawl from Paris. Then silence——

"Mah boy's done hurt his arm—dis is lef'-handed writin'," Delilah had wailed, inserting the card in the wire rack of them she was accumulating. "Mah sweetest boy from all de war done hurt his arm an' dar ain't no good ahead when he gets home, God help his mammy's soul."

Perhaps. Perhaps not. But whether or no, there persisted the feeling of clairvoyance which she applied to the destination of so many of the boys who passed through her experience, never to be seen again or even heard from again, except by a vagrant postal card, perhaps, falling like a star out of the night of her crowded memories.

Some of those boys were not returning on the transport from Brest, nor would they ever. Delilah, with her boastful, aggressive, not-to-be-daunted clairvoyance, practiced a voluble omniscience:

"Dat little red-headed boy from what's dat town, dat we let sleep at de house de night he was feverin' up for his sciatica—what was dat town—Ipepcac—Ithica?—dat chile never comed home from de war, Miss Bea. Mark mah word, dat boy's been took to Jesus. De big, long, red-haired one dat de boys called Shank, dat et me out of house and home in powder' sugar on his waffles—he's got back to dat dar horse-like-lookin' maw out in Kansas he showed us in de picture. Mah chile, Allen, is back wid his maw. He didn't have no time to stop by an' see us on his way out dar—but mark mah word, Miss Bea, dat boy Allen Matterhorn has got hisself home——"

Be that as it may, coming and going, those boys, eager to be off, and on the return, desperately anxious and eager to forget, had contributed by their patronage to all this well-being of an apartment on Central Park West, with gadgets and trimmings, that actually, if the truth were known, represented less than she could really afford.

Those boys, including who knows how many of them left in Flanders fields, had helped bring it all about; those boys, Delilah, and, to be sure, her own fanatical capacity for riding an idea to its conclusion.

This last had helped enormously, but at ironical cost to one who had been forced to learn to tear herself reluctantly from four walls she coveted. By now, the equivalent of any high-power business man, the order of her day was to rush out mornings before her pretty child opened eyes that were accustomed to finding her gone, back again evenings, in time for the fag end, or part of the last hour, of her daughter's day.

And the greater part of the time, scarcely that. It was not unusual for her to return long after the apartment was quiet of every living thing save the ponderous lumbering about of Delilah, for an evening meal which she ate from a tray at one end of the living-room table.

Things had shaped themselves into that crowded kind of pattern. Three B. Pullmans in New York, one in Atlantic City, Baltimore, and Washington, with Cleveland and Chicago in the offing, to say nothing of a candy-and-syrup merchandising enterprise, which, it is true, had become merely complementary to the B. Pullmans, but which was rapidly taking on proportions that meant immediate extension of the two-room office suite and candy-kitchen in an old ramshackle office building in Front Street. There were four salesmen out of that office and a mail-order experiment with Delilah's Hearts that had become, within two years, a department of detail and growing profit.

It was beginning to be said of Bea, rather privately at first and within the sanctum of her business offices, where her clerks and salesmen were her devotees, that everything she touched turned to gold.

Even the candy-kitchen, in the hands of a small corps of girls trained by Delilah, who herself had become too heavy on her feet for long hours over the kettles, started to outgrow its quarters.

With the exception of Cambridge, Massachusetts, where a B. Pullman designed to undergraduate appeal had mysteriously failed and been withdrawn, the little flock of the remainder of them was moving ahead at self-generated and generally exciting momentum.

Already the idea and equipment were sufficiently standardized to make rapid duplication a comparatively simple matter. Floor space, approximately eighteen by forty, although variations would answer, with show window and entrance giving onto important corridor or thoroughfare, were to be found in the arcades, shopping districts, or railway stations of the average large city.

With Delilah on hand for the initial period, and young Flake, who was rapidly taking over the road management of the business and who had the hound's quick faculty for nosing out desirable localities, the results, with a facility that she found actually a little embarrassing, had come to be almost automatically to the good.

To be sure, there had been the quick demise at Cambridge, a failure so difficult to understand that it served to keep the precariousness also well to the fore of both her mind and young Flake's, but on the other hand, take what Bea called her stepchild B. Pullman. Located in New York, within a stone's throw of a large new hotel which invited the exclusive patronage of men, nothing of what she and Flake had anticipated happened. The men who had prompted the choice of location remained conspicuously away, apparently not attracted by the rather playful idea of the diner. It was after three summer months of desuetude that the select girls' schools in a neighborhood characterized by them, literally fell upon and swooped the B. Pullman unto themselves, storming it into sudden and lasting success.

The year that Jessie began to lisp to the small playmates she encountered in Central Park that her mother was B. Pullman and that the Delilah on the candy-boxes was her Delilah, that strange sporadic creature known as her parent, who had so little part in her day and was perceived evenings mostly through the heavy-lidded mists of sleep, was confronting the phenomenon of a twelve months' net profit amounting to fourteen thousand seven hundred and forty-six dollars and eighty-eight cents.

"Delilah, we're rich!"

"Go 'long, Miss Honey-Bea! If we was rich you wouldn't be workin' your laigs off thisaway. We're rich in the luv of the Heavenly Host, if that's what you mean."

This conversation had taken place in the narrow confines of the little apartment on Amsterdam Avenue, where the bulk of Delilah had actually repeatedly been known to get itself wedged into the narrow railroad hallway and where the children and the old gentleman had been placed, in shifts, upon the fire escape, for airing.

"What would you like best, Delilah, if we could afford to do something with our profits this year, instead of pour them back into the business?"

"I'd lak to see you, honey, rest up them achin' bones of yourn."

"No, no. What would you like best for yourself?"

"I'd lak dat for mahself."

"That's not what I mean."

"Lak? I'd lak to see mah white chile and mah black chile git——"

"No, no. Just for you."

"I'd lak if I could see mah ole gemmeman, wid de grace of de Lawd, walkin' around on his two feet dat's made whole. . . ."

"For yourself."

"For mahself? Law, chile! what I wants mos' of all, more'n an' above everything, is to go home to mah Maker in glory. I wants to go ridin' up to him in de finest funeral a nigger woman ever rode home in. I's seen 'em down Richmon' an' Natchez way, an' in Harlem, so fine dey'd make your eyes bug out. I'm payin' lodge-dues an' I'm savin' mah own pennies for to be sent home and delivered to de glory of de Lawd wid plumes and trumpets blowin' louder dan rhubarb would make growin'. When I drives up to dem pearly gates, Saint Peter's gwina say, here comes Delilah payin' glory to de Lawd who she served on earth an' will serve in heaven. Dat's me, Miss Honey-Bea, as I sees mahself every night of mah life when I lays dis here hulk down to sleep. Ridin' up to heaven in a snow-white hearse wid de Lawd leanin' out when He hears de trumpets blowin' to see if I's comin' in a white satin casket pulled by six white hosses."

"But, Delilah, what about until that happens . . . ?"

"Git us somewheres to live, Miss Bea, near for me to wheel mah ole gemmeman and mah chillun out for a bit of green. We misses our ole ocean, cooped up here where mah middle is wider dan de middle of dis house. . . ."

It struck Bea appallingly how little the narrow coop of these years had mattered to her. There had been no time. The daily grind had been too rapid. The rushing out after a snatch of breakfast into mornings of wintry twilight or pale city sunrise, and the fagged return after the waking day of her child had begun and ended, too bone-tired for more than her nightly round of inspection to the sleeping forms of her father and child, to even give alert attention to Delilah's detailed recountings of her child-ridden, old-man-ridden day.

The years in the narrow coop on Amsterdam Avenue had sped, like monotonous scenery past a train, leaving few definite impressions except those of mileage toward destination.

Home was a halfway house in which to steam up for the new day, the new quest, the new decision. Catch up on sleep. Snatch at the luxury of a warm bath, to soak the ache out of bones. Plan tomorrow. Wrestle with the problem of getting in Mrs. Wexler, practical nurse, who, just when most needed, was so dangerously likely to be occupied with another case, to come in and take over the household, while she and Delilah bustled out to Cleveland or to Baltimore, to inaugurate a new B. Pullman. Long evenings of credit and debit on the backs of envelopes. Credit. Debit. Months, even years of those evenings, seated beside a small table in the front room she shared with her child, a bit of old black shawl draped between the electric light and the crib.

The years marched on that way. Insidiously. There was the event of her first credit from the bank. There was the event of young Flake. There was the event of an invitation to confer with the Department of Home Economics at Cornell. There was the event of a voluntary loan of three thousand dollars from Hiram Prynne, Senior, who was to die two months later without her ever having clapped eyes on him. Events marched, all right!

Before she was seven, Jessie, snatching a hoop away from Peola one day, had shouted in a small shrill voice a word she had picked up that morning in Central Park. "Nigger, you!" Following that incident with rather frightening closeness, Peola had undergone severe scalp operation, the result of a hot iron simultaneously cutting and burning her as she was secretly trying to iron out an imaginary kink in her straight black hair. A campaign of newspaper advertising, dreamed by Bea, planned by young Flake, was about to make Delilah's face, Delilah's name, Delilah's smile, one that reached from coast to coast. Months of boiling down advertising copy into the phrase that was to prove succinct and magic. Delilah Delights. And strangely enough of developing within herself so marked an aptitude, that when the B. Pullman advertisement became a full-page feature in metropolitan newspapers throughout the country, she was still writing her own copy, in a sort of rhythm that started a fashion.

Your neighborhood B. Pullman is a rest cure! Read why Delilah delights.

One of her favorite and most successful feature pages was a catalogic summary of those reasons.

1. Delilah is the most indulgent hostess in the world.
2. Delilah loves to spoil you.
3. Delilah has a mother-complex.
4. Delilah cares.

Sometimes there were thirty of these notations. After a while, at her suggestion, the public began to coöperate. One thousand dollars to be given away in prizes for best statement not to exceed ten words, why Delilah delights.

"You've an ear for hokum; you mix it almost as well as Delilah does her batter," spoke young Flake, whose amazement at the fecundity of her copy continued to mount.

Perhaps. It was that, of course. Hokum. American raucous hokum. High-speed advertising. "Well, they like it!" Except that deep down in the reaches of her, from where she surveyed with a seriousness she was not to outgrow, everything pertaining to this strange incubus of business which had obtained strangle hold upon her life and time, she believed her ballyhoo. Felt it, dreamed it, lived it.

A B. Pullman represented achievement, the best of its kind. Under the superlative tutelage of Delilah, its corps of ample, immaculate Negro women graduating into the Pullmans of various large cities was not to be outdone for those qualities which made the enterprise immaculate, popular, and outstanding. If, as young Flake put it, she wrote gorgeous ballyhoo, it was because her copy was weighed with the quality of conviction uncoated by even the priceless veneer of sense of humor.

It was rumored at one time, considerably later, that she had been offered fifty thousand dollars a year to handle the advertising account of a national baking concern. The rumor was true, but it came at a time when, on the basis of relative values, it was to provide her office force amusement not unmixed with a certain amount of subdued hilarity.

Oh, events marched all right. The World War, which straddled that period, had sometimes, quite horribly to her contemplation, seemed to bend a persistent rainbow over her enterprises.

It was as if a harassed world found just the pause she had planned for it within the warmth of her amber-lit, fragrant booths. You stepped off a milling thoroughfare of war-burdened faces into a tiny recess in the day's turmoil.

It was not so simple to analyze the growing momentum of the maple sugar and Delilah's Hearts, except in terms of this same phenomenon of a riddled world eking for itself small gratifications.

In any event, here was the evidence in fourteen thousand dollars net profit for that Armistice year, when the renting of the eighteen-hundred-dollar-a-year apartment on Central Park West was to be the last conservative move out of the mood of a lifetime of conservatism which up to this point had enveloped her.

Overnight, as it were, unloosing what must have been latent dogs of war within her, she seemed to have tasted the blood of big business.

The secret of her success, said the wiseacres of no wisdom, lies in the fact that she does things on a large and daring scale.

Large and daring scale! She knew better. Flake knew better. Up to this point, every knot of the progress from harbor to open sea had been nosed by inches, not ells.

It was as concrete as this: I've got to get over being penny wise, she told herself one August noonday of a humidity that was felling horses in the streets, while she stood in the center of the sea of asphalt of Columbus Circle; stood in the relentless heat, debating whether to take a languid cross-town car or a taxicab, to the place of a business meeting which was to involve a transaction in her affairs mounting into six figures.

Yes, events were marching, and through it all, as if symbol of littleness from which she needed emancipation, her little father, clapped into his body like a druid into a tree, regarded her constantly with his silent eyes.

·26·

The more or less quiescent problem of Peola lifted its head the day that Jessie caused to explode off her lovely lips the ''nigger.''

It was a Sunday morning, one of the rare ones that did not find Bea indulging in the boon of the hebdomadal quiet of her office, usually with Weems, her head bookkeeper, or with young Flake during his intervals in town, going over odds and ends of affairs that had found no place during the week's hurly-burly.

Windows were open to an April sun of drenching warmth that flooded the front of the apartment. In one of them, wrapped in blankets, leathery as a crocodile, his small eyes all for his daughter, sat the old gentleman, ready to lift his threatening cane, in the only gesture left to him, at practically every expression of her solicitude for his comfort.

On the floor beside him, in, about, and around his wheelchair, reckoning with him only as a fixture of environment, there romped the children when the epithet came.

From her chair beside the window, her drying hair, already long and reactionary-looking in a world of women who were beginning to dock theirs, lifted itself, as if individually, from each follicle, of its electric vitality. It was pleasant to alternately open and close eyes upon the scene of the bright frail lacework of new greens in the Park across the street; shouts of children on roller skates, soft new smells, splashes of light on a powder-blue Chinese rug, her flushed and agile Jessie at play with Peola, who was more agile.

And then it came, bursting across the quiet like shrapnel, because immediately from the kitchen, as if part of it had struck out there, was Delilah on the scene, standing stunned and stockstill in the middle of a strange new silence.

"Nigger! No fair! You pushed! You're a little nigger and you've got no half-moons on your finger nails. Nig-nig-nig—ger!"

Nigger! How, how, had the word dawned into the tiny horizon of this household. Nigger.

"Jessie, how could you? Come here, my poor little Peola, to Miss Bea. . . ."

My poor little Peola, not at all! Something as agile and ready to leap as a leopard was out in Peola. Backed almost immediately by the enormous bulk of her mother, her hands flew together and clasped behind her back, so that her thin arms twisted like pulled twine, the small face settling into lines of a fury ridiculously too old for it. Actually, standing there in an anger ready to spring, she made a hissing sound.

"Honey-chile, your mammy's here. Take it standin'. You gotta learn to take it all your life that way. Nigger is a tame-cat word when we uses it ourselves ag'in' ourselves, and a wild-cat word when it comes jumpin' at us from the outside. Doan' let it git you."

"Jessie, apologize!"

"No, no, Miss Bea. 'Tain't no use makin' either one of dem make too much of dis. Peola's got to learn. What's happened is as nacheral as de tides. Dey been creepin' up on her since de day she was born, and now de first little wave is here, wettin' her feet. Jessie ain't to blame. God ain't, 'cause He had some good reason for makin' us black and white . . . and de sooner mah chile learns to agree wid Him the better. Oh, Miss Bea, doan' you remember 'way back when she was a baby, mah tellin' you de itch in her heart mah poor chile was born wid?"

Suddenly there turned upon her mother the small gripped fury of Peola. "You! You!" she screamed, the flanges of her nose whitening and spreading like wings as she beat small fists against the checkered apron frontage of Delilah. "You're so black! That's what makes me nigger."

"Peola, my child, how can you talk to your——"

"Hole a minute, Miss Bea. She doan' mean it no more'n her whitish pap used to mean it. Nobody can tell me dat white nigger married me 'cause he knew I'd slave for him. He could 'a' got plenty. He married me 'cause he knowed I jes' cain't help a-lovin'. Ain't nothin' gonna make me quit lovin' dis chile. She's got her pap's curse. Hating what

148

he was. And it's a heap easier to be black when you're black lak I am, Miss Bea, dan it is to be white when you're black lak mah poor baby. Folks said I worked dese hands to de bone supportin' her pap 'cause I was proud he was white. Proud? De biggest curse what ever hit him or me was his whiteness. Oh, mah honey, cain't you see de Lord done had good reason for makin' you black? Oh, mah honey, cain't you see de glory in de Lawd's every move?''

Into the checkered fold of apron flowed the heat and bitter salt of her child, and finally into the thawing warmth of vasty bosom.

"Sh-h-h, mah baby-chile. Jessie didn' call you nigger wid her meanness. She called you dat wid her blood. Forgive dem 'cause dey know not what dey do is de Lawd's way for makin' it easy for us to bear our cross, as he bore hisn. Doan' cry, mah baby. If you let go of tears for every time you're gonna be called nigger, your tears will make a Red Sea big enough to drown us all in.''

"Jessie, sweet, you don't know what a dreadful unkind word you just used to Peola.''

"Peola is a nigger, Mother, isn't she? But I never meant to be bad.''

"She is a negro, just as you are a white. Go over to her and tell her how naughty you have been to pick up a horrid street word without even knowing its meaning.''

"No white chile cain't be comin' apologizin' to a black and puttin' ideas into her ahead. Stop dat tremblin', Peola, and walk over dar, and tell Jessie you're proud of bein' a nigger, 'cause it was de Lawd's work makin' you a nigger. . . .''

"I won't be a nigger! I won't be a nigger!''

"Got to, mah baby. The further 'long you go apin' whites and pleasurin' wid dem, de more you're letting yourself in for de misery. . . .''

"Won't! Won't!''

"Then brace your heart, mah baby, 'cause breakin's ahead for it. Brace your heart for de misery of tryin' to dye black blood white. Ain't no way to dye black white. God never even give a way to dye a black dress white, much less black blood. Never you mind, mah chile. Some day, on the white wings of a white hearse, wid white plumes and the trumpets of a heavenly host blowin' black and white welcome alike, we'll ride to glory to a land whar dar ain't no such heart-breakin' colors as black and white. Quit cryin' out your little heart. Sh-h-h-h. . . .''

"Delilah, stop her. She'll have a convulsion. Oh, Jessie, how could you!"

"I didn't mean nigger to be a mean word, Mother."

"Then don't dare to use it again! See now what you've done. Peola, you mustn't hold your breath!"

"I won't be nigger!"

"Yes, you will, baby, long as de Lawd is stronger dan you are."

"I won't! I won't!"

"Got to, mah baby. 'Tain't no tragedy unless you make it one. Dar is good black happiness in bein' black. Your maw's done found glory in de Lawd's way. She's gonna learn it to her baby. Remember, honey, some day on de wings of a white hearse—sh-h-h-h, mah little black baby will be carried to her heavenly host."

"She'll have a convulsion, Delilah, if you don't stop her."

"Better now dan when she's old enough to have grown-up ones. It ain't de bein' black, honey—it's bein' black in a white world you got to get your little hurtburn quiet about. . . ."

"I won't be black! I won't be nig——"

Off the small lips, which shuddered the word like a defective coupon out of a machine, spun foam.

"Delilah—the little thing—she's fainted . . . !"

She had. Quite stiffly and into a pallor that made her whiter than chalk.

· 21 ·

One day a glib young reporter from the *New York Mail,* still in the coat
to the khaki uniform she had worn ambulance-driving in France, shot
a question at her, out of a mental kit-bag of them she was using in a
"CAREERS OF SUCCESSFUL WOMEN" series, which left Bea flabbergasted.

"And, now, Mrs. Pullman, at the close of your busy executive day,
what are your recreations?"

They were seated in the new B. Pullman offices situated in the prow
of the twentieth story of the Flat Iron Building, the city laying itself
out from its triple exposure, its gigantic pattern weaving across the
frame of another day.

They had been much in the public print, these offices, keyed to the
pitch of the flamboyant success story.

FEW KNOW THAT B. PULLMAN, KNOWN BY NAME THE COUNTRY
OVER, IS A WOMAN.
WOMAN EXECUTIVE, SEATED AT DESK IN HER EXTENSIVE OFFICES
IN FLAT IRON BUILDING.
SPECTACULAR RISE FROM TINY WAFFLE SHOP TO AN INSTITUTION.

"It is difficult to realize that the comely, mild-mannered woman who
rises from her desk to greet the visitor, is the B. Pullman whose name
has become . . ."

At first, as the identity of B. Pullman began to take on ballyhoo and
feature-story value, this sort of thing had struck her with the usual shock
with which publicity assails the hitherto obscure.

Delilah, who by now could scarcely appear on the streets without recognition following and pedestrians frequently stepping up to confirm their suspicion of her identity, was one matter. Her face glowing above the alliterated euphemism, "Delilah Delights," had stamped itself against the public mind, but as for Bea herself, having one's picture in the paper was somehow not the thing. Mother had even not liked it when on one occasion their figures had stood out quite boldly, if anonymously, in a view of the Boardwalk which a photographer had snapped on them unawares, and which subsequently appeared in the Sunday section of a local newspaper. You left that sort of thing to the actresses and women who achieved the front pages through actions which invited notoriety. You never saw the women members of the really exclusive Atlantic City families in the papers, unless for social events of a high and distinguished order.

Otherwise you got into the newspapers if you were missing like Dorothy Arnold, or divorcing, or kissing Hobson, or wore your hair short, or chopped with a hatchet like Carrie Nation.

It was young Flake who was to hold out for the advertising value of dramatizing the personal equation behind the rise of the B. Pullman from a waffle to an institution.

The ten-year almost general misapprehension of the sex of B. Pullman, the Atlantic City girl who started out on a can of maple syrup; the place of Delilah Who Delighted in the hearts of thousands of doughboys; the University of Delilah, where nearly as possible replicas of herself were trained for B. Pullman service; all a gold mine of free advertising, which, according to Flake, money could not even buy.

Already there were three or four handsomely-bound scrapbooks of clippings on a table in the waiting-room outside the private offices of B. Pullman.

Yet, withal, here was this young squirt of an ex-ambulance-driver putting in her cocksure manner a disquieting question to B. Pullman, that for the moment staggered her.

". . . What are your recreations?"

"Recreations? Why—er—of course." What did one do after business hours? Sundays? Week-ends? During those vacation periods she was constantly planning for herself and the personnel of her staff, but to which she herself never quite got around. Recreations? Now, what? Curious. Most curious. Come to think about it, she had none. In all the years since the death of Mr. Pullman, her father's growing impotencies, the birth of her child, the birth and development of her business, recreation had played no part in her scheme.

Recreations? For years the majority of her evenings had been commandeered for the quiet intervals they afforded for going over her affairs, particularly of late, with Flake, on the occasions when he was in off the road, or in clearing up odds and ends of long accumulation with willing members of her growing staff, Miss Weems, Miss Lejaron, or any of a score of the competent ones with whom she seemed to have developed a talent for surrounding herself.

Bea's jerry-flappers, Jessie was to dub them, several years later on the occasion of the joint celebration of the tenth anniversary of the service of three such invaluable women—Miss Weems, Miss Lejaron, and Mrs. Van der Lippe.

Of course there was the aspect of recreation to all this, especially the periods spent with Flake, whose road to ultimate general managership was paved with his bestowal upon the affairs of B. Pullman of practically all his spare time.

The all too few hours with her child were recreation, but now, with Jessie about to be entered into a boarding-school, which but a few years ago it would have seemed fantastic to ever be in a position to afford for her, even those few spare hours at home would dwindle to the sole performing of offices for the old gentleman.

Recreations? The question off the fresh young lips of her interrogator left her flabbergasted.

Recreations, zero.

However, it gave her pause. Magazines and the feature sections of the Sunday newspapers were constantly serving up the success formulæ of the great and near-great, chiefly as they existed in the minds of press agents bent on celebrating their clients into celebrity.

Knowing all this, having swung back often enough revolted from the printed palaver of herself and her enterprises, there persisted, however, just enough of the conviction of inexact journalism to set going within her a sense of the need to do something about this recreations, zero.

According to the inexhaustible folk-biology of Delilah, you shed your skin, like a snake, every seven years. "Yas, ma'am! New skin creeps

153

up on you and shoves off de old widout anybody but de Lawd knowin' it. You's shed yourn all right, Miss Bea. Mah same Miss Honey-Bea underneath, but a shiny new one on top.''

That was true. It was impossible to live and move in an ever-enlarging world of business women and not both consciously and unconsciously ape their accouterments of dress and good grooming. It was as if, too, she could feel the accouterments of her success. You buckled into them as part of the business day's armor. The bells, the straps, the nickel plating. The large *de luxe* offices, which had grown out of the insistence of Weems and Flake rather than her own volition for the symbols of achievement. The rigmarole of inner and outer, private and public, offices, conference-rooms and secret sanctums. The dramaturgy of Weems, who in her early days had studied for the stage, was responsible for most of these outer trappings. They constituted a success technique to which Bea, resistant at first, was gradually to conform.

No doubt about it, they, that hydra-headed public, wanted it that way. They expected it. They demanded it. Nothing short of it smelled of success, and making your success succeed was by no means a negligible aspect of the strange tribute it exacted. Business appointments staged by Weems or Flake to take place around the lunch tables of expensive hotels. Largess in what you did and how you did it. To the manner born in transactions of growing vastness and importance by one who most of her life had reckoned conservatively and without sense of irk, in her parents' and then Mr. Pullman's world of nickels and dimes. A Weems-and-Flake generated talent for the apparently large and easy spending of the executive who will not stint in the tremendous trifles of keeping up appearances.

You drove your bargain to the last penny amid settings and gestures that seemed to toss them far and wide.

Penny-foolishness and pound-wisdoms developed with overwhelming suddenness in one who still practiced secret and almost appalling personal economies.

The debate with self over the cross-town street car or thirty-cent taxi fare to keep the rendezvous of a one-hundred-thousand-dollar-lease transaction she was to consummate with a group of men she had invited to lunch with her in a private room at the Plaza. Bargain-bin stockings and expensive modish-looking shoes which she bought in Thirty-fourth

Street basement shops that specialized in "slightly imperfects" and in which she trod the expensive Chinese rugs of her elaborate offices. On those days when there were not business appointments over the Waldorf or Holland House or Plaza or Gotham lunch tables, she snatched her bite in a lunchroom on Twenty-third Street called Sweet's Inn, or often as not took it standing up in the form of a chocolate milk-shake and vanilla wafers before a drug-store counter. There was a Tiffany glass-set on her broad-topped walnut desk, but a sack of jelly beans in her beautifully planed right-hand drawer.

Yes, something should be done about it. Constantly you were reading the recreations of John D. Rockefeller, Mary Pickford, Virginia Eden, Anna Held, President Wilson, Valentino, Caruso, Gaby Delys.

No modern woman, up and doing, celebrated after a fashion, could afford to let herself feel thus flabbergasted before the question of a chit. Recreations?

That was the small situation that sowed seed for the elaborate white-tile gymnasium, sunken pool, handball-court, electric riding-horse, rowing-machine, punching-bag, to be installed in the B. Pullman offices, considered quite an innovation at the time and which was to be flashed as a news story from coast to coast.

Incidentally, too, it laid the beginning of the friendship with Virginia Eden, author of one of the most alluring and remunerative phrases of modern industry, "Beauty culture," who, unsolicited, asked permission to install, gratis, into the B. Pullman office gymnasium, one of her beauty grottos, a cabinet of mirrors so cunningly devised that you beheld the back of your neck as casually as you ran eye down the length of your nose and elaborately fitted out with shelf after shelf of the famous creams, lotions, powders, astringents, perfumes, and manicure paraphernalia that bore the famous Eden imprint.

"The gymnasium is yours," Bea told the women members of her office force, who at the time numbered only forty-six. "Use it. Feel at home in it. Get yourself trim in it and keep there in it."

They adored her, these women employees, for a time with a dangerous kind of intensity which took the form of anonymous gifts and letters which ultimately had to be ruled and ridiculed out of practice by Flake. A situation which could easily have become obnoxious and of which Bea herself had remained almost absurdly unaware.

At twenty-seven, despite pores that had been bared to years of city soot, body that had never known massage or periods of rest or respite, and which was never to avail itself of the gymnasium which Weems declared was the source of a fad that was to spread rapidly among men executives, who on all sides were installing punching-bags and electric horses in conjunction with their high-power offices, the B. Pullman who had looked twenty-three at seventeen, looked precisely that twenty-three now.

Through little, if any, effort of her own, she had managed to linger behind her years, her growing symptoms of inner tiredness, her buffeting about the marts of men, her combat with a world which she had dared before she comprehended, to the contrary notwithstanding.

The year that she appended to her offices the elaborately explanatory "recreation," she looked easily, in the lay of her flesh without shadow or crinkles along her bones, in the way her strong glossy hair, when she brushed it a few hurried strokes, continued to stand out strand by strand, and in the stride of her strong firm legs, not a day older than the twenty-three.

Except that imbedded in her bones, packed into their marrow, there nested the growing fatigue that, mysteriously, seemed not to be of her body, yet hung in the very center of her being, like a clapper to a bell.

· 28 ·

The first even incipient friendship of these militaristic years of expansion
and growth was Virginia Eden.

Characteristically, in the events leading up to the installation of the
Eden Grotto, an invitation to lunch had arrived, in the last word of the
prevailing mode of a large mauve florist's box, containing a corsage of
Parma violets with a red-rose center.

It struck Bea with a sense of the growing inner dreariness which
sometimes now seemed to dangle down the center of her, that it was
the first corsage she had ever received. Its cold fragrance filled her
office, and later the sitting-room at home, when she unloosed it in a
bowl and managed to keep it alive a week by storing it in the ice-box,
nights.

They met for lunch in big hats and cloth-topped shoes amid the plush,
carved wood, gilding and heavy mahogany of the Waldorf-Astoria on
Fifth Avenue. There was something exciting to Bea about this occasion.
It was the first time she was experiencing personal and semi-social
encounter with that then comparatively rare bird, woman in big business.
To be sure she knew women general managers, departmental heads,
tearoom and candy-shop owners galore, but years previous, before the
word "beautician" had arrived, she had read somewhere that only one
person in the beauty-culture business had paid income tax. That one
was Virginia Eden, a fact which her appearance delightfully belied.

"Why, I thought you were much older!"

"I thought the same of you."

"I would have recognized you anywhere."

"Your pictures don't do you justice."

They might have been any two of the throng of women meeting in

Peacock Alley, with husband's allowances in their pocketbooks, for lunch and matinée. They flushed, they fumbled among gloves and handbags, fluttered over choice of table, fought, with two waiters standing attention, for the privilege of granting the other the chair with the most desirable view of dining-room, spilled excess emotion, motion, and vitality over trifles.

Within the next few years, by way of one of the major financial interests of the world, was to come to the small ash-blond woman facing Bea, whose face so frail had the look of a sheet of fine-grained writing-paper with careful erasures almost marking out what had been written on it, a cash offer of eight million dollars for her imprint Virginia Eden, which had become a household word.

In fact, five years hence, the combination of Virginia Eden and B. Pullman would have created a stir in any smart public dining-room of New York, and even then, rather unprecedented figures were these two who with their teeth into the wind, were riding farther and farther into the uncharted seas of big business for women.

My, but here was some one in this little trick of a Virginia Eden. A dancing doll on a string, her arms, her legs, her tongue, and the whites of her eyes all seeming to synchronize into an ecstasy of vitality. The way she called, "Waiter!" and, adding first, dashed off her name on the check. The manner in which, relative to a business proposition they were discussing, she flashed a gold pencil out of her bag and did additions right on the heavy damask tablecloth. The circumstance of her being paged by a row of gilt buttons, who bowed her toward a telephone booth. There were rings on her fingers, fine ones of large carat, animated sparkling tips to her nails, and two circles of color on her cheeks that seemed run up there by the high pressure of her bounding heartbeat instead of having been achieved by her already world-advertised cosmetics.

There were no halfway measures with Virginia Eden. Even then, her sureness was quite terrible.

"My dear, you are the one person in New York I have wanted to meet. Not just because I want you to have one of my grottos, and you can take my word for it that I come bearing you some gift—of which, I may add, I expect magnificent free publicity. I'm that way, m'dear! To the point."

She was! Like a streak.

"Five years from now we won't be quite so special as we are now. From now on, women in big business are going to be common everyday, as they should be. But just the same, we're a nose ahead of the gold rush and that's why we've a right to be in on the ground floor. See?"

You bet B. Pullman wanted to be in on the ground floor. It gave meaning to years where all too often meaning had been obscured. All these years of blind pulling at the load must have been heading her toward this. Toward something other than just the blind ploddings. . . .

Sitting here in this red-and-gold dining-room that overlooked Fifth Avenue, lunching with one of the few important business women in America—in the world, come to think about it—brought home a sense of significance.

Who would think it of them, that in all that vast dining-room, so festively agog with millinery and music and fresh flowers, the two youngish women cutting into mushroom omelettes were in a peculiar and exciting class to themselves.

You bet B. Pullman wanted to be in on the ground floor.

"You know, Pullman, they'll tell you that women cannot work well together, and God knows most of them can't. Yet. But we can. I know it by the way you do things. By the way you handle your employees and your fork and your publicity. By the way you swing a real estate deal and sign leases where angels fear to tread. Single-track mind. Want what you want when you want it. That's you. That's me. I want love. I want money. I want success. I don't know you well enough yet to know what you want, but whatever it is, you're after it. How much ready cash can you tap?"

This amazing woman! How did one know so patly what one wanted. How dared one demand so patly. Love? Of course one wanted it. Down underneath the recurring sense of the futility which one kept jammed down so tightly into the recesses of the mind, that want somehow would not be jammed and stilled. One would no more admit to Virginia Eden, who had it, the extent to which her days and endeavors and even her successes were devoid of love in the sense of the word that had lain so apparent in the Eden eyes when she pronounced the word. Cash on tap, now, was another matter—cash on tap—well—er——

"All right. Don't commit yourself. We won't talk any more about it until I have put the grandest array of facts before you that one business man ever placed before another. I've a scheme, Pullman, that will lift you off your chair. Are you a home-wench?''

''A what?''

''Are you crazy about houses—homes—dig-ins?''

Was she! Was she!

''My car is outside. You're going with me to look at a certain parcel of property in this town that is going to put you with me in on the ground floor. You and me ought to work together, Pullman. You make women fat and comfortable. My job is to undo all that and make them beautiful. You're grist to my mill. I want to be grist to yours. Look, I brought you a present. A little Aladdin's lamp. Rub it when you feel blue. It's solid gold. Wear it on a bracelet. When I was seventeen I rubbed mine for the first time and fell into my first love affair, and have been falling in and out of them ever since. Most of them have ended badly, but they've been worth it. See, it's my business trade-mark. Cute, ain't it? I have them made up in gold to give away to my friends. You're my friend, now. Look me in the eye, Pullman, and tell me. Isn't success ridiculously easy, once it begins to succeed?''

She had thought so a thousand times. Yes, after the strain and sweat and pushing until the very groins of your being shrieked protest, something like momentum happened. It took your wits and your concentration and your continued willing sweat, of course, to keep it going, but the success of success had ball bearings. You steered, but in time your energy was strung with nerves along which flowed the mysterious generating currents you had somehow got started back in days when success had not yet been born.

What a smart, shrewd, on-to-herself girl was this one, scooping up peach melba with the quick dips of a bird. Life was a matter of definition for her. She took frequent inventory not only of her business, but of her days, her emotions, her gratifications, her fulfillment, her destination.

Catch her using up the days, the weeks, the months in just the dogged procession of time. Part of life's yield of riches must be love—pastimes——

What are your recreations? How shrewdly, quickly, and to the point Eden could have answered that! She not only had them, but chose them each with purpose. My bridge and golf are equally bad, but playing them at all enlarges the scope for meeting men that matter. Life owes me a living worth living. Yes, Eden regarded life as her debtor, she its relentless paymaster.

By contrast, she made B. Pullman to herself, seem its slave.

Learn from a woman like Virginia Eden, no older, no wiser than herself, but who seemed to have so many more responding surfaces to her mind. All in a breath she talked of life, happiness, and love as if they were the rightful facets to the diamond she called life. Life. Happiness. Love. Not just living along, although there was plenty of homely family pattern in Virginia's life, too. Children by two different fathers whom she adored. Retainers. Hangers-on. A stepfather with a silver tube for a larynx, whom she housed in a special suite especially built on the top of her house on Lexington Avenue.

Yet even more than those kinds of loves were demanded by the imperiousness in Virginia Eden's eyes. Neither was she content to give or receive solely in the coinage of these. Greed for the transcendent of all loves, which begot life and which begot more love, was in the imperiousness of Virginia Eden's demands. Love and happiness, as she said them, made what had been going on through years of a petty and mundane routine seem imitation of life.

Except, there was Flake! Dickery, dickery dock; the mouse ran up the clock. Just so, the name ran up Bea's spine. It was at this time, with scarcely more than the shiver, that she first began to permit thought of him, eight years her junior, to penetrate the tremendous inhibition she erected against it.

My, though, what a lot to be learned from a woman who put under appraisal, demanding value received, pretty nearly everything connected with love and happiness. How typical Virginia Eden's remark: "Life is a feast for those who insist upon forcing their way to the banquet-hall. Think of all the centuries women like you and me have had to sit back and wait for men to manufacture their destinies for them. I'm going to help you manufacture some of your own destiny this afternoon. And you're going to help me. Ever heard of Fishback Row?"

Fishback Row proved to be a city block composed of a regiment of twelve narrow tenement houses with homely, pock-marked faces and unsightly rears that sloped in unkept grass plots down into the East

River which washed and lopped against their clayey flanks. At first sight a dreary line-up of impersonal-looking filing cabinets for city dwellers, washlines flopping their uniforms of poverty, and dirty children with shaved heads playing about the sagging stoops.

High above the heads of these houses, a suspension bridge, jerking Long Island to the acquisitive flank of Manhattan, stalked across the skyline in quite a magnificent geometry of steel and arch. A dramatic effect of high-flung, girdered webbing, bending above these narrow-faced houses as they bathed their dirty feet in the hurrying river.

"Now," cried Miss Eden, bumping her smart sedan along the cobbled, unpretty, and soot-blown street, "what do you see?"

Where, previous to the descriptive eloquence she had just heard from Virginia Eden as they drove along, she might have seen precisely the literal picture that blew so coldly against the naked eye that raw November day, there slid now a vision that transformed the pock-marked tenements into a row of Colonial houses along what Miss Eden described as "the London Embankment all over again, what with Blackwells Island across the river bed, giving a House of Commonsy effect."

What an idea! The new houses to be built hind-side around, with kitchens facing the drab slit of street and the clayey back yards becoming inclosed gardens which marched in well-graded terraces down to the river and which would then face the lovely fronts of these lovely homes.

To one with that perpetual hurting nostalgia for a house and a bit of green, and that sense of security within four dear walls that were meant to inclose happiness, here in the heart of this city of granite bosom, was a bit of small intimate soil, washed by and smelling damp from a friendly river. Not the impersonal grandeur of the Hudson, but just a stream that cut through back-yard dirt.

In such a bit of yard Father could sit and sun himself, the children shout at play.

The children! It was becoming constantly necessary to jerk the mind to the new reality that Jessie only returned home nowadays at long and stated intervals from Miss Winch's Tarrytown School for Girls, and that a surprisingly long-legged Peola marched off for public school these mornings from a household long since empty of either of their day-long needs.

The children did not shout any more at play. Up to the time the encroaching problem concerning them had made necessary the choice of separate ways, the hitherto inseparable youngsters, destined so suddenly and so irrevocably to fly apart, had already reached the stage of conversing in quiet, little-girl tones.

But in any event, it was easy to visualize Jessie, arriving with her school-girl luggage and her bright hair that would never bear restraint, flying, to a home into which she could be proud to bring a chum. Here, off the central lanes of a city forever in the throes of building and rebuilding, in these old-women houses literally standing in their footbath of river water, was somebody's chance to create a colony of new homes. Her own. Virginia Eden's. At least a dozen of homes. As Eden said: "somebody's chance to reap the easy rewards of starting a bright new fad in a city that loved to succumb to them."

What a chance!

Simultaneously, as on a thunderclap, their eyes, hers and Virginia's, met.

"I knew you'd see it! Anybody with imagination would! That's what makes it such a dangerous idea, though. It is a miracle nobody has seen it before. This block, darling, can be purchased for under two hundred thousand dollars! We can start something this town will remember. All we need is one bell-sheep to come in on it and watch the rest follow. I know a woman now—client of mine, you'll know her name right off—who is ripe to sell her Fifth Avenue house and start a colony somewhere that looks as if it's for fad and for fun, instead of for thrift. Can't you just see the layout? Homes and gardens and the right ten or twelve people to make it the smart thing to up and move away from the beaten old trails, and us in on the ground floor of it all, with our own homes costing us not a cent!"

Bea could!

"It isn't really my idea! Except it took me to pounce on it. A girl in my cosmetic department—poor dear, she died last month—got the pneumonia and I came here to see her. She lived in the fourth house, there to the right. Had a back room—can't see it from here, but one facing the river and the Island. She saw me looking out of the dirty window toward the river, with the boats moving up and down it and the bridge arching it all. "Somebody ought to buy up these tenements, Miss Eden," she said, "build homes with gardens, and start a fad. It's like the Thames in London, where I was born.'' That put the idea in my head. I've been back every day since. Poor Claire, I didn't speak any more about it to her before she died, not knowing how sick she was. Figured there would be time to give her a share of credit. Meant to give her a room of her own in my new house overlooking the New York Thames. She's gone now. But you're here. Are you interested?''

Was she! The thought of this real estate venture, whetted by her own previous forays into rentals and leases of her various B. Pullman sites, came rolling at her like a tide.

A two-hundred-thousand-dollar proposition! Two hundred . . .

Never, never be overwhelmed. Things need not be what habit made them seem. There was a time when even contemplation of the scale on which she now did business would have floored her. Never be overwhelmed. Stretch the mind. The imagination. The will. Find a way. Here was a project into which the imagination flowed like wine into its carafe. Here was Jessie's home, about to be born. Here, then, in this row of frowning witch-like houses, was the meaning of everything that had gone before. Nothing ventured, nothing gained. Nothing ventured, nothing lost.

Well, venture everything!

· 29 ·

There were to come periods, during the three years of the labored and reluctant fruition of this project, when, laid low of what she was to call her chronic Fishrow headache, she was to wish herself well out of it. At least so it seemed to her when time and time again circumstances attendant to Fishrow were to take on what seemed a spirit of vengeful design to obstruct. Actually, however, during their darkest destiny, she was to refuse two offers to buy her out. One from the firm of architects at work on the plans for reconstruction; the other from the very building loan association that was helping float the enterprise.

Now indeed were money worries, what with her business up for collateral during fifteen long months of uncertainty, and staggering and unforeseen impedimenta to teach her the terror of the squatting of sleepless nights upon her. Yet even these were subordinate to the devilishness of certain realizations of the human equation, that were to come in a terrible sort of dawning.

The single-fisted years had been one matter. One schemed, fretted, maneuvered into action on the one-man plan. But suddenly now, in this partnership, with all the new and vast corollary interests, so vast that they threatened, there for a time, to engulf her own original enterprises, there began her grim education of how men sharpened their teeth for throat-to-throat contest in business.

Virginia Eden's teeth were as pointed and polished and incisive as a terrier's, and with them, when she sank, she drew blood.

They were to sink, during those nervous, harried, and yet withal adventurous months, into B. Pullman, drawing from her blood of disillusionment and almost defeat.

"I feel," she told Flake during this period of critic intensity in her affairs, and when it seemed to her she had reason to regret the hour she had ever laid eyes on Fishrow, "as if I am doing business by ear. I hire expensive lawyers, I listen here, I listen there, but in the end I go ahead on my own judgment. Such as it is. Such as it is. Such as it is!"

"I've faith in it," he said.

They were seated at lunch at Sweet's Inn, and she felt herself flood with color and the world jump.

"I couldn't go on if you didn't."

It was the most emotionally freighted remark she had ever made to him. They served at Sweet's little canary-bird bathtubs of pickled beets before the arrival of the meal proper. She began to jab into hers, spattering little crimson drops on the tablecloth.

"Look what I've done," she said, feeling the same crimson mounting to her eyes.

"Technically," he said, resuming, in a voice smooth as glass, where they had left off, "Eden is within her rights. The contract provides, corporation shall not be responsible for unsuspected fissures, rock formations, underlying obstructions. . . . "

In the end, and at the risk of financial jeopardy that for a period of five months threatened to dash her onto the rocks of bankruptcy, it was B. Pullman who swung loans and terms to enable her to buy out the Virginia Eden share of Fishrow, Inc., at a top price which was handsome justification for all the beautician's prophecies, that windswept November day when the two of them had viewed the properties from her sedan.

It was a close and to-the-swiftest race, with two sets of expensive lawyers chuckling over the spectacle of Virginia Eden and B. Pullman waging a fierce, amicable bargain with apparent satisfaction to both sides concerned: Apparent satisfaction to both sides concerned, because even with knowledge that the final terms were mulcting ones, and that the Eden profit on the investment was netting her eighty-two per cent, there was elation and relief in feeling herself out from under a partnership that had become something worse than irksome, free now to swing this project with the single-handed precision of one who has always walked alone.

The stand taken by Virginia Eden with regard to the need to suppress the fact of an immense rock stratification running under part of the property where important excavations were planned, was what had thrown the pall of incompatibility over the partnership. Division of legal opinion inclined toward the Eden attitude. The Fishrow block had been purchased under what might or might not have been the knowledge of the former owners concerning the presence of rock. Legally, it seemed fair enough to pass on that suppositional ignorance, even though these disclosures threatened to double, if not triple, the cost of building to those who had bought lots. All within their rights, and, as Virginia Eden had not been slow to reiterate, shrewd and legitimate business. In fact, the gamble, the zest, the quick-wittedness of big business lay in just such sleight-of-hand. Besides, the type of person who had been induced, mainly by Eden, to buy in on the novel project, could afford to take the additional financial punishment.

Perhaps. But stubbornly, doggedly, threateningly, B. Pullman opposed the suppression of the fact of the rock stratum.

"There is a difference between integrity and just out-and-out dumb business," an equally resistant Eden fought back. "If anybody asks me if there is a rock stratum below the point of present excavation, I'll say yes. But I won't go out of my way to advertise the fact, and neither would one single shrewd business man of my acquaintance."

"I'm not saying you aren't within your rights, Virginia. It's just that we don't feel the same about it. I've never done things quite that way."

"Babe-in-the-wood luck may desert you at any moment, you know."

"I realize that. But just the same, there is something in me won't let me see that corner lot going to your Mrs. Kan Casamajor, I don't care how many millions she has, without letting her know the foundation for a house the size she plans is going to cost her about four times more than we originally estimated for her."

"Darling Exhibit-A, chances are she'll never even know the difference! Do you think she stews over her account books the way you and I do?"

"Perhaps not, but that doesn't change my rôle in the transaction."

"Starting Fishrow is just a fad for her. She'll live in her house a few years and then pass it on to one of her children. But to us it means everything."

"Neither would I do it to Hedda Owen. At least she has had to earn her fortune."

"Preaching thrift to an actress! What does she know except that as long as it's there it's there to be spent! Why do you think I, who haven't personally given a facial in years, made Owen the talk of the town in twenty treatments, if it wasn't to knead into her flesh and bones the idea of Fishrow?"

"Then why, if it makes no difference——"

"Because where you and I might not back out for the sake of the extra money that rock strata will cost, these women, once they learn about it, even though ordinarily they wouldn't ever miss the difference, are rich enough and famous enough to make themselves cheap for the sake of a few thousand dollars. And without Casamajor and Owen, where do we stand for making Fishrow the fad of the town. Oh no, you don't do this to me!"

"They won't renege on us, Virginia, even if they know the truth. Neither will the Baileys nor a single lot-holder."

"Maybe. But we don't take that chance!"

"I do."

Their eyes met.

"You do it alone, then."

How calmly and irrefutably that decision settled itself. How outside herself. There was a sureness, and underneath all, as she and this small-faced, determined little nugget of a Virginia Eden faced one another across a directors' table, a sense of rightness, that had dictated so many of her previous and lesser decisions.

Something stubborn and sure held out in her, even in the face of what seemed irrefutable evidence.

Eden was right enough. No use pretending, even to herself, that years in the conflict of the business world had not taught her that. *Caveat emptor*—let the buyer beware—was phraseology she had picked up among the marts of men. What was not specifically guaranteed was not guaranteed at all. Unless ethically, and the great ethics of business, as you approached its upper reaches, was to be legally protected.

Mrs. Kan Casamajor, oil magnate's widow, whose initial purchase of the large corner lot and the adjoining one was to start off the Fishrow project as one of the smart new residential fads of the town, might undoubtedly be the sort to raise hue and cry should certain facts of the rocky lay of her land reveal themselves to her. But in the end, legally helpless, she would take her punishment. So would they all.

B. Pullman, facing Virginia Eden across the long table of a private room their bank had thrown open to them for this hurried discussion, realized this. Realized this as well as she had known, five years before, that a certain interpretation of a clause in a contract with a firm of candy-box manufacturers would, had she availed herself of the loophole, have saved her eleven thousand dollars.

Here it was again, the curious, rather frightening rigidity of her adherence to certain mysterious and unplotted tenets of her behavior.

"We've come to a deadlock, Virginia."

"Well, what are you going to do about it?"

"Buy you out."

"Good. Pay me the percentage of profit I've figured has got to pay for my initial genius in this affair, and the Fishrow baby is yours, hook, bait, and sinker. I'm never interested in anything that looks sure-fire, anyway. And besides, my darling, oh, my darling, I'm in love! He doesn't know it yet. In fact, he doesn't even know I exist. But you can see for yourself—how can I let my business interfere with my life . . . ?"

If only, if only, if only, she thought, smiling back at her brilliantly— if only, if only, if only mine were the kind of life with which my business could interfere—if only——

"Make me an offer, Pullman, remembering that I come high, but within reason to friends——"

"As one business man to another, name your price, first and last."

"Two hundred thousand buys me out, first price, last price, so help me God."

"Piracy. But said. Done."

·30·

Christmases, Easters, and Thanksgivings, except the last two of them, when she had visited her roommate in Baltimore, Jessie came home. The summer vacations of her tenth, eleventh, and twelfth years, however, were spent in the Switzerland summer branch of Miss Winch's school, along with about twelve of the boarding girls, who were escorted by Miss Winch herself and a Miss Askenasi, junior member of the highly successful firm known as Miss Winch's Hudson School for Girls.

Admission into Miss Winch's school had been something of an achievement. With no prestige other than a business one, which in the nature of the case might have been a deterrent, the by no means simple circumstance of entrance to Winch's was achieved in a manner that mattered with intensity to Bea, because it seemed to place her under the first tribunal of her young daughter's judgment.

It had long since become evident to everyone concerned that the problem of the day-by-day propinquity of Peola and Jessie was one that would no longer keep laid.

"One of us has got to get t'other away from t'other, Miss Bea. Dem two chillun is turnin' black an' white on us now, in earnest. Your chile cain't go startin' in the same public school, tagged on to by mah nigger child—'tain't no good for both."

No argument to that. The time had come for the parting of two tiny ways which had converged successfully enough up to that point.

"You doan' want no public school for yourn, nohow, Miss Bea. Ain't you affordin' one of them fancy boardin'-schools for her?"

A small neighborhood girl who walked with her nurse in the park and sometimes invited Jessie to tea parties off miniature fine china in her own elaborate nursery, had already inculcated into a pair of laid-back and listening little-girl ears the magic of the name Miss Winch's School.

It was during those days of need of decision and action regarding boarding-school for Jessie, that Bea, rather than risk direct application at Winch's, keyed herself up to a piece of aggressive letter writing not easy for her.

> MY DEAR MRS. GRENOBLE:
> I read of your activities with much pleasure in the Atlantic City papers.
> I wonder if you remember me and my first B. Pullman booth for the First Church Fair of which you were patron many years ago. You recall, we left cards at one another's home.
> My little daughter is quite a young lady by now, and I desire to enter her in Miss Winch's Hudson School for Girls. Excellent references are necessary and, knowing yours would be that, I am, for old times' sake, requesting that you indorse my application.
> Thanking you in advance, my dear Mrs. Grenoble, for any assistance you may give me in obtaining entrance for my daughter into a school of such fine rating as Miss Winch's, I remain

The reply, which immediately she began to await as something which was to determine so much of her status with her child, came with alacrity and enthusiasm.

So when she was seven, a rather lanky, knob-kneed little girl, whose first blondness had dimmed into a freckled sort of eclipse from which it was to emerge again, was entered as boarding student in a school that was practically to monopolize her, body and spirit, for the next decade of her life.

At the period when the circumstance that Jessie was almost the identical height of her mother was still a shock and a surprise to them both, there was not yet much to indicate the Jessie to come. Gone was that quality of golden childishness which had once made it a delight for Delilah to appear with her showy charge among the nursemaids in the park, leaving only a glow of pallor over a child almost conspicuously a gawk. For the several years of this transition, Jessie, as Flake once put it, teasing her, hung from the joints, knees and elbows dominating her young weediness. There was not so much length, as looseness, of limb; a predisposition, too, not unlike her mother's, had been toward premature growth, except that there was something slab-like and boyish to her kind of slimness. Tender and tiny were these early maturities of Jessie, only half awake, reluctant there in the lathe-like flatness of her pallid body, with its budding breasts slow to emerge from the dream of sleeping flesh.

Even at fourteen, in her manner was something of the startled unease of a boy in a roomful of strangers—half shy, half rebellious, wholly inarticulate. Her blue eyes with their extraordinarily large black pupils darted, her breathing came short, and always her head was half thrown back as if to give ready momentum to imminent flight. A startled-looking little girl, as if her ears were laid back to sound as slight as the falling of a leaf, her eyes wide apart and unquiet, her expression listening, her attention cocked, like a squirrel's.

Time and time again the thought rolled over her mother: The child looks surprised about something. Perhaps she was born with some of my surprise that anything so different—so—so like a bird, could be her father's daughter. Or, for that matter, mine. We never imagined things together. We didn't know how. Us—to have begot her!

Strange were the feelings she engendered in a mother whose imagination had been unprepared for her. It was like holding a bright foreign bird captive in the hand and feeling it breathe fast of all sorts of fears and uncertainties, and then loving to release it and watch it hop exploringly around the house and sometimes actually come perch upon the shoulder.

And as she grew older, and her visits home from school more and more intermittent, especially when the summers in Switzerland became almost part of her school routine, that quality seemed out over her more and more.

She talked so little; so little that her mother came to have secret awe of her silence.

I am one of those mothers who isn't supposed to understand. There are probably teachers, that Miss Askenasi or Miss Winch, in whom she confides. She is more at ease, no doubt, in the homes of her school chums. She never brings them here. She will some day, though, when I give her the proper background. I wonder if I am educating her away from me. That will be a terrible thing, and yet I will go right on doing it. I wonder what she thinks of me. Or if she thinks of me. After all, in my world I stand for something. Wonder just how she feels about that. She never wants things like other children. Almost as if it embarrasses her to be beholden to me. I want to give her. Those are the things that draw parents and children together. Giving. If only there were something she terribly wanted. The right kind of home to which to bring her chums? She never complains. Only doesn't bring them. If only she were of a temperament to come to me, wanting things. We're so formal. It would even be darling if she would nag. Perhaps I am just one of those tired business men to her, wanting to buy my way into her affections. I'm away from home so much. Must seem terribly preoccupied by outside worries. Why, Delilah is a better mother to her Peola than I am to mine! Next year I am going to start a regular campaign to spend more time with her. Next year——

It was just about this time, though, when Jessie was her stand-offish fourteen, that she did something that amounted to a darling and tremendous trifle.

Home for the Easter holidays, a little strange about the house, noncommunicative, except with Delilah, whom she followed from room to room; or with her grandfather, who, even while a babe herself, she had babied, she suddenly, out of a clear sky, began what to Bea turned out to be the delightful inauguration of addressing her as "B. Pullman."

"Hello, B. Pullman!" she had cried, kissing and greeting Bea the evening that, appalled, overwhelmed, and almost unbearably excited, she had entered the apartment after catching Virginia Eden's proposition on the fly.

A dozen methods of procedure for raising the initial down-payment of good-will moneys, mental maneuverings for collateral for loans, were pressing against the hot and troubled inner surface of her forehead as she turned her latchkey that night, conscious that what she needed was to forage, face down, into a bed Delilah would turn back for her, and confront, in a spangled darkness and concentration created by tightly squeezed eyes, the gorgeous dilemma into which a stubbornness of purpose, over which she seemed to have no particular control, had crowded her.

Fishrow in her lap! Wanting it with all her intensity, she nevertheless felt pinioned, appalled, frightened by it. This dazzling project of Fish-row! As if already the arrival of her child for the Easter holidays had not been relegated to a corner of her mind by circumstances that kept nudging and crowding at her for attention.

On top of her latest determination to open a Pullman in the Wall Street district, with a lease pending for precious footage in the financial district, with Flake in Detroit following up an important location lead there, and the final payment of a twenty-eight-thousand-dollar note to Frazier Bank to be met that week, here an additional something had developed, of her own stubborn volition, it is true, that staggered her.

Partnership acquisition of a good parcel of land, its subsequent sub-division and resale under highly restricted and profitable conditions, was one thing; lone-hand operation another. No two ways about it, whatever of considerable and canny acumen she, Bea, had been able to bring to the immensely difficult task of the purchase of a block of individually owned lots, with prices mounting as suspicion of a pro-moting project developed, Eden's indispensable contribution had been the important list of the right names she had been able to commandeer as purchasers of building lots in Fishrow.

Twelve lots in all, eight of them, including the double one to Mrs. Kan Casamajor, had been sold according to Eden's insatiable lust for names.

Due to certain perceptions in Eden, perceptions entirely lacking in Bea, the quite remarkable balance of at least two of the town's foremost social and professional signatures had been appended to Fishrow deeds.

To swing so growingly important a project alone from this point on!

"You play a lone hand best," Flake had repeatedly told her, after her involvement with Eden had started to show up fissures in their common ground. "It is sex o'clock in the garden of Eden. It is just plain six o'clock in yours. One of you will have to get out."

Well, it had been Eden.

Walking into her home that evening, weighted with this new aspect of an old fear of that perpetual bugaboo, her aloneness, it seemed little short of blessed dispensation to be met by the lovely phenomenon of her young daughter, thawed, of her own sweet will, into the sweet nonsense of: "Hello, B. Pullman! What's the use having a national institution for a mother unless you cry it out loud!"

Jessie's favors, when they came, could be quite lovely. Her over-consideration for her grandfather was one of them. During what was to amount, from this time on, to a practically sustained period of absences at schools in and out of America, not a week was to pass without some token, from a postcard to a package, finding its way to the old gentleman.

"It's so pitiful to me that some poor quirk in Grandfather's brain denies him the happiness of loving you," she told her mother once, a remark which Bea was to keep polished by constantly turning it over in her memory.

It is doubtful if he was ever to place quite definitely in his brain the identity of his granddaughter, except that his eye loved to rove over her, much in the fashion it would follow a mote of sunlight dancing along a wall. Her brightness moved and laughed and danced, like light. There was a male nurse, now, for the old gentleman. John, a taciturn middle-aged Scot, who was to remain with him until Mr. Chipley's demise some sixteen years later in Helsingfors, Finland, of all places, at the age of ninety-two.

Jessie's holidays meant long hours of relief for John, while she wheeled the sack-like figure of her grandfather in the sunny lanes of Central Park, or, with the serious, unamused face of a preoccupied adult, cut rows of paper dolls for him. Alas, they meant these holidays, the most curious exhibition of class consciousness between her and her erstwhile playmate of all hours, Peola, which Jessie now tried to meet with too much show of affability and the dark child with too much sullen reticence. It was for Delilah, however, that she reserved an almost demonstrative adoration; Delilah, who in turn paid her the perfect tribute of reciprocal devotion by emulating in Peola, as far as her sense of propriety dared, Jessie's clothes, hair-dress and color schemes.

Demonstrativeness toward her mother was sufficiently rare to make the episode of the "hello B. Pullman" memorable. Extraordinary the quality of formal restraint between these two. Always had been. To the mother, who in all her life-time had almost literally refused her nothing, her requests came timidly, if at all, and then usually by way of Delilah.

"Delilah, you ask the B. Pullman for me, when she comes home tonight, if I may spend Christmas holidays with my roommate, Madelaine Stanhope, at their camp up in the Adirondacks." "Delilah, you ask the B. Pullman for me if I mayn't have one of those fur skating-jackets the girls are wearing.'' ''Delilah, it would help a lot if you would talk up with the B. Pullman the idea of another Switzerland summer for me.''

''Law', chile-honey, why doan' you up and warm your mammy's heart by askin yourself.''

She never did. Or rather, she never could. The inhibiting something between these two kept them timid one of the other.

Sometimes it seemed to the mother, thwarted and yet adoring, adored and yet thwarting, that if literally she could hold the yellow head of this girl close to her for as long as she wanted—and that would be days, weeks; hold it as long as she wanted—that something inside her, the something that hungered, would reach out and draw this child of her being back again into the warmth of a body that yearned for it.

''You and your chile is too polite to each other, Miss Bea. What you need to git acquainted is some good old hollering fests, lak me and mine. We yells our lovin'. You two just hurts yourn.''

True. It hurt terribly, to be shy of the child you loved. It made seem doubly precious any indication of thaw in her.

''Now is that nice? To address your decrepit old mother that way? What put it into your head, Puss? Where is your respect for the aged? Hello, Bea Pullman! The idea!''

''Well, you are, aren't you, everybody's Bea Pullman. Why not mine? Every time one of the girls or a teacher learns for the first time you're my mother, their eyes turn cartwheels!''

The thought smote her for the moment that their eyes might perform the phenomenon referred to, because of the indefinable snobbery that exists in all school worlds. In her own time, even back in the Atlantic City public school, children of mothers who ''worked'' were in a subtly relegated class. But none of that here. There was pride in Jessie's voice. Jessie was admiring her.

''I wonder, child, if you wouldn't like to come down one day, while you're home on this vacation, and see our new offices?''

''You bet!''

Actually the child seemed to want it!

If only there were time tomorrow. She would walk her through the offices—not exactly to show off, but for the girls and boys to have a look at her in her natty little velveteen suit, long black-silk legs, blond hair escaping her velveteen cap and flowing over her shoulders.

Tomorrow! Dread of it came surging over her like an engulfing wave. The very dawn of it would be tangled with problems almost too staggering to be faced. Too staggering—yet exciting—yet alluring. "Hurry, Delilah, my dinner. I've heavy going tomorrow."

"Here it is, Miss Honey-Bea, pipin' hot, and I'll turn your bed down."

How well Delilah knew! Hours ahead face down into her pillow, lying there fully dressed, concentration pinioned, the darkness soaring in Katherine wheels before her squeezed eyes, until, finally, exhausted, she rose only in order to go to bed.

Her child had been sweet tonight. Something seemed to have pushed up through the fresh young earth of her. A budding of something that seemed to make her shyly but surely aware of Bea.

One must follow up this something so sweetly and newly begun between them.

But at the moment, so much more so even than usual, there was heavy going ahead.

Meanwhile, Jessie must wait.

·31·

Ultimately, it became noised about that B. Pullman Company, Inc., had gained exclusive control of the Fishrow enterprise.

What actually happened was the reverse, because for a period of over three years B. Pullman, Inc., became literally a mortgage, held as collateral by Fishrow, a complicated deal which was to harness that period in financial exactions that took heavy toll of peace of mind.

It was not that subsequent developments were not to more than justify this strange leap into the dark of Virginia Eden's proposition and the subsequent mortgaging of the B. Pullman enterprises. They were, and with brilliance. But it was that sense of the suspended private ownership of her short string of standardized B. Pullmans that had grown, as it were, from the intimate flesh of the palm of her own hand, which kept unease her running-mate.

There were urge and hurry, presence of fear and dread of disaster, over these years, due chiefly to the involvements which complicated her state of mind as well as her state of affairs.

There simply could be no peace to the period of the suspended ownership of her business. Fear hung like a dagger into the mortgaged days. Immature business instinct motivated these fears. Her experience in a fluctuating commercial world dominated by loan and notes, mortgage and collateral, did little to come to the rescue of these amateurish anxieties. With the passing of her sense of complete ownership of her Pullmans, persistent unease was born.

It lay on her heart, it motivated her days, it drove her strength; captured for its own purpose every ounce of her vitality. Needlessly to the extent that it did, because from the very first, events practiced conformity to her pattern for them.

Mrs. Kan Casamajor, social dowager whose fancy at seventy-six had been captured by Virginia Eden's carefully massaged-in idea of a new residential center removed from the usual restricted area of the socially mighty, took the news of the serious rock strata impediment across the most important excavating section of her property, so casually that she did not even trouble to reply to the report of the surveyors' findings. It is doubtful if she did more than toss it half-read along with other matter pertaining to her entertaining new pastime.

Already, with the new venture in its incipiency, the dowager Mrs. Kan Casamajor had become the subject of publicity and speculation.

Let it cost. The new venture was proving amusing.

Miss Owen, influenced chiefly by a turn in her own domestic affairs, which was ultimately to result in divorce, demanded, upon learning of the additional expenditure of thousands to be occasioned by the difficulties of excavation, release from the transaction, a junior member of the architectural firm which designed the external layout of the block, buying in immediately.

Within three weeks after the announcement of the Kan Casamajor purchase, what amounted to two city blocks of lots had been sold to persons likely to keep to the mood of Virginia Eden's original project, and on a basis calculated to yield B. Pullman her property free. Making up the carefully planned motley of Fishrow were a Wall Street broker, internationally known as a turfman; a spinster, with a lower New York Street named after her forebears; the granddaughter of the dowager and her artist husband; a songwriter who had married the daughter of a bishop; Ned and Lyne Esty, a brother and sister of local social and athletic fame; the junior architect; and to B. Pullman's amused delight, the remaining plot to Virginia Eden, at a price none other than the one she herself had originally determined it must yield.

Ironically, long after the blue-print version of Fishrow was to become brick and mortar reality in the finest Colonial tradition, one lot only, Number Nine, Bea's own, was to remain empty, filled in, fenced in, and waiting, for the first spadeful of dirt to be turned toward the erection of her house.

Almost, it seemed, before her senses were prepared to receive the full impact of the phenomenon of Fishrow, it had begun to be a moving concern of clearance of tenements, wreckage, blasting, excavation, blue prints, brick and stone.

Fishrow, with the exception of her own well-dreamed house, which must now await the easing of the great financial pressure of these mortgaged years, was almost too easily becoming reality.

Every growing aspect of it never ceased to amaze and stun her. The meeting of the stockholders to agree to the last detail upon the architectural stipulations of Fishrow. The dowager's handsome gift of a pair of Vermont marble and limestone gates, as portals to Fishrow Gardens. The negotiations with the city of New York for certain riparian rights concerned with boat-landing at the base of Fishrow Garden. The decision of the stockholders to inaugurate their own steam-launch service between Fishrow, Wall Street, and points intermediate.

Promptly this enterprise, which B. Pullman found herself swinging single-handed, became a publicized, not to say spectacular, project; residential land values along a hitherto ignored edge of the city started rapid response to inflation. Almost immediately promoters began buying up adjacent rows of tenements, none of which, however, could claim the peculiar river-front advantages of Fishrow.

Here was a ground-floor achievement. A Wall Street journal carried this quip:

IT IS NOT GENERALLY KNOWN THAT THE B. PULLMAN OF WAFFLE AND FISHROW FAME IS A WOMAN. THE NAME B. PULLMAN, OF COURSE, IS GENERALLY KNOWN, WITH EVERY INDICATION OF BECOMING MORE SO. HAVE YOU SEEN THE LATEST B. PULLMAN ON BROADWAY NEAR TRINITY CHURCH? THE LAST WORD OF ITS KIND. THERE ARE NOW TWELVE DISTRIBUTED BETWEEN NEW YORK, PHILADELPHIA, BALTIMORE, ATLANTIC CITY, DETROIT, BUFFALO, NEW HAVEN, CLEVELAND, CHICAGO, KANSAS CITY, AND TULSA. WATCH THIS. ALSO WATCH FISHROW. AND MOST OF ALL, WATCH B. PULLMAN.

Here it was, happening all right, all about her. The success of her success. She, who had scarcely been aware of the woman-suffrage movement as it came to fruition, importuned now on all sides to address business and professional groups of her sex, eager to take cue from her; she to whom everything outside the home was interference with the ordered rightness of the dear private things that mattered. Achievement, built upon the shoestring of those days when the dimension of her dream was no larger than an ultimate bungalow at Ventnor on an income which was to be wheedled from the back doors of Atlantic City!

The piling of those days into weeks, into months, into years until now . . .

"Miss Bea," said Delilah, after John, the male nurse, had read her the item in the Wall Street journal, "dat's grand, but dar's something powerful lonesome-soundin' about it."

"What do you mean?"

"Outta all dem men down dar in Wall Street, supportin' and lovin' deir wimmin, you ain't one of 'em."

"What under the sun kind of an idea is that?"

"I want some lovin' for you, honey—some man-lovin'."

"Delilah!"

"Yes, wasn't no slipperance of de tongue. Man-lovin' was what I said. All dis here gittin' us upper and upper is all right, but 'taint gittin' mah child nawthin' for herself."

"Why, Delilah! Hush!" She felt hit. As if suddenly she had walked into the edge of a door standing open in the dark. As if there had been an accident and this was her first moment after the crash.

"Ain't nothin' wrong in what I done said, Miss Bea! After all dese years, I want some man-lovin' for mah chile. . . ."

"Delilah, I've never heard you talk like this before. It's not nice. It's vulgar. . . ."

"Right kind of man-lovin' ain't vulgar, honey. It's de Lawd's patent for makin' enough babies to keep de world goin', wid enough left over for wars and cyclones and drownin' and fallin' off de tops of build-in's. . . ."

"I've had my share of that sort of thing."

"Man-lovin'? No, you ain't, honey. You jes' know you ain't. I doan' know nothin' about Mr. Pullman, honey. You ain't never mentioned him much. I ain't nevah asked, knowin' mah place. But I've seen his picture, honey. You ain't nevah had your share. Nothin' lak your share. You doan' know nothin'. It ain't in your eyes, honey."

The thought flashed through her that sometimes her eyes felt like the carved ones that kept sculpture such a dead art to her.

"I's jes' an ole nigger woman, honey, but I's had it and I's done wid it, but I's had it while it lasted. I's laid wid a no-'count nigger, knowin' I was no moh to him dan a washin'-machine and a ironin'-board dat he married to save ever havin' to shuffle a bone again. But in lovin' dat no'-count, I's had de t'ing dat ain't come up in your eyes yet. And knowin' dat, I wants mah Miss Honey-Bea to have it. No matter what you got to pay, its worth it. Doan' wait too long, honey. Cotch it!"

Cotch it! Here relentless pursuit did seem to imply the overtaking of something. Of what? Cotch it! Cotch security, home, opportunity for her child. Cotch it! Cotch life. Success. Fishrow. B. Pullmans. More B. Pullmans. Detroit. Philadelphia. Chicago. New Haven. New York. Kansas City. Springfield, Massachusetts. With still more Springfields in the offing to conquer, what with Flake already casting his location eye over the Springfield of Illinois. Cotch it! Round black faces as nearly as possible in the image of Delilah shining over the waffle irons of the cities of a nation. Maple-sugar hearts. Mail-order shipments of more and more gross of them. Gray-squirrel coat for Jessie. Fishrow for Jessie. Switzerland for Jessie. Success. Cotch it! More, bigger, and better Pullmans. Man-lovin'. Cotch it! Dickery, dickery dock, there was that little fugitive thought that, like the mouse, ran up the clock. Only the clock was her spine, stinging to the scuttling thrill. Man-lovin'. That dream had been dreamed dubiously and lay for what it was worth in the small sealed casket of her dimming yesterdays. Within it, the image of Mr. Pullman was dust. Sometimes, on those rare occasions when she attempted to try and piece together her memories of his features, his precisions, his habits of speech, his heavy-breathing habits of passion, his gaitered heaviness of tread, the bits of love's young dream, lay squashed into that dust, nor would they revive into pattern. Cotch it? Gone!

The act of teaching Jessie the final clause of her nightly prayer had been little more than a mental gesture. "God bless my mama and my gramp and Delilah and Peola and dear gramma and papa in heaven."

The mere thought of the dear dust of Adelaide Chipley lying in the small plot of Atlantic City cemetery, beside the decorous remains of

Mr. Pullman, was tender to tears. But somehow, his memory could not seem more than a small pebble pressing the memory but faintly, the heart not at all. In just such proportion as he disintegrated into featureless, then faceless dust in the memory, the need to resurrect his image for the growing Jessie sporadically presented itself.

The child had remained uncurious but politely attentive to the cabinet-size photograph which her mother took occasion to hold before her from time to time.

"Jessie, I am going to have a copy of this photograph of your father made and framed for your room at school." Or, "Jessie, it is twelve years ago today that God called your dear father to rest."

Once when she was six, her reply indicated no relevance of idea to the theme.

"Did you shave my pap?"

"Pap? Who is he?"

"Pap is my papa. Delilah calls papas pap."

"Never mind what Delilah calls him. You are to say papa, or better still, father-dear."

"Did you shave my papa-dear, the way you shave Gramp?"

"No, dear. Your father was not ill and helpless. He shaved himself."

"Did my pap spit, like Mr. Vizitelli?"

"No, Jessie. Your father was not the sort of man to chew tobacco."

"Did my pap——"

"Father-dear! Now say it after Mother, Fath-er-dear!"

"Faw-ther de-ar!"

It had not been easy to keep mental image of Mr. Pullman hung in either the child's or her own gallery of portraits.

From the very beginning "Grandma" had tripped lightly from the fastidious sills of Jessie's little lips. Not so, Fath-er de-ar.

"Man-lovin'. That chapter is closed, Delilah."

·32·

Without anyone knowing it, except the strange little crypt herself, Peola, at eight, had "passed."

By one of those feats of circumstance that seem to cerebrate and conspire, one Peola Cilla Johnston, entered into a neighborhood public school one morning by B. Pullman, as she paused long enough in her morning rush to enroll the child, was actually to pursue two years of daily attendance, unsuspected of what she chose not to reveal.

In a public-school system where the northern practice of non-segregation was common, it must have been a simple, if coolly calculated, little procedure, for the eight-year-old Peola to take her place without question among the children, never by word or deed associating herself with the handful of negro pupils in the class.

Only in a city whose density of population could make possible so fanciful an anonymity could this child's small ruse have been possible. Be that as it may, for over a period of twenty-eight months, living within a three-block radius of a public school made up of district children, the fact of Peola Cilla Johnston's race remained unbeknown to school-mates and teachers alike.

As Delilah, with her face fallen into the pleats of a troubled mastiff, reiterated over and over again: "if I'd 'a' only known all dem months dat my chile was a-cheatin' on color! Swear to de good Lawd who is mah Saviour, Miss Bea, I'd 'a' turned in mah grave if I was dead. Cheatin' on color jes' because de Lawd left out a little drop of black dye in de skin dat cover up her black blood. How kin I git mah baby out of crucifyin' herself over de color of de blood de Lawd seen fit in His wisdom to give her. Lawd, have mercy on mah chile's soul, Miss

Bea! She cain't pass. Nobody cain't pass. God's watchin'. God's watchin' for to cotch her."

The manner of the upset of Peola's little apple-cart came ultimately by way of an incident treacherously outside calculation.

A sudden freak rainstorm, little short of cloudburst, precipitating itself into the midafternoon of a day that had begun in sunshine, played such havoc in parts of the city that streets were flooded, cellars and subways inundated, and at certain intersections traffic, paralyzed, stood hub-high in water.

Alarmed as she viewed a wind-swept, tree-ravaged section of Central Park, Delilah, in a cape that gave her the appearance of a slightly asthmatic rubber tent, set out for the school-house with galoshes and mackintosh for Peola.

"I starts out for her, hurryin' to git dar before school closin'. Her pap died from bronchitis he cotched in jes' such a storm. When I seen dem trees twistin' and heared water roarin' down de streets like Noah's flood, I started footin' it fast as mah laigs would carry me for mah chile, known' her pap's weakness in de lungs. . . .

"Miss Bea, all of a sudden, standin' dar in de door of her schoolroom, askin' for mah chile, sweat began to pour on me lak it was rain outdoors. Dat Peola's little face, sittin' down dar in de middle of all dem chillun's faces, was a-stickin' up at me when I asked teacher for mah little gal, lak a little dead Chinaman's. Mah baby turned seventy years old in dat schoolroom. . . . Lawd help her and Lawd help me to save her sinning little soul. . . ."

This was strangely and really quite terribly true. The straight-featured face of this child, Peola, had the look to it of hard opaque wax that might have stiffened in the moment of trance and astonishment following the appearance of Delilah in that schoolroom, into something analogous to a Chinese masque with fear molded into it.

Bea Pullman, walking into the typhoon of hysteria that followed the arrival home after the thunderbolt which had smashed a small universe to smithereens, heard the first commotion while riding up in the elevator.

Facing Delilah in the center of the kitchen, her dark lips edged in a pale little lightening of jade green, was fury let loose sufficient to blast the small body that contained it.

Low-pitched fury, grating along on a voice that was not a child's voice.

"Bad mean old thing. Bad mean old devil. They didn't know. They treated me like white. I won't ever go back. Bad mean old devil. I hate you!"

"O Lawd! O Lawd! saw a brown spider webbin' downward this mornin' and know'd mah chile was comin' home brown—O Lawd! . . ."

"Go away—you! Yoo—yoo—yoooooo!"

The words out of Peola's fury became shrill intonations of the impotence of her rage, and finally with her two small frenzied fists she was beating against the bulwark of the body in the rain-glossed rubber cape, beating and beating, until her breath gave out and she fell shuddering and shivering to the kitchen floor.

"May de Lawd," said Delilah, stooping to pick her up as you would a plank, and standing there with her stiff burden outstretched like an offering, the black chinies of her eyes sliding up until they disappeared under her lids, something strangely supplicating in the blind and milk-white balls—"may de Lawd Jehovah, who loves us black and white alike, show mah baby de light, an' help me forgit dat mah heart at dis minute lies inside me lak a ole broke teacup."

"Oh, my poor Delilah!——"

"Poor Delilah ain't no matter, Miss Honey-Bea. It's poor Peola."

They wrapped her in warm cloths, with memory of methods used in a previous attack similar to this, and chafed her long, slim, carved-looking hands, and, despite dissuading from Bea, there was a smelling muslin bag, with a rabbit foot attached, that Delilah kept waving before the small quivering nostrils.

"Dar's shameweed in dat bag, and asfidity. Shame, mah baby. Lift de curse from off mah baby. Lawd, git de white horses drove out of her blood. Kill de curse-shame de curse her light-colored pap lef' for his baby. Chase it, rabbit's foot. Chase de wild white horses trampin' on mah chile's happiness. Chase 'em, shameweed. Chase 'em, rabbit's foot. . . ."

"Delilah, that's terrible! That's wild!"

"It's de white horses dat's wild, a-swimmin' in de blood of mah chile. Drive 'em out, Lawd. Drive 'em out, shameweed. If only I had a bit of snail water——''

"Delilah, take away that horrid-smelling bag. Try this brandy—force the spoon between her lips——''

But in the end the services of the physician, with offices on the ground floor of the apartment building, were hastily enlisted.

"This child is in a state of nervous collapse. Has she had a shock?''

"Yes, Doctor. A little upset at school."

"Look at that eye," he said, rolling back the lid. "Rigid."

Poor Peola!

"You have a highly nervous little organism here to deal with, madam. You know that?''

"We do, Doctor."

"Public school?"

"Yes."

"Remove her. Let her have instruction at home or at least where she will receive individual instruction. Get me a bowl of good hot water, Mammy, so I can immerse her feet and get some circulation started."

"Get the one from my room, Delilah."

"Is this your only child, madam?"

"Why, Doctor, this is the daughter of the woman you just sent for the hot water! Peola is colored."

He screwed the top onto his thermometer, slid it into his waistcoat pocket, and reached for his bag.

"I see. My error. Sometimes difficult to detect the light types. Keep her in bed overnight. She'll be all right for school in the morning."

In the doorway he encountered Delilah with the bowl of steaming water.

"Innything else I kin do, Doctor, for to make her free of de spasms?''

"Spank her out of them when you see them coming. Gently, of course. Then dose her with castor oil. She may not be so inclined then to go off into them."

"Ain't you gonna put her into dis heah footbath I brung you, Doctor?''

"A night's rest will fix her up. Good evening."

"Miss Honey-Bea—what—how?"

"Dear, dear Delilah! . . ."

But it was out of the wretchedness of this was born one of the few desires Delilah could ever be inveigled into expressing.

"Miss Bea, I'd love it, when mah chile gits well, for to send her away to school like Miss Jessie. Not no boarding-school, of course, but dar's a colored school teacher in Washington I used to work for could tell me whar I could find a private learnin'-school for mah baby. . . ."

Two weeks later, as boarder and pupil, Peola was installed in the home of Miss Abbie Deacon, daughter of a colored professor of mathematics at Howard University and herself a teacher in the public schools.

·33·

One aspect of the B. Pullmans was most pleasurable of all.

Personal contacts, practically the only ones for which there had been time during the straining years, had grown out of the Eastern Seaboard Pullmans, chiefly New York and Atlantic City.

It started during the war. Tired doughboys, homesick troopers, regiments coming and going, formed the habit, dear to her, of making the Station B. Pullman and the one on Madison Avenue tiny and informal headquarters.

Pen and ink and writing-paper were on hand; B. Pullman engraved stationery with the imprint of Delilah delighting, in the upper right-hand corner. Mail was received and held for the soldier boy who chose to give B. Pullman as his address. It had not been unusual for a few of these boys to accompany Bea to the tiny apartment she had occupied at One Hundred and Thirteenth Street and later to the larger one on Central Park West, there to sit for an additional hour or two around the tiny open fire to more good coffee and more of Delilah's waffles. It struck her with a sense of inner disquiet, one day after a large newspaper story of her largess to these boys had appeared, how much selfish gratification was mixed up in these contacts.

Crowding them into the confines of her narrow little home puffed her up like a mother hen. It was good having them there. Their nonsense and cubbishness subtracted from her loneliness. Sometimes they brought ukuleles and banjos. Sometimes Delilah, not to be coaxed out of the rear end of the apartment, would consent to sit in her dark kitchen, firelight on her eyeballs, cheek bones, and surf of white teeth, and sing through the open doorway her version of "When Jesus wuz totin' de cross up de hill to Calvery":

> *"Mus' Jesus bear de cross alone,*
> *An' all de worl' go free?*
> *No, dere's a cross for ebbyone*
> *An' dere's a cross for me."*

Or, how these youngsters did love to succeed in getting her started on her John Henry legends. Sitting out there in the semi-darkness of her kitchen, huge body rocking and winding to the rhythm of the on-and-on of it, was their delight——

> *"John Henry said to his captain,*
> *Well, a man ain't nothin' but a man,*
> *An' befo' I'd be beaten by dat ole steam drill*
> *I'll die wid de hammer in my han',*
> *Lawd, I'll die wid de hammer in my han'."*

"More, Delilah!"——

> *"Some said he came from England,*
> *Some said he came from Spain,*
> *But it's no such thing, he was an East Virginia man,*
> *And he died wid de hammer in his han',*
> *He died wid de hammer in his han'."*

"Go on, 'Lilah!"—

> *"John Henry was killed on de railroad,*
> *A mile an' a half from town;*
> *His head cut off in de drivin'-wheel*
> *And his body ain't never been found."*

"Tell us, 'Lilah, about Polly Ann!"

> *"John Henry had a little girl,*
> *Her name was Polly Ann.*
> *John was on his bed so low*

She drove him wid his hammer like a man,
Drove him wid his hammer——''

" 'Lilah, come on in here and give us 'Whistlin' Sam'.''
"Go on, you boys; I got mah sleep to git."
With the increasing of her great bulk, as the years settled themselves more and more in terms of flesh over along her vast body, her major activity, except for the trips she was obliged to make for the proper inaugural of each new B. Pullman, had chiefly to do with training new recruits to preside picturesquely and efficiently above the waffle-irons. It was no small task to find types of black women who combined sufficient of waffle-iron technique with the something benign and effulgent which must approximately, at least, correspond with the nation-wide trade-mark of Delilah in her fluted crown.

It was after the almost enforced retirement of the great hulk of her back once more into the hinterland of her own kitchen, that more and more, after the war, there drifted into the household, not only the doughboys themselves, but a growingly miscellaneous company of un-attached and more or less lonely city souls to whom a B. Pullman offered friendly and sociable refuge.

"Some day there will be a B. Pullman alumni, or a B. Pullman American Legion," Bea was fond of prophesying when taking stock of the myriads of letters from her boys, from their mothers, from lonely city figures who during the years had passed through and passed on.

Passed on. Some to anonymity, some as from the cloud of a temporary and stranded loneliness into such assorted ultimate destinations as the navy, the farm, marriage and the home, and in the case of one young fellow with a Southern accent and a poetic shyness, who had found the adventure of New York rooming-house by night and a haberdashery shop by day not to his liking, a trading-post north of the Yukon, from where he wrote enthusiastic post cards.

Regina Elmp, invaluable emissary of her supplies department, had come out of the ranks of solitary women who had learned to regard the neighborhood B. Pullman as a sort of club from which she was reluctant to be ousted at closing-time for the narrow confines of a rooming-house.

Several of the traveling salesmen were recruits from the ranks of boys who had returned from war unshot, but with scars in the depths of their eyes.

There was a stack of letters and telegrams from the mothers and sisters of these boys, and all the miscellany from the boys themselves, alphabetically arranged in the jewelry-drawer of Bea's dressing-table.

Delilah owned a stack of them, too. One, postmarked Seattle, written on lined paper, was framed and mounted in a little silk portfolio she had made for it.

> *Darling Mammy Delilah, My boy Allen has told me all about you. He is not ashamed to say that without your kind substitution for his old mother, he could not easily have found the courage to face the dreadful days following his sailing from New York. Bless you and the dear lady who employs you. The inclosed little gift I knitted myself from my invalid's bed and it goes to you with the love of Allen, who is at work in the fields but whom I am proud to add is also studying civil engineering at night. Your friend, Addie Matterhorn.*
>
> *P. S. To think of your dear lady letting him sleep in her own bed and tending him like a baby the night he was taken with chill. I remember you both in my prayers.*

The memory of that boy—his name was Allen Matterhorn—blond and slim and nineteen, frightened and influenza-bitten, remained a favorite image in a mind that was filled with dimming pictures of the secretly suffering youth who had passed in transient troops through those days.

"De Lawd chastised dat boy wid homesickness and fear and body misery more dan enny I seed sail away, an' it is in mah tea leaves, de Lawd ain't done chastisin' him yet."

"Delilah, you read his mother's letter. He's not only safely back on the farm, but preparing to become an engineer."

"Dar ain't no safely back anywhares for dat boy. It was writ in his eyes de night he lay shakin' here wid chill. He got himself out of de war, but dar is more chastisin' ahead for dat boy in de battle of dis life. I know it, and when I knows a thing wid my knowin', I knows it."

No use to try to dissuade Delilah from one of her oracular and prophetic convictions. She lay back in them as into a warm bath and let the waters of portent wash over and immerse her.

"Dat boy Allen had doomnation in his eyes. May de Lawd relent and save him the sufferin' ahead. May de Lawd spare his maw, layin' out dar on her death-bed, knowin' it."

"Death-bed, Delilah? Invalid's bed doesn't necessarily mean that."

"Her is on her last bed. I knows it wid mah knowin'. No use. Doomnation for Allen."

But for others in her gallery of memories of doughboys, which memories she kept as brightly scrubbed as the aluminums in her kitchen, was sprightliness in her heart.

"Wonder why dat cuttin'-up Micky boy from Altoona dat used to pester me life and soul to sing him 'Whistlin' Sam' has quit writin' us postals every Armistice Day? Sure as fate dat boy's too busy gittin' hisself rich and happy for to have time for postals cards." Or: "Bless mah soul if it ain't a funny valentine from dat red-headed Kentucky mountain Harry who could eat one waffle in exactly two mouthfuls. Jes' you watch dat dar boy take care of hisself in dis world. What you bet he's got a wife now makes his waffles faster'n he can gobble 'em."

Frank Flake came later. It was considerably after the Armistice that the square-shouldered, lean-hipped young fellow with a spare square face that in profile was as sharp as a blade, began to repeat evenings, at a corner table of the Madison Avenue Pullman, crouching there over what might have been medical or law books and making annotations into a loose-leaf notebook. So many of the unattached and apparently detached young frequenters were like that, some of them medical or law students or from the dental school around the corner, but more, usually, men just beyond the student age, often following business vocations and studying evenings toward some profession.

Flake fell into the latter category, by day an expert accountant for a wholesale glass-and-china firm on Seventeenth Street, a medical student by night to the extent that he spent his evenings either at libraries or beside the B. Pullman corner table, hunched over books on his chosen subjects.

This came out slowly in the first few casual passings of the time of day which Bea took pains to exchange with her repeaters, during those years when she made it a rule to alternate her evenings between one or the other of the local B. Pullmans.

It pleased her when young Flake took finally to leaving overnight some of his books on a small shelf at the rear of the Pullman, and to talking less reservedly as she drew up opposite. It meant that once more someone was burrowing gratefully into the kennel warmth she had achieved in these retreats.

Flake, back from the war, reluctant to return to East St. Louis, where an uncle and sole relative had died during his absence, diffident, in-articulate in the rather terrible way characteristic of so many of the returned boys, was another lone hand being played against a vast im-personal background.

Not that it appeared that way to him. To one through whose head still roared cannon noises and whose eyes were not clean of horror, feeling tucked into the anonymity of new life in a city he had never seen before, embarking from it for war, was like one of those incredibly quiet French dawns, too unreal to hold portent of the reality of the days' impending cannonading.

He often said of these first years in New York, that with all their external din he was sitting in the midst of a world that was quiet as a graveyard with the memories of the dead buddies that were stacked higher in his eyes than reality. Higher even than the memory of all the days of his life in East St. Louis; in the home; in the public schools; and finally in the hotel-supply business of an uncle's who had died during his absence at war and left the entirety of a not inconsiderable fortune to the Christian Science Church. Higher even than a strangely thwarted and secret passion for the fifteen-year-old daughter of an East St. Louis clergyman, who two years before Flake's return from overseas was to become wife of her father's assistant curate and mother of twins.

A mountain of dead bodies, to dwindle slowly, rose between him and such realities as loneliness and detachment.

He was too deeply in the trance of his peace. Uncannonaded days led to these uncannonaded evenings in candle-lit, amber-colored warmth.

There was no February chill sufficiently icy those first two years, for him not to feel himself thawing of the war horror and war terror and war dread that had ridden him like witches.

Just to move along the hurly-burly days of a hurly-burly city, even at tasks not congenial to him, on into quiet evenings where for the price of good strong coffee served in decorated pottery cups he could sit in a sense of warmth and security, was to feel dread lifting.

"I must have been even more of a coward throughout that mess than I realized, because I can't seem to get over my relief at being out of it," he once confided to Bea, as the shy regalia of his constraint began to wear off.

She had seen them come home shell-shocked and dazed and with strange wooden masks over their erstwhile careless faces, but it did seem that the sustained look of relief on Frank Flake revealed what must have been his quite terrible terror throughout the period of his two years and ten months.

Yet the young private had come out of it a first lieutenant, with two citations and an honorable history of active fighting on two fronts.

Apparently he did things that way. Certain amount of indefinable doggedness which a quality of frailty in his looks belied. It surprised her to learn he was then earning sixty-five dollars a week with the china-and-glassware firm, in the hotel-supply department.

You hesitated before you took pity on a youth who could afford to do so many of the things for which he apparently lacked only the inclination.

He seemed older than his twenty-eight years, was another reason why she had to curb the impulse to invite him home for an hour before her fireplace one evening at ten-o'clock closing, along with a Miss Elmp who nightly shunted off as long as possible the return to her hall bedroom. Much older, with quite a tracery of blue veins showing beneath the pallor of his angular blond face and bright blue eyes the color of the carbon flame that comes spluttering off good coal.

It occurred to her, exchanging the pleasantries of weather with him one evening as she hesitated beside his table, that he was quite beautiful, and then felt a shock that somehow the thought was not sufficiently shocking to her. A beautiful man! And yet in a way, quite strange and surprising to her, she kept admitting the beauty of Flake. Nothing effeminate about him. A bridge or a ship or a storm or a foundry at night might be beautiful. Young Flake had beauty in a handsome way. That putting of it satisfied something disturbed in her.

It was about along in here that she caught herself increasing the number of her evening visits to the Madison Avenue Pullman, and in an ashamed orgy of self-discipline remained away almost a week. At the prospect of Flake sitting there in his corner, his spare figure hunched in a way that had become familiar to her, something rose like a tide, carrying a small rush of excitement right through her.

Well, why not? There was something about a well-cut young fellow like this Frank Flake to just naturally point up the anticipations. Pleasant to have about. Interesting to have about. Still——

It was during one of her subsequent chats with him, that something he said in regard to a plan he had under way for working out a line of reproductions of early American glass for his firm, put an idea into her head.

Why not have Flake devise something new and novel in the way of china equipment for her Pullmans! The soft, imitation-Spanish potteries she was using were not only being imitated by a rapid influx of tearooms, but their easy chipping and high breakage was a growing problem.

Something he had said about white glass recalled a quaint and early chromo of an American plate that had belonged on a shelf in her mother's dining-room. A white glass plate with scalloped edges, through which was run a strip of pink satin ribbon. Why not install a new scheme entirely, harkening back to Colonial wares. White glass! Heavy, durable, quaint. White table service. Napery. The heavy white glass plates with the design raised. White goblets. White cream-jugs. Tiny individual butter-dishes in the design of a setting hen. Americana.

Even now, with the Central Park apartment still fresh as paint, was beginning to be borne upon her a sense of the stereotyped. By a process of observation and assimilation, she had outgrown, almost before entering into it, the home so lovingly furnished in blanket department-store fashion.

Fishrow, the beautiful general design of the architects, restricting each plot-holder to conform to a certain unanimity of Colonial scheme; conferences with the architects, decorators, builders, had awakened something new and exciting in her. Visits to the Metropolitan Museum and private access to handsomely bound reproductions of famous interiors of homes and palaces, began by now to clearly define her dream of her ultimate house in Fishrow.

At present it stood there a yawning vacant lot, between the already realized homes of the Wall Street turfman's and Virginia Eden's, except that forming and growing in her mind, in terms of American Colonial for which her mind's eye accounted brick by brick, was the ultimate lovable and beautiful reality of Number Nine Fishrow.

Now take a young fellow like this Flake, just sort of thinking out loud to him and watching his nice lean sensitive face flash into understanding, made it doubly exciting to plan. . . .

No wonder one looked forward to the evenings. . . . Natural. . . . Why shouldn't one? . . . Now, why?

Take the matter of white glass which was ultimately to lead to her famous all-white table service—except for those evening's chats, there just wouldn't ever have been white glass. . . .

It was out of white glass grew not only the largest order of young Flake's career, but two years later, with his china-and-glassware firm trying to retain him at a price that topped Bea's offer, he was to accept the position of general manager for the B. Pullman, Inc., interests.

·34·

Virginia Eden's house at Number Eleven Fishrow had been completed three years, while Bea's empty lot continued to give to the handsome compact block the effect of a missing tooth.

In some respects, Number Eleven was the most outstanding of all, not even excepting the Casamajor home on the double corner lot, with its fine Georgian façade and heavy marble pillars that bore out handsomely its Greek lineage.

Virginia's home, of less than half the Casamajor frontage, gave to the street a rather pinkish pressed-brick face, fine convex windows of carefully collected Tudor panes with lavender fires in them, a white door with a fanlight that had been considered one of Charleston's finest, and from what had once been the littered rear of a row of tenement houses, an awninged terrace with silver balls that flashed in sunlight. Bird baths, flagstones that wound under trellises, led from the French windows of Virginia's drawing-room, down marble steps especially imported by Mrs. Casamajor from the neighborhood of Villa d'Este, to a gaily painted community boathouse.

Thus had Virginia Eden, who had been born Sadie Kress in Jersey City, succeeded in making this sunny, terraced, pretentiously simple home along its imitation Thames Embankment her own.

She occupied it with a second husband whom she had twice divorced and twice remarried; a mother-in-law who throughout these fluctuating episodes had taken sides with her son's wife; the stepfather of the silver larynx, two daughters, a sixteen-year-old son by this husband's former marriage; a Miss Tweedie, secretary, cousin, and inseparable companion to Virginia Eden; six cocker spaniels and a corps of servants who overran the house as informally as a brood of children home for the holidays.

In demanding of those about her more of everything than might be considered the just lot of one person, Virginia gave with even a higher and freer hand than the one with which she commanded.

Her servants quailed before her tantrums and reaped the harvest of her quick spasms of self-reproach which she expressed in the form of showered affection and gifts. She enjoyed neither their deference nor what might be termed their respect, because the sense of their familiarity mixed with contempt and affection, saturated, and in a sense made ridiculous, her household.

But predominantly they adored her, and in that one respect, like her husband, left in frequent huffs, only to return on a more intimate and more firmly intrenched basis.

"If I can't have people around me whom I love and who love me, then I prefer to wash out my own shimmies," was the Virginia Eden succinct summation of the curiously tropical and storm-infested atmosphere that surrounded her. The same applied to her business. Her hairdressers, manicurists, masseuses, and saleswomen clamored for her favor, fawned, won it, went down before her Siroccos of rage, departed from her service, protesting at her tyrannies and returned to it chastened.

It was said that her stepson, vowing he would rather break rock than endure the hierarchy of her roof an hour longer, did literally that, fracturing his leg in an upstate quarry the very first day of his drastic alternative.

Chartering a plane, she flew to his side, returning him to her hearthstone by way of a twelve-thousand-dollar motor-launch which she purchased for him in fierce mood of restitution.

There hung over Number Eleven the surcharged atmosphere of a woman who demanded on every side assorted loves, from the effusive canonization of her employees to the mute, inglorious adoration of her lean and lame stepson, to the sporadic fidelities of a handsome and somewhat wastrel husband whose major virtue was his frank realization of his merely ornamental rôle in the history of her success.

It was rumored, and rightly, that certain capitalistic interests had already offered Virginia Eden five million dollars for Virginia Eden Beauty Products, Incorporated.

A wag in a New York tattling weekly had it: Certain capitalistic interests are reported to have offered Virginia Eden five million dollars outright for world rights to her business. Pocket money for Virginia. It costs that to keep her vassals in tin spears and her court in Fishrow going.

Be that as it may, the household of Virginia, crowded with hothouse flowers, sunlight, sycophants, objects, *objets d'art,* jangling telephones; a household of excitements, waste, easy intake, easy outgo, it was one to never cease to amaze Bea, on her infrequent, always diplomatic, visits to it.

Diplomatic because between these two, shunted by circumstance into the curious sistership of pioneer rôles, was deep and intuitive realization of the importance of at least surface amity between them.

"Where two men might be able to afford to publicly agree to disagree without further comment, let us so much as yea the other's nay, and they'll have our hairpins flying. You and I have to be friends, Pullman, and like it."

Grimly they acceded that, with laughter.

"I won't be treated by them like a Pekingese who has learned to walk on his hind legs," Virginia was fond of reciting. "I won't be patted on the back by a man's world. Let them pat me on the bean. Here, around the brain-pan."

Despite, however, such perilous incompatibilities as had sent them skywise in the project of Fishrow, there did exist between these two a quality of mutual attraction not unlike that between parent and the offspring which most markedly reproduces his own characteristics.

Every move of Virginia Eden's was of vital interest to Bea, and *vice versa.* Bea knew of herself that if she so much as picked up the morning *Times,* a reference to Virginia, even though incorporated in fine print in the body of a long column, would spring at her with the velocity of a headline. What this woman did, how she lived, loved, achieved, were matters of transcendant interest, with all this equally true of Virginia Eden, who had been watching Bea steam into the scene even before Virginia had begun to dawn with such potency upon the latter.

The racy ingredient of competition lay folded into the psychology of all this, tempered, however, by the fact of the two fields of separate commercial endeavor.

If anything, it was rather easy for Virginia Eden, who by now was imbued with her mission of high priestess of beauty, to take on a magnanimity toward an enterprise which had flowed to its fruition from the sugar buckets of Vermont.

The Virginia Eden School of Massage; the Virginia Eden Mask for Facial Rejuvenation; the Virginia Eden Delphic Studios; the Virginia Eden Electro Gymnasium; the Virginia Eden Institute of Beauty; the Virginia Eden Aesthetic Preparations, showed plainly the trend of the mind behind these vast commercial interests.

When Virginia Eden addressed her assembled employees, disciples of her cult of beauty, there was high priestess in her bearing, and mind you, in her heart.

The fact that her cult grew out of the aggressively eager effort of one Sadie Kress of Jersey City to earn a living for a family consisting of one pair of shiftless parents, one paralyzed sister, one gang-running brother, all of whom broke her heart by dying an assorted array of deaths within a year or two before she began to come into her own, seemed in no way to impede her growing sense of self-ordainment to the cause of beauty.

Her mission in clearing up the acne from the faces of women, cleansing them of the ravages of living in a world too much with them; her dedication of self to hours in her laboratories, experimenting, along with highly paid chemists, for preparations warranted to bring new sheen to old bodies, had kindled strange fires of fanaticism in the quick eyes of Virginia Eden.

Interested as she was in every aspect of the strangely analogous career of B. Pullman, so like hers, so strangely alien to it, she could nevertheless afford to be widely charitable.

"There is a woman hard to fool in dollars and cents, but life has short-changed her every inch of the way and she can't quite locate the deficit. She doesn't know she is on earth, chiefly because she isn't. She doesn't ask for what she doesn't see, but she wants it mighty bad without knowing it. If I've got to be cheated, I'll take my licking in dollars and cents. She's taking hers in love and life. No wonder she's got such hurried-looking eyes. She's got love and life coming to her and none too much time to collect!"

On the basis of sex solidarity, one could afford a public and conspicuous intimacy with one of the outstanding business women of her day, even though, where the intimate aspect of life were concerned, she was a wooden Indian. There were hidden, intimate subjects to be shared and discussed with the sort of girl-friend confidantes with whom Eden surrounded herself. With Bea, now, you didn't know where you stood, or rather where she stood. Was her life merely what it seemed to be? Probably not. The stilly kind usually had it "behind their ears."

But at any rate, her gesture of affiliation with B. Pullman in the Fishrow enterprise had been a dramatic amalgamation. Withdrawal, as circumstances developed, had seemed the canny part of discretion. Let Bea hold the bag, if bag there was to be held. Nor had the subsequent success of the enterprise soured or embittered anything of the external attitude of Virginia toward her friend.

More and more, even to the extent of trailing them about her own drawing-room and posing in them with groups of instructors in her plastic classes, the painted velvet robes of the high priestess, instead of the tailored suits of the business woman, were enveloping Virginia.

Yes, even with what might be regarded as Bea's *coup* in this matter of Fishrow, it was something to be well out of it, sitting pretty in a house that, if you counted just one of her recent successful forays into Wall Street, had cost her from its cellar to its mansard roof not a penny. Also, there was something about the outstanding friendship of two outstanding women that should be regarded as touching, splendid, generous, as-it-should-be. A brilliant rebuttal to the popular theory that women did not get on well with rival members of their own sex.

Less complicated were the reactions of Bea Pullman to the tenacity with which Virginia Eden held out for the friendship.

First to grant Virginia precedence in both her public and private achievement was Bea.

There was something willful in the manner in which, by availing herself of every opportunity to look in on Virginia's, she exposed her own life to contrast.

There was a woman for you! Virginia Eden! A woman toward whom life flowed like sunshine over the fields and meadows it was fructifying. Light, gayety, easy friends, easy laughter, easy adoration, flooded that household. A husband who was naughty but whom she adored with a kind of intermittent and adolescent infatuation, kept her boudoir a bower of flowers; a stepson who followed her movements with the tragic worshiping eyes of one who found her splendor heartbreaking to endure.

Her servants called her undignified, diminutive, endearing names, and worried over her diet, her fatigue, her moods. The out-and-out admiration of young men and young girls, oldish men and ageing women, kept further patine on a life that apparently had never lost its luster even with Virginia within view by now, of her menacing forties.

There she goes! was the applause-laden atmosphere through which daily, at home and in business, Eden walked in adoration.

More and more, by contrast, it was beginning to be borne in upon Bea, that for her, life was like a furnace that had not worked very well. She was cold.

·35·

When Jessie was sixteen she wrote to her mother from Zermatt in Switzerland, "All that I am I owe to you." To be sure, it was embodied in the commonplace comment of a usual fortnightly letter of running inconsequential patter concerning the pleasant routine of life in a Swiss school for girls, and came hard upon an urgent plea to be permitted to remain abroad over another summer vacation. But to Bea it seemed a pair of arms flung out of the girlish scrawl of that letter, firm and true and tight about her neck.

This was the year that the Fifth Avenue B. Pullman, on a lease negotiation that over the interim of years would amount to three quarters of a million rental, opened heavy, copper-trimmed doors that were designed to simulate the entrance to a *de luxe* observation car.

Half a year of the concentrated efforts of herself and Flake had conspired toward the creation of this *tour de force* in B. Pullmans. Its equipment, not the standardized, had been especially designed, redesigned, built, rejected, rebuilt; its minutest details, color, walls, ventilation, plumbing, gadgets, supervised by them both, during days of standing by the debris of plaster, paint, lumber, and scaffolding that achieved the transformation of the premises from eighteen-by-forty feet of space to an observation dining-car of elegancies not exactly adapted to the rigors of the road-bed, but delightfully and poetically licensed for the boulevard.

A *tour de force!* Ideally suited to its purpose, it ran through the block from street to street, with entrances at both ends, its lighting, its simulated scenery, its novelties in upholstery, china, menu, and atmosphere, luxuriously distinguished from the pattern of B. Pullman construction in use by now the country across.

"It's too grand," had been Bea's private indictment to Flake, the day of the much-publicized opening. "If it doesn't pay, we'll tear out the elegance and just go plain diner again."

But it did pay.

During the first month, for the few hours a day that her limbs would support, without becoming unbearable stabs of pain, the heavy bulk of her, Delilah herself, household trademark come to life, presided at the shrine of her waffle-iron.

It was at the end of the first month, when by chance Bea found her hidden and shuddering in the locker-room, where it was revealed she retired at close intervals for the relief of letting the shooting pains have their way, that the popular innovation of the personal appearance of Delilah was discontinued and a trained disciple installed in her place.

The Fifth Avenue B. Pullman, with its varied innovations, including full-fledged menus, higher price list, rather amusing display of Americana along the walls, cloudy and clear glass reproductions, quickly followed by replicas on East Forty-ninth Street and an even more sumptuous one in the arcade of the new Father Knickerbocker, became quickly and remuneratively the popular rendezvous of the surprisingly large class of upper middle-class women who still shop, foregather, attend matinées, hotel bridge parties, and while away hours out of the heart of the city's congested workaday.

It seemed to Bea that Jessie's letter, with what for her amounted to effusion, coming as it did on top of a school of successes such as these, to say nothing of two-hundred-thousand-dollar net Fishrow profit, plus her own building lot which had cost her exactly the price of registering the deed, was the crowning touch to a series of circumstances almost frighteningly benign.

She even talked it over with Flake, with whom she discussed everything except such private affairs as these, and let him read the letter.

"Thought you might be interested in seeing the kind of letter my girl puts up," she said, tossing it, with over-elaborate carelessness, across her desk. "Of course I know what those summers over there mean to her. Hiking trips, sight-seeing, and visits to her roommate's home on the Italian Riviera, but it's the third successive year abroad. She's a darling and will come home at the drop of a hat if I say so, only I suppose the rascal knows I won't say it. Just thought you'd be interested in her description of the trip she took with Miss Winch and Miss Askenasi to Lausanne.''

What secretly and ingloriously she desired was the moment when, seated opposite him, she could see his eyes trail the third to the last line ''. . . realize it's my third consecutive summer, but next year I'm finished and home for good. Of course I'll do as you say, dear, *all that I am or hope to be I owe to you.*'' . . .

High time young Frank Flake knew where she stood with this daughter. It had not been easy, carrying around this blank, casual exterior where Jessie was concerned, not even mounting her photograph in silver on her desk (the one, for instance, in her beret and the wind-blown hair!) the way so many of the business executives did wives and children and sweethearts.

It was almost as if she felt the need to wait, with this daughter of hers, until they were better acquainted. More time for each other, ultimately in the home of that now aching void of a lot in Fishrow— Jessie out of school, herself out of business. Yes, yes, herself out of business.

It was better, having waited this long, to hold off on the erection of the home that was going to be the ultimate kennel; the house beautiful which she had been most of her life in the dreaming. Not the largest, but the most perfect house in Fishrow. At auction, steered by the ubiquitous Eden, she had already purchased a fine example of Duncan Phyfe tea-table, a museum-piece maple candle-stand on tripod, a six-legged burl-walnut highboy, a Hepplewhite sideboard with a knee-hole front, and a pair of Sheraton inlaid knife urns to adorn it. And for an early American girl's bedroom that was to look out upon a plane tree, flagstones, and a pair of stiff knickerbocker garden benches beside a river, a spool bed and a tambour desk beautifully inlaid with satinwood in the original patina.

It was high time she permitted herself the luxury of showing that letter to Flake.

He responded, too, warmly, something he did not always do, now that his rôle had rather automatically fallen along lines of controlling the erratic movements of a chief whom he had apparently determined to indulge as a genius of sorts.

''If I'm to be worth my salt to you, I figure that you are to follow your heart up to a point, and then I'll step in with a bit of head. Geniuses are not expected to function with run-of-the-mill horse-sense, the way most of us ordinary mortals have to try to do.''

That was his attitude spoken and unspoken, when, for instance, he put what he called the ''kibash'' on a sudden impulse of hers for what might be considered the unwarranted expenditure of impulsive decision.

This species of his authority dated to the occasion, some three years previous, of his having saved her a sum that would have mounted beyond ten thousand for certain electrical installations in the Pullmans, falsely represented to her as falling within range of fire regulations. Repeatedly he had steadied what he considered her erratic and emotional susceptibility to having the wool pulled over her eyes by the sycophants and inevitable double-crossers of business.

Then, too, it had been Flake who gradually took over the aspect of the business for which Bea was notoriously unfitted, the ruling and regulation of disbursements.

''You're a genius, Chief. I'm an accountant. Your place is at the prow. Mine is at the till, seeing to it that you are pound, as well as penny, wise.''

The implication embarrassed her, yet diffused her through and through with the warmth of wine. Of course it was not true. She had worked fiercely, ploddingly, and without any particular talent, except that of self-dedication in a life which offered nothing much else to do.

Along with the cumulative quality of the plodding, single-track years that had subordinated everything personal in her life, events had managed to shape themselves propitiously for her business success. That propitiousness, added to an industry born of loneliness, was the luck part.

Industry. Luck. The moment. A certain spirit, what with life none too sweet, to risk all. Act in haste but only after you are convinced that there will be nothing much to repent. Rather simple ingredients out of which to concoct any pretense of genius.

As ridiculous was the portrait of Flake at the penny till. If I've genius, it manifested itself when I attached Flake. You don't ordinarily look for efficiency behind a pair of almost startlingly purplish eyes and under a thatch of coarse heavy hair the color of bantam corn. This last, to the consternation of the entire organization, he did something about, shaving his head and wearing it bristly as a convict's until heat and cold alike conspired for his discomfort.

Yessir, perhaps it did take genius of a sort to find somewhere in that conglomerate of blond and dreamy boy, doing his job with the china-and-glassware firm by day and poring over second-hand medical books by night, a general manager of the rapidly accruing B. Pullman interests. And what a one, gathering in almost immediately, and with what seemed a rather loose rein, the organization under his discipline!

In constant perambulations from city to city, little seemed to escape the diamond-bright quality of the cutting observation of those curiously colored eyes of his. They scratched through the gloss of externalities; they uncovered debris of falsified accounts which had been costing B. Pullman, Inc., years of unexplainable deficits; they concentrated on high breakage, faulty location, discipline, contributory causes to the greater or less success, or the occasional out-and-out failure of each B. Pullman with regard to clientele, prestige, and service.

A constant stream of minutiæ, calculated, unless cleared, to clog and impede, flowed beneath his observation. With all the contradiction of his personal appearance, and with the surgeon's impulse latent in his long hands, he presented the further paradox of hawk-like astuteness for detail.

No aspect of the business too lowly for his calculation. Why, for three consecutive years, had Cleveland's Euclid Avenue B. Pullman shown an almost identical falling off for April and May? Something about the inability of the St. Louis Grand Avenue B. Pullman to keep one of its imitation Delilahs for more than a period of two or three months, that needed ferreting out. How to enlist Mary Pickford and Marion Davies and John Gilbert into inaugurating Hollywood's B. Pull-man as a gay fad, instead of just the popular snatch-a-bite for studio extras it was almost sure to be, otherwise. Why did Delilah's Hearts turn over daily in Philadelphia and move not at all in Chicago?

In Chicago once, during a highly local visitation of pink-eye upon the personnel of both Pullmans there, he alternated between Michigan Boulevard and State Street, himself tossing waffles and presiding at percolators. For eleven successive evenings he had sat with his legs wound about a bookkeeping stool of the New York offices, angling for a balance of nineteen dollars and forty-five cents, which in the end was to lead to revelations of deficits mounting to thousands.

This was the case which resulted in the apprehension of one Frank Cass, bookkeeper, whose falsifications amounted to forty-one thousand dollars and who Bea refused to prosecute. Cass was to remain in her employ fourteen years longer, repaying eleven of the forty-one thousand, and dying at his desk with his face on a post card she had sent him from Shanghai.

"Blue Diamond," Delilah, in one of her inimitable flashes of the pet phrase, was to dub this fellow Flake. "Dat boy's got a pair of blue-diamond eyes dat could gimlet hell open!"

Sometimes it seemed to Bea that the eyes of this fellow cut the initials of a certain disdain against some of her newly acquired little veneers.

For instance, he would concentrate that diamond-hard, not unamused gaze of his against the carved-looking artificial hair wave which Virginia Eden had decreed as necessary to groom her head into smaller and smarter contour. Was he saying to himself, you are a fool and a slave just like all the rest of the women, or was he contemplating a new look of youth in her. She would passionately have liked to know.

He seemed anything but unaware, although consistently silent, concerning the many small subterfuges she practiced against his pronounced judgment, such as extending credits in what almost invariably turned out to be unworthy directions. Just as he knew, to the individual, but without gloating, the number of dismissed employees she had reinstated against his memorandum to the contrary notwithstanding, only to once more find them disastrously wanting. Flake was smart.

It was small of her to want him to know the contents of this letter from the never too effusive pen of her daughter. Doubtless the diamond of his steady perceptions was cutting right through her impulse of pretentiousness in showing it.

Just the same, for no reason she could quite articulate to herself, she wanted him to know it, and there he was, running his eye along a page written in Jessie's free hand.

. . . because all that I am, I owe to you. . . .

Sometimes she wondered if this cold blue narrow young man, so versed in her petty foibles, so versed in his strangely mature knowledge of her impulse to leap too soon after looking, her emotional and sometimes harmful generosity, her tendency to over-buy, over-stock, over-pity, was himself sufficiently versed in those larger qualities of daring captaincy and intuition which were so much more powerful, than the deterrents which he sought to control in her were damning.

As a matter of fact he was.

"You don't actually need a pettifogger like me around, except to do your mental chores. I pretend that these things matter, so you won't see how unimportant I am. You're a genius who does things from the inside-out, and no amount of coaching from the outside-in matters a great deal. For every trifle you do wrong, you do ten big things, inimitably right. Nobody alive could have told why, for instance, you leased that store on Peachtree Avenue in Atlanta, right over my head, after being in town about two hours when I'd been there studying the ground for two weeks. But you did and cleared eight thousand on the lease the next week. From that day on I realized that my job was to check up on the chicken-feed and laundry-soap problems of this concern and carry the queen's train."

Well, despite protestations such as this, Flake, at under thirty, was monitor of her foibles, and as such merited to be jerked to occasional reminders of wherein lay her strengths. All that I am or hope to be, I owe to you. . . .

This from her sixteen-year-old daughter. The lovely yellow timid stranger who had spent practically no years of her young life in a home environment that might have deprived her of the graces she was beginning to wear like the points of a crown.

By now Jessie wrote and spoke French, German, and Italian as glibly as the mother tongue. There were photographs of her in fencing, skiing, dancing, driving, and riding garb standing framed about the house, and she had sent home a phonograph record of her small, clear, careful, and bird-like voice singing "Ah, fors'è lui che l'anima."

All that I am or hope to be, I owe to you. . . .

·36·

It was surprising, the number of evenings she was beginning to have to herself. Quite terribly to herself. The work days of her organization ended like clockwork. At five, covers were clamped onto typewriters, dozens of young men and young girls hurried toward locker-rooms and telephone booths, eager for the release from routine. Even the men and women of managerial rank of one sort or another, clerks, office boys, long files of employees from the mail-order department, hurried for trains, subways, and evening diversions for which they had engaged themselves ahead; a business world eagerly facing homeward and pleasureward.

For so many years, evenings had meant no other respite from the arduous activities of the day than delivering the heavy packages of sugar and syrup through the back streets of Atlantic City, or the long worrying hours of figuring on the backs of envelopes.

Now, not so suddenly, perhaps, as it seemed, business duties, responsibilities, worries, fitted themselves fairly well into the pattern of a well-organized workaday. Always plenty to be done, of course, if one insisted upon remaining after hours and keeping a clerk or two, or Miss Weems on extra duty, or fussing around at home over reports from various cities. But actually, there was little to be accomplished that could not be attended to within hours, by able members of her force. Her executive committee met, at stated intervals of more or less formal conclave, around a directors' table in a room for that especial purpose, which had been fitted up with table, chairs, Maxfield Parrish frieze, water-pitchers, and wall maps, and for some time Flake had been reminding her that her Haroun al-Raschid rôle, in and out of the various B. Pullmans, as in the days when she had dropped into a chair opposite a young man poring over second-hand medical books, no longer synchronized with her rôle as head of a corporation.

Evenings, suddenly, had become entities in which she sat rather appalled at the cessation of the day's activities.

Around eight o'clock the elevator in the apartment building began to take on an air of festivity which had never before particularly struck her one way or another. Men in evening dress and women without hats and in bright-colored wraps and slippers began ascending and descending. Whistles of doormen summoned taxicabs. Traffic through the Park and streets started to flow toward the theater districts. From the corner window of the apartment, a faint watermelon pink lifted rosy fingers over the roofs of the midtown district. The old gentleman liked to watch this glow deepen, like a strange sunrise across the night sky. It made him laugh, and laughing he was like an old stuffed gunny sack with some of the grain settling. Every night and in practically the same words Bea pointed it out to him, and most usually in response he raised his threatening cane to her in the only gesture left him.

"Look, Father, that is the Times Square district lighting up. That is only about twenty blocks from my office. You should see it from there!"

Sometimes when she repeated that, her heart cried within her. For over fifteen years this felled figure had sat leaning in this chair. Life had stopped and sort of backed in him like old waters in a clogged pipe. How long, O Lord, how long?

A thousand times during those years Delilah, dreaming the glory of her own funeral, had plotted his, lovingly, with detail, with grandeur. "Mah chair-chile knows when he goes ridin' up to de Lawd in glory, dat de misery is gonna fall from his laigs like scales and he's gonna walk de pearly streets of de white city one of Gawd's chastisedest and holiest. My ole chair-chile knows. . . ."

What was it he knew, that she, Bea, did not. Something. She could have sworn it. It flowed across the milky fluid that was beginning to obscure his sight. It hung thin as gauze in a mask before his stricken being. Something was faintly luminous about his old ruined hulk of Father. Something about him gleamed like the eyes of a cat in a clothes-closet. Even as she could have cried out her heart for him, something about him hung triumphant before the hulk of himself, making tawdry her tears.

Did he know what her heart cried out he should know? That come what might, here, there, everywhere, in happiness and despair, she would never leave him? Once, when she had planned a trip to Switzerland, which had failed to materialize because of pressure of home events, every provision had been made to transport along the bulky hulk of Father.

Did he know? Father, I will never leave you—

What was he seeing from this fallen tower of himself? What was there, as it hung in that faintly luminous gaze, that Father was knowing and she did not know! . . .

Sometimes, in the vacant evenings, after his male nurse had wheeled him away, she continued to sit in the dark beside the window, pondering something of the secret that seemed more and more to envelop the ruin of her father in a kind of light. Usually Delilah, her last pan turned in a kitchen around which she navigated with difficulty, routed the nurse to early bed in order that, as the old gentleman slept, she might pray over him with a Baptist fervor that made it necessary to close doors and windows.

"May de Lawd have mercy on mah ole gemmeman's soul and sanctify it in heaven for its sufferings on dis mortal earth. Bless him, O Lawd, in heaven for seeing fit for to bed-ride him on earth, and may he ride up to meet you to de blessin's of doves an' music."

Night after night, through the apartment, as she swayed over her dish-washing, as she turned back beds, sat, because of legs that did protest too loudly against her weight, on an improvised throne before her ironing-board, the prayerful improvisations of Delilah, chanted to her own syncopation, rose like a vapor off the day.

"God have mercy on mah babies. Lead 'em to de fold, O Lawd, in glory. Ride us all in de white hearse and de flowin' plumes to glory. Bless mah chile-of-de-chair, O Lawd, and make him whole when he gets up to de pearly streets. Rain your blessin's down on mah white chile, Miss Jessie, and cause her to walk, Lawd, in ways dat will bring her closer to you, Lawd, and to her mother who done worked her fingers to de bone, idolizin' her.

"Keep sleepin', O Lawd, the white horses in de blood of mah

baby. Make her contented wid her lot an' pour love of de Lawd in her soul while she's down dar in Washington, learnin'. Bless mah bigges' baby, Miss Bea. Keep her from denyin' herself, O Lawd, de good things dat she deserves. Bless all her doin's an' give her man-lovin'. . . ."

Sometimes, as Bea lay in bed, it took crowding of her pillow up around her head to shut out the sounds of the invocations of Delilah, and on some occasions to crowd down the ridiculous tears—of self-pity—bless all her doin's and give her man-lovin'. . . .

One way to while away these evenings which, if left to herself, Delilah could cram with these high articulations, was to drive with her, in a taxicab, to Fishrow, and there, parked against the curb, wrapped in evening as they contemplated the empty lot of premises Number Nine, sketch into the darkness the ultimate dwelling.

"Look, Delilah, just imagine that we're looking at the front of the house, although, of course, from here, you will only really be able to see the rear—"

"Dat certainly is something new to me. De back side of a house facin' de street, so every chicken giblet in de kitchen can be stared at from de sidewalk."

"Imagine the Colonial pillars down the front, Delilah, and a little farther down in the garden, tall stone gate-posts topped with stone pineapples that I've already bought from a house in Charleston that was built before the Revolution."

"Honey, God's pearly gates was built before de Flood."

"Hand me those blue-prints out of my bag, Delilah, and hold the searchlight. See, now my idea is to have a sort of little second-story balcony inside the columns, leading off Miss Jessie's room. . . ."

"Law' now, honey, you ain't changin' de face of dat house again?"

"I'd like it a lot if her room could open on to a little balcony."

"Git your egg hatched fust, honey. Git dat chile home. Doan' go loadin' yourself up wid a big house, honey, jes' for to have it feel empty on you. Dat's what I say about mine. I ain't goin' to set mah heart on nothin' until I sees her comin' back to me wid de fear cast out of her heart, and blackness, widout darkness, in it."

"I wouldn't dream of turning even the first spade before Miss Jessie comes home, but I want this house of ours to be the snuggest, the most secure, the most beautiful, the most everything kennel in all the world, Delilah. Some day, when I sell the business, and there's time for real living, we're all going to retreat here. See, right there in that space of darling empty lot is homeland, Delilah, where we're going to face the music of growing old!''

"You's de one has got de growin' old ahead of you. I's in it."

Dear Delilah, seated in the gloom of the cab, black, gargantuan, a tent, there were suds of white already scattered into the kink of her mossy hair and deep in each breath, like springs coiled about the heart, asthmatic wheezes.

"I's steamin' into port, honey. Not dockin', mind you. I ain't fit for to meet mah Lawd yet, by a long shot. I's jes' steamin' wid de pearly shores in sight."

"Aren't we all?"

"No, honey. You ain't rounded de curve yet. Life ain't ready to slip out of your hands, unless you jes' won't go out and cotch it. De trumpets ain't blowin' for me yet, but dey's raised and ready."

"Delilah, how you talk!"

"I ain't crying about it. I's jes' summin' up. An' dat doan' mean I ain't goin' to be right here a-waitin' when mah Peola comes home for to say, 'Mammy, I's through wid it all, now, except bein' what I am, where I belongs.' I's gonna be right here to hang curtains in dat house we been sittin' here on dis curbstone, dreamin' a different dream about every week for de last three years. I's got to live on. I's got babies, one, two, three of 'em . . . besides de one God give me out of mah own flesh. . . ."

It was five years since Peola, en route to Seattle from Washington, had palely darkened the threshold of the apartment on Central Park West. Five years and, as Delilah knew to the day, six months and twenty-one days.

"Jes' you watch! Mah chile passed her 'zaminations for Howard University, but you jes' watch, she won't enter no black college an' she ain't goin' to take de chance of a white one not openin' its doors to her." Which was precisely what happened. At sixteen, Peola, from the Washington home where she had been tutored, succesfully passed librarian examinations and, after one year as second assistant at Wilmington, Delaware, Public Library, had accepted first assistant librarianship at Seattle.

Every month there came a letter, chiefly of thanks for Delilah's bounties, and every Christmas, gifts and the promise of that impending trip home.

"After all, I'm not so much better off than you, Delilah. It's Jessie's fourth summer abroad."

"Yes, you is, honey. Your chile ain't a-buckin' de whole world. Yourn is honin' herself for to fit in wid it."

"Delilah, dear, I do want so terribly to make up to you for the way life has behaved to you. I owe you so much more than I can ever repay, even if you let me. Do you realize that instead of the hundred-dollar-a-month slave you insist upon being, you could be working for me under any financial terms you name? What is there Delilah, I can do?"

"You know what I wants most, honey-chile. Something dat money cain't buy. I wants to drown dem white horses plungin' in mah baby's blood. . . ."

"Suppose I were to get on a train and take a trip out to Seattle and see just what is what with Peola. How she is living. What . . ."

"Not even you, Miss Bea, can brung mah chile home to her race. I doan' know how she's livin' out dar. I'm 'fraid to know. I doan' know what she's passin' herself off as. I only know when she comes home to her race an' her black God an' her black mammy, she's got to come of her own free will. Got to come 'cause she's seein' de light. Nobody cain't brung her."

"Then, Delilah, I've begged you for so long to tell me, what is there you most want for yourself, your own darling self?"

"Honey-chile, you talk like you ain't made life a white-satin padded cell for Delilah. Everything I wants, money for to send mah chile, money for to dress in de purple. I doan' want nothin' else on dis earth 'cept peace an' honesty for mah chile."

"But, if you had a wishing-ring, one you could turn and wish for anything except, of course—Peola—what would you wish? Think hard."

"I'd wish for to meet mah Maker lak a queen comin' befoh de throne of de Heavenly Host. I'd wish for a funeral dat would make de eyes of dis heah New York's black town bug out for to see. I'd wish for de whitest hearse wid de longest plumes an' de prancin'est horses an' de brassest brass band to blow mah name right to de ears of de Lawd. I want to meet Him ridin' on a snow-white bier wid lilies and doves of peace an' righteousness. Dat's how I wants to go for to meet mah Maker. Ridin' through de streets to de tootin' of bugles an' de hallelujah of de best nigger voices in Harlem:

> *'Swing low, sweet chariot,*
> *Comin' for to carry me home.*
> *Swing low, sweet chariot,*
> *Comin' for to carry me home.'*

Ridin' to mah Maker in glory. Comin', Lawd! Comin' in a big white hearse! Dat's de mansion I got mah eyes on. 'Taint in Fishrow. It's de heavenly mansion of de Lawd!''

"I hope, Delilah, you'll occupy the Fishrow one many years first."

"Jes' doan' you worry, honey. I ain't ready yit for de pearly gates. Mah baby may be needin' me, and mah Miss Honey-Bea, mah Miss Jessie, and mah old chair-chile. Dat spook-house on dat dar empty lot ain't gonna be manned wid no low-down shif'less servants dat I ain't got de pickin' of.''

"I wonder if it would be enormously expensive to add another story and make all the second floor rooms two stories high so we could have a balcony running all the way around the living-room.''

"Law' now, you cain't go changin' dem dar blue-prints no more. No wonder you got to keep waitin' for to build 'til you can afford what keeps on growin' in your mind. Dis here house has already et its head off in the cost of blue-prints. You kin have rooms two stories high if you've a mind to. They's your rooms. But I'll take mine de way de Lawd intended rooms should be. Ceiling jes' far enough away for to hold de chandelier. Dat's de way I's house-minded.''

So during the week-after-week of evenings, Bea often descending from the cab to prowl into the neatly inclosed vacant lot or into the sweet-smelling rear gardens, was planned and built, planned and rebuilt,

217

the castle that was to fit into the space of that twenty-five by one hundred feet of Fishrow.

"Delilah, it's a lonesome evening. Let's drive over and work on the house."

"Miss Bea, whyfore doan' you go git yourself some one who will make your mawnin's and your evenin's de way God meant for dem to be. Filled wid de right kind of man-lovin' which is something you deserves and doan' know nothin' about. Even if you has to take a husband thrown in, Miss Bea, I's for man-lovin' to make a body forgit life ain't all beer and skittles. Some one for to make over you and for you to make over, even if you knows in your heart ain't no man livin' worth makin' over. . . . Lawd, honey, if I do say it as shouldn't, in mah day I shore could make over 'em. What you want ridin' around evenin's with ole 'Lilah? Go cotch yourself a beau."

"I've an idea for the garden, Delilah! I want the steps that lead to the boathouse to be chunks of marble set into the terrace the way they are in the snapshot Miss Jessie sent of herself in the villa on Lake Bellagio. I want violets to grow around those steps in spring, and anemones, that will make it darling and difficult not to step on them."

"In de garden of de mansion of de Lawd, honey, is where you walk on violets and jasmine and magnolias and honey-suckle."

"I'm going to have one of those electric clothes-chutes they're showing at the Architects' Exhibit at Grand Central Palace this week. I've worked out a place for it under the stairs."

"Yes, chile, earthly robes needs washin'. It's de heavenly mantle of de angels of de Lawd dat doan'. Honey-chile, it will shore seem a funny world up dar widout washin'. If de Lawd's robes only needed launderin', I'd do His tucks de way he's never seen 'em done."

"And there is a sort of Chinese Chippendale bathroom on exhibition at the Architects' Show, too. Amusing dragon wallpaper. Little Chinese porcelains set into the wall over the bathtub, and all the gadgets and faucets of black onyx. I've decided on it for Jessie. Girls love little nonsenses like that."

"Gawd bless de Lawd, in mah day de Chinese Chippydale bathroom was a kidney-shaped tin tub in de middle of de floor every Sad'day night, and more squawkin' black chillun a-shyin' away from it than you could shake a hickory stick at."

Sometimes, to fill in the vacant evenings, dressing herself in the well-made chiffons she was affording now, fluffing herself in a scarf of beige-colored tulle which at the moment it was the fashion to wear across the shoulders, and binding down her beige-colored hair with a band of the same, she attended a theater with Weems or, during those intermittent periods when he was in town, with young Flake.

For a while, there, Virginia Eden had taken to inviting her to some of the frequent functions at her new house in Fishrow or to large dinners at the hotels or popular night clubs, where Virginia, as it became the rage to hobnob with her, presided with brilliance and eccentricity.

But in every instance timidity overwhelmed Bea's impulse to accept and her curiosity to look upon the worlds so nonchalantly invaded by Virginia.

In the long years since her marriage, every one of them spent in urban communities, it occurred to her that she held the unique record of having had part in not one social function of any nature whatsoever.

The evenings with young Flake, five or six of them in all, were the nearest approach. Usually, in seats ordered during the day from a speculator, they attended one of the popular musical productions of the season, dining beforehand in the rather solemn splendor of the Hotel Gotham.

It had been in the sonorous atmosphere of this dignified hostelry's dining-room, overlooking Fifth Avenue, that two officials of an enormous mortgage and loan association, meeting with herself and Flake over lunch, had made possible her Fishrow venture.

Thereafter, it became her favorite dining-place in general, and her invariable rendezvous with Flake on those evenings they set out together for a theater.

It must have been around this period that there not only began to dawn upon her the extent to which her interests were narrowed, but to what degree they had begun to concentrate, away and beyond her control, on anticipation of Flake's periodic returns from his almost continual circuits of inspection.

On one occasion she found herself deliberately creating a business exigency which ordinarily she would have solved for herself, but which now she used as pretext to recall Flake to New York.

The evening of his arrival on a long jump from Denver in response to this summons was the one upon which Delilah, observing her attiring herself in a beige-colored velvet, with a gold turban and gold slippers to contrast, exclaimed:

"Chile, what's happened? You look lak someboy has lit de Christmas tree. . . ."

Somebody had.

·37·

Incredibly, in this sixteenth year of her widowhood, it now began to be borne upon her, from the evening of Flake's return from the trip she had terminated on pretense, what was happening, not only from this occasion alone, but from the strangest conceivable silence upon a certain subject from Delilah. Never again after this, as if fearful that her merest gesture might startle something as elusive as a deer, was word or innuendo to escape her.

Deep down in the dark shaft of her personal loneliness which Delilah had so long deplored, a Christmas tree of timid tapers had been lighted, all right, burning at first so feebly that the faint circles of inner glow, warming her, were conceived long before they were perceived.

Suddenly, in the routinized drama of her business success, two huge new forces were at work, bowling her over.

Flake! A perception that trembled in her like a leaf and roared through her in thunder.

Now, too, following the enormously exciting event of the stock-market listing of B. Pullman shares, spreading all about her were rumbling the beginnings of the rumors of determination on the part of Usa—Universal Sales Association, to attempt the out-and-out purchase of the B. Pullman enterprises.

Months before these rumors became fact, thoughts that she could no longer keep jammed down crowded for place into the fore of her mind.

Suppose, just for the sake of argument, private argument, argument, in fact, so private that it did not emerge beyond bas-relief from the recesses of her mind—suppose a man like Flake were freed suddenly, to follow the desire which he so seldom permitted himself to express in her presence. What were four or five years out of the life of a young fellow at his peak. He had the hands of a surgeon. The books piled beneath his office desk bespoke the untamed dream. What if! How easily the floor plan of Number Nine, Fishrow, could be changed and given over to consulting offices, X-ray laboratories if need be and — and——

Once the mind rollicked on like that it had to be checked, peremptorily; more than that, puttied in, sealed, as it were, against the vagrant mouse-like thoughts finding their way through chinks and peepholes of her consciousness.

The sale of her business for a seven-figure sum that even now staggered her! "Dr. Frank Flake" on a tiny metal plate at the entrance of Number Nine, Fishrow. Or no: Frank Flake, M.D. By appointment. The present plan for a kitchen should be a waiting-room instead, paneled in a lightish knothole maple to avoid that lugubrious atmosphere. There should be a separate professional entrance and a private one connecting with the living portion of the house, so that between patients, as she arranged flowers in bowls or sat at sewing for Jessie, who would be young and gay, Flake might steal into the living-room to stoop to kiss her or indulge in private husband-and-wife nonsenses as she ran fine tuckings into an underthing for Jessie——

Good God!—I'm getting senile!

There were letters on her desk to be answered. Dear Flake: In regard to your wire from Miami about the Triangle matter, I have decided to sit tight. . . .

A rival and imitative company, called Hot Cakes Triangle, had sprung up, specializing in obtaining triangular corners at busy intersections where triangle-shaped hot cakes were served on triangle-shaped plates. For the moment it had seemed the better part of policy to contemplate buying out the competitive corporation, which had started with quite a nation-wide spurt. But suddenly, on what Flake termed one of her tips from Mars, she decided to sit back and let the new enterprise flare and die. Which it did.

All about, even with the wear and tear and the anxieties and worse, that from all sides assailed each business day, was the steadily mounting phenomenon of success succeeding.

And now, in a layer bright as gold beneath her workaday consciousness there ran the something that was mattering more than any item in any day of all her days had ever seemed to matter before!

Her ruse of recalling Flake from Denver off what was by no means the last lap of a six weeks' tour, under pretext of the need to consult him on the Triangle matter, after she had clearly and cleanly decided it for herself, coupled with Delilah's exclamation as she dressed to dine with him the evening of his return, were what jerked her to concrete evidence of what was happening to her.

Flake was! This young fellow, eight years her junior, of a most marked power of business acumen which she felt sure would have brilliantly manifested itself anywhere, yet so strangely dominated by this passion for surgery, inherited no doubt from an ancestor, Major Basil Flake, cited for outstanding accomplishment in the medical corps of the army of the Confederacy. Flake. The thing was abashing, incredible, not to be countenanced, even by her secret innermost thoughts. Mother of a grown daughter, head of a big business, caught thus in the beginnings of an infatuation that would have belonged more properly to any of the girls in the office force who giggled and thrilled in the locker-rooms over the personable young general manager with the straight, stern, intensely blue-eyed face and the long, supple hands that looked boneless but gripped with strength and decision.

Jessie, forgive your ridiculous mother. It's enough to make me want to run from myself. It's because I'm so terribly lonesome. I'm ashamed. I'm ridiculous.

Nevertheless, standing there before her mirror, contemplating herself in the gold turban and the beige velvet, Delilah's remark about the Christmas tree smote her awake.

Flake was the answer! Flake. Flake. Flake. Young Flake. Clear-eyed, incisive-eyed. The mouse ran up the clock. The thrill ran up her spine. Flake was the answer. Young Greek, whose premature return, falsely motivated by her, was causing Delilah to exclaim over her shoulder: "Chile, what's happened? You look lak somebody had lit de Christmas tree."

Sanity must return, would return, of course, long before she found herself sitting opposite to Flake in the gloomy grandeur of the Gotham dining-room. But meanwhile, for the instant, while Delilah placed across her shoulders the tan-and-gold brocade evening wrap which she was wearing for the first time, something absolutely without precedent was tumbling through her.

Flake was back.

. . .

They met at the hotel, she with the seniority of manner which she cultivated against a tendency to exhibit toward her employees too great a humility, on the basis of the gratitude she felt toward the least and last of them.

I am in love with Flake, she said to herself, as she sat down opposite him, cracked open a hard roll, and simultaneously began buttering and realizing all over again the incredible ecstasy that was happening to her.

In the last year he had taken to contributing his share to the rather formal decorum of these combination business and pleasure evenings by appearing in semi-formal dress, which gesture, unsolicited by her, had prompted her to do likewise. The effect from the first had startled her, enhancing her pleasure in the young blond beauty of this fellow who combined business astuteness with so many qualities that seemed to run crazily into the geometric pattern of his precise kind of mind.

Here, mixed in the person of this young fellow whose hair set onto his brow as if carved there after the fashion of waves leaving their print on sand, and whose face was shaped like the sole of a lady's narrow square-toed slipper, was the curious conglomerate of expert accountant, very expert disciplinarian, organizer, and efficiency man, all straddling, like a super-imposed viaduct, the stream of his stubborn desire for surgery.

I love him, leapt and flickered in the newly lighted tapers of her consciousness as she forced her eyes against the menu. I love Flake.

Outwardly and with lips that moved coolly and evenly and straightly, she asked him about a Pullman on Olive Street in St. Louis, which, for reasons Flake had especially gone there to analyze, was continuing stubbornly to stand in the red of the debit side of its monthly statement.

For the better part of an hour she listened to his recital of the generic and minute matters which made up his chronological report of the ground covered before her wire had curtailed the last three weeks of his trip.

In the beginning, her judgments had seemed to him to come snap, hit or miss, so quickly they followed upon the heels of a report. He had come to learn differently. What actually happened was that the wealth of detail which he recited or read from closely documented reports sprang into immediate pattern, enabling her to see the whole.

Facts and statistics which he shoveled before her eyes were the dots composing the lithograph. With the curious talent of the block-reader, salient points marched out, disassociating themselves from contributory lesser ones. Long since, Flake had learned to defer to the tuning-fork of her intuition, which, responding almost immediately, pitched her for quick action.

What a curious conglomerate, this B. Pullman. But not of difficult stripe, once you learned to reckon with the fact that only Pullman the business woman was the phenomenon. Herself, apart from the strange acumen, ability to meet immense issues with what seemed no realization of their immensity, her almost instantaneous perceptions, curious quality of throwing out casual dictums involving enormous transactions, her baffling tricks of largess and contradictory economies; apart from all these, she was, as Flake put it himself, nothing more than a girl with her skates. A rather blowy girl in her thirties, who wore her new grooming like a shellac from which her fluffiness of hair and figure and nervous manner would escape, but withal, a delayed kind of prettiness out all over her.

I am in love with this boy, thought Bea, feeling some of this prettiness, and trying to behave, deep down to herself, as if the realizations, sweeping over her, were not flooring her. I am in love. For the first time in my life. Why not?

It was as if she needed to feel, at the inner admissions, the flood of her shame. But instead, slicing down into steak, forking up peas sauté, and permitting the secret intoxication to mill through and through her, she sat coolly listening to his perfectly submitted territorial report of maple-syrup and maple-candy distribution west of the Rockies.

I love Flake and I am glad of it, and not even my child shall deny me! And nothing smote her, not even shame, except the quite incomparable sensation of sitting there in her beige velvet, her hair soft, brown, and with electricity in it, curving out from beneath the gold turban, and more beige, fluffed in tulle over the bare white bosom revealed by her decolletage, blocked squarely into his vision.

As a matter of fact, he had taken on the habit, these last months, or was it years, of slipping, without change of tone, and certainly without change of manner, from the intimacies of business into a strange, paradoxical, kind of impersonal intimacy that had to do with her appearance.

"Is that hat hurting you or is it supposed to be worn on the back of your head that way? Looks like the devil." He had bolted at her one day following immediately upon the heels of a discussion they were holding in her office over the idea of simultaneously invading Los Angeles with a Wilshire Boulevard, Sunset Boulevard, and Seventh Street B. Pullmans.

She had felt slapped and her hand had flown to her head. Devil! Tease! He knew it was not hurting, but that she had pushed it so, as she invariably did when the rim felt hot and bothersome.

A paragraph in one of the gossip weeklies had recently referred to her as a "big business dame" and disciple of the Queen Mary School of Millinery, "who, it is rumored, is considering a seven-figure offer for the Paddy Cake Business."

He must have read that wise-cracking nonsense! Her hand which had flown to her hat began tucking away the strands of her hair, which she still wore, except for flattened pompadour, precisely as she had worn it all of her adult life, and then down to her bodice, along the diaphragm, which for some time she had been noticing rolled in a little ridge of flesh above the corset line.

"Why? What do you mean?"

"I mean just that. Talk it out with Virginia Eden. She's high priestess of that sort of thing. They tell me she actually uses her own preparations. It pays to advertise, if you can sell your products to yourself."

That had been more than sufficient. She could scarcely wait, that day back there when his first comment had fallen, to hasten, in her sense of humiliation, from her office and from his sight.

What a figure she must cut, for him to have ventured that much! Even her child, in a recent letter, had affectionately admonished her not to forget to "squnch" her hat down. Probably that same copy of the gossip weekly had fallen into her hands. For months Virginia Eden's urgings, "Come in and let us do you over. You need to be taken in hand," had failed to penetrate. Now suddenly, now immediately, nothing mattered quite so much as to somehow, some way, convert those aspects of herself, such as the bulgy diaphragm, and the blowy hair of which hitherto she had been half, but not sufficiently, aware.

It needed no more than this word of terribly embarrassing suggestion from Flake to whip awake the half perception that, prettier than ever though she might be at this period of her life, she was nevertheless letting herself go blowy.

The defensive impulse of the thirties had apparently had no chilly dawning. Up to the time of the veiled inventory that lay beneath the remark of Flake, there had been only the private pangs of plucking out the first gray hairs which had not multiplied, and that latent sense of the thickening which was manifesting itself in the bulge above her corset line.

Just the same, I am a prettier woman than I was a girl, she said back to her reflection one day as she stood noting herself in the full-length mirror mounted onto her bedroom door, and self-embarrassed, snatched up her handbag and gloves and made her rush for the subway.

Then Flake's remark, of the some months previous.

And now: The security of sitting there opposite him at dinner, and feeling with every inch of her the grooming and creaming and waving and slimming she had endured at the hands of the chorines Virginia Eden had loosed upon her! Flake's penetrating appraising eyes, as they swung, as impersonally as he swung his voice, into the channels that more and more, of late, he was permitting himself:

"That's a handsome outfit."

(He means I am handsome!)

"Those browns and golds are clever. Whatever it is you have been doing, is all to the good."

For him, to whom words came sparingly, where she was concerned at least, here was fulsome praise.

The sense of being admired lifted itself from the dusty places within her. The gift of blushing lit across her face and for a painful instant she was conscious that she had giggled upward like the girls who had crowded about her the week before, after she had delivered a talk at the Advertising Show, on Women in Business.

Women in business! What did they matter! Women in *love!* Ah, women in love set!

Brilliantly, blindingly one thing mattered. I am in love with Flake!

·38·

The head of one of Great Britain's largest corporations had stated in an interview that women make erratic executives, and two or three of the news services were hard after what reply B. Pullman would make to this.

Quonta Club, national business women's organization, was wanting B. Pullman as guest speaker for the Philadelphia Convention.

National Weekly invites article: What Price Business Career to a Woman.

Weekly *Wall Street Journal* requests interview: Do Women Really Want Business Careers?

For the first time in its history, *Advertiser's Monthly* had departed from its standardized green cover, for one in three colors that blazoned "The Face That Has Become A National Institution" (Delilah's).

At the expiration of the period between the lugging of the tins of maple syrup through the back streets of Atlantic City, to this culmination of shipping-rooms, mail-order departments, luxurious B. Pullmans that were idealizations of even the most *de luxe* dining-car, a wave of business-woman consciousness seemed to have struck the press.

Considerably after the event, the achievements were suddenly being heralded of women who for a decade or more had deployed their activities well over the commercial scene.

"Dey didn't pay no attention to us in de years when a little of dis here free advertisin' we're gittin' now, and that we can afford to buy, would have saved us corns on our hands and souls."

Right enough, but the year that B. Pullman, Virginia Eden, and such women as Hanna Gronauer, reputed to have conceived and promoted an aggregate of thirteen miles of model tenement buildings in the larger

American cities; Faith McDonald, founder and president of eighty-eight Cutie Dress Shops; Fanny Mason of the Mason Savings Bank System— came in for flare after flare of publicity, the B. Pullman enterprises almost doubled profits.

"It pays better to be advertised than to advertise," she remarked to Flake the evening they dined, in celebration of the results of inventory, across lighted candles in the dining-room of the apartment on Central Park West, a dining-room long since gone chromo in her estimation, but which pending Fishrow, she refused to refurnish.

It was months now since the strange rhythm of being in love with Flake had swung itself to her consciousness. Months of constant procrastinations, with herself and with him, of one trumped-up alibi after another for maneuvering to keep him from important territorial surveys and the routine of inspections which were part of his indispensability to the firm.

Time after time he had turned restive, while she parried for time and subterfuge.

"There is something brewing in my mind that I am not quite ready to discuss, but I don't want you off on territory until I have settled it one way or another." Again: "No need to start south yet. Reports are good and the Atlanta situation can be handled from this end. With all the rumors flying that Usa is about to make us an offer, it might be just as well for you to remain here for a while. . . ."

And then suddenly, as if to legitimize her procrastinations, there came, not the rumored move by Universal Sales Association, but a proposition from Imperial Chain, the British corporation that had recently flung its indictment that women make erratic executives, to simultaneously spread the B. Pullman novelty through six European countries, with further expansion in immediate view. Six European countries, and Orient, enterprise to be launched by Imperial Chain in coöperation with B. Pullman, Inc., with minimum three-years agreement, the president herself to personally inaugurate the overseas chain.

Rome to Singapore! Three years of city-to-city, dotting the world with B. Pullmans. Rome. Monte Carlo. Budapest. Vienna. Munich. Berlin. Deauville. Paris. London. Sydney! Singapore!

Terms, the flattering perfection of terms. The world literally this time, an oyster to be pried open from Rome to Monte Carlo. From

Budapest to Vienna. To Munich. To Paris. To Peking! An oyster to any woman except the one with her eyes on a kennel with a small brass plate beside the door, and a sitting-room with a private door through which a put-upon surgeon could escape from his office. . . .

But suddenly, here into her lap, with a time clause allowing four months for decision, was sufficient controversial material to justify her procrastinations with Flake. Big decisions pended here.

Deep down inside her tiredness, imbedded into her fatigue, her every impulse turned its head away. New worlds, but old life stretching ahead in them. Sugar-sugar-sugar. Sites. Delilahs.

Boats, trains, hotels, conferences with strange men divided from her by strange languages. Boats, trains, hotels. Planes because time would be priceless, instead of long and sweet and slow and utterly, darlingly worthless, except for purposes of private and personal happiness; lazily her own, in a home agog with such unroutinized delights as the comings and goings of a young daughter. With the comings and goings of a— of a young husband. Flake!

She dared now, in the innermost recesses of her, speculation that set nostalgia for what she had never known, fizzing along her veins. The business sold outright to the home corporation, Universal Sales Association! Fine ample revenues from six-figure investments. Life to be lived now, perhaps tardily, but fully, dearly, rightly.

More and more her mind began to fasten itself upon the possibility of Usa. For months, filling the air like missiles, had persisted the rumors of this impending offer from a corporation backed by the second largest money interests in America.

Where a year or two before she would have given only the slightest credence to any one of the insect army of such rumors that in one form or another buzz into a busy day, now suddenly, it was difficult not to concentrate hopefully upon them.

Was Usa actually about to swing open its monopolistic jaws in the direction of B. Pullman, Inc.? Theoretically, the idea had for years been anathema to her. All about her was the spectacle of business after business, built up out of lives and brawn, slipping down impersonally into the gigantic maw of a new industrial monster that seemed to have appetite only for what somebody else had created.

Virginia Eden, with her eyes on unridden seas, had already refused, according to what Bea knew to be more than rumor, a four-million-dollar outright sale of her interests to Usa.

It was fair enough to assume that at this period of their ripe maturity the B. Pullman enterprises might also fall within the gargantuan appetite of monopoly.

In the years before this impulse to be free of the vast incubus of business had ridden her, the dream of finding herself in a position to refuse an offer mounting into the terrific millions had dramatized itself across her imagination.

B. Pullman refuses Usa offer of ten million. . . .

Jessie abroad, her teachers, her colleagues, would read it as a news dispatch.

Her entire organization would know it one morning as she strode through its outer offices to her private one, where piled messages of applause and congratulation would await her.

Only eighteen months previous the entire run of her consciousness had been something like this: Usa? Sell now? Indeed! If B. Pullman is a household word, wait! Five years hence will see a B. Pullman in every town of a population of twenty-five thousand and more, that intervenes between coast and coast.

Nothing, it is true, so daring as the British Imperial Chain idea, had entered her reckoning. But there was Canada yet to be invaded. Ottawa. Toronto. Montreal. Then, too, the dream that lurked back of all this. An ultimate negotiation of national scope, whereby a B. Pullman buffet car would be part of short-run train service the country across.

If Jessie seemed to marvel now at the large accomplishment which lay behind every advantage she so lavishly enjoyed, the next five years would reveal how comparatively puny had been the hitherto achievements of the parent she called B. Pullman.

What with annual business bulking into millions, B. Pullman negotiable shares not only holding their own, but brilliantly rising in a fluctuating market, the rumored Usa offer had been one to covet chiefly in order to reject.

And now, all that was changed!

Instead, the rumored offer from Universal Sales Association, continuing to linger in the limbo of mere hearsay, was becoming a matter of acute anxiety; part of the general frenzy of mind that mingled so confusingly with the elaborate mental tissue of maneuvering to keep Flake at home.

The time had come to "cotch." Cotch life! She intended to. Yes sirree! Cotch it on the rebound and for all it was worth, and it was worth a very, very great deal. Particularly these days since their relationship had swung from the office, the Gotham lunch-table, to these small candle-lit evenings in the dining-room of her own home.

Evenings like this one, following inventory or preceding one of the long territorial trips, had hitherto been matters of late conference at office with sandwiches and coffee brought in, or across the impersonal rectangle of a hotel table.

Now suddenly, across the highly personal one of her own, a right gay table with twisted blue candles in a pair of crystal girandoles which Flake had picked up for her at a New Orleans auction and which were ultimately to adorn a highboy at Fishrow, the something in her that had leaned shyly out of her manner was about faintly to capture his attention. "What's all this," he seemed to say, scenting, but by no means aware. "What's up?"

A sense of revulsion against something old and predatory within herself swept her as she saw this happening. An older woman was spreading her net for bright youth. The sort of woman that sometimes, in fear of the precariousness of her position, she visualized might ensnare him on the road. You could tell, from the invariable flurry he created among the women of the organization, he was not the man to pass unnoticed, even though his apparent imperviousness seemed almost too perfect not to be simulated. The voices of the older women, Weems and Lejaron, and even Mrs. Van der Lippe, no less than the youngsters, whose manners were coated with sex when they had occasion to address him, curved, where Flake was concerned.

The older women. She was one of them, not so old as Weems or Mrs. Van der Lippe, but sufficiently older to feel this boy's youth flaming between. At that though, only eight years! . . . She had worried so at the thought of those eight years, that finally reduced and distorted in her mind, they existed there soluble and shrinking under the constant self-justification.

What were eight years? Between a woman twenty-five and a youth eighteen, yes! But the span narrowed as they grew older. Now both she and Flake were in their thirties! And a woman with a sublime reason for needing to keep young, can. Does! In mind, in body, in spirit! Oh, Flake, will you think I am crazy, when you know?

And something of knowing was flickering across this youth. Within a fortnight his manner, which seemed to say, "What's all this?" had been scenting. Flake was no fool. He must be seeing for himself what at first may have seemed unbelievable . . . what's all this? . . . what's up? . . .

" . . . Rome to Singapore! Enormously flattering, but there isn't money enough to tempt me!" She was saying to him, explaining over and over again, under pretext of needing his advice on a matter definitely settled in her mind, the elaborate details of the Imperial Chain offer. "There are things in life besides bigger and better business. Bigger and better living counts for something. I'm beginning to realize that."

"I don't suppose it would make much of an impression on Imperial Chain if you were to explain to them that while you are disinclined to devote the next several years to knocking about the cities of the world, you've an extremely efficient young fellow to offer as substitute. A genius blushing unseen—"

"Why, Flake," she said on a rapid gush of words too quick for her, "I had hoped you might have the same reason for not wanting it that I have. Surely there is nothing to years ahead to traipsing around the cities of the world doing the things over and over again that we have already succeeded in doing. We—I see such different things ahead—don't you?"

Well! There it was said. Anyway, so much of it that she sat back in the sudden rush of silence, breathing as if she had been running.

Well? well? well? her alarmed kind of waiting seemed to say. Well, I've said it, now what are you going to do about it? You can't kill me for being ridiculous. Loving you is not a criminal offense. I do love you. Flake! I want to stay back here, for happiness, with you.

Of course what he said out of a silence which seemed to gather around him as if to clothe him in the decent shadows of reticence, was along lines that steered them back into the unembarrassment of casualness. But from this point something in Flake had been reached. Ever after, it was to spread its essence over his manner. She had been casting pebbles against his consciousness, and suddenly a shade had been raised and a man was looking out at a woman. . . .

"Mighty fine of you to feel that way about it," he said. Under his skin appeared a tinge of pallor that made it hard and smooth as marble. Under her own, it seemed to her she could feel the entire stream of her blood coagulate and redden her. Well? Well? Well?

"I'll take up this matter with Jones of Syracuse by long-distance telephone, since you think it best for me not to start off on schedule," he said, folding a sheet of figures that had lain in a space cleared of dishes, and over which they had been poring.

Well? well? well? her silence seemed crying, and as if irked by it, put upon by it, ill at ease almost beyond endurance, he lifted the embroidered chiffon edge of her sleeve, fingering it.

"New?"

New! Within the past three weeks, she had not only spent more on clothes than within any similar given period in her life, but had actually tripled any annual budget she had hitherto allowed herself.

New? Every garment! The very new-fangled boneless corset which lay to her body like a coating of tallow was being worn for the first time. It had cost eighty dollars, and accustomed as she was by now to similar items that had come to seem just casual on the mounting bills that came in from Jessie, the price for her own had come as a shock to one who never in her life had paid more than three dollars for contraptions that seemed adequately enough to fill their corset's purpose.

The smart couturière who had literally outfitted her from tip to toe had exclaimed in shrill French at the stiffly boned corsets in which she had stood revealed the first day of her fittings, jerking them off and holding them up gingerly to marvel at their antiquated architecture.

The new foundation felt sleazy and light under the lingerie and gown built so snugly to conform to the new flowing lines of the figure it created.

Were those new things? The apricot-colored chiffon, set off with jade belt and jade shoulder ornaments and jade satin slippers, in which she sat opposite him in the soft light of table candles, had cost five hundred dollars, not including the whispers of the fine underthings which lay so ingratiatingly to her body.

She knew now, that really, regardless of what had gone before, for the first time in her life, along in her difficult thirties, she was feeling herself delectable for a man.

All the more so because in these difficult thirties, more and more, she was realizing the barrenness of every moment that had led up to them; more and more was being borne in upon her the travesty of herself, in a marriage that now stood revealed as a pallid mating with a man who had not even faintly roused her from a somnolence of senses destined to stretch over the first thirty-five years of her life.

I am entitled to this! My child, who is forever berating me for getting too little out of life, will be the first to entitle me to it. I have been half-dead in a half-dead world. Flake likes me. He can be made to love me. In books—and of course in life, too, it happens that way. We are both in our thirties! The few years' difference this way or that do not matter. He is not the sort to run after fledglings. Never has been. I am tired. My bones are tired. My marrow is tired, and he is bringing me to life. I want to be free of all this. Sell out. I want my home in Fishrow. I want my child in it. My husband. Delilah. Flake.

All along, under their talk, as she handed fresh fruit out of a silver bowl inscribed, "With the affection and admiration of the office. Christmas 1924," the runnel of her thoughts beat and flushed her face.

"Flake, has it ever occurred to you that if the Imperial Chain offer were even double what it is, I've had enough?"

"You mean?"

"I mean that if the proper offer to buy outright, comes from Usa, or any similar source, for that matter, I'm ready! I know when I've had enough, Flake."

He crushed his napkin on the table, half pushing back his chair, and rather too elaborate in his gesture of surprise.

"But I've heard you say repeatedly that you could imagine no reasonable offer large enough for you to accept."

"That is true, Flake, of the years gone by. But people change."

"Yes, yes, of course."

"I've changed, Flake."

She fastened her eyes on him then, as clearly and unblinkingly as she could manage, amazed at the implication her gaze seemed able to muster, because as she held it she could see his face, where it started to quiver slightly in little jumping nerves along the jaw line, set itself against it.

"Why shouldn't you get out from under? You've worked long and hard. Too hard. You've built up your monument. You're a rich woman."

She sat there leaning slightly forward, conscious that Delilah had shut the door to the kitchen, and absolutely breathless with desiring something different from what he said. He had not followed up the challenge of her retort. On the contrary. She had not, somehow, the womanish talent to make him toe the mark of her passionate desire to keep him personal.

I'm tired, Flake, she wanted to say with the sob in her heart making itself felt in her voice so that he must, must, see all the way into the meaning of her maneuverings. I'm tired. You are the meaning of rest to me and happiness, and everything that life hitherto has not meant for me. Don't you see? Won't you see?

What she actually said was a string of words; little shrill words that clattered like coals off the chute of her lips.

"I want to live, Flake. I haven't ever."

Either the lines that flickered in and out of his face were the almost too terrible ones to be endured, those of a man retreating before the advances of an older woman, or they were the worried ones of a man concerned chiefly with thinking about his job. Either, she was saying to herself, he is saying to himself, The old thing is after me! Or: Well, that will let me out. New management if she sells. Reorganization. What of me in all this?

Here it came!

"Well, the day you step out, I do, too, no matter what. With you gone there will be nothing left of it all but its bigness and profit. Imagine B. Pullmans without the B. Pullman."

"Frank, you don't need to imagine anything without the B. Pull-man—"

"Oh, I'm for your decision. You're right. Dead right. What does business amount to, if not as a means to an end."

"The end is our—"

"I'm in a position to take my medicine. I've saved. I may seem a little too old to branch into new worlds. Perhaps, but not much. I've never let myself dwell on stepping out while you. . . . ''

"While I, Frank?"

"Not that I've entertained the idea that I'm indispensable."

"You have been! You are!"

"Nonsense! You're too shrewd a business woman not to understand the big-business principle that no one man is ever indispensable. But let me tell you that these years in association with you have been indispensable to me."

"Flake, Frank, they've been more than that to me."

"Stuff and nonsense! Part of your success has been your talent for employees. I don't know how you do it. I doubt if you quite do. But practically everybody who works for you, now that the girls have got the nonsense kink brushed out of their minds, becomes your Delilah."

"Not you, Frank. . . . ''

He reached over and patted the back of her hand.

"Yes, me. And I've liked it. As a matter of fact I've liked it so much that your decision to sell may turn out to be the blessing in disguise for me that will start me on the road doing the only thing for which I have any real talent or desire. The fact that I feel sure I could pass my state medical examination right now isn't going to help me much, if I don't hustle out and get a diploma to prove it. The day you get out from under, I enroll for that diploma."

She had a desperate and overwhelming feeling that somehow she must push back the strange tides she had so unwittingly released.

"But, Frank, what I mean is . . .''

"I know what you mean. You're dead right. From now on, you want to begin to use your success, instead of going on creating more. You've already more than you want for your needs. Get yourself the things now that your money and leisure can buy. Get that girl of yours home. Enjoy her. Enjoy yourself. God knows you've managed life well enough for everyone around you. It's time you remembered you're living a life, too."

"But, Frank, without the lives of those about me, Jessie, you—I need——"

"You've it coming to you. If she's anything near the gal she ought to be . . .''

"And you, Frank—you're built too solidly into my life by now for me to . . ."

"Never fear. You'll have a hard time to shake off this old relic of your business life, even if Weems and Lajaron and Van der Lippe are to be sold up the river with Universal Sales Association."

"How can you!"

"You know what I mean—passed on to the new ownership, you'll have them and plenty more of us, who owe you too much to quite know what to do about it, yapping around your ankles, long after you would have done with us. And mark my word, with your interests in the condition they are, you'll unload to Usa or some corporation as big, for somewhere around six million, and it is coming to you every cent."

"That's the least . . ."

"Funny part, I know it is. You don't begin to realize anything about yourself."

"That's not quite accurate. I'm just beginning to."

"You've kept your nose so close to the grindstone that you actually haven't taken time off to realize what's happened to you. Or have you any kind of inkling that what has happened to you and the handful like you, probably hasn't happened to women in the history of the world. Name me a woman, with the exception of the few in your same class today, who have built up businesses anywhere approaching the magnitude of yours. How many women, in the whole history of them, have ever proved themselves to be the business man you are. The stage hasn't been set for it. Wasn't set for it when you steamed in, for that matter, and set it for yourself. Go as far back as you like and find me the equivalent of a woman about to be offered millions for a business she built up out of a can of maple syrup. What you need is time off in order to get on to yourself."

Oh, how wrong, how cruelly, how even ludicrously wrong had been her tack. Here he was talking to her after the manner of a toastmaster introducing her at a Woman's Business League dinner.

Here she was, calling to him from the arid desolations into which none of these things he recited had reached: Frank, I love you. All the reward and all the meaning of my success lies centered in you and there you sit talking to me of my achievement. You and my child are my

238

achievement. I am ready for you both now. Can't you see what I am driving at? Won't you see?

Suddenly, as if the stimulant of what was happening had only just reached him to the core, he reached over across the table and closed his hand over her wrist until the bracelet bit in.

"If you sell the business, you're releasing me for something I should have had the courage to do five years ago on my own. I didn't. The job here interested me and the salary solved a lot. Besides, working for you was one of those privileges a fellow doesn't easily throw over. The day you step out, though, I step into medicine. In my way, this Usa offer, when it comes, will mean as much to me as it will to you!"

There was something of the compensation of self-flagellation in continuing to sit there in the candlelight, twirling the jade bracelet that his clutch had made dig into the flesh and planning with him, far into the midnight, the sale of a business that would release them both.

·39·

The night that, unannounced, Peola walked in, Bea, who had come into the apartment about ten o'clock after a monthly round-table dinner with her staff managers, was standing before her mirror in one of the new fluffy peignoirs that had lately replaced her cotton crêpe kimonos, braiding her hair into the two identical plaits she had worn to bed all of her adult life.

Through the open door of her father's room, she could hear his rumbling breathing, which was as definitely part of her night as the ticking of a clock. Once indeed, the night of his second stroke, both she and Delilah had darted from bed on no more alarm than the unwonted silence of his having skipped some of the breathings.

Whe-e-eze, it was going through the apartment the night that Peola turned unexpectedly up, as Bea stood in the immemorial attitude of a woman making a braid over one shoulder and binding it with a wisp of combing.

It was three and a half years since Peola had passed through New York for a two-day visit on her way from Washington, D.C., to Seattle, Washington, to accept the new position as librarian.

Her appearance, following a late ring at the door, answered by Delilah who had been moving about the kitchen at her nightly rite of peeling a cold red apple for Bea before she retired, had been the occasion of an instantaneous outcry and clatter of an apple bumping its way along the hallway.

"Praise be de Lawd Gawd Almighty for bein' in His heaven! It's mah chile come home to her waitin' and prayin' mammy! Lawd, you answered mah prayer. I knowed you would. Come out here, Missy Bea! Didn't I tell you mah chile would come home to her mammy?"

As a matter of fact, she had not told her. Bursting through the immense stress of this moment came the revelation of what must have lain crouching beneath the shell of Delilah's silence concerning this protracted absence of Peola.

Never a word out of her at all the delayed Christmas visits, procrastinations, postponements, except an apparently almost indifferent justification, difficult to ever have quite believed, yet so puzzlingly convincing.

"Mah chile ain't comin' home dis heah Christmas, after all. Sent her de money, but ah tole her to keep it and git herself something for to wear, her a-havin' de stylish jimjams lak all of 'em, includin' Miss Jessie, who ain't comin' home, neither. It's re-cat-a-log-in' time out dar whar she works. Is re-cat-a-log-in' something as fine as it sounds, Miss Bea?" Or: "If de chile didn't go git herself mumps so she cain't come home nohow, Easter time. We doan' want no mumps traipsin' in, gittin' cotched by mah chair-baby or Miss Jessie if she comes home from school. Well, ennyhow mumps is something easier on de mind dan re-cat-a-log-in'."

Not an intimation of that chronic ear-strain for the postman's footfall; of the long arid intervals between the neatly typed envelopes bearing the Seattle postmark. One to every ten or fifteen of Delilah's, as they went out in their cramped immature scrawl, bearing, in spite of every effort to convert her to a checking system, inclosures of bank notes pinned to the letter sheet.

And now here was Peola, straight as a blade, her banana-colored pallor standing out beneath the brim of the modish hat, walking into the routine of Delilah preparing to deliver the nightly polished apple on its nightly polished plate.

Flood gates went down, sweeping the one reticence known to Delilah, the secret inner hurts, turmoils, fears, and anguishes concerning this offspring of hers, along the surface of released tears.

"I knowed mah baby would come home to me. Every night, when I prayed to God, I knowed it. Dar's a knife jumped right out of mah heart when I opened dis door jes' now. Jumped plop out an' quit hurting when I laid eyes on mah chile. Gawd Almighty, praise be de Lawd, mah chile's come home. . . ."

The wide expanse of her face slashingly wet, the whites of her eyes seeming to pour rivulets down her face like rain against a window pane, her splayed lips dripping eaves of more tears, her throat even rained against, there was apparently no way that Delilah could capture the face of her child in an embrace. Rigid-eyed, it swung, the banana-colored mask, this way and that, away from the wetness. It eluded, it dipped, it came up dry and powdered with pallor, fastidiously untouched in the perfection of its maneuvers to escape the great wet crying surface that was after it.

"Mah baby. I knowed she'd come if I waited and prayed and prayed and waited. Mah baby, come home to her mammy, and nobody askin' it of her."

The dry inscrutable face, wrung and silent, stared across the vast shoulder of her mother; stared and stared at the figure of B. Pullman standing on the edge of that scene of the revelation of the pouring forth of this soul, this vast reticence of Delilah.

Here was the silence of a late evening suddenly strewn with the secret debris of all the released torments that during the years must have pressed against the infallible outward exuberance of Delilah. A crucifying kind of pity for it looked out from the face regarding Bea above the enormous mound of her mother's shoulder. Pity and a veritable nausea of revulsion. Peola was suffering that embrace, a demonstration against which her flesh and her staring eyes seemed to curl.

"Miss Jessie's letters comed oftener, but mah baby brunged herself instead of any letters. Look heah at mah honey-chile, Miss Bea. Miss Jessie never come home in no more style! Look at dat fur tibbet, will you! White wid black tails lak kings wear. Ain't she de fashionest-plate! Uh-uh, gimme dat valise! Doan' you spoil your pretty hands luggin' dat luggage. Gawd Almighty, mah chile's come home—an' will you look at dat tail to her walk. Struttin', I calls it, an' struttin' ain't none too good for her.—Gawd Almighty, mah chile's come home!"

It was obvious enough that what happened with such immediate sequence had not been planned by Peola at all, as she opened stiff lips to try and make manifest in the first few lines of her dreadful little preamble.

But somewhere her intentions, as revealed by her luggage and the late hour of her arrival, were failing her. The vast wet surface of a face that threatened to suck hers to it, the arms loaded with flesh that crowded and pressed her, the pronouncement that the small spare room off Delilah's which she had occupied on the rare occasions of visits to her mother was now preëmpted by the male nurse. Her intention to remain even overnight was failing her, failing her as she stood.

"Come right into your mammy's room, honey-chile, and take off your things and let your mammy feed and rest you. Ain't no place, wid mah chair-baby's nurse cluttering up de little room, for you to sleep tonight, exceptin' where you belongs, in your mammy's arms in your mammy's bed . . . something I wouldn't take ten million dollars for . . . mah baby wid her mammy in her bed. . . ."

"No. No. No. I mean, I couldn't. I can't. I mean, you see, it's better this way. Quickly. Let me talk it all, right here. In the hall. Standing. It will be better then for me to go. Please, Mrs. Pullman, you stay too. Please. You must. I've traveled three days and three nights to see you both this way together!"

"But, baby-chile—ain't you gonna let your mammy git you fixed and comfortable fust? You looks dead-beat, baby. Missy Bea and me will wait—not Mrs. Pullman, honey; dat ain't no way for to call—your best friend."

"Please! The sooner this is over the better for—everyone."

"Baby, you ain't in trouble?"

"Not unless you decide that I am."

"Lawdagawd——"

"Please! You—Mrs. Pullman—Missy Bea, tell her we must talk quietly and at once."

"But, Peola, your mother is happy and excited——"

"Jes' so happy, baby, I don't know where to turn fust."

"I know you are, dear. But I need so much to talk to you, now—at once—quietly——"

"I'll leave you and your mother alone, Peola."

"Oh no, no! No, no, please! Won't you please stay? You have to be here. That's why I've come. To see you both."

"Then come into my room. Don't bother with those heavy bags now, Delilah. Come."

"If it's because you got to sleep wid your ole mammy dat you don't want to stay tonight now dat you got your bags here, I kin roll mahself up on de floor."

"Delilah, you'll do nothing of the sort! Come into my room."

No sooner in, behind closed doors, than the daughter of Delilah, facing them, jerked off the small hat that revealed suddenly with startling distinctness the straight black hair and straight contrasting pallor of straight brow.

"Help me, you two!"

"Lordagawd! . . ."

"There is nobody but you two who can. Help me to pass!"

"Lordagawd!"

"I've been in Seattle four years now. I'm liked there. I've made good there. I've passed. You must have known that all along, Missy Bea."

"I've suspected it."

"There's nothing wrong in passing. The wrong is the world that makes it necessary."

Suddenly Delilah began to sway, throwing her apron up over her face and talking softly into it as her body rocked.

"Lordagawd, it's come! Give me strength. De white horses have cotched her. Lordagawd, give me strength."

"You'll never know," said Peola to Bea, as if trying to make herself heard above the noise of a crying child, "how I've dreaded all this. The wailing. The dreadful sounds—the awfulness. . . ."

"Lordagawd, forgive me for wailin', but after all dese years of mah prayin', you've seen fit, in your wisdom, for it to come this-away——"

"There is nothing wrong about this way. What the world does not know, will not hurt it. I'm not ungrateful. Please try and understand that. I know how good you are. Twenty thousand times too good for me. Twenty? Fifty! Fifty times fifty times! Everything you've given me has been more than I deserve, and you've given and given and given me since the day I was born. . . ."

"Oh, mah baby, a-givin' you has been the meanin' of livin'. A-givin' you, seein' you git fine and educated an' into what you are now, even if in de end it crucify me, is God's meanin' for puttin' breath of life into dis black hulk——"

"Then you do want me to be happy——?"

"I does, baby. . . . It hurts lak dis ole heart was a toothache, wantin' it."

"You do, you do, of course you do. And yet you know as well as I know, that with all you've given me over and above what I deserve, since the day I was born, I've been the most wretched . . ."

"Doan' say it, baby. It's de knife back in mah heart."

"I must say it in order to make you understand."

"Doan'. . . ."

"You at least can cry. I can't. You've got tears left. I haven't. I've cried myself dry. Cried myself out with self-loathing and self-pity and self-consciousness. I tell you I've prayed same as you, for the strength to be proud of being black under my white. I've tried to glory in my people. I've drenched myself in the life of Toussaint L'Ouverture, Booker Washington, and Frederick Douglass. I've tried to catch some of their spark. But I'm not that stuff. I haven't pride of race, or love of race. There's nothing grand or of-the-stuff-martyrs-are-made about me. I can't learn to endure being black in a white world. It might be easier if I was out-and-out-black like you. Then there wouldn't be any question. But I'm not. I'm light. No way of knowing how much white flows somewhere in my veins. I'm as white under my skin as I am on top. Sometimes I think if my pap were living he'd have things to tell me——"

"Peola!"

"Lord Gawd Almighty, it ain't mah chile talkin'—it's de horse in her neighin' out through her blood. . . ."

"Listen. You scarcely know me. I've gone my way, able to do so because you have been good and indulgent and generous. I haven't been a good daughter. I know that. I haven't been anything you deserved to have me be——"

"You're mah——"

"But as things go in this world, I have been a good girl, morally or whatever you want to call it. I've worked. I've studied. I've tried to make the best of myself. And all the time with the terrible odds against me of knowing I could never get anywhere I wanted to get!"

"Oh no, Peola!"

"Yes, Missy Bea! What do you know about the blight of not having the courage to face life in a black world? You've succeeded in a world that matters to you! Give me that same chance."

"What do you mean?"

"I've got on out there in Seattle. Librarian in the city's finest branch. I've been careful. I've watched my every step, made no false ones. I'm not black out there in Seattle. Nobody knows anything, except that I'm an orphaned girl out from the East earning a decent living. And now, and now—the test has come. Sooner or later it had to come. I've got to go on forever that way, or be thrown back into something I haven't the courage to face. You can help me. You two. Only you two and Jessie, who will, if you will. For God's sake make her stop those moaning sounds. I can't stand it. I wouldn't hurt a dog that way. Make her stop it. . . ."

"Delilah, you must give Peola the right to state her case. . . ."

"Lord Gawd Almighty, I'm breakin' in two! I cain't hear it no more. Lovin' de Lawd dat made me black, I bring mah baby-chile into a race dat I'm proud to be one of. A low-down, good-for-nothin' race of loafers, lots of 'em, but no worser dan loafers of any other color. Lovers of de Lawd and willin' servers is mah race, filled wid de blessin's of humility—a singin', happy, God-lovin', servin' race dat I loves an' is proud of, an' wants mah chile to love——"

"I can't! I've nothing against them, but I—I can't be what you want. I'm not the stuff. Not in a white world. If your skin is white like mine and your soul is white—like mine, there is no point to the needless suffering. I've got to be helped. You two can do it. And I need to terribly—now—now!—to pass completely."

"Lawd have—"

"Delilah, you must hear Peola out! What do you mean by 'now,' Peola?"

"It's the crisis that had to come sooner or later. You know what I mean. Oh, not what you're thinking. Not that. Just the ordinary inevitable crisis. . . ."

"Marriage?"

"Yes."

"White?"

"Yes."

"No, no, no! Gawd don't want His rivers to mix!"

"Please make her stop, Missy Bea!"

"Delilah, dear good Delilah, you're making it impossible for us to talk this thing out. Sit down here, next to me, and give me your hand—and hear Peola out."

"If mah hand ain't good enough for mah chile, if her runs away from sleepin' wid her ole black mammy,'tain't good enough for to touch yours!"

"My dear, oh, my dear! Why, of course! Of course—my dear—" But what she attempted was apparently simply beyond Peola. Stepping around the small chintz chair that stood between them, she half described the gesture of taking her mother's hand and stood there locked in the midst of an effort that flooded her eyes, her face that would not flood with color, stamped with the tell-tale story of an aversion that was stronger than she was.

"Won't you please—won't you—release me—let me go—my way?"

"Let go what I 'ain't never had——"

"I need so terribly what it is in your power to grant me. I am safe except for you. He needs me so. Not even he realizes how much. Regardless of how much I love this boy, and I do, I do, I dare not risk letting him lose me by knowing. Neither dare I risk it for myself. I couldn't live. . . ."

"Black wimmin who pass, pass into damnation. . . ."

"O my God! What chance have I, Missy Bea, against her swamp and voodoo nonsense? . . ."

"Dat ain't swamp talk. Dat ain't voodoo. Dat's blood talk. Dat's de law-of-de-Lawd talk. You cain't go ag'in' de fallin' of de rain and de crackin' of de thunder. They're there. You're there. Black! You ain't lovin' nobody but yourself in dis here passin'. Your man will live to curse de day when your lie comes out in your chillun. . . ."

"I've taken care of that!"

"Peola!"

"I'm not ashamed. There are millions to populate the world besides me. There is no shame in being sterilized in the name of the happiness of another. He knows, without knowing why, that I can't have children. I want my happiness. I want my man. I want my life. I love him. I'll follow him to the ends of the earth. Which is practically what I propose to do."

"What end of the earth, Peola?"

"He's an engineer. We're going to Bolivia. I'll see to it that we stay there. His happiness will be the meaning of my life. I love him. He loves me. Knowing would blast his life and destroy mine. Nothing can happen to destroy us except if you . . . won't . . . help——"

"Lordagawd give me strength. . . ."

"Try, dear Miss Bea, to stop her. It's like a horror in a jungle—it's like—everything I'm trying to run away from. For God's sake—don't do that—stop swaying—stop praying——"

"Doan' leave me, baby. Doan' pass from me, baby. Even if I ain't never had you, doan' leave me. . . ."

"You're good. All my life I'll carry the memory of it locked up in my silence. But let me pass—Mammy——"

"Mammy! She called me Mammy—I's in her blood—she cain't help it.—Honey-chile, come to your mammy——"

"Don't you dare! You can't hold me. Blood can't, because there isn't enough of it between us. I don't care what you say. If my father had lived he might have had something to tell me that not even you know. Let me pass!"

"You cain't pass! You cain't! You cain't! God'll know it, even if nobody else does, and what you gonna do when you face him on his pearly throne. . . ."

"Let me take care of God! All that I want is your pledge. Both of yours. To let me pass, in silence. Give me your solemn oaths that so far as you are concerned, so far as ever entering my life with my husband is concerned, you do not know me, have never seen me, have never heard of me. It is that, for me, or nothing. It is life for me, or death. Promise me never to know me if you should meet me face to face in years to come. I'll see that you don't, but just to allow for the arm of coincidence, promise me!"

"O Lawd, was ever such words listened to——?"

"I know it sounds terrible. But, oh, my poor dear, it's in your power to give me my happiness! My freedom. Let me go. Let me pass. I need the promise. The oath. You've more than my happiness in your hands. You've my life."

They made a strange center, these three, to that conventional bedroom of taffeta, Circassian walnut, and unelaborate fixings of its unelaborate occupant. The furniture stood off at stiff angles from them as they held the formation of an unequal triangle, the rather cold remote light of a crystal chandelier packing them into a kind of pallor.

"You'll be well rid of me. I've been no good to you or for you."

"Lordagawd, you're a-askin' more of me dan to bury mah chile in her grave, but if dat's your will. . . ."

"I'm not worth your tears. I'm not worth a single one of them. I'm as vile in my own mind as I must be in yours. But somehow I'll make it up. I'll make it up to A.M. I'll make it up in trying to bring complete happiness to at least one human being. I'll make up for the rotten child I've been by making A.M. the best wife God ever made a man. He's just a darling, clean young boy, Mammy, a farmer kid who studied engineering when other fellows would have been hitting it high with his free time. He got to coming to the library evenings, after his mother died last March, leaving him without a tie in the world. Lonely kid. Darlingest clean fellow. Wonder if you know what it means, leading the lonely careful life I had to. All of sudden—all of a sudden the whole world bursting open, like a flower. I never dreamed—I never tried for him. It was just a case of a lonesome kid coming to the library evenings and the lonesomest girl in the world——"

"De makin's of misery—de makin's of misery——"

"I tell you no! He's gassed, to say nothing of half a hand he lost in Flanders. He's never yet shaken the hell of war out of his eyes. He needs change. We're going to make a fresh start. He's got this engineering chance in Bolivia. Thousands of miles from anyone who knows us. We'll get our roots down, there. What he doesn't know about me cannot ever hurt him. What he does know will bring him all the happiness there is. It's not a sin, Mammy, where there won't be children. It's all or nothing for me. You two have my life or my death in your hands."

"Oh, Peola, it isn't fair to put it that way to your mother."

"Don't you think I know that? Don't you think I've sweated agony before I took the train to come here? But it's all there is left. Life doesn't mean much to me, Missy Bea. Never has, until now. I couldn't go back to having it mean little again—and live on. Mammy's got you. You've got Jessie. I've found A.M. He loves me. I love him. I've done the—the right things—about the possibility of children. Never mind how. You couldn't believe how! It hasn't been easy. It's been terrible that—well, without him, I couldn't face a life that would be as sterile as I am.''

"How have you dared!''

"One dares everything when there is nothing to lose and everything to gain. His mother died and he began studying on his evening engineering course at the library. He couldn't find the right lodgings. I got him a room where I was boarding. We got to sitting together on the stoop evenings, after library. Walking. Talking. He needed to be nursed out of a state of mind he'd gotten into about that half of hand. He's been so terribly gassed too. To show you the kind of boy he is, his mother never knew that, up to the day she died. Not a boy to go gadding around. Lonely. Me too. Self-conscious about his hand. I cured him of that. Mining engineers don't read much outside their work. I got him into the habit. We began to go rowing Sundays. With a book. A.M. is such a kid. Used to his mother——''

"Mah chile dat's gonna throw away her own mammy is a-lovin' him now for a-lovin' his mammy!''

"It's life, I tell you. Me clutching at life! You've got to let me pass into a new world. I haven't told him anything different than I've told everyone out there. Practically nothing except that I—I'm alone, too. They like me out there. He—loves me. He depends on me. He's out there now—waiting for me to come back before we set sail. He's got this South American job. It's a five-year one. A big chance. Most of it in jungle country. Once I get A.M. there—away—safely alone—mine—he need never know. Thousands have done it. He'll never know anything except how happy I can make him. And will. Oh, don't look at me like that, the two of you. What do you know of what I've been through? I know what I'm doing. It's all or nothing for me. For us. Oh, you two—please . . .''

"Lordagawd, help me—do for mah chile what she wants——''

"I want you to let me pass. I want your oath. Never so long as you live, if you meet me here or there—in the jungle or on the high seas, to recognize or own me. I leave you no name. No address. We'll have to live along on engineer's salary instead of your darling generosity. I'll have to learn to forget. You'll have to. If you have mercy, Mammy, and you have—let me pass.''

"Dar's spikes through mah hands and dar's a spike through mah heart if ever dar was spikes in de hands and de heart of anybody besides our Lawd. . . .''

"Peola, you are asking of your mother something too terrible to be borne. . . .''

"As if everything she had to bear connected with me hasn't always been that. Let me go. Let her be free of me. There is nothing for either of us this way. Mammy, I beg—I beg—on my knees I beg. . . . I'll kiss your hands—I'll wash your feet. . . . Let me go——''

"No, no, no! Git up. Your mammy cain't bear dat. Git up for de love of Gawd. I got to let her go, Miss Bea. Lordagawd must help her from now on. Lordagawd and my prayers dat won't never leave her alone in de jungle. I got to let mah chile go, Miss Bea. Does you promise, too?''

"Yes,—Delilah——''

"Lordagawd, forgive mah chile, for she knows not what she does. Bless mah chile. Make happy mah chile. Strike me daid Lordagawd, if ever on dis earth I owns to bearin' her. . . .''

Seeing Delilah faint was the equivalent to beholding a great building slump to its side of earthquake.

·40·

"You must be a luvver of de Lawd if you want to go to heaven when you die."

Delilah desired, passionately, to go literally to a literal heaven when she died.

There were not many of the kinds of conveyances she had in mind, to be seen in street processions. Back in her childhood in Natchez, at every demise of a lodge member who had not let dues lapse, out came Ditmar's livery-stable hearse with the glass flanks and wooden plumes and three white if spavined mares, to the leadership of a major-domo with a fur mountain on his head and the flash of a silver ball before his eyes.

Once, only once, in all the years had she beheld such a procession move through the streets of New York. The funeral march had come winding up to her kitchen, on One Hundred and Thirteenth Street. Rushing, she had leaned the hulk of her body far over the sill, and there, down below in the street, proceeded the cortege.

Tra, la, la, la. Tra, la, la, la.

Moving along the cleared street, silver ball dancing, lodge uniforms gleaming, horses moving with fore knees lifting high and slowly, boom, a soul was riding to de Lawd.

"You must be a luvver of de Lawd if you wants to go to heaven when you die."

Delilah was. Oh, more and more, the love of Him wrung her. The love of Him and the vision of traveling toward Him between plate-glass flanks and to the bouncing of the silver ball.

"Lordagawd, mah baby has done You wrong. No meanness in her heart ag'in' You, but she done You wrong. Lordagawd, spare her, 'cause her mammy's gonna bring You atonement. Lordagawd, show her de light.''

It was important to guard against talking aloud to herself as she moved about at self-inflicted chores. It made folks tap their brows and smile. Most of the time she succeeded, lips firmly compressed in the presence of John or the young housemaid who worked under her surveillance.

On those occasions which she relished, when she had the old gentleman, during the male nurse's periods of off duty, to herself, she poured out to his dimming face growing exultations.

"You and me is going to Lordagawd, pore ole baby you, a-lovin' Him jes' as if we ain't been crucified on dis here mortal earth. You and me ain't holdin' nothin' ag'in' our Lordagawd, 'cause we knows His ways, even when dey hurt so, and tie us down to chairs, and tear out chillun from us, is divine ways. Mah baby-chile who couldn't get de scales offn her pappy-colored eyes has done wrong, Lordagawd. 'Lila's gonna atone. . . .''

Along in here was the beginning of curious slyness in regard to money affairs, asserting itself in one who hitherto had drawn her monthly wage only in order to send the most of it, outside of lodge and church dues, in wads to Peola.

Atonement now took the form of monthly contributions to the Baptist churches, not only of Harlem and Brooklyn, but Richmond, Natchez, Washington, as well as the most amazingly indiscriminate donation to the many black causes that began pouring in upon her.

"Delilah, you simply can't handle money if you are going to give it out willy-nilly to everyone that comes along. Don't you know those darkies aren't always honest with you? Word of you has gone out among them, and now see this deluge. . . .''

"I didn't give a penny to dat prowlin' deacon from de Order of de Angel of de Lawd. Angels of de Lawd ain't snoopin' in back doors, pinchin' pretty hired gals' laigs . . . an' dat's what I cotched him doin'.''

"Well, you've broken your promise somewhere along the line. Here is exactly eighteen dollars left in your purse and that leaves over one hundred and ninety to be accounted for outside your churches and lodges.''

"Honey-chile, dem niggers dat thinks I's jes' anybody's easy mark doan' know it, but I's atonin'. Lordagawd won't hold it ag'in mah chile

253

so long as her black mammy loves Him twice. Once for herself and once for her baby-chile what couldn't see de light. . . .''

And so it went, Delilah, except for her shares in the B. Pullman Company which reposed in a box in a vault, diverting the funds that had once flowed toward Peola, this way and that into the crush of begging palms that soon came to surround her.

"Let her alone, dear. After all, it's hers to do with as she likes," Flake had advised one evening after Bea's remonstrance at a gift of fifty dollars to some fantastic and unvouched-for Order of Liberian Ewes of Christ.

The noun spun around her like plates off the hand of a juggler. "Dear" from Flake!

She tried to keep down the slightest evidence of her almost unbearable excitement while he went on sorting over a book of snapshots which Jessie had sent of a skiing party of herself and classmates at Zermatt!

"Looks like a live crowd of girls."

She had never before come even anywhere near capturing such a moment as this, and now the precious thing had fallen at her very feet. "Dear." The desperate need to somehow hold it made her for the moment seem more than ever to herself, and revoltingly, the angling older woman. And yet she was saying:

"Flake, put that album down. I want to—talk."

He closed it with a little bang, crossing his long slim legs and slumping in his chair in a way that she loved to think was intimate. They had just completed a meal that Delilah, who doted on him, had prepared to the perfection of his liking. Lamplight was on his grave cool face and formed pools of shadow on his hair and in his deep eye sockets.

"Flake, has it ever occurred to you how impersonal we are?"

They had been discussing, up to the interruption of the Delilah incident, a cable received that day from Imperial Chain, enumerating certain aspects already included in the original offer, and expressing high hopes of ultimate decision: "We have further decided that this project should be pushed into Scandinavian countries, possibly as far north as Helsingfors."

"You see what I mean by impersonal, Flake. Here we are, talking about this offer just as if my not wanting to tour the cities of the world had no private important reasons bound up intimately with my own life. With our—lives——''

"On the contrary, it seems to me that the entire discussion about this Imperial Chain matter has been based upon the highly personal. If you were a different temperament, I would be urging you to accept the opportunity to travel, see the world, roam from Rome to Helsingfors.''

"But, Flake, aside from temperamental reasons as you call them—''

"They are the major ones. You have reached the stage in life where you can afford to do the things you want to do. Why on earth you should go traipsing over Europe, just at a period when you are not only uninterested in this entire business of establishing B. Pullmans the world over, but anxious to unload your American interests as well, is beyond me. Certainly we are reckoning with the personal equation, *you*. Not to mention, perhaps, a little of my own personal equation thrown in. Each of us, in his own way, wants to begin to live.''

"Oh, Flake,'' she said, and put a hand on his knee, "that's it!''

There was no mistaking it then. Like a man on his guard, he sat suddenly erect, as if something had startled him.

"You see, Frank, everything from now on, in my business, even European success, would be anti-climax. I'm tired. I want to rest. I want my personal life to take up where my business life leaves off. Frank, I want us—you—Jessie—me—to have everything we want. I want to begin to build my home, for my child, for me. Must I say it Flake, for us? I have the insane idea that perhaps you know what I am driving at. I want to break ground for our new lives, Flake, as well as for our new home.''

During a silence roared into by the strophe and antistrophe of the old gentleman's breathing, who in his perpetual attitude of sitting up was asleep across the hall, Flake held the position of flecking an ash off a cigarette end, as if shocked into an immobility from which he could scarcely unlock. So did she, her bare shoulders laid over with lamplight, her body tilted toward him and held there as if the falling of his ash would precipitate her forward.

All of her senses, of humiliation, seemed to stop in their tracks; her breathing, her rush of sensation to hang, massed, her being to pause as if in a second of death.

Frank was sitting there knowing. She could feel it as she slowly limbered and could move. He was knowing, beyond any doubt now, as he sat there with ash suspended. Flake with his cool, lean, undesiring face, was knowing that here was a woman awake to him and, under all the pretense of the heavy paraphernalia of affairs, in love with him. Suddenly he had tautened into knowing. The ash hung. The silence hung. Her humiliation alone was churning. He knew now. The procrastinations, the too eager alibis for postponing his departures for territory, were but the immemorial devices of the female maneuvering. . . .

To herself, quite horridly, the arms and the legs and the torso of her felt old and leathery. Something not young was reaching out for youth . . . a woman who had been awakened deep down inside the hitherto motionless jungle of her emotions was sending out to him the mysteriousness of her message. Terror of his having caught it flooded her. Whatever he might hitherto have suspected, he was knowing now. He would be knowing as he got up and went away. He would be walking down the street, away from her, a bad taste along his tongue, with knowing.

All this talk, all this hullabaloo, all this anxiety about the prospect of Universal Sales Association and selling the business; her reiterated and perhaps unnecessarily reiterated unreceptiveness to the idea of the European chain; underneath it all, surely by now, plain to him as the nose on his face, Flake! The A-B-C of it must be before him in the kind of flash of events said to blaze against the panoramic vision of a drowning man.

Poor Flake, was he a drowning man before the onrushing designings of an older woman? Here was one eight years his senior (oh, but they were both in their thirties!) awakened by him to the new consciousness that life had slipped her by. Marry me, Frank, flowed just beneath the thin surface of her silence. Build with me what is left of my life and I will build for you. I'm tired, Flake. But not from life. From lack of it. I have been cheated. I want to salvage. I want marriage. With you. I am finished with building a business. I want now to build happiness. Frank! Flake! I have been living in an attic room of myself all these years. I was married in that room eighteen years ago. The house of me has never been opened. You have ripped up the blinds and let in the light. I want to lay with you, Flake. To love with you, live with you, build into our future with you. . . .

He in this instant must be sensing all that. . . .

"Must I use words, Frank? Or perhaps, like the Imperial Chain, I should say to you, 'We do not press you for an immediate decision. Give yourself six months' time. . . . ' "

She tried not to breathe into the gossamer web of the silence. . . .

He tore into it by rising, and stooping for the act of kissing her lightly against the forehead.

She could hear him fumbling in the hallway in a crazy kind of haste, open the door with a small click, close it after him without any.

·41·

The days of that spring came in shod like Mercury. Wing-tipped days that sped of their own strange and excited momentum.

I mustn't let myself act like a schoolgirl, swung like a semaphore in her mind.

It was April, and as she dressed, leaning for longer and longer periods into the mirror, a box of orchids had arrived from Flake.

In the eight weeks since his lips had pressed against her forehead, and without more ado, or anything pushing forward the incident, except the arrival on two occasions now of a pair of formal orchids with his inscribed card, stream of life flowed along its rutted channel of days laden with their usual burdens of decisions, executions, conferences, inspections, meetings, except that suddenly its waters were charged!

I am the same, she told herself, only something is shaping itself to change me. He is!

It was then, leaning into her mirror to fasten the orchids in a trial cluster at her throat before she put them on ice to await her dinner with Flake, that the trill of laughter escaped her.

"I mustn't, I mustn't let myself act like a schoolgirl——"

But after all, laughter lay on her air. It hovered in the drapes Delilah was that week removing against the onslaught of impending heat. It came in perfumed efflations off the thawing soils of Central Park which had suddenly become soft and high like a nursing mother's breasts. It hung into the days like the net curtains that divide heaven from earth in amateur productions of church allegories. It lay in something sly and sudden in her father's old stone eyes. She could feel it pressing against the china whites when his gaze seemed to follow her. He could not roll his eyes. They were locked into two fixed lights in the centers of their balls, but they were crowded with seeing, seeming to follow her to every corner of the room like the painted eyes of a trick portrait.

"Father," she cried, one day, kissing his pebble-hard cheek and ruffling his immaculately brushed hair until his old eyes crowded up with thunder, "can you understand? I'm happy."

Delilah came running with his hair-brushes then. Baby-fine ones that she would not even permit the male nurse to apply.

"Doan' muss mah chair-chile's hair, Missy Bea. He knows what's goin' on inside you, widout mussin' up his hair."

Delilah knew, too. The knowledge lay in the dried beds of her eyes and across her smitten face.

Bea stepped gingerly between the knowing ones of the household, satisfied that they knew, yet fearful before what was about to befall her as a young deer can be at what it sees reflected in the water when it bends to drink.

Besides, how much was her imagination and how much did they really know?

For months, also, the approaching of the return of Jessie had been animating that small household. By all the devious methods of reiteration, Delilah's private jargon, passing of snapshots before his rigid eyes, exhibition of letters in young and florid handwriting with foreign postmarks, the old gentleman had been appraised of the impending event of his granddaughter's return.

A new mink lap-robe covered his legs even these spring days.

"Honey-chile, you doan' want Miss Jessie to come home and find her grandpap sittin' under nothin' less finer dan a min-ik lap-robe, lak dem fine babies in de park lay under."

His new ball-bearing chair: "Dat gran'chile of yourn may be wantin' to roll you out herself, an' de bes' ball bearings ain't none too good for her to push."

By the device of cutting a door, a room and bath from an adjoining apartment had been transformed into quarters for Jessie.

"Thar ain't gonna be no room in de Fishrow house more fittin' for a princess dan de one we got for Miss Jessie to come home to right in dis heah little ole flat. Dat chile's been livin' over whar dar's kings and queens. Her's gonna come home to a room decked out as good as if she were Princess of Switzerland."

Part of the admixture of the sense of high excitement of these days was undoubtedly Jessie; the pending return of a native into a fold from which she had virtually been absent for the eight or ten years of her school life.

The prospect of meeting Jessie, whom she had not seen for nineteen months, this Jessie of the gay, unthoughtful, photographic letters; the many snapshots of her slim foreign-looking little self with companions at pastimes and sports so alien to the small household on Central Park West, was an impending experience which, as the time approached, sent overwhelming excitement, dread, and almost unbearable impatience racing through Bea.

In this return, up to a few months ago, had seemed to be vested the entire meaning of life. Now too, of course, except, with all the difference in the world!

How would this girl, this strange, slim, quite beautiful product of her indulgences, this child who had only flashed through her life, fit back, now that the time had come, into the pattern . . . a pattern suddenly shot with hues of nobody's foreseeing.

They were such strange strangers. Years of gay enough letters, descriptive of travel and study, after all, told so little. Endearments tucked into many of them. "Mother-the-Magnificent, the thought of returning such a not-beautiful-and-dumb-belle into your august midst fills me with stage fright." And: "B. Pullman, what will you think of your vacuum called daughter when she returns to you from all the expensive education mills?" "Dear Household-Word, I am one of those pale carbon-copy offsprings of the great. I haven't an ambition in the world to do anything except be gorgeously and outrageously happy (Winch dubs it rank hedonism, but between you and me she is somewhat of a dub herself!) preferably in the castle in Fishrow we are to build together but which I am too lazy to even plan—preferring to leave it all to that famous brain of yours. Except I do want windows I can lower without getting out of bed. Years of life in Switzerland have taught me the man who invents that device is the true world humanitarian." Another: "Bea, try not to be too disappointed in an offspring who would rather see, than be, a person with an urge. Tell my darling old Delilah (poor lamb, what a terrible kind of courage she has), anyway, tell Delilah, I's her dumb chile still, hanging to her skirts while bye o'baby bunting, mamma's gone a-hunting, to get a lot of ermine skin to wrap her baby bunting in! The summer ermine I bought in Paris, just does wonders for my dirty-dish complexion. But seriously, does fate think it funny, I ask you, to continue to indulge her peculiar sense of humor by serving up to genius one minus-quality offspring after another? There's Arabelle Dijon, here at school. Daughter of the poet. Well, Arabelle just doesn't retain. There's me. Daughter of the B. Pullman. Jessie is a nice enough girl. Sort of regular, but who would ever think she had B. Pullman for a mother? But, dearest, I'm the only girl at Winch's (the wench) with a real pearl necklace. Home in May, Bea. Oh, pain-in-the-pit-of-me, what does one say when walking down the gangplank to meet the distinguished B. Pullman who happens also to be one's mother whom one hasn't seen seen in nineteen months! Darling, it's most unmodern of me, but way down in the pit of my tummy I'm most frightfully in awe of me parent.''

This Jessie coming home into the maelstrom of the new emotions with which she must greet her! Little wonder that waking these mornings was like a dive from a springboard, into water that rushed to charge over her in great confused breakers.

The days began with the sly new manner of Delilah, wise with knowing she knew not quite what; with the eyes of her father that seemed to follow her without shifting their stiff white setting; with the barrage of eyes that followed her as she strode through four rooms of outer offices, aware of an awareness concerning her that subtly seemed to have stirred within the alert little army of clerks and stenographers.

The eleven-o'clock conferences with Flake, preparatory to sending him now on his two months' deferred territorial survey! There was an actual kind of eagerness now to have him gone, the impending trip over with, before what was trembling between them came to its consummation.

True, what happened the morning before his departure, in her private office, with slate-colored uncompromising light swimming against the window panes and threatening her with that sense of tired flesh which more and more she was beginning to combat, practically constituted a darling and definite seal upon her happiness.

A first direct communication from Universal Sales Association, signed by the president, requesting an early conference over the lunch table of the Sky Club, on the roof of the Universal Sales Association Building, lay on the desk between them, adding its burden of suspense, excitement, and thrill to this day of Flake's departure.

Flake was leaving. Universal Sales Association was making its first gesture. Jessie was on the Atlantic. A second cable within the week from Imperial Chain was baiting about in terms which would make her ultimate gesture of refusal dramatic, not to say sensational. Rome to Helsingfors to Singapore! B. Pullman shares, due to rumors connected with Usa, were rocketing. The city, responding to cunning wires that were under her thumb, had granted the Fishrow riparian rights, the boat-landing to be located directly at the foot of her garden. And on this morning, fairly crashing with the thunder of its burdens, Flake, in the instant before leaving, timing it so that the secretary to whom they had been dictating had scarcely more than closed the door, kissed her his good-bye, this time against the lips.

"When you come back, Frank, everything will be set."

What she meant was, by the time you come back the Usa offer will almost surely be in my hands. Meanwhile, my child must be made slowly and beautifully to know of you so that her share in our happiness will at once become apparent to her. The dream of our home will be ready for its first spade into the ground. Here is your surprise which I shall save for you, darling. The top floor, instead of a solarium, is to be your medical library. Only you do not yet know that. You do not know half the dear things that I know for you.

She lifted back her lips that had been kissed, placing in turn her fingers against his mouth.

"Frank—"

They flew apart then to the click of an opening door. The secretary who had just left was announcing H. Prynne, Jr., Vermont member of her board of directors.

Greeting him as he entered, Flake passed out on the first lap of his long overdue six weeks' territorial survey of points south and west.

· 42 ·

The first intimation came out of the long tunnel of a restless night in which Bea had lain half wakeful.

It was not easy to sleep, when the break of any day might usher in the victory or defeat of the weeks of negotiation with Universal Sales Association.

These were difficult and harrowing nights, filled, as they were, with the immense desire to be free of this incubus of a business; filled as they were with new dreads, the strange, almost terrifying dread that was slowly moving like a tide over every expectation connected with the return of Jessie.

Was this girl, in whom the hopes of eighteen years were centered, about to find herself returning to the simpering spectacle of a mother angling a man eight years her junior into marriage!

Was that the spectacle of herself as others would see her!

Was that the spectacle with which she might unwittingly be preparing to confront her returning child?

Was it her sensible middle-aged rôle to turn aside from these belated stirrings? Dared she risk revolting the high-strung youth of Jessie with desires which all these years must have lain squirming in the damp cellar spaces of the vast structure she had erected?

She had built a colossus, when all she had ever wanted was a home-life behind swiss curtains of her own hemming, with a man who had awakened her as Flake had. . . .

Dared she, whose flesh felt old, risk revolting youth, any more than she dared risk facing a future of superlatively more and superlatively bigger business.

Or worse: Suppose—just suppose, she were to decide on the European chain, which at its ultimate peak could only mean repetition of her initial victory. Rome, Paris. Helsingfors. Shanghai. Hotels. Father, to be lugged like so much baggage. Conferences with strange men in strange languages. Hotel rooms. Hotel fare. Hotel life. . . .

Into such a night, filled with its fevers and its fears, its intermittent despairs and brilliantly high optimism, there came Delilah's cry, as croaking and as hoarse as a crow's, grating a silence habitually torn with the breathing of the old gentleman as he slept upright.

What was that! It seemed to Bea, sitting up in the dark, with her father's night-light lying palely across her face, that such a cry had frequently come through to her before, possibly through sleep. And yet again, it seemed to her that here was a cry too strange and in a measure too terrible to ever before have found articulation. A croak from a floor; from a ground place. A sob from a mole in a hole. Waiting, there it came again, barking through!

In one leap from bed, her nightdress streaming back against her legs like the marble drape to a marble body, she and her father's nurse met in the hallway over the vast semi-prostrate figure of Delilah, who had evidently been making her way on all fours, toward the room occupied by John.

"Delilah!"

"Go back to your bed, chile. Cotch your deatha . . . John—misery's got me more dan I kin stand. . . . John—give me something——"

As the lights went on, Delilah there in her huddle on the floor, a heterogeneous twist of pain, her back in an arch, her torso writhing, was the color of her own gray eyeballs, her enormous neck, with a cleft in it from a mastoid operation, running with sweat that rolled onto a clean red-and-white-striped bungalow apron that evidently served as nightgown and gave her something of the appearance of a bathhouse on a beach.

Manipulating her vast hulk to the living-room couch reminded Bea rather grimly of motion pictures of whales being hauled ashore after a catch. There was no way except for the two of them, John and herself, to drag away for dear life, until, panting and exhausted, Delilah lay ballooning and moaning upon her divan.

"Git away, honey-chile. 'Lilah cain't suffer her own way wid you aroun'. . . ."

"John, call a doctor! Not the one on the ground floor. There's one across the street. Quick!"

"No, no, ain't no doctor gonna gitten his hands on mah misery. I's lived alone wid it for three years, day and night. An' de wusser it gits, de closer it gits me to my Lawdagawd——"

"Delilah, you mean you've had attacks like this before? Can't you tell me what it is—where it hurts. . . . Drink this down, Delilah. It's brandy——"

"Lordagawd, honey, if tonight it hadn't pinched me jes' a little wusser dan I could stan' it, I wouldn't have made a nuisance of mahself bawlin' out. O Lordagawd, ease it while mah Missy's standin' by—O Lordagawd! . . ."

"Oh, my poor Delilah—can't you tell me where—what——"

"Doan' wipe dat sweat off mah face, honey. It helps me hurt. Git yourself back dar to bed. Maybe it won't cotch me ag'in tonight. Jes' lemme lay here quiet and not take no chance on dat ole debbil bitin' me ag'in. Sometimes I kin skeer him wid dis heah ole rabbit's foot. . . ."

"Oh, Delilah, tell me about all this. . . ."

"Nothin' to tell, Miss Bea. Ole debbil, I call him, 'cause he jumps aroun' inside me lak a debbil wid a fork and tail. Cain't tell when he's gonna strike—mostly nights. . . . I jes' musta let mah cryin' slip out tonight——"

"I've heard you! I know now, time after time, and I've always thought I was dreaming. Oh, Delilah, and you've suffered all this in silence——"

"No, I ain't, honey. Lordagawd has had to lissen to me night after night——"

"Where does it hurt?"

"Feel."

"O my God!"

It was hard, upon touching, with a gingerness for which she despised herself, the great swollen protuberance under the striped-awning nightgown of Delilah, not to curl up and surrender to an impulse to faint.

This growingly mammoth Delilah of the last several years was not huge with additional flesh, but was a woman carrying the protuberance of something growing.

"Delilah, why haven't you told me this!"

"Lordagawd's way is mah way!"

"And you let your child go—knowing that! O, my God!"

"Lordagawd's way is mah way. He's a-havin' mercy on mah baby wherever she is, dat's all I'm askin'...."

"Why, oh, why doesn't John come with a doctor?"

"Ain't nebber seen one worth his salt. I's got herbs in mah room in a tin box under mah mattress. Knockout drops for ole man debbil inside me. Uh-uh, honey-chile. O Lordagawd, have mercy! Ole man debbil ain't nebber befoh chased me lak dis!..."

There they came again, the croakings! The terrible guttural croakings that seemed to come from ground and marshy places, and as if the divan could no longer contain her pain, the bulk that was Delilah began to ease itself once more to the floor, where it could writhe against its hardness.

"Delilah, a little more courage. John is coming with some one to help you."

In the din of her battle she was past hearing now, her suppliant eyes rolling in their straining whites and the living-room floor the dreadful spectacle of the mutiny of agonies long pent up.

"O Lordagawd have mercy! De River Jordan is on fire and a-runnin' down mah soul! O Lordagawd, have mercy!..."

"Shh-h-h Delilah! Doctor is coming to help you."

"I's a-comin', Lordagawd, in a white hearse wid plumes an' de tootin' of horns proclaimin' I's a luvver of de Lawd for havin' mercy on mah chile. Ain't I a-comin' to de Lawd thataway, Missy Honey-Bea?..."

"Yes, yes, Delilah, but not now!"

"I want you and mah chair-chile a-ridin' open and before de worl' in de fust carriage. Hear me dat, Miss Honey-Bea? You kin hoist him to de carriage in his chair.... Diden' I tell you mah chair-chile would live to follow his 'Lilah to her grave? Hear me dat, Miss Honey-Bea—you an' him?..."

"Yes, yes, Delilah, I understand..."

"... a-ridin' behind me in mah snow-white hearse an' de band a-playin'——"

"Delilah, save your strength."

"Lissen.... Come here—I knows something. I dunno. Guess I

dreamed it—or does I know it?''

"Delilah, you're in too much pain to be quite clear. Wait.''

"Lissen. Sometimes I thinks it. Sometimes I dreams it. A.M., 'member? She called him A.M. Don't you know? Ain't you knowin'?''

"Knowing what, Delilah?''

"Come heah. Come heah close. Dat's mah blue-eyed boy out dar in Seattle what we nussed through de 'fluenza. 'Member? Wid de mammy who was layin' on her last bed when she writ me and sent me de knittin'. 'Member? A.M. Dat's our Allen sojer boy we nussed through the 'fluenza! Dat's *Allen—Matterhorn!*''

"Delilah, you're imagining——''

"Didn't I tell you dar wasn't no good ahead for him? He's her man down dar in dat white man's jungle. Doan' tell me no different. A.M. Dat's our Allen boy. Lordagawd! to think dat mah chile, a-passin', should pass to Allen boy. . . .''

"Delilah, that's nonsense! . . .''

"No, 'tain't. It's writ in all mah tea leaves dataway and I's close 'nough now to de Lawd's book where it's writ, to read it. Lordagawd, have mercy on mah chile and Allen boy——''

At six o'clock in the morning, on a pallet two doctors and John managed to contrive for her on the floor, Delilah, lifting herself out of a hypodermic-induced sleep, begin suddenly to pour hot broad kisses against the bare ankles of Bea, who stood by.

In that act she died.

·43·

So far as the spark which set off the forest fire could be traced, the news-
paper-reporter brother of one of the sixty-five stenographers in the outer
offices, scenting a story in the demise of the famous trade-marked face,
started rolling the ball of furor occasioned by the passing of Delilah.

Broadcast over the face of the press there flashed the laughing black
face in its tiara of fluted organdie and every conceivable pose of copy-
righted Delilah, in the savory act of flopping the waffles that had made
her a national institution:

WAFFLE QUEEN WHOSE FACE IS KNOWN TO MILLIONS DIES IN
HOME OF B. PULLMAN.

PASSING OF FAITHFUL NEGRESS UNDER WHOSE LAUGHING IMPRINT
THE B. PULLMAN ENTERPRISES DEVELOPED FROM A WAFFLE TO AN
INSTITUTION.

RUMORED TO HAVE LEFT LARGE BEQUESTS TO BAPTIST CHURCHES
OF HARLEM, BROOKLYN, RICHMOND, VIRGINIA, AND NATCHEZ,
MISSISSIPPI.

ELABORATE FUNERAL PLANS AFOOT.

FAMOUS BLACK WOMAN LIES IN STATE IN HARLEM CHAPEL WHILE
THOUSANDS PASS IN REVIEW.

This last was literally true.

For two days, in unbroken procession, young and old, black and white, wound around the bronze, silver-handled bier that contained the enormous and smoky clay that was Delilah.

Mounted in state against a stained-glass version of Peter receiving, which occupied one wall of the chapel, streamers of indigo, garnet, mint, jasper, grape-purple, poured down like reins, onto the chariot of Delilah's coffin.

Potted palms led in an aisle to her. Lilies banked her. Blankets, from which mounted the scented miasma of great numbers of roses exuding in heat, tucked her in up to the chin, and there, through the glass window of her coffin, darkly, quite grandly, in the fluted cap in which, reiteratedly throughout the years of her anticipation of this occasion, she had requested to be buried, shone the polished teakwood mask of Delilah. Patine high on the cheek bones, the curious quality of her dignity out on the pale pink shelves of lips along which had moved so constantly the name of her Host.

Harlem, of which she had never been part, except by gestures of patronage and munificence, poured forth for the spectacle of this dead face of one of the humblest members of its race which had become an affectionate daguerreotype against the consciousness of a nation. School children, black, filed, and left each a carnation in a mound at her feet. The Order of the Sisters of the Rising Star spread a banner the size of a wall, and two hundred marching members of the Amalgamated Lodges of the Sons and Daughters of David, turned out in caps with visors and spears tipped with tin foil.

Fourteen hundred employees of B. Pullman, Inc, sent illuminated resolutions on parchment and a floral piece of lilies and white stuffed doves.

Every hymn, including "When I Die," "Asleep in Jesus! Blessed Sleep," and "Rock of Ages," that she had sung through the days that dated back to the early ones in Atlantic City, rolled over the scene of Delilah lying in state at this her last earthly station on her way to the Host.

All of her guttural ecstasies were folded into the salve of stanza after stanza, her polished face, resting on fluted satin under glass, floating, like a dark lily pad, upon the rivers of pouring voices.

> *"Swing low, sweet char-i-ot,*
> *Comin' for to carry me home.*

Swing low, sweet char-i-ot,
Comin' for to carry me home."

"I look'd over Jordan, an' what did I see,
Comin' for to carry me home,
A band of angels comin' after me,
Comin' for to carry me home."

Hallelujah! Death had come for Delilah in a chariot of bronze and lilies, reins of fire pouring down from St. Peter on his stained-glass throne to hitch her chariot for the flight. Hallelujah!

Not one lodge, but four, into which, atoningly, in the name of pride of race, she had poured funds, lined up before the splendor that was Delilah, trumpets poised, horns with fringed banners tilted, major domos in two-foot hats, ready.

The pastor of her foreordained choice, flanked by deacons, extolled to ringing rafters the godliness, the goodliness, the churchliness, the holiness, and the righteousness of Sister Delilah Cilla Johnston.

"Oh, yondah come the chariot,
The horses dressed in white,
The four wheels a-runnin' by the grace of God
An' the hin' wheels a-runnin' by love."

sang fifty from a choir loft, the whites of eyes moving in shadows like the searchlights of a posse in fog.

"She should have had it in her lifetime," sobbed Bea into her handkerchief.

In their roped-off pew, the hand of Flake, who had returned by plane from Kansas City, reached out over hers.

"Don't cry, Bea. Remember this is her jubilee."

"You're right, Frank. It is. Tell that to Father. He'll understand."

From his chair, which had been wheeled into the aisle, Mr. Chipley, his rigid china eyes frozen into their centers, seemed, nonetheless, to forge ahead with them.

"Mah ole gemmeman is gonna outlive me, see if he don't, and ride behin' mah procession to de Lawd one of dese days, big as life. Dem ole eyes don't miss a trick. Ain't gonna miss no trick when 'Lilah rides to heaven.''

Locked within the hulk of himself, was it possible he was seeing and hearing and feeling and, down in the secret areas of his sensation, crying. Doctors disagreed on what degree of sensitivity was left him. Only Delilah had been sure. . . .

> "Oh, yondah comes Sister Mary,
> An' how do you know it's her?
> A-shoutin' Hallelujah,
> An' praises to de Lamb,
> Yes, bless de Lawd, praises to de Lamb.''

Slowly, on the twenty white-cotton palms of bearers, there rose from its lilies, the bier of Delilah for its lofty ride down the aisle.

Fifty school children, trying to keep eager, curious eyes cast downward, lifted shrill voices in the words she had loved, "They crucified my Lord, an' He never said a mum-ba-lin' word" and scattered rose leaves down the aisle. Organ music rolled, and closed her over like a sea. At attention, caparisoned in lodge aprons, buttons, caps, fringes, arm bands, insignia, sunlight trembling, brass of instruments trembling, the members of five orders flanked the steps that had been cleared of crowds that leaned, tightly packed, on the side-walks against the cordons established by police.

Four motorcycle policemen in goggles, whined down the cleared asphalt of the avenue. Delilah's escort! A white horse-drawn hearse, plumed, with purple drapes, gold-fringed, backed a pair of elaborate doors against the curb.

May sky, pale, clear, aloof, and a little colder than spring, spread high and speckless over the scene of the pressing of crowd, the prancing horses of mounted police, the cleared strip of street down which dashed the motorcycles, the long borders of narrow brown buildings, their windows packed with brown leaning faces, before which presently would pass the glory of Delilah.

Enormous, on high, tilted, rode Delilah on the springs of white-cotton hands, the faces of the men who bore the extra-size, extra-weight casket, springing into ready sweat.

> *"An' He never said a mum-ba-lin word,*
> *Not a word, not a word, not a word,"*

sang the children, trying to keep lowered their white eyeballs as they strewed.

"Sistah Delilah, Sistah Delilah, Sistah Delilah's on de pearly road!" chanted and swayed a woman spectator standing wedged into the sardine-pack of the sidewalk, and suddenly, so chanting and swaying, to the rolling ocean of shoulders getting the ecstasy, the surf of thousands of voices began to roll and boom beneath the borne aloft bier of Delilah.

"Sistah Delilah, Sistah Delilah, Sistah Delilah's on de pearly road. . . . O Lord!—O Lord!—Sistah Delilah's on de pearly road. Delilah. Delilah. Delilah's on de pearly road——"

Hoisted, chair and all, into the fore of the open automobile, chained to his silence and his immobility, a strange prow to this procession, probably seeing all, knowing all, rode the old gentleman, first, along with Bea and Flake, to lead the procession of Delilah.

"They mustn't make you ride this way in an open car!" Flake had expostulated.

"No. It's the way she wanted it. Don't let anyone else in except John, beside Father. That empty seat is for—someone. Delilah wanted that—place empty. Peola's."

Led by the two brass bands, by the bearers of the banners of the societies honoring the deceased, twenty-five carriages, filled with only about one-fiftieth of the preachers and deacons, brethren and onlookers, who had fought for place, the horse-drawn cavalcade moved into slow procession along the highway of upper Seventh Avenue which had been screamingly cleared by the motorcycles.

"Great Scott! this is awful! Look on the roofs. They are taking movies. Look at that crowd down there!"

"She would have wanted it."

"I know, dear, but it's terrible for you. Let me have them put the top on the car."

"No, Frank; she would have wanted it this way."

"Didn't know there were so many in the world. There can't be any darkies left anywhere."

(Except one. In her white man's jungle.)

"Poor Bea," he said, and felt for her gloved hand. "It will be a queer world without Delilah."

She pressed her tonsils to keep down tears, and under the motor robe could feel the knee and the flank of him, warm as life.

"If only," she said, trying to talk through her tight throat—"if only she could have waited a few more days. Jessie—terrible for her not to have her Delilah to come home to. . . ."

"She'll have you, darling. Poor dear darling. . . ."

Da, da, dada, da, dadadadadada. Boom, boom, boomboomboom— Marche Funèbre. There were tears so far down she never could finish getting them cried. . . . Delilah. . . . The knee and flank of him, warm as life, so near and dear to her—Frank. . . .

· 44 ·

Not even the barrage of snapshots during the past three summers, nor the flying visits home previous to that last sustained period, prepared the way for the slim marvel of this adult Jessie.

"It's your legs, darling! They're so long when you stand and so adorably short when you sit. You're 'mah baby-chile' as you sit there, but when you rise to your feet I need an introduction."

"That's kind of the way I feel about you, Bea. You're just as you as you can be, except in the ways that you are—different. You've grown so young! All the things I've been nagging you to do for years you've done and it frightens me! What a lamb to do it for me!"

(I'm a fraud, Jessie, and presently you've got to know it!)

"I miss your whaleboning, darling, and your starched panties, and much as I admire the new way in which you make connections with your hats, it doesn't somehow seem you without one perched on your head as if it bore no particular relationship to B. Pullman. I love you chic, but I can't get used to you."

The mutual adventure of rather timid exploration took place that first week between two, to whom the bend of each new hour of the day revealed surprises.

"Bea, look at this letterhead I found! I'd no idea you were on the board of trustees of the Alton Trust Company!"

"Jessie, I do believe you speak with a little accent! Mamma'll spank!"

"Mother, you never wrote me a word about this presentation silver service! 'To B. Pullman, Upon The Completion Of Her Fifth Year As Our Beloved President, With The Grateful Appreciation Of Business Women Of The Eastern Seaboard.' How divinely horrible."

"Why, child, what are these? Water-colors signed by you, and I never even knew you could hold a brush!"

"Darling, not really. Please don't look at them. Just some views of my darling Bellagio. They're putrid, really."

"Why, Jessie, I love them! I'm going to hang this sailboat one in the front room."

"Over my dead body. You see, sometimes when I feel driven to live up to being my mother's daughter, I try to cultivate an urge. But I haven't one really, Bea, except to be just outrageously happy. I think that's how I managed to stay across so long, Ma, keeping the family skeleton out of sight. No ambish' is what ails me."

"No what?"

"No cosmic urge, beyond a low-down yen for a castle in Spain or Bellagio or in Fishrow, where I can dig in for all the swell permanent things that are said not to interest my hell-bent generation. Just a plain home girl, Ma, willing to unbuckle her hip-flask and her dancing-sandals for any simple home-loving lad who can support her in even greater style than that to which she is accustomed."

"Jessie, talk to me really—about the things you think—and are."

"Of course I will. I'm finished being awed by you. You're grand and make me feel like a jello dessert, but, darling, if you don't mind my telling you, there's something almost human about you these days."

"Is that nice?"

"Fresh, aren't I? But what I mean is, you're as grand as ever—a bit grander—but—dearest, if I could trust myself to say it without going off into hysterics, I'd say you're in love, or you've made peace with your Maker, or you've finished with cosmic urge, with which, oh, parent, you have utterly failed to endow me."

"Jessie, now that you're making it easy for me, there is something I do so desperately want to say to you."

"I know. You're dead right. Don't feel delicate about rubbing it in. I've been rubbing it into myself for the last two years abroad. Winch-the-wench, and Askenasi feel about it as you do. I'm a lazy, aimless fluke——"

"No, no——"

"Yes, yes. Up-and-coming American girls simply don't jell, like me, into weak sisters. I suspect that Winch-the-wench must have written you reams about her efforts to 'stimulate me to self-realizations,' as she puts it, before dumping me back on your hands. No matter who you are nowadays, you're supposed to have an urge. Muriel Stroheim, in my class, with twelve million in her own name, is learning to make beds and change dressings in the American hospital in Paris. Vicky Ness, whose father owns half of Buffalo, is coming back to beg a job on one of his newspapers. If I had any gumption I'd be your right-hand man by now. Or at least, out on my own, making good. If only I could begin to want to be something besides a pleasant sort of an oaf, whose chief ambition is to lie in the sun like a lizard and be happy. . . .''

''You don't understand, darling! I don't want you for my right-hand man or anybody's right-hand man, except right-hand man to your own personal happiness. That's what I'm coming to, Jessie, this matter of personal happiness. You see, dear, I've reached the point in my life——''

''Speaking of right-hand men, where is the immaculate snowflake? The boy beautiful who has developed into the boy wonder—the whole works! That's the kind of thing I should have done. Daughter of B. Pullman dons overalls and starts in to learn business from the ground up. . . . Daughter of famous woman magnate is shown no preference. . . .''

''Flake will be back from his last territorial for the year any day now. That's why I want so terribly to talk to you, Jessie, before——''

''Mother, you're asking a zero to sprout a stem and behave like a nine. Perhaps I can, dear. I need to, if I'm to be saved from the crushing inferiority complex of being your daughter. I'll face Flake. I'll face knowing more about everything pertaining to you and yours. Only, let me get my bearings first. Let me get used to being at home, to being my mother's daughter.''

''Jessie, I want to tell you what kind of a mother the daughter has——''

''I wonder if you've any idea how much time I've given to studying this daughter's mother. I never thought I'd ever find myself telling you about it, but you're so darling and human this time. Not but what you've always been, but not in this new softy way that is knocking all my silly old inferiorities skywise. I know more about you this minute than you probably know about yourself. . . .''

"Perhaps. But there's one thing— Oh, Jessie, why am I so desperately anxious for the Universal Sales Association opportunity to sell my business? Why am I passing by this astonishing opportunity to travel and see the cities of the world and establish a European chain! Why am I giving up everything in order to build our kennel in Fishrow?"

"Because you're tired—fed up——"

"Oh, darling, so tired!"

"If I thought it was all on account of me, I'd fight it to the death. But I know. You want what you call your kennel more passionately than you've ever wanted anything in your life. You're having the sense to set about building and creeping into it while you're still young enough to enjoy it."

"And, Jessie——"

"Berlin, London, Shanghai! More big business and more big enterprise are just anti-climax for you from now on. I'm enough of a bug-in-a-rug to understand. You want the things you haven't had and out of which your success has cheated you."

"Berlin, London, Shanghai. I can't bear the thought any more, Jessie. I'm too tired. I haven't the energy left, the fight, the vitality. Jessie, a part of my body, a part of my spirit, a part of my mind that seems to have never come to life, is actually awake now. I'm greedy, Jessie, for what I've missed. I'm demanding it of myself. I'm demanding it from you."

"Hear! Hear!"

"I'm begging it from you. Your rights still come first, but granting me mine will rob you of none of yours—on the contrary, will only enrich you. We'll build our kennel just the same, dear. The most beautiful kennel in the world. You and me and—and——"

"You darling wonderful human, Bea! I don't know what it's all about, but I'm for it. Who in Heaven's name am I, to do anything but throw my cap into the air, if you want to climb out from under? Why shouldn't you? You're at your best!"

"Oh Jessie——"

"You've earned the right to everything good."

"You think that?"

"Do I! And I'm here to see that you get it!"

"Then, darling—the thing that I want mustn't surprise or revolt you——"

"We'll dig into Fishrow together, Ma. No London, Paris, and, of all places—what is the last one they sprung on you?—Helsingfors, and points continental for us! No Laps lapping our waffles, or whatever it is Laps do up there near Helsingfors. No trunks for hearthstones, but the home fires burning!"

"If only I could explain to you, darling, what it means ——"

"Excuse my headline kind of mind. Woman magnate to retire. B. Pullman interests absorbed by Universal Sales Association."

"Shh-h-h! It hasn't happened yet!"

"Retirement of B. Pullman stirs Wall Street. Declines offer to establish European system of B. Pullmans. Why, who knows, darling, you may even decide to settle down to the anti-climax of romance. Only I couldn't bear that! cries the selfish bear. I've found you. I've got you. I mean to keep you."

It was no use. It was simply no use. The way to plunge into the telling of this thing would have to be by way of leaping fearlessly into the middle. Jessie, I am in love with Flake. I want to marry him. I promise to subtract nothing from your life but to add immeasurably to mine and yours as well.

That way she must plunge.

With all this unspoken, she tucked Jessie, who had been sitting at the foot of her bed in yellow lace pajamas and her matching hair spread in a fan across her shoulders, in under covers.

Walking to her own room through the strange silence of a household that did not contain Delilah, there awaited, across one end of her dressing-table, a box of thirty-six red and white roses and a telegram from Cleveland, announcing tomorrow's return of Flake.

· 45 ·

It was, Bea told herself again and again during the sleepless watches of a night through which her child and her father were sleeping uninterrupted, it was better so.

Especially now, with the telegram putting forward the return of Flake by at least two weeks. There would be so much less to explain, once Jessie had observed with her own eyes the phenomenon of her love for Flake transcend all possible disparities.

Let them meet first. They were little more than dim images to one another. Let them meet now. Then gradually—gradually—oh, it was better so. . . .

And that was precisely how it seemed to happen. If at first the full-fledged maturity of Jessie had the effect of creating a certain reserve in one whose chief memories of her were the result of the transient visits, usually in the hen-like wake of Delilah, of a chick of a child to the office, the same was true of Jessie. Flake, squarer and older in rimmed glasses by now, and with the curious, almost imperceptible heaviness of a man who has matured into power, was someone to become acquainted with all over again.

Thank God, thought Bea to her fevered self, that first stiffish evening the three of them dined at the Gotham, that I didn't tell her anything in advance and harness her up in self-consciousness. Gradually it will come to seem to her just one of those natural things. . . .

How inexpressibly near and dear, having them both within easy radius of her greed for them. It was as if her heart, pouring simultaneously in two directions, must drench them in the flood of her poorly concealed emotions.

"Would you have known her, Frank, if you had met her on the street?"

"Only if the eyes had come along by themselves."

"There's an idea! Two eyes on stilts stalking down the gangplank!"

"If I had met her at the docks, I would have searched for the same leggy youngster Delilah used to cart into the office."

"I'd have known you, glasses and all, except that I might have taken you for your older brother."

"You got so darned pretty."

"You got so darned handsome."

"You should hear, Frank, some of her ideas for the house! Tell your plan for grandfather's solarium, Jessie. They build them with sliding roofs on the Riviera——"

"Yes, I've some hot ideas for the house, Frank."

"A castle in Spain?"

"Not a bit of it. A castle in Fishrow that will make you and Bea want to build a bonfire of all the blue-prints you have on hand."

"Let's drive over to the lot after dinner, Frank. There's a moon and Jessie's new ideas make it exciting!"

"Yes, let's. The days of castle-building in Spain are over for the Pullman family. I hereby nominate we three as the Break Dirt Committee for Number Nine Fishrow!"

We three. How blessedly deterred she had been from making last-night revelations. How much more rightly it could happen this way. We three! The possessive in her rose chokingly. These two were hers. Her eyes, with the impulse for tears across them, felt thick and warm as she fastened them on the yellow radiance that was Jessie. Underneath the table, for the first time, she let her hand grope out and rest lightly for an instant on Flake's knee, then dart back, frightened as a bird.

These two were hers!

Later, as they drove in a warm plush of darkness to Fishrow, her gloved hand, holding on to Jessie's in a little pressure, the flank of her body conscious of the long lean flank of Flake, she gave back, ever so slightly, what seemed to her to be his message of pressure.

Why not? Jessie would be the first to understand! A married spinster had begot Jessie, of a stranger called B. Pullman. Locked into her, frozen in her up to now, had been the stream of life.

Rigid, as unthawed as in her undelightful girlhood, she had moved through the subsequent years, until now, blessedly, before it was too late, hidden rivers in her had been released. Stream of life was flowing in her, pounding, dancing, desiring to carry on its released bosom ecstasies of which she had never even dreamed. Ecstasies but faintly indicated by the feel of this flank of youth against her. My lover. My child. Centers of my universe. I will give, gladly, even more than I receive.

The lights of Fishrow, except for the Pullman empty lot, shone in lamps at windows, in fanlights above doorways, and curving like the spine of a straddling monster, the steel arch of the bridge, crawling with traffic, flickered with constant movement and rose immensely against the sky.

"Block Beautiful" born of her travail, her sleepless nights, her machinations, negotiations, loans, notes, mortgages, collaterals, perils and colossal unease, was now about to yield her a castle in which to live out her undreamed riches.

How often had she and Delilah, seated in this same soft gloom, erected that castle. And presently, now these three of them, hand in hand over the spongy dampness of her vacant lot, were dreaming this castle between the tall stiff walls of adjoining buildings.

"It's too beautiful! Fancy living right in the heart of New York with the river lapping your garden wall. If only we had more width! I've the grandest idea! Bea, is the Grinnelle place next door for sale, now that he has died?"

"Yes."

"Why don't we buy it in and tear it down."

"Why child, that house is only three years old!"

"It's a comic!"

"Possibly, but they are asking two hundred thousand——"

"Well, what of it?"

"But it just isn't done, Jessie. Fancy tearing down a handsome place like the Grinnelle house even though you think it a comic, just because we want a few feet of additional width."

"But why isn't it done, Bea? We're rich, aren't we? Frightfully, now that you are about to sell outright. Didn't you spend all morning drawing up a rough outline of a letter you intend to send turning down a million-dollar offer to start the European chain? What's two hundred thousand to us, darling? Isn't it for your home? Who has earned the right of everything she wants, if you haven't?"

"I never thought of that."

"Of course you haven't. I've come home to do it for you. With those extra feet of width, look at the frontage we'd have. River rooms for every one of us, even for Frank when he wants to week-end with us. My idea of an ugly-mug is a narrow Colonial house with room for only two or three pillars down its front. Just look at that Bailey place. It's spindle-legged compared with the lovely flowing lines of the Casamajor house. See what we could do with proper footage, darling. . . ."

"By Jove! the girl's bright. Buying in the Grinnelle place won't be a luxury; it's a necessity. I never realized before how wrong pillars might be before a house as narrow as Number Nine."

"Look, Frank, how we could manage! By dropping the dining-room a few feet lower than the living-room, and doing away with walls between, you get the sweep of one huge room and yet the effect of two. . . ."

"And say, why not carry out the same idea upstairs between your bed- and sitting-room? . . ."

"Exactly. And I know the darlingest way to do convex windows! A girl I visit in Nice lives in a Normandy villa where every window is slightly convex, so that it does nothing much in bulges to the exterior of the house, but creates all sorts of adorable little bays within. The same could be done in a Colonial . . ."

"Say, that's great! Give me a room with window-seats, every time."

"Shows your lazy temperament."

"You don't mean that."

"Every word of it. But seriously, Frank, come here and I'll show you what I mean. Stand with your foot on that clump of dirt. Look up. Imagine that room up there. Say it's your week-end one over the library. Both your windows, in case you want to sit around of an evening, or fool with your medical books, or whatever it is you're gaga about, will jut out just enough to form a little bay. . . ."

"In case I want to sit of an evening with medical books or—with you——"

"Of course, if you won't be serious——"

"Getting back to b-e-a-u-x windows——"

"Disgusting and puerile form of alleged wit. With twice the frontage that you and this darling tight-wad old Bea have been content to figure on, see what we can do. Let's hurry back home and figure it out!"

"Don't look at me like that. I am capable of only one idea at a time."

Who would have thought Flake could unbend like that to such nonsense? Go on! Go on! Go on!

Once or twice on the drive home she gave back shyly, speeding through the Park, what seemed to be the nudge of his body against hers, while the two of them, her two, having struck between them the key of a delightful persiflage, spun laughter into the darkness.

· 46 ·

Following that first noncommittal but significant lunch at the Sky Top Club, where the major issues in the minds of all concerned were skirted but never skated upon, flurries of rumors began to fly and thicken.

Negotiations for the out-and-out sale of the B. Pullman interests, while carefully guarded from the press, became "Street" rather than general conjecture.

There was anxiety on the part of Universal Sales Association not to have leak out beyond the inevitable confines of Wall Street and interests vitally concerned, the passing into new hands of a concern so intimately associated in the minds of the public with the name and personality of its founder.

Both on the part of Universal Sales and B. Pullman, Inc., statements, interviews, or comment was denied, and for ten days, while two sets of corporation lawyers sat in preliminary conferences, B. Pullman, target for skulking reporters, remained virtually a prisoner within the walls of her apartment.

They were ten days laid over with a simulated enchantment of what amounted to a game she played with herself.

Suppose, just suppose the deal were through and that she was awakening, this string of quiet secluded mornings, to days that were absolutely freed of her labor and consecration. Days devoid of reports and conferences, telegrams, cablegrams, adjustments, maladjustments, long-distance and local problems, chronic and emergency complications, quick decisions, locked committee meetings, personnel and staff considerations, moneys, notes, stocks, loans, mortgages, leases, releases, insurances, breakage, overhead, claims, shipments, accidents, prices, wear and tear, innovations, renovations, Cleveland, Toronto, Hollywood, Denver, Chicago!

This brief and enforced seclusion in order to escape the press, the immunity from the usual office telephone calls of widely assorted inquirers, promoters, cranks, interrogators, made possible for her a little oasis of days the like of which she had actually not enjoyed since the days when, as a small-waisted, large-pompadoured bride she had sat in the box of a house on Arctic Avenue hemming window curtains that were to be laundered and hung before the heavy-footed arrival home of a heavy-handed husband.

"I suppose," she confided to Jessie, as she trailed about in pastel finery her daughter had brought her from Paris, "that I ought to feel like a caged lion, stamping to get back into the marts of men. I don't! So far as I'm concerned, except that they lead to the end, these preliminaries could go on forever. There's a word my mother used. I've never heard it since. 'Huck.' I want to 'huck' right here at home. I want to 'lay' as long as Delilah, bless her! used to beg me to. I want to dig in, cozily."

"Oh, Bea, if your public and your business women's organizations and your inquiring press could only hear you now!"

"I'm a curtain-hemmer at heart. A toter of some man's carpet slippers for him when he comes home of an evening." There! (Oh, darling, aren't you ever going to help me to get it said? I can't hold him off much longer. But I need so terribly to have your sanction first, baby.)

"Bea, were you ever in love with my father?"

"Why, Jessie!"

"Oh, don't pretend. You're modern enough to stand up under a question like that."

"I don't know what you mean?"

"You do. Only the Arctic Avenue in you won't let you be simple and frank about it. I'll answer for you. No, you weren't."

(Now, now! Now, was the time! Jessie, you're right. My marriage to your father was the marriage of a sleeping spirit and a sleeping flesh which he never succeeded in awakening. That had to wait eighteen years. For Flake. That's why I'm greedy. I'm forty, Sweet. Let me have what is left. I'm not sure that Flake is any more awake than I was twenty years ago, but I feel so sure of what I have to give. He's mine, Jessie, for just the lowering of the last bar which I must let down to him. Let me have him, Sweet.)

Here, if ever, was opportunity to tear these words out of her silence. Here, if ever! The two of them hunched in their soft things on the *chaise longue* in Jessie's room. These comparatively peaceful shut-in days of security against intrusion. The growth of this something so right and normal between them, after the delayed and frustrated years of intimacy. The need to talk to Jessie. Opportunity was at hand.

Next week this time, steam-shovels would already be biting into the waiting dirt of Fishrow. New life, as if waiting for the signal to raise the curtain, was about to begin. . . .

"Jessie, you and I, because of the strangeness of our lives, the immense thing that happened to me when I thought that all I was doing was trying to keep a roof over our heads, haven't had the opportunity, up to this perfect and precious present, to get really acquainted. . . ."

"Don't I know it! It's been long-distance awe for me and being impressed by the grandeur of a parent who turned out to be a swell exhibit A of my idea of a regular mater. No two ways about it, Bea, something just perfectly grand has happened to you this time. Up to now I've always sort of shared the idea of the girls and teachers at school and of everybody who ever heard I was my mother's daughter. Thrilling and all that to be the daughter of a famous mother, but rather too grand for comfort. But it's this selling the business or—something, or perhaps my discovering for myself how darlingly human you are, has thawed all the awe and still kept you the darlingest person in the world."

"Oh, my dear! . . ."

"I'm crazy about you, Bea. Not just admiration and being impressed. I think you're such a darling. Remember how Delilah used to say to Peola—it's so hard to remember not to mention her—remember how she used to say, 'Chile, ain't you ashamed to be so naughty when you got a missus is sech a darling?' . . ."

"Oh, Jessie, now that we are this way, so blessedly close—things that would have been so terribly difficult to discuss have suddenly become so——"

"Don't I know! Easier to say. Easier to confide. Easier to just crawl, old darling, into each other. Bea darling, I'm so happy, so ridiculously happy this very moment. Oh, Ma, don't look at me. I'm silly and full of giggles, and if you look at me twice, I'll cry."

"Jessie, what do you mean?"

"Nothing; that's the ridiculous part. I only know that I'm happy, Bea. Happier than I've ever been in my life."

"Silly! Has it to do with being home?"

"Yes. Yes-yes!"

"With me?"

"Yes."

"Is it—Fishrow——"

"No. Yes-yes-yes, in a way. Oh, Bea, don't you see?..."

Strangely enough, to what was to be her subsequent and almost insane despair, she did not see.

· 47 ·

That she did not see was almost immediately to be borne in upon her humiliation in hot and heaping coals.

The growing and grim tautness of Flake, which at first she attributed to the importunings of Universal Sales Association that, in the event of sale, he remain on with the new combine for a minimum period of three years, was obviously of stranger and deeper source.

There was something that seemed startled and apprehensive in the manner he carried about. He entered the house that way evenings, during the retreat of Bea following the all-too-heralded rumor of sale. He paled under it, grew reticent under it.

And then came the occasion, as she entered the room one evening where he sat poring over blue-prints with Jessie, that Bea, placing her hand lightly on his shoulder, had felt his body spurt to its feet, as if to throw it off.

And still in the enormity of her lack of realizations, the dear thought struck her that the time was at hand when every taut suppressed nerve in his body, instead of retreating, would relax against hers. The suspicion of a desiring Flake repressed actually smote her body like fingers across a lyre.

Here was every indication that under the strain she was imposing upon him, the weeks of procrastination, her failure to see him alone, the holding off rigidly for the sake of a sanction she could not bring herself to proceed without, Flake was breaking. Jessie or no Jessie, the time was at hand, the time had come!

But there was Jessie.

From her position on the other side of what had been the concealing figure of Flake as he rose at that touch, it was almost as if—why, it was almost as if Jessie, who now sat spread like a flower on a cushion at his feet, must have slid there from his knees.

The thought smote her, the thought stopped her heart, and then, too ephemeral to endure beyond the batting of an eye, died back into the recesses of her consciousness. Why, these two were giggling! they were feet apart and apparently had been hard at the blue-prints for Number Nine, because the curled sheets lay between them, and as for the lovely brightness that lay on the face of Jessie, that was constantly there these days, like a flood light.

Like a flood of brightness; but still she did not see.

Over years of strange dark foreign nights filled with the most tormenting musings, she was never to cease to marvel over that.

Over years of letters from them, of regularity, of affection, of deepest nostalgia for her return, and later, over the first precariously scrawled letters of their children, all three born in Fishrow, she was never to cease to marvel at what had been the paralysis of her perceptions. . . .

The seeing, when it did come, had to happen so literally as A-B-C. A for apple. B for biscuit. C for Cat.

It had, so she cried out to herself from the fastnesses of hotel suites at Deauville, the Crillon in Paris, the Savoy in London, the Australia in Sydney, to be ground into her consciousness as concretely as gravel under a heel.

For years, to the constant peregrinations of her affairs, while, as it were, her enterprises joined hands to almost literally encircle the world, Madrid to Rome, to Vienna, to Berlin, to Paris, London, Sydney, Shanghai, that thought, like a hangnail against peace, was to continue to prick and torment.

She practically needed to be told, in words of one syllable, when an ounce more of blessed intuition would have spared her son-in-law a future of unease and abjectness in her presence. As a matter of fact, would have spared them both that harness of insurmountable self-consciousness which was forever to caparison their mutual manner and which was ultimately to condemn her more and more rigidly to the prolonged absences from the home in Fishrow where her grandchildren were growing up to regard her as a magnificent legend.

It kept happening and happening that night, the feebleness of her perceptions, when she should have been able, not only to grasp, but to hold, the revelation that Jessie, at her entrance into the room, had slid from the embrace of Flake.

Not only, as she walked in upon them, did the flash of her initial impression of these two in the propinquity of an embrace streak across her mind and then out, but immediate contrition for the snide thought flooded her.

Plain to see all that had happened was this:

Her touch upon Flake's shoulder, spurting him to his feet, had been something goading, something more than he could bear. Jessie or no Jessie, the time had come!

"Jessie, I need to talk to Frank. Will you leave us alone?"

"Of course," said the yellow spread of skirts from her cushion, with the brightness out over her face in its flood light, and also, too, as if glad to be released from a moment that had caught and captured her into discomfort.

"Frank," she said, in their sudden aloneness, and went toward him.

Since her return, Jessie had rearranged the lights of the living-room so that they were dimmer and pinker, and suddenly, and because of what she was about to say, she felt grateful to them for wrapping her in a protective kind of tulle.

"Frank!"

There was that pallor again against his face like a steel light, and the stiffening she had noticed of late, which was his manner, these days, of meeting her protracted technique of evasions.

"Frank, I know you're hurt with me. I know you're baffled with me. But it's nothing, except that I've been stuck in the mud of a psychological hole. Frank, the reason I haven't let this thing happen as—as it started to before Jessie came, is because I've been playing for time. Too silly! She'll be the first to think so. I've wanted to tell her—prepare her—silly nonsense somewhere in me of thinking I owed it to her. Frank, am I being awful—or mistaken about everything—or just humanly honest about what won't stay pent up in me any longer? Shall we both tell Jessie—now—together? Frank, my dear, am I being terrible? . . ."

To stand there was to feel, as nearly as the human body is capable of feeling, that the heart was a pump forcing blood up tight against the roof of the head, rushing it down tight, close, pressing, into the legs, making them want to burst. Up. Down. Up.

"Frank!" Surely and terribly there lay that steel light against his face!

"If I've been insane, crazy, dreaming, tell me, boy. One can no more than be incinerated of humiliation. Only I thought—you see, all, everything between us—all the more so because it has never quite been spoken out—has been there—as surely as your hand is there on that table. Frank, are you about to tell me that the thing that has been between you and me has existed only—only in my craziness?..."

"Good God! a man like me—one-tenth your caliber—to have to tell a woman like you—the lay of land between us. You're right. After the first realizations began to crack in upon me that things could actually be what they were seeming to be, I did come to understand that matters could come to their head almost any day. Of course I came to know what was brewing in that blessed head and heart of yours. I—was biding my time—glad that you were biding yours, in order to make sure that what was happening to me was not some quirk in my brain, making me see things. A man, I kept telling myself, would be insane not to want it. A woman like you. Me, actually having the power to interest a woman like you. I don't know, Bea, being as honest with you as you deserve I should be—I don't honestly know how it all would have come out. Only now—now I know what a terrible mistake has possibly been averted—for you as much as for me, Bea. God what a mess!"

She tried to draw his palms away from grinding against his tightly closed eyes.

"Why, Frank, are you misunderstanding? There is no mess. Everything is what it has been, only infinitely more. Don't you see, I'm through now, playing for time. I haven't any pride where you are concerned. Only humility, Frank, and the passionate desire to try to return to you some measure of the incredible happiness you have given me. Age is not necessarily a matter of years, Frank. The eight years between us need not be eight. My capacity for living and loving——"

"For God's sake," he almost screamed, his teeth bared beneath the grinding of his palms against his eyes, and this time no mistaking the tense turning of the pillar of his body away from her—"for God's sake—don't make me have to be plainer. . . ."

On his turning, the door swung open to Jessie in her canary-colored frock.

"Did you call? Of course I know you didn't. But I've been so afraid he might be the first to tell you, or that he wouldn't tell you at all, or if things got into a jam there would be no sweetheart to guide him. Darling, has he? Of course he hasn't! As a matter of fact, he hasn't quite told himself. I've done all the tolding. He's a terrible lover, Ma. Doesn't know his own mind. Blows hot. Blows cold. In God's mortal awe of you. Temperamental as a barber. Would escape if he could. Couldn't if he would. Wouldn't if he could. But I love him and he loves me. Relieve his terror, parent; give us the maternal blessing with caution or I may pass out of the pressure of too much happiness."

Here was the scene which was to be preserved so perfectly in the retina of her mind's eyes, that looking back, looking back at it across the years, the living picture of it, even to the yellow of a frock and the smear of anguish across a face, were never to dim.

They were so young, standing there . . . so right. . . .

THE END

NOTES

Notes are keyed to pages of the novel.

1 *tintype*: An inexpensive type of photographic portraiture extremely popular in the United States after the Civil War.

2 *Janice Meredith*: A best-selling Revolutionary War romance by Paul Leicester Ford (1899).

    When Knighthood Was in Flower: *When Knighthood Was in Flower, or The Love Story of Charles Brandon & Mary Tudor*, was a popular historical romance by Charles Major (1898).

    Richard Carvel: Revolutionary-era romance by Winston Churchill (1899).

    Mill on the Floss: George Eliot's 1860 novel about an intelligent and imaginative young woman who struggles with the restrictions and narrow-mindedness of her provincial world.

4 *I weep for Adonais, he is dead*: The first line of "Adonais: An Elegy on the Death of John Keats" (1821), a pastoral elegy by the Romantic poet Percy Bysshe Shelley (1792–1822).

5 *Welsbach lamp*: Invented in 1893 by Dr. Carl von Welsbach of Vienna, the Welsbach incandescent lamp was fueled by gas. Its extraordinary brightness rivaled that of electrical lamps and helped finalize the technological leap from oil lamps.

9 *a Sousa or Creatore band*: John Philip Sousa (1854–1932) and Giuseppe Creatore (1871–1952) were both leaders of successful and patriotic marching bands in the early twentieth century.

11 *Free Silver*: The Free Silver movement stood against the Gold Standard and "bimetallism" in the debate over the standardization of U.S. national currency. This debate was a central issue in the presidential election of 1896 and continued in the years that directly followed.

Dewey's candidacy for the Democratic nomination: Admiral George Dewey (1837–1917), commander of the U.S. Navy's Asiatic Squadron, became a national hero after leading the attack on the Spanish at Manila Bay during the Spanish-American War. He briefly flirted with the possibility of running for president in 1899, but decided instead to support McKinley's reelection bid.

Gold Standard Act: Ratified March 14, 1900, after a lengthy debate, the Gold Standard Act established gold as the only standard for redeeming paper money.

Klondike: The Klondike River in Canada's Yukon territory was the site of the gold rush of 1897–98, which attracted tens of thousands of fortune seekers.

President McKinley: William McKinley (1843–1901) served as the twenty-fifth U.S. president from 1897 until his assassination in 1901.

Galveston cyclone: The Galveston cyclone and tidal wave of September 8, 1900, devastated Galveston, Texas. An early motion picture by Thomas Edison's film company, which was advertised as "a most picturesque mass of wreckage," featured the devastation.

trusts: A volatile issue at the turn of the twentieth century; many Americans were deeply concerned with the power and influence wielded by business monopolies, also called "trusts," in an increasingly stratified society.

16   *Mark Hanna*: One of the most influential political figures of the late nineteenth and early twentieth centuries, Marcus Alonzo Hanna (1837–1904) was a prominent Cleveland businessman who was instrumental in getting McKinley elected to the presidency in 1896. He became a U.S. senator in 1897.

the Maine: The battleship USS *Maine*, was blown up February 15, 1898, while moored in Havana harbor. The act helped to catalyze the onset of the Spanish-American War, declared April 21, 1898.

Panama Canal: Originally conceived in 1880, the Canal, with heavy U.S. funding, was finally opened in 1914 after a lengthy, expensive, and dangerous period of construction.

"Tom Platt Silverites": Thomas Platt (1833–1910) briefly stood as boss in the New York Republican political machine, and later served two terms in the U.S. Senate (1897–1909), where he was a central figure in the gold standard debate.

G.A.R.: Founded in 1866, the Grand Army of the Republic, an organization of Union Army Civil War veterans, had over 400,000 members by the 1890s. The organization came to wield tremendous political power; five of its members became U.S. presidents, and it was said that nomination to the Republican ticket was contingent on a GAR endorsement.

Battle of Manila Bay: May 1, 1898, one of two major U.S. naval victories in the Spanish-American War.

Boer War: In a bid for control over South Africa, the Boer War (1899–1902) pitted the British against the Dutch Boer republics of the Transvaal and the Orange Free State.

Rough-rider fellow: Theodore Roosevelt helped build his political reputation as a manly, rugged, and iconoclastic American with his instant best-selling *The Rough Riders* (1899), an account of his Spanish-American War adventures in Cuba with a diverse group of soldiers.

18   *Steel Pier:* Opened June 18, 1898, and billed as "the handsomest and most luxuriously appointed pier in the world," the Steel Pier helped to solidify Atlantic City as one of America's most popular tourist destinations of the early twentieth century.

19   *Hume . . . Treatise on Human Nature:* David Hume (1711–1776), Scottish philosopher, wrote his *Treatise on Human Nature* in 1739 and is considered the primary and founding figure of modern empirical philosophy.

22   *Wanamaker's:* Founded in Philadelphia in 1876, John Wanamaker's was the first American department store.
     David Harum: David Harum: A Story of American Life (1898), a humorous popular novel by Edward Westcott.

24   *Book of Facts:* In 1912, Harry Peck published *The Standard Illustrated Book of Facts; a comprehensive survey of the world's knowledge and progress, with a historical, scientific, statistical, geographical and literary appendix.*

26   *Blüchers:* Functional and convenient half boots; so called after Field Marshal von Blücher (1742–1819), Prince of Wagstadt, who popularized the boot while a commander of the Prussian Army in the Napoleanic War.

27   *a college professor:* Woodrow Wilson taught jurisprudence and economics at Bryn Mawr College, Wesleyan College in Connecticut, and Princeton University. In 1902 he became president of Princeton.

28   *Woodrow Wilson's first election to the Presidency of the United States:* The reformist Wilson first became president in 1912, in an election he won against the former president Theodore Roosevelt, the socialist Eugene Debs, and the incumbent Republican president, William Howard Taft.

30   *"Hiawatha" . . . "Where Was Moses":* All popular songs of the late nineteenth and early twentieth centuries.

31 *"Stars and Stripes Forever"*: The official march of the United States of America, composed by John Philip Sousa, according to legend, on Christmas Day, 1896.

33 *congress gaiters*: Low ankle boots with elastic sides popular in the nineteenth century.

38 *Vigorous Manhood*: An obsession for many at the beginning of the twentieth century, "vigorous manhood" became a term that described the strength of both a man's physique and his character, as in Senator John Sherman's 1896 description of then candidate McKinley: "William McKinley . . . is now in the prime of vigorous manhood, and his powers of endurance are not excelled by any American of his age."

69 *sen-sen*: A popular "breath perfume" first developed in the late nineteenth century.

80 *chatelaine*: A clasp or chain commonly worn at the waist, used to hold keys, a watch, a pad of paper, and so on.

82 *Hominy*: Southern food made of hulled and dried kernels of corn, prepared by boiling.
  Cracklin': A well-browned, crisp snack, made when melting pork fat down for lard.

83 *pickaninnies*: A disparaging term for African American children.
  "Doan' talk . . . Bloody Bones!": "Raw Head and Bloody Bones" often appeared in cautionary folk tales and lullabies originally told among African American slaves.

105 *a Pullman car*: Bea first imagines modeling her restaurant on the luxuriously appointed railroad sleeper cars called "Pullman cars." These cars commonly employed black men to work as Pullman porters.

107 *the car tracks along which the last "Owl" had passed*: The "Owl" was the name given to railway trains with late-night runs.

113 *Carrie Nation*: A leading, militant member of the Women's Christian Temperance Union. The hatchet-and-Bible-wielding, six-foot-tall Nation (1846–1911) became a dreaded figure and a national icon as she led her followers to destroy saloons with the cry "Smash, ladies, smash!" Lobbying the Kansas House of Representatives to pass anti-alcohol legislation during the time before women's suffrage, Nation reportedly explained to them, "You refused me the vote and I had to use a rock."

129 *the new Grand Central Station*: Manhattan's new Grand Central Terminal on 42nd Street was opened on February 9, 1913.

135 *armistice*: On November 11, 1918, the Armistice was signed by the Allies and the Germans, ending World War I. This date was celebrated as Armistice Day from 1919 until 1954, when Congress changed the holiday's name to the more-inclusive Veterans Day.

151 *Flat Iron Building*: Built in 1902, this triangular skyscraper was understood by many to be the architectural embodiment of a forward-looking modern Manhattan.

152 *Dorothy Arnold*: Arnold, a 25-year-old aspiring Manhattan writer and heiress, disappeared on December 12, 1910. She was never found.

155 *John D. Rockefeller*: John Davison Rockefeller (1839–1937) was for many years the world's wealthiest — and perhaps most reviled — man. From modest beginnings, he built the Standard Oil Company into a massively successful corporation.
     Mary Pickford: Born Gladys Louise Smith, Mary Pickford (1892–1979) became one of the biggest movie stars of the silent film era.
     Anna Held: The first wife of theatrical impresario Florenz Ziegfeld and a member of Ziegfeld's famous *Follies*, Anna Held (1872–1918) was one of the leading stars of the musical stage in the late nineteenth and early twentieth centuries.
     Valentino: Rudolph Valentino (1895–1926), Italian movie star known for his smoldering acting and exotic looks.
     Caruso: Enrico Caruso (1873–1921) was the most prominent tenor of his day.
     Gaby Delys: Gaby Delys, aka Gaby Deslys (1881–1920), was a popular French actress and dancer known for her risqué behavior; in the early years of the twentieth century she scandalized Broadway with her performance of a striptease. She appeared in some American silent films before her untimely death.

158 *Peacock Alley*: The name given to the 300-foot corridor that connected the Waldorf and Astoria hotels. In the first decades of the twentieth century, fashionable New Yorkers and tourists alike would go there to parade the latest styles, to see and be seen.

162 *London Embankment*: Responding to "the great stink" of 1858, members of the British Parliament approved the construction of London's first city-wide sewage system. Upon completion in 1870, the city's waste would

no longer be dumped directly into the increasingly foul-smelling Thames River. The largest sewage pipes were built along the Thames, and were then covered to create a scenic embankment, complete with gardens and a promenade.

189–190   *"When Jesus wuz totin' de cross up de hill to Calvery"*: Delilah is singing a version of Thomas Shepherd's 1855 hymn "Must Jesus Bear the Cross Alone?"

190   *John Henry*: According to legend, John Henry was born a slave in the mid-nineteenth century and grew to be an enormous man. He later worked as a "steel driving man," helping to clear the way for the laying of railroad tracks in West Virginia. The popular folk ballad about him, probably originated in the 1870s, tells the tale of Henry's exploits working for the railroad, including beating the steam drill in a contest and then dying from the effort. The earliest known written version of the ballad appeared around 1900, and it became the most recorded ballad in the history of American folk music.

204   *Zermatt*: A mountain village resort in Switzerland, at the foot of the Matterhorn.

208   *Marion Davies*: Born Marion Douras, Davies (1897–1961) became one of the most adored film stars of the 1910s and 1920s, appearing in some twenty-nine films between 1918 and 1928.
       John Gilbert: "The Great Lover of the Silver Screen," Gilbert, born John Cecil Pringle (1899–1936), was the highest-paid actor in Hollywood in the late 1920s. He made nearly a hundred films before his death at age 37.

211   *Maxfield Parrish frieze*: Parrish (1870–1966), a painter of dreamy, lush landscapes, was one of the most prominent figures in what is now referred to as the golden age of American illustration. In 1922, his painting *Daybreak* was a sensation, selling an astonishing 200,000 prints.
       Haroun al-Raschid: A courageous warrior and a compassionate leader, Haroun al-Raschid (786–809 C.E.) was the most celebrated of all Muslim caliphs.

218   *Grand Central Palace*: Manhattan's Grand Central Palace was a huge exhibition hall at Lexington Avenue and 42nd Street. The building was demolished in 1963.

Fannie Hurst (1889–1968) was a novelist,
screenwriter, and short story writer. She is best
known for her novels *Imitation of Life* and
Back Street.

• • •

Daniel Itzkovitz is an associate professor of
English and director of American Studies at
Stonehill College. He is a coeditor of the
collection *Queer Theory and the
Jewish Question.*

• • •

Library of Congress Cataloging-in-Publication Data
Hurst, Fannie, 1889–1968.
Imitation of life / Fannie Hurst ; edited and with
an introduction by Daniel Itzkovitz.
p. cm.
Includes bibliographical references and index.
ISBN 0-8223-3324-4 (pbk. : alk. paper)
1. Single mothers — Fiction. 2. Race relations —
Fiction. 3. Women domestics — Fiction.
4. Female friendship — Fiction. 5. Mothers and
daughters — Fiction. 6. African American
women — Fiction. 7. Restaurateurs — Fiction.
8. Restaurants — Fiction. 9. Widows — Fiction.
I. Title.
PS3515.U78514 2004
813'.52 — dc22   2004013142